I0796996

ATLAS CREED

JAX

Armitage is a work of fiction. Names, characters, businesses, organizations, places, events, and incidents either are the product of the author's imagination or are used fictitiously. Any resemblance to actual persons, living or dead, events, or locales is entirely coincidental.

Cover Design by Gammatrap aka Brandon McCamey

Edited by Elizabeth Merck
Interior Formatting by Atlas Creed

This book has been rated Adult (A) by the Independent Book Rating System (IBRS) for strong language, violence, and graphic depictions of sexual assault and attempted rape. See content warning page for more details. Visit www.indiebookratings.org for rating details.

Names: Creed, Atlas, author.
Title: Armitage : Children of Arcanum, book one / Atlas Creed
Description: Second Edition | IAX [2024] | Series: Children of Arcanum series ; 1

For information contact ; address : www.atlascreedauthor.com

ISBN: 979-8-9877453-2-8 (paperback),
979-8-9877453-5-9 (hardcover),
979-8-9877453-3-5 (ebook)

CONTENTS

Content Warning

Please note, some of the content warnings listed below may indicate spoilers, proceed with this in mind.

Your mental health is my priority, and while this story contains adult language and depictions of violence and sexual assault that some may find uncomfortable, my hope is that you are aware of potentially triggering content. This content includes:

Self-Harm
Attempted Suicide
Blood, Gore, and Violence
Language
Sexual Assault
Attempted Rape
Accidental Cannibalism

Indie Author Appreciation

Authors succeed most when communicating, supporting, and helping each other. I am fortunate to be part of a community with so many wonderful and talented authors. I'd like to take a moment to praise a few indie authors who I enjoy and who have inspired me along my journey.

Megan Mossgrove, author of *The Wingbreaker*
Mikel Melwasul, author of *Paragon Exordium*
S.M. Campbell, author of *Corrupted Tides*
J.C. Ceron, author of *Death of the Ice Angel*
Daphne Parker, author of *What Lies Beneath the Tide*
RSK, author of *The Adventures of Hemera Nyx in the Galaxy of the Future!*

If you are looking for other books to enjoy, these are authors that I recommend along with one of the books they authored. Please, share your generosity and support with my fellow indie authors.

This subject is dedicated to my family and friends. I have struggled through much, many things unknown to you, but you are the reason that I am here today. For that, I owe you my life.

"There is hope, even when your brain tells you there isn't."

- John Green

PROLOGUE

The figure emerged beneath a spear of lightning, cloaked in black and wreathed in smoke. Rebekah sensed its stare from beyond her rain-stippled bedroom window, and a chill raced across her skin, leaving her flesh prickled with goosebumps. Another flash ignited the sky, and the phantom vanished.

She pressed her face against the glass, both desperate and trepid for the entity to return, for some inkling of proof to confirm what she saw. But with each strike of lightning, the street below remained empty. Dazed, her hand extended beyond the open window as an offering to the storm. Water ran down the branch of her arm and trailed off in twisting spires at the ends of her fingers.

She must have imagined it. That was possible, right? And yet, a morose sense rallied against her denial.

There was nothing there.

You didn't see anything.

She hoped, through sheer repetition of repressions, the memory would wisp away, but despite her mind's attempts to placate her, the image remained. She had seen something…

Her door crashed open, shattering the mirror of her vanity. Her father stood beyond the threshold, exhausted impatience riddling his face, absent any notice of the broken mirror. Instead, he looked beyond her, and she followed his gaze to water pooling along the baseboard. She turned back in fear as he snatched a towel from the hallway's linen closet.

"Are you out of your damn mind?" He ripped her from her perch and slammed the window shut. "It's pouring outside. There's water running everywhere—down the wall, all over your floor." He bunched the towel along the baseboard to soak up the liquid. "I thought you'd know better than to open the window when it's pouring rain."

"Sorry, Dad, I—I—"

"Yeah, yeah, you didn't think. Why am I not surprised?" He took a composing breath. "Your mother has dinner ready, so make yourself presentable."

He left Rebekah sprawled on the floor and stormed from the room, though he hesitated at the scattered pieces of glass. "And clean up this fucking mess."

Gleaming tears filled her eyes, and she glanced back toward the window at the water racing down in rivulets. She'd always found a comforting symmetry in storms. Often, they inspired freedom, much like the freedom she imagined Andy Dufresne felt in the rain beyond the walls of Shawshank. But the rain that night brought sorrow.

She exhaled a tremulous breath. Despite the years of blind callousness, she still found herself tirelessly vying for her father's approval without success. The relentless naivety of a child's longing for love and affection, though the novelty wore thin. Steeling herself, she made her way to the glass mosaic that decorated her floor.

Brushing pieces into a pile, she caught a jagged shard of glass with the heel of her hand. The cut stung sharply. Rebekah examined her injury, watching the blood begin to pool beneath her skin in a crimson patch, little beads cresting on the surface. The pain quickly subsided as the glinting rubies clotted the wound, leaving nothing more than a fading memory.

She caught her reflection in the broken fragments and recoiled. Grief had aged her. At only fourteen, she looked miserable. Bags sank beneath her eyes, accentuated by heavy, dark circles. Seeing her face, and not recognizing the soul behind it, was deeply disquieting. A foreign voice found its way into her mind.

It's your fault, it hissed at her. *She's dead because of you.*

Rebekah rocked back on her knees, exhaling deeply. Closing her eyes, she clenched her fists as labored breaths fought their way through the pressure in her chest. She struggled to reclaim herself, battling the monster that crept its way into her head, whispering evils to her.

The vanity drew her gaze. Blades of glass decorated the edges of the frame where the mirror used to be, and a single photo remained, torn nearly in two. While the side of it still anchored to the frame was resolute, the other half dangled threateningly by a sliver. She plucked her favorite picture of her and her sister from the mirror.

Her sister had been dead for years, but some part of her still denied it, holding on to the possibility she might still be alive. She had gone missing four years ago at the beach her family used to visit every summer, but they never found her body. So, there was hope, right?

She folded onto the floor, white knuckles gripping her knees. The torn photo hung from her trembling hand as she cried, but in the corner of her room, the miserable figure watched her, choking out the light and darkening the atmosphere. Its voice echoed in her mind.

Beside her sat the jagged shard that cut her, still coated in a faint trace of blood. She reached for it and positioned it so she could see her face once more. Beneath tendrils of wild, curly black hair, she found her eyes, rimmed in red and lifeless, no shine of happiness. Even the crescent-shaped, silver mark of her iris—prized as a unique characteristic—brought an unwelcome feeling.

"Rebekah!" Her father summoned her from the kitchen, his tone blanketed with irritation.

The voice in her head whispered to her—commanded her—and a strange sensation took control. With a trembling hand, she tightened her grip on the glass, making the sharp edges dig into her palm.

She placed the fragment against her wrist and slowly worked the rough edge deep through her flesh. Blood ran from the wound like a crimson drape, cascading with the same ferocity as the rain streaking down the window.

The voice laughed. *I see you, Guardian*, it hissed.

Her hands fell to her sides, and the remnant of glass skipped across the hardwood floor victoriously. The fog of turmoil in her mind dissipated as the sinister voice shrank into the distance, becoming muted beyond Rebekah's waning consciousness.

1
THE MAN

Three years later…

CHAINS CLINKED IN THE dimly lit room, a macabre symphony that painted the atmosphere. The man inhaled the chemical overtones of bleach and ammonia that concealed the bitter tinge of iron, a scent that settled on his tongue. Old blood. The subtleties excited him, like secrets hidden in the nuance.

He collected his tools, which he had cleaned and organized with meticulous detail, their significance interwoven with decades of memories. Settling into his seat at the workbench, he ran his fingers over the surface, feeling the stories etched into every gouge, dent, and scar. Every mark, a testament to his history, lent a textured tapestry to his craft.

Precision guided his every move. It was a code he lived by, carved from a blend of study and fear. Deviation spelled death.

Unrolling the canvas sheath on his workbench, the cloth pattered across the stainless-steel table with dull thuds. The polished knives concealed within reflected the soft glow of the room. He spared a moment to admire his work, turning a knife over in his hand, finding no flaws. Then, he donned his apron and gloves before reaching beyond the table for the switch, igniting the room with brilliant white light. An electric hum sizzled from the fluorescents.

His gaze fell upon his victim, Edward Smith, a young man whom he'd followed and studied, as his process required. He stole him from his vacation, though not with family. They were never with family, as his past mistakes had taught him. No, Eddie came with a small group of college friends who were in a perpetual state of inebriation. In his drunken stupor, the ketamine was excessive, but his code required it, and the code was gospel.

The room bore witness to the carefully orchestrated setup. Plastic sheeting veiled the walls, leaving no gaps or flaws, while the drainage trench remained exposed, a deliberate choice to ease the cleaning. The mixture of animal blood would conceal any damning evidence, he reassured himself.

Approaching Eddie, still dressed in his beach attire, the man went to work. His shears sliced away the vibrant tank top and board shorts, revealing the canvas upon which he would work. He paused at the seashell necklace, drawing a whisper of disdain from his companion.

Pathetic.

Silencing the voice with a thought, he unclasped it and set it aside with a manner of care.

Your trophies work against you, evidence of your perversion.

Giving no pause to the voice, the man pressed on. He freed the body from clothing and other accessories, prepping it for a sponge bath, and cleansed away any traces of the outside world. The gentle rise and fall of Eddie's chest stood testament to the potent cocktail of drugs, though, the effects would soon fade, so there was no room for error.

Beneath the table, leather straps awaited their purpose—to bind the body. As he tightened the final strap, a flicker of life stirred in Edward Smith, and the man's pulse quickened with anticipation.

Steady, the voice cautioned.

"Quiet," he reminded his companion.

Let me speak with him, the voice within persisted.

"No."

"What—What's happening?" Eddie attempted to move, but his bonds bit into his flesh, restraining him. With clenched fists, he wriggled harder, drawing a groan from the heavy metal table. Beneath grunts and screams and pleas, he struggled. Futile attempts to free himself, but soon he fell into exhausted defeat. His eyes darted around the space until they found the man, watching him patiently.

"Who the fuck are you? Where am I? What are you doing to me?" Eddie desperately pleaded for answers.

The companion within the man, an unseen force clamoring for control, slithered forward, hungry to assert itself. "Don't," he hissed, trying to restrain it, fighting for command.

The weight of the creature's presence intensified, bearing down on him like an invisible hand, suppressing his will. Eddie's eyes widened as the man's voice surrendered, and the companion's guttural tone poured forth.

"Silence." The command echoed.

Eddie obeyed, his defiance quelled by the unseen puppeteer manipulating the man towering over him, peering into the depths of his soul with unsettling curiosity.

This is my life, my body, the man thought, but his concern was brushed away.

"Your eyes," the companion uttered in a gravelly tone.

"What? What are you talking about?" Eddie's voice quivered.

"They are not your own. One different from the other."

He leaned closer. Panic painted wild strokes across Eddie's features as sweat beaded along his flesh. Desperate eyes danced in widened sockets.

"It's a condition." Eddie trembled. "Heterochromia."

"A rare occurrence," the voice acknowledged. "When two souls inhabit a single body, their presence can manifest in many ways. The mind can break or separate. The body can deform. Your fragile minds struggle to bear the pressure of coinhabitance."

Stepping back from the tableside, the steady pulse of the man's footsteps clapped against the plastic lining on the floor. Eddie jerked his shoulders against the bonds, still chasing the hope of escape.

"Do you believe in gods, Edward Smith?"

"I—I don't know."

"Your ancestors did," the man said, walking in ponderous strides. "Your ancestors were pious. Primitive. They built great monuments to beings like me, and my kin became infatuated with their adulation. But times have changed; you and your ilk have grown callous, seeking distraction from the world, lost in bickering and wars over misplaced veneration."

"I don't know what the fuck you're talking about, man!" Eddie screamed. "Let me go!"

With a sharp thud, the man slammed his fist on the metal table, silencing Eddie's protests. He leaned in, his breath hot against Eddie's cheek, yet his voice remained calm.

"Mortals have shown their true colors, but that is not why you suffer." The man leaned back. "I believe you are harboring someone, Edward. I do not believe you are aware of your coinhabitant. You are simply collateral. But in your sacrifice, your connection to this plane will be severed." The man pressed a button on the side of the table, turning Eddie feet over head. "You will be free from this hollow, wretched shell. A new beginning, a gift that few have ever been blessed with."

"No, no, no!" Eddie cried. "No, stop. Please! Fucking stop! I don't want to die." The whir of the actuators accompanied his screams.

Is it him? the man asked his companion.

We shall see, the voice replied, surrendering control.

Amid Eddie's continuing cries, the man shuffled back to his workbench. From beneath the table, he retrieved a box intricately carved from burled wood. Opening it and removing a cloth wrap revealed an archaic, curved dagger, its handle fashioned from bone, and a blade of white opal glimmered with an otherworldly allure.

He turned the dagger over in his hand, heavier than it looked, and watched the fluorescents glint their prismatic pattern off the opal blade. Unlike the influence of his companion, the power radiating from the dagger held a subtler allure, a haunting charm that had gone unnoticed at first but, once felt, latched onto him like an addiction.

He returned to the inclined table and approached "wrong way up" Eddie, whose head hung precariously above the drainage trough. He cried, still pleading for his life, tears rolling over his brow—a cacophony of sound the man had become adept at tuning out. With resolute purpose, he made a swift incision, starting at Eddie's ear and trailing up to his collarbone, cutting deep into the throat. Blood spewed forth, dousing his gloved fingers, coating his apron and rubber boots. Swiftly stepping away, he spared himself the worst of the carnage.

Blood spurted from Eddie's neck and cascaded down the curves of his skull, painting his face a macabre color. Gurgling and coughing on his own gore, Eddie tried to scream, staring from horrified eyes. The table trembled as its occupant writhed in a final desperate plea for freedom. The veins in his head bulged from strain as his flesh drained of color to a pale, sickly white.

As Eddie's struggle waned, his eyes rolled over to find the man, watching him patiently. The hint of a smile toyed with his lips, a glimmer of satisfaction amid the horror. The man's heart lightened with the hope Eddie would be the last, yet a darker part of him craved more, a part he tried to suppress. The conflict was what his companion played on. He despised the duality, the lack of control over his own desires. Eddie's body slackened, and his eyes drooped, gravity holding them open in bulging surprise.

Turning to the workbench, he set the blade aside, lamenting as he rested his hands on the table. In that moment, a pressure released from his head and an uncomfortable silence settled. The brief, fleeting quiet was the only reprieve the man had, where an echo of himself could be found. He held his breath and yearned for his companion to remain absent, hoping his task had reached its end. But as swiftly as it had gone, the pressure returned. It gripped his mind like a vice, accompanied by the familiar presence he could never escape.

It was not him, the voice said.

2
REBEKAH

LAUGHTER BROKE OUT IN response to Devon's joke, dragging Rebekah from her soul-searching and bringing a measure of joy she'd been lacking. It had been a difficult road to recovery over the last few years, and she longed for a return to some semblance of normal. As if to spite her, though, her grief for her sister lingered, and tremors from that night found their way to her still.

Her motley group of friends sat around the table, enjoying their meals and discussing the movie they just left, *Thirteen Ghosts.* It was the third time Rebekah had seen it. She developed a strange interest in it since her own ghost encounter years prior. Examining the jagged scar on her wrist, she ran a thumb over the rough texture and smiled.

"So, Becks, any plans this weekend?" Anna turned to her. Excitement edged her tone. The question was a courtesy to not seem conceited—she clearly had news to share—but Rebekah had grown accustomed to it.

"My dad has me on lockdown," Rebekah said.

"Ugh, again? Why?"

"You wouldn't believe it, but I had an opinion *different* than his." Rebekah laughed.

"No way!" Anna joined in, giving her a wry smile. "How dare you."

"I know. How careless of me." Rebekah thumbed her scar again. "No, I plan to enjoy the weather, if we get any snow. We're almost out of winter. I hope we get something this year. It would be nice to sip some hot cocoa and catch up on my reading. I have a few books that I'm really excited about."

"Always with the reading," Anna jested. "Get out a little more and enjoy life."

"Life is bland. Books add spice. You should try it."

"I think it's nice," Devon chimed in, scraping the last of his food up and shoveling it into his mouth.

"Charming." Anna mocked disgust.

"What?" Devon slackened his jaw, exposing the mushed contents within.

She looked away, shielding her face from the vulgar display.

"You're disgusting. Close your mouth!" Rebekah said with a smile.

Devon gave a crooked grin and resumed chewing. Josh chuckled at his friend, hovering over his own plate.

"What about you?" Rebekah looked at Anna.

"Well," Anna started, snuggling Josh's arm and casting him an endearing smile. "Josh is taking me with his family to their cabin at Whitetail."

"Oh, fancy. Have you ever gone skiing before?" Rebekah asked.

"Nope," Anna said. "So, I will definitely have a sore ass when I get back."

"And not just from skiing," Josh said, sending the two boys into a roar of laughter.

Anna slapped him on the arm. "Gross!"

"Okay, okay." Josh threw his hands up, cringing from Anna's assaults, but with a smile decorating his face. "Yo, Devon, let's get some ice cream."

Devon nodded, and the two boys fled the table.

"Bring us something back!" Anna called.

Josh waved in response as he exited the restaurant. Rebekah sipped her drink and held her wrist again. The cool condensation from the glass wet her hands, and it felt good against her arm. She drew a pattern around her scar with the dots of moisture that collected on her skin.

"How are you doing?" Anna raised her eyebrows in concern and gestured toward the scar.

"Oh, I'm fine," Rebekah replied, letting go of her wrist.

"Have you had any...thoughts lately?"

"No." The thought of confessing to Anna tempted her, though. "I mean, what happened back then was—"

"Scary," Anna finished. "It was scary, Becks. We were all so worried about you. You know, you're not alone. I'm always here for you if you need to talk."

"Thanks," Rebekah said.

The idea of coming clean retreated behind her guard. She often couldn't rationalize what happened even to herself and wrestled with the thought that it had all been in her head. She could only imagine how Anna would respond.

"You don't have to worry about me, though," she said. "It was a difficult time for me, that's all. I was a different person then."

"Yeah, but the way your family acts...I'm worried that your dad might push you too far again."

"It wasn't my dad. I mean, he can be an asshole at times, and he drives me crazy, but I wouldn't kill myself because of him. You know that's not me."

"Well, I *thought* I knew that, but..."

"Anna." Rebekah gave her a steady stare. "I'll be fine. Trust me. I just...wasn't myself. You don't have to worry."

And that was true. She hadn't seen the figure since that night, except in scattered nightmares throughout the years like lingering echoes. The time spent at the hospital had been the worst. The constant questions and caution, like she would spontaneously combust, and the mandated therapy was miserable. But she did her best to forget and move on.

"You sure?"

"I am." Rebekah gave her a weak smile. "So, Josh. How's that going?"

Anna smiled, and her cheeks flushed. "I don't know. Good? I mean, I like him, and we have fun together."

"None of that sounds bad."

"It's not," Anna said.

"So, why do I feel like there's a 'but' coming?"

"But," Anna emphasized, "I want to go to Roanoke, and he's got his scholarship to Madison."

"So? JMU isn't even two hours from Roanoke, and doesn't his brother go there?"

"Yeah."

"So, he has more reason than you to travel, or you can drive to visit him. It's not like you're in different states."

"Maybe I'm overthinking things," Anna said. "I mean, it's only been a few months, but what if he meets someone else?"

"Between his course load and basketball?" Rebekah raised an eyebrow. "Plus, who's he gonna meet that's better than you?"

"Aww," Anna mocked. "You're tho thweet."

"Shut up." Rebekah prodded Anna's arm. "I'm trying to cheer you up. Don't be weird about it."

Anna smiled. "I know. Thank you."

"But..." Rebekah mimicked Anna's mocking tone.

"God, okay!" Anna laughed. "I'm still worried. How often do high school relationships last?"

"Well, with that attitude..."

"Okay, you know what?" Anna gave a devilish grin. "What about Devon?"

"What *about* Devon?"

"You know he likes you."

"Obviously. What's not to like?" Rebekah exaggerated a hair flip. Ego wasn't a color she wore often unless she decorated it with sarcasm.

"Fair." Anna chuckled but glanced down at her hands, rolling her glass between them. "But seriously, Josh wanted me to talk to you about it. So, what about Devon?"

"He's nice," Rebekah said.

"But..."

"Okay, enough of that." Rebekah giggled, shaking her head at the inane and overplayed joke. Coming down from the jovial high, her smile faded as reality settled in. "I'm not ready to let someone into my life. I'm just starting to get comfortable with me again."

"Maybe that's exactly what you need," Anna said. "Someone to drag you out of your sour moods and add a little light to your life."

"Uh, excuse me." Rebekah threw up a sassy finger. "I am an independent woman, and I can mope around all I want. Plus, isn't that what you're here for? What else could I need?"

"Hate to break it to you," Anna said, "but I am *not* gonna be the one to snatch that v-card."

"Oh, so the truth comes out!"

"Girl, have some fun. We're almost in college, and you don't know what you're missing." Anna gave her a self-aggrandizing smile.

"You lost yours like a month ago, so relax," Rebekah said. "I'll just have to live vicariously through you because that is *not* happening any time soon."

"Treat yo-self." Anna took a sip of her drink. "Look, I'm not telling you to go on a sexcapade." She cracked up at her own joke. "I'm just asking you to consider him. Just go on one date."

"Maybe."

"Fine." Anna set her drink down. "I'll take a maybe. Baby steps. Ah, just what I needed!"

Josh and Devon returned with four small cups of ice cream. Josh slid into the booth next to Anna, and Devon slid in beside Rebekah, offering her a cup. She took it.

"Peanut butter cup," Devon said. "Josh said you like that flavor."

Rebekah shot a look toward Anna, who zipped her fingers across her lips, and a smirk teased the corners of her mouth.

"I do. Thanks." She smiled at him.

Silence fell over the table as they all indulged. Rebekah glanced out the window at the gray skies hoping for snow. They finished their desserts and said their goodbyes. Devon walked Rebekah to her car. They didn't talk, but the silence wasn't uncomfortable. Maybe Anna was on to something.

On the drive home, she danced along to her "angry music," as her parents called it. Emo was what everyone at school called it, but it calmed her, so who cared? The first flecks of snow started to fall, and Rebekah craned her neck over the steering wheel to see, her heart racing with excitement.

When she got home, she stood outside, looking up at the gray-cast sky, watching the small white petals of snow drift down and melt as soon as they hit the ground. She smiled and took a deep breath, smelling the icy chill of winter. Without further hesitation, she raced inside, hung up her coat, kicked off her shoes, and bounded upstairs, already mentally picking out a book to read.

As she crossed into her room, she stopped brusquely. A memory hit her like a hammer, siphoning the wind from her lungs, and her heart sank. Propped against the dresser in a pool of her own blood sat her younger self. The youthful Rebekah from her vision looked up at her with glossy eyes and pallid, waxy skin. A low, rattling breath escaped her lips.

Rebekah clapped a hand over her mouth and sank to the floor, tears filling her eyes. All thoughts of reading or cozying up by the fireplace vanished. All the joy from her venture to the movies with her friends seemed a distant memory. As hard as she tried, the tremors from that night always found her.

A knot formed in her chest, and she started to cry harsh, painful sobs. Running her fingers through her hair, she grabbed a handful of her curls, pulling them tight behind her head. Mrs. Harrity, her therapist, had given her breathing exercises to soothe her anxiety, a placebo she retreated to for comfort but not something she had any faith in. It had been a long road to recovery, but what happened to her all those years ago—that was the death of her innocence.

3

NIKO

THE MONOTONOUS NOISE OF the office was maddening, and Niko hadn't even had his morning coffee yet. Distant chatter, ringing phones, and the irritating buzz of his CRT monitor crowded the atmosphere. *Government budget hard at work,* he thought. He slumped into his chair, examining the mass of notes and clutter littering his desk. A headache was already settling behind his eyes.

It's going to be a long day.

"You look like shit, Ortez."

Kevin Brindle nestled into his seat across from Niko, draping his blazer over the back of his chair.

"Yeah, thanks."

"Long night?" Brindle set his cold brew aside and logged in to his computer.

Niko sighed. "Danielle was up my ass about visiting her parents. I don't have the time or interest in torturing myself with another size-up from her million-dollar family."

"Whoa, detective," Michael Harrington chimed in from the desk behind Niko. "I didn't know you were into ass play."

"I dabble," Niko replied, "and don't call me detective."

"I take it her family isn't too fond of you," Brindle said.

Niko loaded coffee grounds into his French press. "Yeah, they don't think I'm good enough for their 'trust-fund Barbie.'

That's how they treat her anyway. They have some West Coast anesthesiologist lined up for her. They have for a while now. FBI special agents don't make the kind of money Silicon Valley socialites pine after. His parents are probably in the same yacht club as her parents or some shit."

"You sound real broken up about it," Harrington said.

"Yeah, a total mess." He chuckled and broke from the press, turning to Harrington. "Tell me about your girl problems—oh, that's right." He gave Harrington a slick grin.

"Yeah, real funny. I don't keep 'em around, so they don't bother me any."

"Must be nice." Niko turned away, his interest waning.

"Look, I can solve all your problems for you," Harrington said. "If you're not happy, move on."

"Noted, but I think I'll ration the advice I get and take it from people with actual experience."

"Your loss, man." Harrington shrugged and sank behind his computer monitor.

Niko turned to Brindle. "What about you? Any sage advice?"

He pondered. "You guys have a lot of history. You've been together, what…ten years?"

"Since high school, yeah."

"You've been in it a long time. But Mikey's right. Maybe it's time to call it quits. Like ripping off a Band-aid, just get it over with."

"I'm sorry, but did you just side with me on this?" Harrington asked.

Brindle waved him off. "Don't get used to it. It's a rare occurrence."

Niko shook his head, turned back to his desk to work the press, and transferred the coffee to his thermos. "From the man who had it all."

"If you want your hand held, ask someone else," Brindle said. "Only you can make the decision, but a word of advice—keep your business, your business. What you say to others when you're angry shapes how we see her and guides the advice we give you. Think about it."

Niko considered the counsel, zoning in on his thermos. The steam from the cup danced in the light as particles of dust floated through the wispy tendrils. For a moment, the chaos of the station dissolved into static. His thoughts weaved in and out of trivial notions before he placed the lid on the cup, took a sip, and set it aside. With a final exhausted breath, he turned to his computer and logged in for the day.

The hours dragged about like an ankle weight. The case numbers began to blur: #02-9478—Missing Person; #02-9490—Sexual Assault; #02-9502—Assault and Battery; #02-9555—Attempted Suicide; #02-9565—Bomb Threat. Routine, routine, routine. The same tedium adding further insult to the injury that had become his reputation.

He shuffled through trivial memories to placate his boredom, a tactic his therapist gave him to fend off his anxiety. Keeping his mind busy was never a problem, but all paths led to one memory, and it was the one he most sought to avoid. Such was karma that the haunting memory lingered when it was least desired.

"Ortez," his supervisor, Richard Fleeger, barked from across the room, cutting through the static in his mind. "My office. Now."

Fleeger's broken dialect earned him the infamous nickname "Shatner," but his stuttered tones irked Ortez. He communicated like a dementia patient delivering cryptic messages.

Harrington laughed, mocking him like a child in grade school. "Time to hit the Shatner burner, Ortez."

Brindle shook his head in mild amusement.

Niko stretched back in his chair and took a long swig from his thermos. He adjusted his tie and made his way through the cube farm—affectionately referred to as the bullpen—to Fleeger's office.

"Get the door," his supervisor commanded. Fleeger plopped into his chair and began adjusting the bric-a-brac scattered across his desk, idly maneuvering a picture frame, straightening a pen, moving his stapler, and then moving it back.

Niko closed the door, avoiding the faded cluster of grime formed from years of others habitually touching the same spot. A strange habit that lingered. Sure, he had his share of unusual idiosyncrasies. Who didn't? But his quirks seemed more justified than others.

He took a seat in one of the chairs facing the desk. Harrington referred to them as burners because the only asses hitting those seats were likely getting reamed. The thought pegged him as he sat, causing him to shuffle uncomfortably in the chair. A groaning chorus from the leather cushions followed.

An uneasy quiet settled in the room. Fleeger scanned over emails, ignoring Niko, and Niko examined the office, drumming his fingers on the armrests of the chair. He flicked over the various degrees and certifications framed along the walls. Superfluous trinkets for the position he was in, but they held intrinsic value to Fleeger all the same, even if only to bolster his ego and flex his perceived dominance awarded from years of ass-kissing.

If ruthless brownnosing was an Olympic sport, ole Dick here would be a shoo-in for the gold.

"How long have you been with the bureau?" Fleeger began in his usual droning tone, his eyes still scanning over emails.

"Four years, sir," Niko replied.

"And your probation started…"

"Seven months ago, sir." Exasperation struck Niko already.

"Ah, that's right." Fleeger's eyes glanced at Niko with an arrogant slant, lingering for effect. "It appears family ties don't always guarantee success. As I understand it, your father was quite the accomplished agent. Is that right?"

"It is."

"He retired as special agent in charge at this very station, correct?"

"He did."

"I never met the man, but his acclaim does linger." Fleeger resumed his mindless inspection of emails. The added inflection on every other word drove Niko insane. "He sounds like quite the role model. It's a pity genetics bear no indication on transfer of talent."

"While I appreciate the social visit, sir, I do have a lot of—"

"This station will be undergoing an audit," Fleeger interrupted, "and there are several outdated cases that have slipped out of focus. This is a problem. A select few cases still bear interest. Insistent family members who refuse to leave the past alone. We need someone to follow up on these cases and close them. For a man as renowned as you, this should be an easy task…remedial even."

"Then why not send one of the—"

"This will require some travel. Your expenses and boarding will be provided, of course. Though, the per diem will not be as luxurious as what you are undoubtedly used to from your station in DC. You leave next weekend for Pinnacle Beach."

"I can't do that. I already have a trip planned with my girlfriend to visit her family."

Fleeger held up a hand and peeled his attention away from his screen.

"Girlfriend? So, it's not serious then, and you can make the arrangements." Niko began to protest when Fleeger interrupted him once more. "It wouldn't be wise for a probationer to deny a direct order from their assigned supervisor. Not when they were fortunate enough to maintain an active working status off daddy's reputation."

Niko sat in frustrated silence, wearing a grimace, while Fleeger eyed him carefully. He knew Fleeger was only sending him away out of spite. He had been trying to rile him up to see him suspended for months. Niko couldn't imagine what his grudge was, not that it mattered. He wasn't in a position to argue. He didn't want to sacrifice his career further, so he bore his punishment.

Take it on the chin. Keep your mouth shut.

"Your old boss has requested a follow-up of the incident," Fleeger droned on. "Your six-month report is overdue. He's expecting an assessment of how your therapy sessions are going. As well as a recount of the events from your last assignment."

His extra emphasis on "therapy sessions" added its own insult. Niko stopped drumming his fingers and instead gripped the armchair in dire restraint. "I will get right on it, sir," he said.

Silence settled in again as his nerves began to peak. He jittered his feet.

Niko rose from his chair and started for the door. "If there's nothing else…"

"In fact, there is," Fleeger said. "You have a meeting this evening with the ASACs as well as your old SAC. So, it's best you hurry with that report. Four o'clock. Fifth floor conference room. Don't be late."

Niko lingered at the door, tightening his grip on the handle. His head buzzed with possible scenarios. None were positive. It was irregular for him to meet with his former chief so soon, and doing so didn't bode well.

"Ortez," Fleeger chimed in again. "It's best if you are detailed with your report. And don't expect this to excuse you from your current duties. We still have metrics to adhere to."

Niko exited the office in a rage. He clenched his fists, and his fingers dug into his palms. Biting back an outburst and speeding through the bullpen, he passed his desk, passed the elevators, and burst into the restroom. He slammed his hands on the quartz countertop. "Fuck!"

Wetting his hands, he slicked back his black hair and paced the room. In his anger, he booted the trashcan across the tiled floor, listening to the dull plastic thuds as it skipped around in front of the stalls. He pounded his fists against the wall before turning and leaning back against it, sinking to the floor. His mind sifted through the swirling emotions, absent the fact he sat on a bathroom floor speckled with traces of things he wouldn't want to think about.

Brindle entered the bathroom and swept over to Niko. He leaned his shoulder against the wall and tapped his cigarette pack against his palm, ever defiant of the recent federal ban.

"I take it you heard," Niko said.

Brindle struck a match and lit a cigarette. "No. I didn't need to. There's only one thing I know of that would make you stomp around like that."

"Yeah. Well. I don't imagine it's good news."

"Maybe," Brindle said preceding a cloud of smoke. "But nothing is guaranteed. You need to take a breath and get yourself together, or it won't be. If they see you break down like this, you'll never hold a shield again."

"Rogers will definitely—"

"You don't know that."

"They issued me two years of conditional probation. The only reason they would call me in so soon is because they've reached a decision. I won't be holding a shield again regardless."

"Again, you don't know that." Brindle took a long drag of his cigarette.

"Goddammit." Niko rolled his head back against the wall. "Dr. Rosenberg—it had to be her. She and Rogers go way back. She must have been feeding him notes in the background. I didn't have a chance."

"You're making assumptions."

"The evidence is overwhelming. You know that."

"Actually, I don't." Brindle flicked ash into the sink and ran some water to clear the porcelain. "All I know is Rogers is bringing you in for an early evaluation. Your family name has been in this organization for three generations. Your dad was highly respected, and that earns you points here. Plus, your dad mentored Rogers, so there's a level of respect too."

"I'm far from the agent my father was."

"I disagree. You have the mind for it. You just lack experience, and you're quick to jump to conclusions. You need to pump the brakes on that cynicism. I don't think they'll bar you so early on."

Niko scoffed. "That's highly optimistic."

Brindle shrugged. "I have a feeling it won't be what you think it is." He doused the cigarette under the sink faucet, retrieved the toppled trashcan, and discarded the butt. He squatted next to Niko. "Listen. Pull yourself together and get your report drafted. Start there, and the rest will come together. You're not out of this yet, but you need to show them that your mind is clear…that you aren't holding on to that trauma anymore."

"But I am," Niko replied after some thought. "I can't let it go. What happened was my fault, and because of my incompetence, three men died."

"You know that's not true." Brindle studied him. "There was nothing you could have done."

"I know how I responded." Niko shook his head. "Or didn't. And now I have to carry that with me the rest of my career."

"From what I understand, it happened quick," Brindle replied. "You were the first to get shot, right? Took a hit to the back? You couldn't have seen it coming. No one else did. You can't hold it against yourself.

"Look, I've known you long enough to recognize when you're bottling shit up inside. But the point is not to let them know. You'll come to terms with what happened, and you'll be a better agent because you won't let that shit happen again. Of that I'm certain. But until then, don't give them the leverage, and please God, don't give Fleeger the satisfaction."

Brindle helped him up from the floor, and Niko straightened out his slacks.

"You and I both know that they hold all the leverage already," Niko muttered. "I'm a puppet on a string, baby."

"Christ," Brindle snapped back. "The headaches you get from trying to help people, I swear. Hop off the stick you keep permanently glued up your ass, and pay attention. You're full of assumptions, and not a single one of them is positive. Step out of that pity parade, and get out there, and write your damn review. You're a good worker and a hell of an agent. But you make one mistake, and you let the world crumble on top of you, stomping around like an entitled child. Woe is fucking me.

"Let me clue you in on some words of wisdom your dad shared with me…No one gives a shit. They don't care about you. Most people only care about themselves. You might think everyone is watching, you may even have times where you think people are criticizing you behind your back, but they're not. So, suck it up, sweetheart. Cut the shit, and do what you gotta do."

Niko stood there stunned like a deer in headlights. He expected the eventual impatience but never pegged Brindle as one for the outburst.

"Wow," Niko replied. "I'll be honest, you caught me off guard, Kev. I don't know how to respond to that."

"Good. Then just shut up and listen." Brindle patted Niko on the shoulder. "You've got potential, but you're too in your head. Fix this." He prodded Niko on the temple. "So you can start working with this." He poked a finger at Niko's chest. "Now, if you're finished sucking at the tit of self-deprecation, then let's grab a bite so we can both think straight. I've had my fill of your shit for today. I need a refill if you expect me to keep up my sunny disposition."

He slapped Niko on the back and ushered him out of the restroom. "Oh, and this one's on you," Brindle jested with a playful smile.

Niko tucked his hands into his pockets and chuckled to himself. His inhibitions about the meeting melted away, and the trepid fog in his mind dissipated. His tensions regarding that haunting moment lessened, and he carried it in his walk.

As confidence worked its way back into his mind, he even dared to be hopeful about his upcoming meeting, though uncertainty still played on his anxieties. Choking back doubt with a composing breath, he and Brindle made their way to the elevators, weighing their options for lunch. Guilt still festered, minimizing his appetite, and leaving him to wonder if he would ever be free of its burden.

4

REBEKAH

She faced the room with such aversion she believed it miraculous she'd come at all. Rebekah stood rooted to the spot, enmity in her veins, hand clenched around the door handle, fighting the act of turning it. A burning desire to spin around and go home flooded her, as it did with every visit. But a childish hopefulness urged her to enter. So, she pressed her head against the age-worn green door, breathed deeply, and entered the room.

The tinny whine of the hinges preceded her. She had been attending therapy for over two years, but the sound still caused her flesh to prickle. Her unease kept her on edge, resistant and sensitive to every small thing. Her senses were coated in an indefinable distaste she could only assume was due to the associations crafted in that room. As if the walls carried the acrimony shed from each barrier she'd reluctantly torn down.

Then again, it could be a symptom of the exile constructed by the truth being deflected by contrived attempts at logic. She believed the adults in her life substituted the unknown with rational thinking as a means of controlling that which couldn't be controlled, thus disconnecting themselves from what was possible and what was explainable. The weight of the room was…conflicting.

"It felt odd and poetic and encouraging coming back after so many years, a shape imposing itself on life again after chaos," Mrs. Harrity said as Rebekah entered, though absent of eye contact.

"I'm sorry?"

Mrs. Harrity brought her eyes to meet Rebekah's. "It's a quote."

Rebekah found wisdom in those opaque blue eyes—a wisdom she hated. They gleamed like pale blue topazes, buried in a thicket of wrinkled skin—tiny gems that, under different pretenses, could be beacons for dejected souls. For Rebekah, they were spotlights igniting her frailty, exposing it for what it was. Despite all her wisdom, Dr. Jenorah Harrity lacked perception. She lacked the temperance of what Rebekah felt a therapist should embody, and for that, she was unworthy of Rebekah's respect. That flaw feathered the distance between them.

"The writer is Graham Greene," Mrs. Harrity continued, "while the book…less a book and more of a chronicling, is of his research trips into Africa, compiled out of his journal entries. The quote describes one of his return trips, but I thought it fitting for your own return.

"I am taking my own liberties to manipulate it, of course, as your return is not after years away but a resistant return after some time to what you seem to consider a form of torture. I find it encouraging that despite your lack of desire and faith, here you are all the same. However, the 'shape imposing itself on life after chaos' is where our journey should, hopefully, conclude. Wouldn't you agree?"

"I believe our journey has one conclusion," Rebekah said with a tinge of spite.

Laying her shoulder bag in the chair beside her, as she shrank indifferently into her own.

"As always, I am riveted," Harrity said with a playful smile.

"It is good to have an end to journey toward, but it is the journey that matters in the end," Rebekah said.

"Hemingway." Harrity nodded in approval.

"No," Rebekah said. "Ursula Le Guin, though Hemingway

is more frequently credited. From her book *The Left Hand of Darkness,* if I remember correctly."

"I see." Harrity postured her knuckles under her chin with a smile. "You continue to amaze me. You've always been an avid and passionate reader, a trait I'm quite fond of, but it's the way you carry yourself. I often forget that you're only seventeen." She leaned back in her chair and the leather groaned beneath her movement. "And what is your implication with this quote?"

"You're more interested in shuffling me off to where you believe you're meant to bring me than you are in understanding where you found me. I don't believe this will conclude the way you intend, but if you'd set aside your logic and drop the veil you forced upon me that I'm some delusional child, you'd have a better understanding. Something I think is critical to us moving in a positive direction."

Harrity shook her head and leaned forward once more. "I thought we passed this," she lamented, grabbing a pen and jotting notes onto her yellow legal pad.

"Passed what?"

"The misplaced contempt." Harrity still scribbled feverishly.

Rebekah let the silence linger, allowing her to finish her chronicling. A scornful glare colored Rebekah's face. Never one to pass up the opportunity to make the situation about her, Mrs. Harrity struggled to accept a perception beyond her own. For that reason, Rebekah refused to acknowledge her title of doctor—an achievement that baffled her.

Setting the pen down, Harrity eyed her legal pad once more and returned her attention to Rebekah. She lifted her eyebrows, waiting for a response. Rebekah lifted hers in mocked imitation.

"Okay," Harrity said before taking a deep breath, "let's revisit this then, shall we?"

"Sure." Rebekah folded her arms.

"Rebekah." The therapist brought her hands to her face in frustration. She paused, rubbing her fingers into her temples, and Rebekah could see the impatience edging her temper.

"What is it you need from me to show you that I am on your side?"

"For you to show me that you *are* on my side," Rebekah spat.

"Please, elaborate."

Behind Mrs. Harrity's fierce eyes, genuine concern shone—a sort of pleading for compromise, but Rebekah wouldn't yield. She knew she was acting childish, so she took a calming breath. "I want to be heard," she started, struggling to articulate her emotions. "Or maybe I just want you to believe me. Hear what I'm saying not as a therapist but as a compassionate and sympathetic human being."

Mrs. Harrity considered that. "That may sound easy, but there is no way for me to convince you that I am hearing you as both a therapist and a compassionate human being."

"I disagree. All you understand is point A and point B and how best to go between them. You are so buried beneath your knowledge of the process and response mechanisms that you've lost your humanity. You don't care."

Harrity's brow furrowed in dismay. "That's unfair, Rebekah. I care a great deal. And yes, while I do lean on my education to help navigate these conversations, it is simply to circumvent my own emotional input. My job is to provide you with an unbiased solution to overcome your troubles. I cannot allow my emotions to bleed into the process and provide you with advice that could worsen your situation."

"That's the problem. Maybe the answer isn't in the cold pages of some textbook," Rebekah huffed.

"You're an intelligent young woman, Rebekah." She spoke in a soft tone. "I admire that so much about you. But for all your intelligence, you lack experience with the world."

Rebekah didn't respond. Silence reentered the room, aside from the droning hum of the air conditioning overhead. She hated that excuse; she heard it more than once, and it always came from someone older, as if age and experience were exclusively associated.

Harrity held Rebekah in her gaze for a moment before conceding, shaking her head in disappointment. "You told me about your dreams. You said you see your sister in them."

"Yes." Rebekah shrank back into her chair.

"Could you elaborate? Could you describe these dreams?"

Rebekah groaned. She'd been through the motions. She knew the response she would receive and weighed how much energy she should drain into that empty venture. Beating her head against a stubborn wall wasn't her idea of progress. Still, there was a buoy of hope she desperately wanted to swim for.

"It's always the same," she began. "We're sitting on the edge of a dock, our feet dangling just above the water, and we talk."

"What do you talk about?"

"The conversations evolve. Sometimes we talk about her and how she feels overwhelmed with the pressures Mom and Dad thrust on her. Other times we talk about me and the challenges I'm facing. She gives me advice."

"These are new conversations?" Mrs. Harrity asked with curiosity, her pen poised over the paper.

Rebekah sank into introspection. "No. More like fragments of memories," she replied.

"So, you revisit these moments for comfort."

"No." Rebekah's brows creased in thought. "No, I don't revisit them. It's more like I'm brought to those moments. I don't feel in control, I'm just viewing the moment from the outside, searching for...advice, maybe? Or counsel? Maybe it is comfort."

"In one session," Harrity informed her, consulting her legal pad, "you claimed to believe your sister was actually trying to communicate with you."

"Yeah." Was she mocking her? The thought, as neurotic as it was, left her vulnerable.

"Do you still believe that?" Harrity questioned. "Do you believe that your sister's spirit is visiting you?"

"Would that really be so impossible?"

Mrs. Harrity held her with a pensive stare.

"I never had these dreams...you know, before—"

"Before you tried to take your life?" Mrs. Harrity cut in.

Rebekah hesitated. "Yes." She rejected the suicide attempt

because she knew the truth, but she refused to share that with Mrs. Harrity. She could only imagine the damage it would do to the perceived progress she'd made in her therapist's journal.

Truthfully, she hadn't progressed at all, and blaming it on possession would be devastating. Even she had trouble accepting that reality. But she felt weak—like a weight had pressed down on her. The lies, the avoidance, and the internalization were all so exhausting. An outlet was what she needed, but there was no pinnacle of trust in her life. No one to lean on or share her burdens with. Her friend Anna, maybe. But she feared losing that friendship to a deranged confession. She twisted her hands in her lap.

"I've always found myself drawn to storms," Rebekah said. "There's something calming about them. After my incident, everything changed, and in that moment, when I thought I was dying, it felt more like returning home. I saw my sister. It was the first time she visited me. And from then on, it felt like…I felt like she was there. As if there was some connection to her within the rain."

Rebekah glanced up to study Mrs. Harrity, who watched her with a steady, attentive gaze. Her face remained impassive.

"For a long time, I thought my sister visiting me was what most people saw at the precipice where life meets whatever lies beyond. I told myself that it wasn't her but a guardian angel saving me from a premature death." She chuckled at the absurdity of the thought. "I equated it to people finding religion, and that's what I did. I turned to my faith, after having abandoned it for so long, but I found no answers there. It was after I gave it up for the second time in my life that the dreams became… more, and the familiar comfort of the rain became clear.

"That's when the only answer that made sense occurred to me. The dreams were not manifestations. They were my sister visiting me. My brush with death must have connected me in some way to the other side, like some form of a bridge."

A pause hung in the air like a breath as Rebekah wondered if she said too much. In her mind, she could almost hear the footsteps of the white-clad soldiers tramping down the hall, guns primed with pentobarbital, strait jackets in lieu of handcuffs, ready to cart her away to some padded room. Despite that fear, she continued. She needed to shed the weight, and her words pulled at that thread as if uncoiling her tensions.

"My sister practically raised me. I owe everything I am to her, so maybe I'm not ready to say goodbye. My parents wanted her to be a lawyer or a doctor like them, but she always talked about how she wanted to be a poet or a writer or an artist. And she had the talent for it.

"She taught me wit and sarcasm and showed me how to use my intelligence as a shield against bullies. I still hear them, though. The voices of all the people and the horrible things they say behind my back. I still hear the vile things they whisper about me as I pass them in the halls. They talk about how I don't belong here—that me and my family should be in the slums or in some downtrodden neighborhood with other people who look like me. Other Black families.

"I've been the subject of ridicule my entire life because it makes them comfortable. It's easier for them to view me as a statistic than a person because if I fail, that's just part of the plan. But if I succeed, I'm somehow dangerous to them."

Rebekah paused, head down, picking at the polish on her nails. Tears swam along the brim of her eyes.

"I know these dreams aren't real. I know that," she continued. "But I want them to be. I want so badly for my sister to be here now because I'm lost without her." Her breath grew heavy. "I live in this void—this empty existence. I return every day to a broken home filled with silhouettes of people who used to be my parents, greeted with cold and obligatory formalities. The daughter they wanted, the one they poured all their hope into, is gone, and now…it's just me."

Tears painted a silent tale down Rebekah's cheeks. She wrung her hands together frantically, panic pounding within her.

"I feel empty," she wept between gasps of breath. "I'm so lost, and I need her now more than ever, and she's gone. So, no. I'm not ready to say goodbye. I'm not ready for her to leave, and if these dreams are all I have left of her, then I welcome them."

Silence followed her confession, lending uncertainty to the air. Mrs. Harrity studied Rebekah with a pensive and compassionate stare. It held a mixture of comfort and concern Rebekah couldn't decipher. It wasn't until Harrity moved her knuckles from under her chin and began scribbling more notes in her legal pad that Rebekah settled on which emotion her therapist held more dominantly.

"You must know how unhealthy that is," she said, her voice soft, but her words bit hard. "Memories are wonderful tools, but they cannot replace a person."

Rebekah's panic retreated and a sense of loathing worked its way in. Her eyes turned cold. "Don't..."

"I don't blame you for clinging to some sliver of hope, but you are battling yourself internally." Mrs. Harrity's eyes peered over her glasses. "Consider the child you were. Your closest friend, your sister, was taken from you, followed immediately by your parents abandoning you emotionally. You suffered for years in your own silence until a catalyst appeared, leading you to the only catharsis you could find—which regrettably was to attempt suicide. It was a low, your proverbial rock bottom, and since you never dealt with this grief, it compounded, and the child in you created an imaginary friend, not to be too blunt."

Rebekah clenched her jaw, biting back her explosive outburst for fear of what it might mean if she did.

"It became your life raft in an endless ocean," Mrs. Harrity continued. "Which is why you want so desperately for it to be true."

She paused, allowing the weight of her words to be absorbed. Rebekah's eyes were wide with betrayal.

"But the truth is, you are only hurting yourself to place so much stake in these dreams instead of accepting the reality and moving on. I'm sorry to be so crass, but after two years, at some point the truth must come out. You're afraid to let go because to let go of these dreams would cause you to confront the fact she is indeed gone. I understand the difficulty, and I am sympathetic, but the charade cannot continue. You will bury yourself in this fantasy, unable to reconcile. Your life will have truly ended. Your sister would not want that for you. She would want you to live on to be a poet or a writer."

"I don't think you're quite at liberty to make that decision," Rebekah spat. "She's not here."

"Well, if she does indeed visit you in your dreams, then you have the unique opportunity to ask her."

A moment of tension lingered between them. Rebekah brandished her scowl like a weapon, hatred adorning every inch of her piercing stare. Regret washed over Mrs. Harrity's face, but Rebekah didn't care.

"Fuck you," she said.

Mrs. Harrity recoiled, scrunching her face in offense before scribbling notes on her legal pad. That goddamn legal pad. *Keeping your emotions out of it? Yeah, right.*

"How dare you. You claim compassion, but you dance on my sister's grave, waving around some psychological bullshit—defiling the memory of her so you can try to persuade me to act however you think is best. *Move on,* you tell me. You have no idea what's going on in my life. Two years in this hell, and you haven't heard a damn word I've said."

"Try to view this from another perspective," Harrity said, rubbing her temples in frustration. "First, which sounds more probable, that you are grief stricken from a traumatic experience and have developed methods of shielding yourself from the pain, or that you are being visited by the spirit of your departed sister?

"Second, from a psychological viewpoint, we can explain these dreams you are having and the reason you perceive them the way you do. We have studies to support the diagnosis. But there is no science to conclude the existence of spirits or their ability to communicate with the living in the way you are describing. That leaves us with a spiritual possibility. So, what motivations would your sister's spirit have for lingering? You have given no indication that she is warning you of anything or guiding you toward anything. What unfinished business would she have?

"Finally, which situation has a solution? Which event can we face and remedy?"

What little trust remained fled, leaving a bitter resentment. Harrity had never been an ally to her, though she couldn't deny her attempts. She blamed their gap in age. Their vastly different experiences made it impossible for them to relate to each other, try as they might. Even during the earlier days of family counseling, Harrity resonated more with her parents than with her and every petition Rebekah made to find her a new therapist was denied. She waged a fruitless war, incapable of attaining common ground. Despite that, Rebekah indulged the emotional storm since it gave her some measure of satisfaction.

"The depth of your naivety is staggering." Rebekah's voice was coated in incredulous rage. "You couldn't care less about my struggles or my pain. I'm a paycheck to you. That's all you care about. I'm a puzzle to be worked but not understood—not fixed."

Harrity shook her head. "Two years we've been at this. More than that. I would have thought we'd made a better impression on each other than *that*. I can't believe you think that—"

"It's not a thought," Rebekah growled through her teeth. "I know the game. For two years I've heard how you speak to me, belittle my concerns, and try to manipulate me. You don't listen. You attempt to direct and control me."

Harrity sat in awe at the accusation. The pen dangled from her fingers and her jaw sat slack beneath her wide, unbelieving eyes. Those wise blue eyes.

Rebekah held her in her gaze as one would an enemy, but her mind retreated behind her guard. She sat on the edge of her seat, fingers digging into the arms of the chair, readying herself for the next volley in their verbal conflict. Her jaw clenched so tightly she feared she might break a tooth.

"I don't intend to come off as malicious, though I fear that's how you have written me to be in your mind," Mrs. Harrity said. "I only aim to help guide you out of this dark place you're in, but to do that, you must take the first step. It all begins here, if you're willing to face what scares you the most and overcome it."

The thought of punching Mrs. Harrity was tempting despite Rebekah never being violent in her life. But something clicked in her mind, breaking her anger at the root and a sudden calm enveloped her, something she couldn't place. As if a hand had settled on her shoulder to calm her. The chaotic rattle of her heart steadied, and her fingers loosened their grip.

Mrs. Harrity's words danced in her head as if they held some pragmatic answer. She swirled the thoughts around over and over, lending silence to the room. Her brow furrowed in thought, trying to unravel the mystery forming in her mind.

She rose from the chair, slipping her bag over her shoulder and heading for the exit. As she placed her hand on the doorknob, she turned. "A journey of a thousand miles begins with a single step, Mrs. Harrity," she said before walking out the door.

A calling chorus followed her as Mrs. Harrity jumped up from her chair, beckoning her to come back. The implorations sank into the distant crevices of Rebekah's mind as she trudged down the office corridor and into the elevator lobby.

She floated through the world with an utter lack of awareness of anything happening around her. Her consciousness retreated to the puzzle, ever turning, in her mind. It was as if she was being pulled by a string, guided by some invisible track to an unknown destination. The hand guiding her was softer than the one that had forced her to attempt suicide.

The cool evening breeze greeted her as she exited the building, chilling the tears that wet her cheeks. She paused for a moment, drinking in the fresh night air. The sunset cast a brilliant orange glow along the horizon, lending to a pale blue hue above the clouds.

She exhaled in relief before stepping onto the asphalt of the parking lot and made her way to her car, a forest-green Honda Civic hatchback—the car her sister bought before she died. She placed her hand on top of the vehicle and admired the sunset once again.

Moments like that confirmed she wasn't crazy. She couldn't

have been, could she? She *felt* her sister standing by her. Her presence was so familiar and clear it comforted her. Gave her peace. She closed her eyes and breathed in the evening air once more.

"Tell me I'm not crazy," she whispered. "Please."

Another gentle breeze swam around her, and she smiled. Fresh tears cascaded down the curves of her face. She opened the door, slid into her seat, and started the car. The engine hummed beneath the hood, accompanied by a slight whistling, which sank beneath the music blaring from the radio. Incubus sprang to life, and Brandon Boyd serenaded her.

She sat in her car, sinking into the song and staring off at the horizon. Brandon's words encapsulated her feelings. In that moment, she was happy. Despite it all.

She relaxed in her seat as the fading colors of the sun gave way to the blanket of nightfall. Blue to orange and, at last, to the deep violets and navy of the inexorable darkness. She waited for the few brightest stars to puncture the canopy of night before she finally made her way home.

5

NIKO

THE INCESSANT MOAN OF the overhead vent droned on, accompanied by the rattle of the fan indolently spinning. The air in the room was damp and musty and close. It pressed on him, straining his breathing, which only further elevated his nerves. Niko fidgeted in his seat.

Fifteen minutes late.

Twenty minutes late.

What the fuck? he thought, letting loose a long, disheartened breath.

The stress of the moment gave flight to his nerves. He tapped his feet on the floor and drummed his fingers on his knees.

The door to the conference room finally swung open, and four people filed in. The leader, Niko's old SAC, Brent Rogers, had his head buried in a personnel file Niko assumed was his own. A burly man with thinning brown hair, Rogers wore a suit that looked a size too small, swathed over his muscular frame. Following Rogers were his ASACs, Burton Rodriguez and Jennifer Stewart. Stewart dressed smartly and wore a slackened, distant expression. Her eyes were rimmed in red. It didn't surprise Niko, but he wondered why they had her come in the first place. The person tailing the train made Niko's heart sink—Dr. Shelly Rosenberg.

"I apologize for the delay, Ortez," Rogers started, devoid of eye contact. He and his team made their way to the seats across the table from him. "I was caught up in a press briefing that ran longer than expected. I hope you'll forgive the discourtesy."

Niko swallowed, the dry contraction scraping at his throat. None of them so much as glanced his way until they sat. Dr. Rosenberg was the first to make eye contact, but her face was deadpan, as usual.

"It's not a problem, sir." Niko's voice was raspy.

"I don't intend to take up much of your time, Ortez. So, we'll make this brief," Rogers stated in his gruff voice, finally looking up from the folder. "I received your report concerning your last assignment. Considering this incident was over six months ago, I appreciate the level of detail you were able to articulate. It was noted that your report from today was consistent with your initial after-action report. From the bureau's own investigation into the incident, we found no fault on your end."

Rogers paused to study Niko, who sat stoic, marinating in his own nerves and sweat. He wasn't sure how to respond, so he simply processed the information from beneath what he hoped was an impassive expression.

"I hope this information offers some level of comfort to you," Rogers continued. "The situation was a tragic one, and from what we can discern from your weekly visits with Dr. Rosenberg, the guilt of the incident has been weighing on you. Would you care to share your thoughts on this?"

Niko's heart thumped as the flashing memories haunted him. They weighed like an anchor on his mind, disrupting the train of thought he was trying to summon to answer the question.

"Sir," he began, "I appreciate the bureau's decision of no fault, but that was never a concern for me. I wasn't worried about being held liable. I hold myself accountable in my own way. The training I received should have prepared me for such a situation, but fear kept me rooted to the floor. My lack of response meant officers died, and I feel guilty about that. I'm still trying to absolve myself of that guilt."

Niko wrung his hands together and continued tapping his feet on the floor.

"I have tried to explain away the pain of the incident in my sessions with Dr. Rosenberg. But no matter how hard I try to deflect, the hard truth is that I failed to assess the situation enough to do the right thing. As a result, those men escaped justice."

Niko's eyes met Rogers's. As he peered over his glasses, his hand paused between turning pages in the folder. Agent Stewart shuffled in her seat.

"I may not have been responsible for what happened to those officers, but I didn't act in service of their deaths either. That failure still hangs over me. My ineptitude brought grief to their families, and that knowledge weighs on me every day. I understand this testimony doesn't bode well for my career, but I feel it necessary to be transparent."

Niko paused to take a breath, his voice beginning to shake with nerves. He glanced around the room to see everyone intently focused on him, all except for Agent Stewart, who stared into her lap. He closed his eyes and continued.

"You asked if this decision offers me comfort. While I am relieved to know I'm cleared in the eyes of the bureau, the decision doesn't change what happened. The event has marked me in a way I will never forget, and the lessons learned from this I will carry to the end of my career."

Niko gripped his knees. The piercing stares and the weight of judgment bore down on him. Rogers and Rosenberg began jotting down notes in their files. Rodriguez zoned into the wood grain of the table and Stewart avoided Niko's gaze entirely.

Her eyes glossed over with tears. He wasn't naïve to the reason. He watched her brother die, and that guilt fell on him. He couldn't imagine the pain she was in, having to live through that moment again, and there was nothing he could do to ease her suffering. He found himself wondering again why she was there. Was it by choice or duty?

The droning of the overhead vent returned to drown out the uneasy silence. The squeak of the fan textured the moan like mocking laughter. Niko was relieved at having been honest but not without the supplementary doubt of it—the uncertain course his career would take following his confession. He rolled the dice, and the rest was left to fate. No matter the decision, he swore he wouldn't let himself regret his candor. He couldn't. It was the only sense of morality he felt from the whole ordeal.

Brent cleared his throat, and the silence dissipated. "It's remarkable to me how much like your father you are."

He considered Niko with a steady gaze. Niko flushed with embarrassment and his heart rapped violently at his rib cage.

"You could have lied," Brent said. "You could have paraded with confidence, shrugging off your responsibility under the pretext that the bureau had absolved you of guilt on paper. I've seen agents do it countless times. But you wear your failures with humble admonition. It was in that humility that I developed a great deal of respect for your father. And now for you. I agree with your statement that there is more you could have done, but I also agree with the decision of no fault. We are only human, after all.

"I take comfort in your self-awareness. And it leads me to believe that the weight of this mistake will make you more cautious, or persistent, in the future. I hope I'm not wrong about that."

Rogers returned to his document and flipped through a few pages. The beat of Niko's heart steadied.

"I am providing a recommendation to terminate your probation and return you to active special agent status. This is conditional on the conclusion of your psychological review. Dr. Rosenberg will keep me updated on the results. As I recall, you have three months of counseling remaining."

Dr. Rosenberg nodded. The two ASACs scribbled frivolous notes, reminders of the tasks they would need to complete to get him reinstated, he imagined.

"I hope to see an improvement in your mental state," Brent said. "Carrying guilt is a laborious task, Niko. It has its benefits. But it's a poison that can impair your judgment and dilute good intentions with careless mistakes. Focus on clearing your head."

He stood, followed by his two subordinates.

"Until then, complete your required duties here. Whatever

they need. I know Fleeger can be a bit…abrasive, and that's likely to get worse when this news reaches him. All the same, I expect you to respect his command. We will reevaluate in three months."

Rogers and his team filed out of the room. Niko let out a long, shaky breath, raising his hands behind his head and leaning back in his chair. A weight slid from his shoulders, a smile crept onto his face, and the burden of anxiety uncoiled from his chest. He swiveled lazily in his chair, drinking in the pleasure of the moment. But all such pleasures were forgotten when his eyes fell on Dr. Rosenberg, still observing him from her seat. Her eyes poised, she studied him from beyond her emerald-rimmed glasses.

The tension in the room was palpable—Niko brimming with nerves, and Dr. Rosenberg as reticent and pensive as ever. His eyes flitted over the features of her face, trying to read her, but she kept her impassive demeanor. A necessary consequence of years of analyzing officers, agents, and detectives. The creases around her lips finally relaxed, and she diverted her attention to her notepad and scribbled a short thought. Following a quick breath, she broke the silence.

"I trust you're aware of my position regarding our sessions."

He wasn't. He stared at her, skimming the archives of his memories for anything she might be indicating. She didn't wait for him to respond.

"I decided to omit the issue of your anxiety from my report to Rogers, but it is an issue that will need to be addressed if you expect me to clear you to return to the field. Of course, he's no fool, so he has his suspicions."

Niko shifted his eyes. That was what Rogers was questioning earlier. Of course, he knew. Rogers's career began in interrogation, reading people, and Niko's struggle with anxiety might as well have been a neon sign.

"You won't admit to it, but I'm not a fool either. I've left the issue for you to address at your own pace, but it appears you'll require more of a push before you face the subject. Perhaps this meeting was just what you needed. But I won't endorse your reinstatement if you don't open up."

Niko's chest tightened at the thought of digging into the topic. He hadn't realized he was avoiding the subject, but his reaction gave an indication of why. It made sense, but it didn't make the situation easier. He wanted nothing more than to return to fieldwork, to escape from beneath the power-hungry hand of Fleeger, who would undoubtedly increase the pressure of his perceived dominance while he still could.

He had been holding his breath and attempted to ease himself down with a slow exhale. Dr. Rosenberg nodded as she jotted down more notes.

"We are not exploring the topic today, so you can relax. I wanted you to be prepared as this will be the primary focus for the next three months."

She gathered her documents and stood but hesitated. Her pensive eyes danced in thought for a moment. She gazed at him, her brows creased, and a moment of genuine emotion escaped her, surprising Niko.

"I take great pride in my work, Niko. What I do ensures people can respond in critical situations and save lives. You can understand the weight on me. If I should fail, I bear some responsibility for those deaths. Because of that, I will not grant any exceptions to my expectations. I have heard you are a gifted agent with a keen mind and a careful eye, but that will not absolve you from this exercise. I expect you to take these remaining sessions seriously. Lives do depend on it."

She fled the room, leaving Niko alone with his thoughts. The impact of her words lingered, echoing through his head until the hum of the fan returned, interrupting the growing silence, its drone heavier somehow. His hands rested on his knees, his palms slick with sweat.

Glancing around the empty room, marinating in the conflicting emotions, he tried to make sense of the chaos entombed within him. He knew the challenges ahead so intimately they pressed on his chest. The thought occurred to him it may well be his own anxieties instead. That was followed by the afterthought they were one in the same. His nervousness was a challenge, and the more he reflected on it, the more he realized the impact it had on him.

He stood up from his chair, slid it back under the large oak table, and left the room. Making his way from the building to his car, his mind organized and cataloged, attempting to declutter the mess of thoughts and arrange them into something more coherent.

"Hell, yeah!" Harrington cheered through rosy cheeks, his voice muffled beneath the commotion of the bar. "Dude, that is awesome news!"

He raised his glass and toasted with Niko. He was drunk. Brindle, on the other hand, composed himself a little more cordially. He smiled and nodded as he nursed his whiskey neat, a cigarette resting on a crystal ashtray. Niko gulped back a mouthful of Yuengling. Brindle returned his glass to its black napkin and gripped Niko's shoulder.

"I'm happy for you," he said. "But more importantly, I'm happy I don't have to hear you bitch and moan anymore."

Harrington chuckled. "I'll drink to that!"

"Oh, I'm still going to bitch and moan," Niko said. "It's what I do. It's who I am."

They laughed. Harrington turned his attention to a group of women sitting next to them at the bar, slurring his words through failed one-liners and boozy swagger. Brindle glanced beyond Niko, who sat between the two, to watch Mikey strike out and chuckled to himself when he did. There was something about the arrogance of the young and single he missed, he had told Niko.

It's not that he misses it, Niko thought. *It's nostalgia*. It reminded him of the times he spent chasing his wife in his youth. There was a positive attachment to it that helped him overlook the humiliation.

Niko watched the foam settle in his drink, thinking back to the meeting and the conflicting emotions. He was happy to be reinstated, but the thought of facing his trauma seemed overwhelming. Especially with everything else going on. He bounced his feet on the crossbar of the stool as he rolled his finger along the brim of the glass.

"I need some air." Brindle slapped him on the back. "Let's step outside."

Niko nodded and jumped off the stool to follow him out. They exited into the humid evening, Brindle already priming another cigarette at his lips. He took a long drag, exhaled a cloud of smoke, and pondered the sky for a moment. The shopping center around them was alive with light, but the focus was the sports bar where they stood outside. A popular place called Barry's Taphouse.

"Talk to me," Brindle said.

Niko paced a short way down the sidewalk and turned back toward Brindle, who was leaning against the brick exterior. "I don't want to go home tonight," he replied.

Brindle eyed him, his cigarette hanging limply from his hand by his side. "Okay," he said with a confused glance. "You're gonna have to give me more than that."

Niko ran his hand through his hair and rubbed away the tension in his neck. He paused in his steps, looked up, and breathed heavily. "Today's been chaotic, but so far, it's ending on a good note. If I go home, I'm gonna have to break the news to Dee that Fleeger is sending me on travel the weekend we're supposed to visit her family. She won't like that. She'll blame the fight we had last night and throw some spiteful accusations, likely implying that I never wanted to go in the first place. I just don't want to deal with it. I want tonight to end on this good note."

"You think the best solution is to avoid the conversation?" Brindle took another drag from his cigarette.

"No." Niko sighed. "But maybe…delay it? I don't know."

"It'll be waiting for you when you go back home. Only it'll be worse because you're intentionally avoiding her. She'll like that even less."

Niko didn't respond. Instead, he gave a lackadaisical nod.

"I thought the same way." Brindle flicked his cigarette away and prepped another. "I used to avoid confrontation with Emily. It was easier for me to drag it out until she forgot or just moved on. It was always trivial. I justified it by telling myself I didn't want to have memories of us fighting. Just the good times. But now, I wish I would've spent more time talking to her. Sure, we would have argued, but doing what I did caused a coldness between us. Now that she's gone, that coldness is all I remember."

Brindle lowered his head. Tendrils of smoke wove a delicate dance along his arm, ephemeral spirits captured by the evening breeze. With a tremulous breath, a smoky veil enshrouded his face.

"Don't do what I did, kid. I know you love her. You talk tough like you don't, but I know you better than that. If I've learned anything, it's that if something's important to you, you make the time for it. If you dodge the issue now for your own petty reasons, it'll only widen the distance. You'll miss these moments when they're gone, and you can't get 'em back."

Niko stepped over to Brindle and patted him on the shoulder. He was being selfish. His problems seemed so small in comparison. While he worried about a tough conversation with Danielle, the woman he loved, Brindle was coping with the fact he would never have another conversation, tough or otherwise, with the woman he loved. A tear slid down Brindle's cheek, but his face remained stoic.

Niko pointed at the cigarette. "You know, those things will kill you."

Brindle examined the butt and gave Niko a weak smile and a soft chuckle.

"You're right," Niko said, fidgeting with the keys in his pocket. "I'm gonna head out of here and get this conversation out of the way."

"Smart man," Brindle said, a distant sorrow coloring the depths of his eyes.

"You and Mikey gonna be all right?"

"Yeah, we'll call a cab. Don't worry about us. Just go take care of business."

Juggling his keys briefly, he pondered the man's advice before making his way to his car. He drove home in the quiet. Imaginary scenarios ran through his mind of the conversation he was about to have. He played out different approaches, trying to settle on something sympathetic. He decided to make it up to her with a vacation when he got back. As he turned onto his street, however, his heart sank. There was a car in his driveway he didn't recognize.

6
REBEKAH

DESPITE HER HUNGER AND the inviting smell of the roast, Rebekah's appetite was absent. Sitting at the vanity, which looked worthless with the mirror gone, she reviewed her homework. She had read over the last question a handful of times, but her attention retreated deeper into the caverns of her thought.

Tapping her pen on the notebook with her head slumped into her hand, she listened to Yellowcard over the radio. She zoned in on the peeling black polish on her nails, unmoving and unmotivated. Something in what Mrs. Harrity had said pricked at her, dragging her thoughts down as if a weight were attached to them. It was all she could focus on.

It all begins here, if you're willing to face what scares you the most and overcome it, she had said.

Rebekah wasn't afraid, though, she was curious. She sought the visits from her sister, and on the nights when none came, she woke with an emptiness inside her. Perhaps she *was* afraid; afraid the dreams would end and her connection to her sister, if there was such a thing, would cease. Then what? What would she have left?

Her dad knocked on the door, gently easing it open. "Rebekah, dinner's ready."

"Okay," she responded.

Walking away, he left the door open. He *was* trying. She knew that. But a spiteful voice inside her insisted his efforts were too little, too late. His tone was softer, and he approached her with more sympathy, but his prior disregard for her still lingered. So, she reserved a measure of anger toward him. Tossing her pen aside, she pushed the chair back from under the desk, the feet scraping against the hardwood floor.

As she made her way down the stairs, she paused, as she normally did, near the family photos hanging on the wall and adorning the entryway table. She admired those of her sister, and as usual, her heart sank a little lower in her chest. She continued to the kitchen where her mother was setting a Crock-Pot in the center of the table. Plates were placed at the respective chairs, ornamented with food.

Her parents took their usual seats at each end of the table, while Rebekah sat on the side closest to her mother. They joined hands for their routine prayer, but Rebekah kept her eyes open in mild defiance of the gesture. She remained quiet, however. The sounds of utensils clinking against the dinnerware filled the room as they closed the blessing. An uneasy silence underpinned the scraping of cutlery.

It didn't last long since Rebekah's father dove into conversation a few bites into his meal.

"Mrs. Gorman called today," he said, and judging by his tone, it must have been a trying day. "Your grades have been slipping, and you're three assignments behind in her class. She said she's willing to allow you time to make them up, so I suggest you focus your attention this weekend on completing those."

Rebekah nodded. He didn't care about the grades, she thought. He cared he had to be bothered with yet another one of her inadequacies. It embarrassed him. It cast an unclean light on his ability to control his child. Parenting, he would call it. Dodging his prod, she bit her tongue and kept her attention fixed on her plate in supercilious silence.

Her inaction didn't go unnoticed, and her father responded tersely, "I don't think you should act so recklessly about your education."

"I'm not being reckless—"

"You're ignoring assignments, and it's impacting your grades. That sounds reckless to me."

Rebekah retreated to silence again. He was trying but not then. He was backsliding to the old, impatient temperance with which she was so painfully familiar. Conflict was his therapy.

"I shouldn't need to impress upon you the importance of your education." His knife scraped across his plate. "You need it if you have any hopes of a decent career in the future."

"You mean so that I can have such fulfilling careers as you and Mom?"

She didn't look up, but she could feel her father's glaring eyes. Scrunching her face, she reproved her lack of decorum in indulging him.

Her mom stopped eating. Unlike her father, conflict didn't sit well with her. It disturbed her appetite, even before Nicole went missing.

Stabbing at the meat with his fork, her father took another bite, sighing through his chewing, almost relieved. "You're free to enlist in any career that makes you happy," he said slowly. "But that is no excuse to insult our choices." The battle to remain calm edged his face and settled beneath the bulging muscles of his clenched jaw.

Rebekah couldn't restrain herself from prodding further. "No, you're right. I could start my own family, pressure them to live up to my expectations, and renounce them when they fall short."

"With such biting wit, you'd think you'd have the maturity to back it up," her father said. "But like a child, you can't see past your own emotions."

Rebekah smirked. "Says the man arguing with a child."

"You are a child. You're my child! I suggest you remember that and what it means."

Rebekah glanced up, and they held each other's stare in a competition Rebekah was the first to withdraw from. Her mother pressed her fingers into her temples. After a moment, her father returned to his meal.

"Maybe I can be sued for medical malpractice too," Rebekah mocked. "Like an adult. Right, Mom?"

Her father slammed his fist on the table, and the silverware rattled with the quake.

"Victor!" her mother gasped.

"I will not tolerate you disrespecting your mother!" he shouted.

Rebekah met his eyes once again. They were blazing. She steeled herself, but her confidence wavered, and she cast them back to her plate.

"You know better," he said.

Guilt riddled her once again. Why? Why couldn't she just shut up for once? Her anger, or pride—whatever it was—warped her emotions and abandoned her logic.

"You're right," she said. "I'm sorry."

She looked at her mother, who gave her a gentle smile and patted her hand. Her indifference toward her mother had softened over the last few years. Rebekah had come to appreciate her for everything she'd done to make amends. But her family was more traditional, meaning her father held the gavel and had the final say. He withheld his judgement. Instead, a palpable hush loomed over the table until he finally spoke again.

"While we're on the subject, what thoughts do you have for a career?"

"I haven't given it much thought." Rebekah pushed her food around on her plate absentmindedly.

"Well, you're seventeen," he said. "It may not be a bad idea to start thinking about it. If you choose to be a lawyer like me or a doctor like your mother, it will require a long investment in your education. Your mother and I have talked about it, and we would be happy to cover the costs."

Rebekah sifted through the words to find the catch. Yeah, they would pay, and she would be bound to whatever measure of achievement they thrust on her. Their money, their rules.

"And what if I want a degree in English literature to become a writer or a poet?"

Her father scoffed, and her mother cleared her throat. They met eyes across the table, and she urged her husband on with raised eyebrows. It was an encouragement toward a softer hand, a juggle they adopted three years ago, following Rebekah's "accident," as her mother liked to refer to it.

"If that's the path you wish to take, we will support you," her father said begrudgingly. "But it's a foolishly high-risk path."

"It's the one I'd like," Rebekah replied.

"We'll talk more about it later," her father said. "I don't think it's a choice that should be made so lightly. At least examine your options."

"Well, I'm sorry your protégé is gone, and you're left with me and my disappointing choices."

"That's enough, Rebekah." He sounded exhausted.

"I'll work harder next time to rid you of this burden," she spat. But why did she do that? She could agree and then choose her own path later. So why did she goad and antagonize him?

He tightened his grip on his utensils. "I said enough." Dropping them, he buried his face in his hands. "I won't hear any more about it."

"You haven't heard it as it is!"

"It's not an appropriate conversation for the dinner table."

"If you cared at all, you would listen!" Rebekah shouted. "Why can't you just fucking care? What did I ever do to you?"

"I said that's enough!" Her father slammed both hands on the table hard enough to topple the empty crystalware, cracking one of the glasses as it hit the wooden surface. "I will not have you wielding your *dysfunction* as a weapon to assault your mother and I with whenever you feel the least bit threatened. You have no idea the stress we are under right now. Your mother could lose her medical license if we don't—"

"Victor!" her mother hissed.

He stood, baring over her, using his size to impose his will on her, but restraint battled beneath his stare. Tears brimmed Rebekah's eyes, and her lips trembled, but anger swept over the sense of pleading, steeling her resolve. She refused to let him see her cry.

"Maybe I'm not the only one who needs to think about my future," she muttered before she could stop herself.

He snatched her plate from the table, stormed through the kitchen, and dumped the food into the trash before throwing the plate into the sink. It shattered, and Rebekah's mother winced at the sound, tears glistening on her cheeks.

"Go to your room," her father said.

Rebekah pushed off the table and charged toward the stairs. Pausing again by the family photos, she sifted through the emptiness within her. Her parents' conversation continued in the kitchen, and from the hall, she listened.

"Was that necessary?" her mother asked.

"I won't be disrespected in my own home, Evelyn. Nor will I tolerate her disrespecting you."

"Look at everything she's been through, Victor," her mother said. "It's been rough on her. We've been rough on her. Give her a break."

A chair slid, and a small thud sounded as her father sat. He breathed deeply. Rebekah pressed her head against the wall.

"You're right," he said. "You're right. It's just…at her age, Nicole was so ambitious and motivated. She had her career planned out and was well on her way to achieving her goals. Rebekah is nothing like Nicole. I'm not sure how to reach her."

Rebekah felt a cool spot on her cheek and realized she was crying, although she wasn't sure if the tears were from grief or anger.

"Maybe she doesn't need to be reached," her mother said. "And flying off the handle in an emotional fit isn't helping anything."

"What should I do then? Rebekah is so different than Nicole was."

Soft clinking indicated a spoon against ceramic. She imagined her mother nursing her nightly cup of chamomile tea.

"Yes, they are different," her mother said. Another chair slid against the tiled floor. "But it doesn't make one better than the other. Rebekah may not be where we think she should be, but she's headstrong and tenacious. She doesn't budge when we push her."

"She should," her father said firmly. "She has ideas for her future that will leave her struggling. She's better than that, and she has more potential than that. If she struggles when she's older, then it's her own damn fault."

"Victor. She's still just a child."

"She's seventeen, Evelyn. She's not a child anymore."

"Then why do you treat her like one?"

"I push her to act responsibly, to act smarter," he said. "Don't tell me what she's been through. You and I are managing it fine and so much more. This case is—"

Rebekah pushed off the wall and made her way upstairs. She didn't want to hear any more. It was all too familiar. There was a level of comfort knowing her mom was on her side at least. It was less lonely, but at the same time, the distance between them was wider than ever. While her mom wanted to help comfort her, she didn't know the half of it—the part she had only spoken to Mrs. Harrity about, and what a mistake that had been.

She didn't care what Mrs. Harrity thought. She didn't care what anyone thought, really, but the less people she let see behind the curtain, the better. It was drama and stress she didn't need, no matter how well she could weather it. She hadn't even told Anna about it, and they were best friends. Anna had helped her through the worst parts of losing her sister and was there for her after her accident more than anyone else.

Maybe I should tell Anna. She would understand, wouldn't she?

Rebekah pulled out her phone as she crossed into her room, head down and mind churning through her rampant thoughts. Apprehension rattled her heart as the thought of calling Anna willed itself into her mind. Both excitement and trepidation warred within her, but movement caught her attention, halting her steps, and she looked up.

She froze in fear at the figure darkening the space, a shadow from her past. Its imposing shape consumed the corner of her room. A cloaked apparition with tendrils of smoke cascading down its form and pooling on the floor like a cloud, it gave the impression it was floating as it stared at her. There were no eyes on the featureless face, but its gaze pierced through her all the same. There was no doubt in her mind she was facing the creature she had before.

Suddenly, she felt a tightness in her chest. She wasn't breathing—she *couldn't* breathe. The figure started for her, flitting across the floor, its arm outstretched. Her mouth opened to scream, but her breath stayed trapped in her chest. Stepping away, she brought her hands up to defend herself but snagged her foot on the threshold and fell backwards. Eyes closed, hands blocking her face, she awaited her fate.

But nothing happened.

She opened her eyes and gazed into her empty room. Nothing was there.

Had she imagined it?

No, it was too much like that night all those years ago, and she would *not* let herself walk that path again. But despite her will, paranoia crept into her head, and she began to shudder at every little noise, expecting voices to whisper to her. None did, and her mind remained silent, save for the dull thuds of a creeping headache.

Crawling across the floor toward her bed, she crept under the covers and pulled the blanket close to her face. Her eyes wandered around the room warily. Her breath returned, sharp and panicked, while "Something of Value" played over the radio.

She jumped at another loud clink as her parents, or at least her mother, did the dishes downstairs. Her light stayed on that night. She wasn't sure when she went to sleep, but she spent hours awake in a terrified, catatonic state, and she didn't dream. For the first time in a long time, she was glad of that.

7

NIKO

NIKO'S HEADACHE RETURNED AS dinner came to a close. As if he didn't have enough to deal with. It had indeed been a long day. He only wished it were over. But that was his milieu. Bad luck gravitated toward him like a moth to a flame. Case in point, the surprise visit from Danielle's parents. Better than another man in his bed but not a welcomed relief.

Danielle and her mother stood from the table. They started collecting the dishes, still going about their conversation. Her father, Charles, hadn't said much throughout dinner, but then again, neither had Niko. He only added a few nods or grunts. As Danielle collected the plates, Niko buried his palms into his eyes, trying to smother out his exhaustion. He glanced toward Charles, who stared into the woodgrain of the table in ponderous concentration.

Niko rose and found Danielle hunched over the sink. He slid his arms around her hips and buried his head into her shoulder. Raising a hand to his head, she smiled and ran her fingers through his thick black hair. For a moment, they were statues, bound in each other's embrace. He wished they could stay that way, but unfortunately, the thought of their impending conversation weighed on his mind. His stress wouldn't allow him peace. So, he kissed her neck and let her return to the dishes.

"What are they doing here?" he whispered in her ear.

"Dad had some medical thing in DC." She shrugged. "He said they wanted to come by for a surprise visit."

Niko scoffed. "Wonderful."

"Don't. Please?" she asked. "I don't want to fight anymore."

Niko ran his hand down her back, wishing it were that simple. He sighed and nodded his head. "You're right. I don't want to fight either. I'm sorry."

"Nikolas." Charles stood at the foot of the table. "I'd like a word."

"It's Niko," he muttered back, but Charles had already started toward Niko's office.

Even in his home, Charles never respected him. Niko never thought it worth the trouble to initiate the power struggle. Maybe it was his fault. Despite that, the audacity of it irked him. He groaned and gave Danielle's shoulder a comforting squeeze before trudging off after her father. Why couldn't he catch a fucking break?

He made his way to the makeshift office. It was a quaint room. Bookshelves bordered the walls and at the center sat a grand, antique mahogany desk, which once belonged to his father. Charles poured himself a glass of whiskey from the imitation globe decanter. Elijah Craig. Not a fancy bourbon, and not what he preferred, Niko imagined.

To his surprise, Charles poured a second glass and offered it to him. Reluctantly, and with some suspicion, Niko accepted. He took a sip as Danielle's father returned the decanter to its stand.

"What's on your mind, Charles?" Niko asked.

Charles took a sip from his glass, dipping his free hand into his pocket and rolling the spirit over his tongue. He swallowed and considered the drink for a moment before turning to Niko.

"I never told you, but Lisa and I were deeply concerned when Danielle called us with the news you'd been shot. My daughter was a wreck. She could hardly contain her emotions. It took every ounce of our attention to calm her while you were in the hospital. It was an exceedingly difficult time for us."

"Sure," Niko replied, chasing his anger with a swig of whiskey.

Why wouldn't *it be a difficult time for you? I was the one who was shot,* he thought.

"In fact, it was a great relief to us when we learned you were confined to desk work." Charles swirled the whiskey in his glass. "You can imagine my disappointment when we heard you'd petitioned to be reinstated to agent." He observed Niko from beneath a raised eyebrow.

Niko stared back blankly. He always thought of Charles as a narcissistic prick, but he never imagined he would sink so low. Niko wanted to reply but thought better of it.

"As a father, I hoped you would consider Danielle's feelings on the matter and recognize the stress your job places on her. Her worry is unnecessary, and it's selfish of you to discard it in pursuit of your own…ambitions."

"You're not really one to be lecturing me about Danielle's feelings," Niko replied with a chill in his voice. "You were absent throughout most of your daughter's childhood."

"I was eager and naïve when I was younger, that is true." Charles nodded and turned his attention to the spirit settling in his glass. "It left me with many regrets. But I'm working to make amends for them."

"By controlling who's in her life?"

"By helping to guide her to a future that will make her happy." Charles held Niko with a penetrating stare. "I'm painfully aware that she chose you in high school to spite me. I was ignorant to think she would outgrow you as she matured."

"Outgrow me?" Niko shook his head. "You don't even know me."

"I know you well enough."

"You judge people based on fancy titles instead of their character," he replied. "I'm not a millionaire, I get it, but I love Danielle. As a father, shouldn't that be enough?"

Charles laughed, taking another swig of whiskey before setting it on the desk. "That's a childish notion. To think that love is all a relationship needs. You're young, and there is still so much you don't understand."

"Maybe not, but it's been working pretty damn well for us so far."

"You haven't faced any real difficulties yet," Charles said, puffing out his chest and crossing his arms. "You have no idea how life changes when you have children. Even marriage brings its share of challenges. Adding a job as unpredictable as what you're after only adds to the chaos. Why can't you settle for a desk job? There's security in that. Comfort."

"Because I enjoy being an agent. It gives me pride to know that what I do protects people."

"A noble pursuit, I'm sure." Charles snatched the glass and took another sip.

"Do you have a point to any of this?" Niko asked.

Charles inhaled deeply, contemplating his whiskey. "Two years ago, when you asked for my blessing to marry my daughter—"

"Which you rejected," Niko interrupted.

"For good reason. I made my case clear a moment ago. Your job is foolishly high-risk, and should the worst happen, who would be left to protect my daughter? Or your children?"

Niko laughed. "I don't know what's more insulting. That you think I'm so incompetent or that you think your daughter is incapable of taking care of herself."

"She shouldn't have to!" Charles's anger rose, and his posture stiffened. His hand tightened around the glass. "Lisa and I would rather she live comfortably, without the constant fear of becoming a widow, than wallow in the dregs with you."

Niko wore a quizzical look and nodded his head incredulously. He raised his glass to his lips as his eyes scanned the room. He surveyed his modest home and what little luxury it contained, almost all of which was bequeathed to him with the passing of his father.

Niko scratched the stubble on his chin and responded in a calm manner, "This may not be Beverly Hills, but we're happy here. You forget where you came from. Before your money and acclaim, you lived here in the suburbs of Virginia just like we do. Danielle called this place home before you abandoned it for the sunny hills of California. This is where we met, and many of our friends are still here." Niko leaned his shoulder against one of the bookshelves, dipping his free hand into his pocket. He examined the designs on the crystal glass. "She's a very capable and driven woman, and she'll be incredibly successful one day. She has no desire to play the housewife like you want her to."

Charles considered that while throwing back the remaining whiskey. Pondering the empty glass, seemingly rolling the conversation around his head, he turned and poured another finger.

"You have both grown so much as individuals," Charles said. "Yet you have grown so little within the relationship. You still act like children."

He swirled the whiskey around the glass again. The soft clinks of Charles's wedding band tapping against the crystal underscored the tension. He muttered more to himself than to Niko, "I should have put a stop to this years ago." He looked Niko in the eyes. "I won't allow this relationship to continue any longer."

A sting struck Niko, challenging his temper, but he reverted to his interrogation training. Composure controlled the conversation, so he took a moment to regain his.

"You have no right to demand anything from this relationship," Niko said. "I asked for your blessing as a courtesy, and I have honored your wishes out of respect. But Danielle is an adult. She's not bound to your every want and desire."

"She's my daughter!" Charles slammed his glass down on the desk, droplets of whiskey sloshing over the sides. "I will not see her mortgage her future away with you."

Despite the adrenaline beating at his heart, Niko smirked, fire blazing in his eyes. When he spoke, his voice was steady, deliberate, and composed. "That's not your choice to make."

Charles scowled at him. He retrieved his drink and threw back the whiskey. He placed the empty glass upside down on the desk and made his way to the door, pausing next to Niko. "We'll see about that," he snarled before exiting the room.

Niko remained behind, trying to shed the stress of the conversation. Under heavy, calming breaths, he approached the desk and set his drink down, allowing the façade he wore to melt away. He drove a punch into the durable mahogany, a final remittance of anger. Endorphins muted the pain that met his knuckles, and Niko lifted Charles's glass, wiping up the whiskey ring it left behind.

What a dick.

He retrieved his drink and took another sip, grimacing slightly as the spirit sank to his stomach. Charles's voice resounded from the kitchen, barking commands at his wife. There was a brief shuffle and hurried goodbyes before the door slammed shut on a quiet house, and he breathed in relief.

Niko slumped over the desk, his fingers pressed against the wood. Snatching up the whiskey glasses, he made for the kitchen. He dumped the remaining alcohol in the sink and rinsed the crystalware as Danielle entered the room bemused.

"What happened in there?"

"Just…your dad…" Niko replied, furiously scrubbing at the tumbler.

"You know, he does a lot for us. You could be a little nicer." She leaned against the counter next to him.

Niko coughed out an astonished laugh. He slapped the sink handle down to cut off the water and slammed the crystal glasses into the drying rack. For a moment, he thought he might have damaged them.

"He does a lot for you. He doesn't give a fuck about me." Niko turned to her, drying his hands off on the towel hanging from the dishwasher.

Danielle straightened up. "What? That's bullshit, and you know it."

"He just chastised me for trying to get my status renewed," Niko said. "He thinks I should twiddle my thumbs at a fucking desk for the rest of my life."

Danielle glanced away ruefully.

As the realization dawned on him, he threw his hands up. "Oh, come on. You too?"

"I may have mentioned to my mom that I liked knowing you

were safe," Danielle replied. "That's it. I didn't think he'd try and guilt-trip you."

"Well, he did, and it didn't go over well."

"It's not his fault, okay?" Danielle rubbed her arm nervously. "He's just looking out for me. That's what dads do."

"Yeah? And what do you think?" Niko's emotions were teeming from his earlier meeting, her father, and Danielle's newly discovered hidden feelings.

She couldn't hold his stare. "I like not having to worry about you."

He turned away from her, stomping off. She chased him and grabbed his shoulder.

"I don't want that to stop you!" she cried. "All I want is for you to be happy."

Niko rounded on her. "Well, you know that desk job you love so much? They're sending me on assignment the weekend we're supposed to fly out to California."

Danielle paused, perplexed. Trying to process what she'd just heard, her eyes scanned his face. Anger slid over her like a mask as she realized he was serious. "What?" she asked.

"Yeah." Niko let loose a sigh. "Fleeger is sending me off to Pinnacle Beach to close some cold cases for some upcoming audit."

"And you accepted?"

"I didn't have a choice," Niko replied.

"No, you didn't try to get out of it," she said. "You didn't want to go on this trip in the first place, so you took the first out you could get."

"You know that's not true. My job is already up in the air, and he threatened it further if I refused."

"Bullshit. Especially after tonight with my father."

"That has nothing to do with this!" he shouted. "Fleeger dropped the news on me today before I even knew your parents were here."

Danielle stormed off to the bedroom.

"What are you doing?" Niko called.

"I'm going to meet my parents at the hotel," she said, ripping her suitcase from the closet. "I'll take the flight back with them and stay there for a while since you can't make it anyways."

"You've gotta be kidding me. Don't do this," Niko moaned. "You're being a bit dramatic, don't you think?"

"Ha! Dramatic?" She pointed a handful of clothes in his face. "There's been something festering for a while, hasn't there? I've tried to ignore it, but..." She began furiously stuffing the clothes into her suitcase. "I've been questioning a lot lately, and I know you have too."

"What are you talking about?"

"I'm talking about how we barely talk anymore. There's just some miserable distance between us. You come home, eat dinner, and sit in front of the TV until you pass out."

"Because I'm stuck in this shit desk job!" Niko snapped. "What do you want from me? I'm wasting away, pushing paperwork instead of working on what really matters. Nothing I'm doing makes a damn bit of difference."

"But at least you're safe!" Danielle stopped stuffing clothes in her suitcase. She trembled as tears began to roll down her cheeks. "I'm so exhausted. I've been a miserable wreck ever since you were shot. And I know you're not happy in this new position." She raised her head and dabbed at the tears in her eyes. "I'm so conflicted. I feel selfish for wanting you to stay where you are, knowing that you'd be happier back out in the field."

She collapsed onto the bed next to the suitcase and buried her face in her hands. "But I'm terrified." She shuddered behind a shaky breath. "I can't go through that again. And to think that you could have died...I don't want to lose you."

Heavy sobs broke her words off. Niko sat beside her and rubbed her back. She leaned into him, pressing her face against his chest, and he brought her into his arms. They sat in defeated exhaustion, lost amidst the passage of time. She cried while he zoned out into the distance, trying to process the events of the evening. Sleep weighed heavy on his eyes as a headache rapped at his temples.

What a fucking day.

8
REBEKAH

THE FIGURE HAUNTED REBEKAH'S every thought, though it had been absent since that night nearly a week ago. Still, a presence lingered, and that set her nerves on edge. The terror hung from her mind like an anchor, and the voice of that fiendish apparition beckoned to her. She had convinced herself it had whispered a single word like an echo in a cave, and that word buried itself deep into her mind.

Rylos.

She tried to dispel the thought, but it carried a weight with it that imprisoned her. It sat beneath her subconscious, leaving her always vaguely aware of it. Like an unreachable itch.

She sat alone at the lunch table, tapping her foot and trying to enjoy her meal. But between the incessant headache, the irritation of the word rattling around her mind, and the ominous feeling of being watched, she found little peace. When Anna and Josh joined her at the table, it was a welcome distraction. Rebekah hated being the third wheel, but in her languid state, she found comfort in being around other people. Better if the attention wasn't on her.

Anna dropped into her seat, holding both trays as Josh's hands were glued to her hips. "Hey, girl."

"Hey, Anna."

"You stood us up the other night, and Devon was asking about you."

"Sorry," Rebekah replied. "My dad forced me to catch up on some late homework."

"Say no more," Anna groaned. "Your dad can be a hard ass. I get it."

Rebekah nodded. *That's an understatement.*

"You're almost eighteen," Josh said. "Why do you let him boss you around so much?"

Anna slapped him on the shoulder.

He coughed out a "What?"

"Not your business, okay?" Anna said.

"No, it's fine," Rebekah replied. "My dad is more traditional, and to him, it's their house, their rules. I hate it. But I don't have anywhere else to go."

"Why not stay with Anna?"

Rebekah shifted in her seat. "I don't want to put Anna or her family in the middle of my drama. That wouldn't be fair."

"You know my parents wouldn't care," Anna said. "They love you. They practically treat us like sisters."

"Yeah, I know," Rebekah said. "But it's like Josh said. I'm almost eighteen. I'll be going off to college soon, so I won't have to deal with it much longer."

"Oh, that reminds me! I heard back from Roanoke. I got accepted!"

"Oh wow. Congrats!"

"Have you heard from them yet?"

Rebekah shook her head. "I haven't even submitted my application yet."

"Becks, seriously? We're supposed to go together, remember? I'm not gonna room with some random person. You need to apply tonight, okay? Promise me."

Rebekah laughed. "Calm down. I will."

"If you need help with your essay, let me know," Josh said. "My brother goes to Roanoke. He helped Anna with hers and well…"

"It *is* only April," Anna said. "So, we still have a few months to get your admissions package together before graduation."

"Class of oh-two, baby!" Josh cheered, and a chorus of mocking cheers echoed somewhere in the distance of the cafeteria.

Anna laughed and hugged his arm. "Your grades shouldn't be a problem, right? I mean, you're way smarter than me."

Rebekah nodded but looked away, returning to her food. She shrank into her shoulders.

"Wait. Did you say your dad made you catch up on homework?" Anna asked. "Are you falling behind?"

"A little," Rebekah said. "It's not a big deal. I'm just not feeling very motivated. The work is boring, and I feel like I'm wasting my time."

"A necessary evil, Becks." Anna scowled. "The point is to do the stupid work so colleges know you can do *their* stupid work. Then find a major you're interested in. Something challenging for you."

"That's a good point, but do you mind if we talk about something else?" Rebekah was getting exhausted, and it showed. "I'm sorry. I've heard this lecture from my dad already."

Anna studied her. Her eyes crinkled in frustration and then loosened to sympathy. She turned to Josh, who was wholly invested in his plate.

"Hey, babe, can we have a minute? Girl stuff."

Josh nodded. "Sure."

They gave each other a long kiss, and Rebekah glanced away. She told herself it was out of respect, but public displays of affection always made her uncomfortable. It was never something she was around growing up, so seeing it always seemed out of place.

"Love you," they both said in tandem, and Anna giggled. Josh grabbed his tray and left. Anna watched as he disappeared into the crowded cafeteria. A smirk decorated her face, and her cheeks were flushed when she turned back to Rebekah.

"Okay," Anna said. "Talk to me."

Rebekah's brow furrowed.

"Becks, we've been best friends since second grade. You think I can't tell when something's up? You've been distant and lethargic…You're slipping on your schoolwork…Seriously, what is going on?"

For a moment, she weighed Anna, rolling the conflict over in her mind, but she ultimately decided to confess, come what may.

Rebekah sighed. "I don't really know where to start."

"We just sat down for lunch. We have time."

Rebekah thought for a moment. "Remember my accident a few years back?"

"Um, yeah? How could I forget? I was so worried about you."

"See, that's the thing," Rebekah whispered, leaning toward Anna. "That wasn't me."

Anna's head jerked back, and her face twisted in confusion. "What do you mean it wasn't you? Are you not seeing a therapist because of it?"

"No, I mean…" Rebekah huffed, trying to compose her thoughts. "It *was* me physically but not mentally. There was this…voice in my head. It's hard to explain. Remember when I told you about the ghost from my dreams?"

Anna nodded, raised brows perched over attentive, concerned eyes.

"That's him. He was in my head. He whispered to me, told me I was worthless, and said I'd be better off dead."

"Becks, I'm not following. This is starting to sound a little—"

"Crazy? I know. But it's the truth. I didn't want to hurt myself. I was depressed about my sister, but suicide never crossed my mind. You know me better than that. Something came over me, and I felt like I had no control. And now, I'm seeing that ghost again. I mean, I started seeing it that night, but it's back. Like it's haunting me. I'm terrified, Anna."

Anna's skeptical stare sparked frustration in Rebekah. She knew what was happening to her was real, but seeing the concerned look on her friend's face, the person she thought she could confide in, wounded her. For the first time in years, she believed she might be going crazy. She exhaled and dipped her head. She knew what she wanted to say, and she desperately wanted Anna to believe her, but she couldn't articulate her thoughts. Tears rimmed her eyes. Anna reached out, grabbed Rebekah's hand, and gave her a comforting squeeze.

"Oh-ho, what's this?" A voice came laughing up to the table. "Black-ah and Gingersnaps are lesbians? I mean, I always had my suspicions, but damn."

"Drew, can you not right now?" Anna groaned.

Drew and Mike laughed. The notorious duo was hardly ever apart. Drew sat on the bench next to Rebekah, straddling the seat. Rebekah turned away, wiping at the tears pooling in her eyes while Drew peered over her shoulder.

"You know, I can fix that for you," he said in feigned suavity. "Spring formal is right around the corner, and rumor is you don't have a date."

Rebekah's head snapped back to him, her eyes rimmed in red. Anger flushed her cheeks, and Drew smiled coldly.

Mike chuckled. "Look at her. She's lost for words." He clapped his hand on Drew's shoulder.

Drew kept his eyes trained on Rebekah, still wearing a crooked smile. She wanted to slap him, but her sister's words found their way through the haze in her mind. Nicole had taught her to outwit the bullies, so that's what she did.

"You can't be serious." Rebekah snorted. "You saunter over here, insult me, then have the gall to ask me to a dance? Are you truly that naïve, or is it just banal ignorance?"

Drew's face slackened.

"It means you're unoriginal," Rebekah said as Anna laughed.

"I know what it means," Drew snapped.

"So, it *is* an intelligence thing." Rebekah mocked surprise. "That's a shame. You're a walking cliché, and you lack the capacity to even recognize it."

"You really think you're better than everyone," Drew said, a smirk forming on his face.

"No, not everyone. Just you."

"You got a big mouth," Mike said, leaning over Drew's shoulder. "Maybe I should give you a better use for it."

"That's a disappointing innuendo from someone who likely can't spell innuendo."

Mike's face drooped with an incredulous stare. He had the pudgy, pale-skinned, red-cheeked appearance you'd expect to see on a toddler, which made sense because he acted like a child. Drew leaned toward her, malice in his eyes, but his tone was soft and calculated. A cruel smile was etched onto his face.

"Everyone thinks you should have done it, you know. Killed yourself." His eyes locked on hers. "People still talk about it behind your back. What would it even matter? Just another dead Black kid. Who would care? I mean, who cared when your sister died?"

Rebekah stared at him with a sinister expression as her emotions raged inside of her. Drew's eyes flashed in response.

"I suppose you cared. Sad, depressed Bekah. Unable to move on, moping around school like a whiny bitch. You know, people took bets on how long it would take before you'd try again. I had high hopes for you. I thought you'd make it at least two years. Now, I wish you'd just do it already. Do us all a favor."

Anna shot up from her seat. "What is your problem?"

"Sit down, bitch," Mike said, hands clenched at his sides.

Rebekah stared at Drew, tears stinging her eyes as he smiled darkly at her.

"Is there a problem here?" Josh said, coming up behind Anna.

Mike stepped back. At six-foot-four, Josh intimidated most people, Drew and Mike being no exception. Rebekah glanced over to see a devious grin on Anna's face.

"Nah," Drew said, standing up from the table. "We were just sorting some things out."

"Glad to hear it," Josh said. "Now get out of here."

The two boys backed away, but not before Drew cast a final glance at Rebekah, his face still screwed into a malicious grin.

"God, I hate those guys," Anna said.

"They're cowards," Rebekah stated.

"Unfortunately, they're cowards we share fifth period with." Anna turned to Josh. "Thanks for scaring them off, baby."

They kissed again, but Rebekah was still glancing off in the direction Drew and Mike had retreated. Through the crowd, the cloaked figure watched her, looming in the distance. Panic pressed on her chest again, and her breathing grew heavy.

"Becks, are you all right?" Anna asked, snapping her from her stupor.

Rebekah turned back to Josh and Anna. "Is it true? What Drew said?"

The couple looked at each other, both apprehensive.

"Were people taking bets on when I'd kill myself?" Rebekah inquired.

Anna hesitated before nodding ruefully.

"And you didn't tell me?" Rebekah snapped, her voice shaking.

"You were going through a lot, Becks," Anna replied. "Kids can be assholes. You know that. Everything with your parents and your sister…I was only trying to protect you."

Anger filtered Rebekah's vision, and she ignored the regret that settled on Anna's face.

Anna reached for her. "I'm sorry."

Rebekah jerked away and stood quickly from the table. Anna gave her a sympathetic look, but Rebekah ignored it. She turned away, fresh tears pooling in her eyes. Hugging her backpack, she fled the cafeteria. Her emotions boiled over as soon as she hit the hallway, and it took every ounce of her will to keep from collapsing. She rushed to her locker, dialed in her code with shaky fingers, and opened the door before her legs gave out on her.

She sobbed, clutching her backpack for comfort. Anna was her best friend, and she understood why she kept the truth from her, but there was something about the way she discovered it that reeked of betrayal. And that broke her.

After a while, she composed herself and stood, swapping the books in her backpack with the ones needed for her next class. She wiped her nose and brushed the tears from her eyes, jumping as a hand touched her back.

"Whoa, are you okay?" Rebekah turned to see Devon, his eyes fixed on hers.

"Shit," Rebekah said. "You scared me."

"I'm sorry." He stepped back. "I didn't mean to."

"It's okay," she said, closing her eyes to calm herself. "I'm fine. What do you need?"

"I was worried when you didn't make it out the other night, and I saw you rushing from the cafeteria just now..."

"Oh, right," Rebekah said, turning back to her locker, haphazardly shifting the contents around. "Yeah, sorry. My dad wanted me to catch up on homework, so he wouldn't let me go out."

"Oh, yeah," Devon said, shifting on his heels. "I remember you said your dad can be really strict."

Rebekah chuckled. "It's kind of annoying."

"Well, if you're caught up on your homework, and you don't have plans this weekend..." Rebekah turned to him. Devon fidgeted nervously. "Maybe..."

"Are you asking me out?" Rebekah asked.

"Yeah." Devon breathed in relief.

She hesitated. She was wary about getting close to anyone. She loved her sister, and losing her wounded her deeply. She feared giving anyone else the power to hurt her like that. But she liked Devon. She wasn't ready to be close to anyone yet, but if she was, it would be him. Then the thought of the phantom that haunted her returned.

"Devon, I..." She fumbled, not wanting to hurt him. "I don't know if I'm ready for something like that."

"Oh." Devon frowned. "Yeah, no, I—I get it." His eyes dropped to his feet, and he shoved his hands into his pockets.

"It's not that I don't like you," she attempted, but he kept his eyes fixed on the ground. "Look, I have a lot going on, and it wouldn't be fair to drag you into all my problems."

"I understand." Devon looked up at her, a weak smile on his face.

Extending a comforting arm, she halted as the cloaked figure emerged behind him. Its face, a featureless void, pierced through her soul, igniting a primal surge of terror within her chest. The air grew heavy with the palpable weight of fear, etching a labyrinth of lines upon her face. A step backward, unsteady and faltering, was her instinctual response, but the shadow lunged forward.

Panic urged her to scream, yet the air vanished from her lungs. With a sudden jolt, her foot slipped on something, a macabre obstacle concealed by the darkness. In a desperate grasp for salvation, she clutched at Devon's hoodie, an instinctual tug to pull him out of harm's way. But the phantom passed through him, a chilling spectre untouched by the physical realm, and instead, it reached for her with ghostly tendrils, stealing her from light and plunging her into darkness. Then…

There was nothing.

9

REBEKAH

THE TIDE ROLLING OVER sand stirred Rebekah back to consciousness, and a cool breeze hugged her body. The salt-laden aroma of the ocean carried whispers of distant memories and feelings she had long forgotten, painting a soft smile on her lips. Slowly, she fluttered her eyes open to a night sky awash with the soft glow of moonlight and a tapestry of stars, more than she'd ever seen. Yet, there was something unsettling about the constellations—they were foreign, unrecognizable. She realized with a growing sense of unease she had no recollection of how she came to be on such a strange and unfamiliar beach.

Attempting to sit up, Rebekah met resistance. Panic surged through her as she struggled against an invisible force that held her firmly in place, as if an anchor secured her to the ground. With every ounce of her willpower, she strained to move, but her body remained unyielding. Her frustration gave way to tears, and Rebekah wept.

A voice spoke to her from the caverns of her mind. "You have a strong will, child. That's good."

Startled, Rebekah called out, "Who's there?"

The voice, gravelly and devoid of human quality, replied, "No one of consequence."

"I find myself in a strange place, approached by a strange

man I can neither see nor defend myself against." Rebekah's heart hammered. "I consider you someone of consequence."

The voice laughed, its eerie cadence setting Rebekah's nerves on edge. "Very observant. You possess a remarkable intellect, but you need not fear me."

"Then reveal yourself," Rebekah demanded, her voice strong despite her trepidation. "Show me who you are, so I may decide for myself."

Even her words were foreign to her, with an unfamiliar cadence. The very air surrounding her seemed alien, less substantial. The longer she stayed, the further she drifted from her sense of home.

"Very well," the voice said. "I am Aegeus."

"And what is it you want from me?"

"I am trying to help you," he said.

Rebekah considered his words. There was a peculiar calmness to the man that comforted her, but could she trust him? In the end, trust was irrelevant. She was trapped, and her choices were limited. Trust born of necessity was a bitter pill to swallow.

"Are you here to free me?" Rebekah asked.

"No," Aegeus stated. "Your binds are my doing. I need you still while I work."

Rebekah's heart thundered anew. The pulsing rhythm throbbed in her temples. She made another attempt to move, but her body remained motionless, trapped in a state of paralysis. Or had she been drugged?

"Please," Aegeus said, his voice tinged with urgency. "You do not understand the importance of what I am trying to do, but it *must* be done."

"I don't care." Rebekah struggled again, even if it made no difference. "You are a stranger to me, and I have no reason to believe you mean me no harm. If your intentions are pure, then reveal yourself to me."

"That's not possible," he said.

"If I could rise, I could see you myself," Rebekah growled, her determination resolute. "Will you not let me rise?"

"Even if you were to rise, you would not see me. Now, please. There is much to do." Aegeus's tone was sharper. Impatient.

A deeper voice came from the darkness. "She will not be calm if you lose your temper."

"My temper would steady if she would but listen," Aegeus replied.

Growing increasingly anxious, Rebekah called out, "Who's there?" Had the other man been there the whole time, lurking in the darkness?

Rebekah's chest rose and fell rapidly, and her heart pounded against her ribs. She questioned the reality of her situation. Was it a dream? It felt surreal, like a nightmare she couldn't wake from. For the first time in as long as she could remember, she yearned to be home. To see her mother and father. She sought the comfort of familiarity in that strange and unsettling place.

"You are safe, girl," the new voice assured her. "No one seeks to harm you. I am Numenos. Aegeus is my brother. You are bound for your own protection."

Rebekah's voice wavered as she cried out, "Soft words do not soften your actions! What is this place? Why are my words strange to me? And why have you imprisoned me?"

Numenos made a shushing sound that only furthered Rebekah's terror. "You must be calm."

"Very good," Aegeus mocked. "Why hadn't I thought to tell her to calm herself?"

"Brother," Numenos said. "We have much to do and precious little time. For your safety, girl, you must hold still. Aegeus, if you would."

Defiant as ever, Rebekah continued to struggle. It felt strange to send commands to limbs that remained unresponsive, but she persisted nonetheless. Unrestrained, her body would have been a maelstrom of furious motion, but instead, she lay there, her veins throbbing futilely from the effort.

A sudden pulse, like a vibration, rippled through her from head to toe. Her muscles tightened involuntarily, then relaxed. Another pulse followed. And another. With each tremor, her strength waned until she was too weary to resist.

"What are you doing to me?" Rebekah whimpered.

"We believe you are housing a Guardian," Numenos said as if that explained it all.

"A what?"

"A Guardian," Aegeus huffed. "A protector of the ethereal plane. He is the last of his kind, and we believe he is trapped in your consciousness."

"I don't understand," Rebekah said. "Trapped in my consciousness?"

Neither man offered further explanation, and a disconcerting silence took root.

Rebekah gazed up at the speckled night sky, her breath feeble beneath the unseen weight pinning her down. She lay there in silence, her thoughts a whirlwind of confusion as an eerie presence waded through her mind.

"Brother, look!" Aegeus called.

"Good," Numenos said. "We must act quickly to break the seal."

"What is happening?" Rebekah asked, her voice fraught with fear.

"We have found him," Numenos replied. "We are freeing him from your mind."

A searing pain abruptly seized her temples, and a sharp ringing pierced her ears. She screamed, mentally writhing in reflex, but her body remained unresponsive.

"Stop!" Numenos cried, his voice muffled by the deafening ringing. "Stop, brother. Now!"

Rebekah's agony grew, and the world slipped into the distance. The voices of the two men became incomprehensible as they argued. As the pain subsided, Rebekah's consciousness waned. Amid her delirium, a chilling presence infiltrated her, prickling her flesh.

Rebekah, a voice whispered, one she didn't recognize.

"He's here!" Aegeus's voice snapped into focus. "I'm sorry, child, but we must go."

The tremendous force that pressed down on her suddenly lifted, and her body jolted, responding to its newfound freedom.

Energy flooded her, chasing away exhaustion, and she scrambled to her feet. She scanned her surroundings, but there was no one there. She stood alone on that black sand beach, the tide lolling to-and-fro against the shore, its rhythmic dance shimmering in the moonlight.

Where did they go? She examined the sand but found no footprints. A sense of disorientation crept over her, and she began to doubt her own sanity.

Turning her gaze to where the trees met the shore, an eerie fog slithered through the darkness. Something stirred within it. Her heart raced, and she took a step back. Her eyes darted up and down the shoreline. It was empty as far as she could see. Mountains climbed the sky in the distance beyond where the shore sank from view.

Run, the unfamiliar voice whispered again.

Ignoring it, she watched as the shadow emerged from the fog. She braced herself to face the nightmare that had haunted her for years. It uncoiled itself from the darkness, tendrils of smoke twisting around its shape. An inexplicable force took control of her, propelling her to run along the shoreline. Not looking back, she ran as fast as her legs would carry her. She ran to the brink of collapse. Her muscles burned, her breaths came in ragged gasps, and still, she continued running.

When exhaustion threatened to bring her down, she turned. The spectre bore down on her, black sand billowing behind it like a cloud of smoke. Its cloak whipped violently in its wake. Panic clawed at her chest. She twisted around, but her foot caught the sand, sending her crashing to the ground. Desperate, she scrambled to her feet, but the spectre seized her wrist and spun her. A gnarled hand latched around her throat, lifting her from the earth.

Rebekah fought for freedom. A futile struggle against the phantom's grip. Drawing her closer, the acrid stench of soot and death emanated from it. Yet, she refused to yield, locking her gaze with the void of its face.

The spectre hissed its raspy snarl. "There is no fear in your eyes."

"I do not fear my dreams," Rebekah replied, her voice resolute despite the panic in her chest.

"There are no dreams here, Guardian," the creature said. "Only death."

"No!" Aegeus cried.

With a loud pop, an orb of light flared as the being that must have been Aegeus manifested between them. A scaled creature with a tentacled mane, beard of sea moss, and horns resembling coral curling out from his temples shoved the phantom away with a powerful force. A pillar of water rose from the sea, following the gesture of his hand, and crashed into the figure, hurtling it back beyond the tree line.

Aegeus turned toward Rebekah. His iridescent green eyes locked onto hers, and an unspoken compassion radiated from within. "I am truly sorry," he uttered in a shaky whisper, pressing his palm against her chest.

A soft glow emanated from beneath his touch, coursing through her body like a gentle, reassuring wave. The warmth it brought filled her with a renewed sense of hope. But beyond that soothing glow, the ominous figure emerged once more from the abyss, bearing down upon them. The warmth swiftly turned to searing pain, and Rebekah's body tightened and compressed. The radiance from Aegeus's hand intensified, and a deafening pop reverberated through her senses as she was engulfed in the overwhelming expansion of a blinding light.

10

NIKO

FLEEGER MEANT IT AS a punishment, but Niko couldn't help being drawn into the mystery concealed within the missing persons documents. For days, he delved into them, preparing for his trip, and as he sifted through the files, the traces of a pattern emerged. It was a disjointed and elusive puzzle, missing a crucial piece of information that could tie everything together. The rhythm of the disappearances was too coincidental.

Analyzing the dates, Niko meticulously mapped them out, checking and rechecking the details. "Nearly thirty years," he muttered, "but then, an eight-year gap…"

Reclining in his chair, he pressed his hand against his chin, burdened with the mystery of winding theories. Every time he thought he had the threads woven together, an unexpected wrench jammed the gears. No clear patterns based on race, age, or gender emerged, and no evidence or testimonies offered any leads. The only common thread was their proximity—something that made him wonder if the eight-year gap was deliberately intended to throw off the investigation.

His brows furrowed. *Eight years is excessive,* he thought, weighing his theory of a serial killer. *There must be a reason.*

His thoughts circling like predators on the hunt, Niko couldn't shake the question: Why the gap?

Selecting a file from the stack to his left, he opened it, revealing a picture of a teenage girl clipped to the first page. He studied the case, hoping it might reveal a missing link amidst the chaos.

"What's that?" Brindle leaned over Niko's shoulder.

"One of the missing persons cases."

Brindle nodded and took a swig from his mug before sitting in his cubicle. A heavy tobacco scent piped off him. He never paid Brindle's habit much mind, but a twinge of concern for his friend's health greeted him.

"Still obsessing?" Harrington asked from behind Niko. "They're ancient unsolved cases, man. Contact the families and close them. You aren't going to find those people."

"They're cold cases of missing people. I can't just close them," Niko replied, somewhat forgiving of Harrington's naivety given his background as a data analyst. "Besides, I think there's more to it than that."

Harrington brushed off Niko's determination with a dismissive wave. "Whatever. You're giving Fleeger the satisfaction. He handed you those cases to torture you. He knows you won't just follow up, take some notes, and move on."

Niko turned to face Harrington. "There's something here," he asserted. "All these disappearances happened within a four-mile radius—the entire stretch of boardwalk. Two people vanishing every year like clockwork, almost predictably. No, there's more to this."

"People disappear at the beach all the time." Harrington shrugged. "The boardwalk even more so."

"Kids, maybe," Niko said.

"Yeah, and that there looks like a kid." Harrington pointed at the open folder.

"Nicole Daroh?" Niko turned back to his desk. "She was seventeen. The youngest to go missing and the only one that year. She's an anomaly. I think that's where they slipped up."

"Slipped up?" Harrington questioned. "Are you thinking serial killer?"

"I don't know," Niko admitted. "Maybe. All I know is this case stands out. The others look…routine, I guess. But this one. I don't think they planned this one."

"And you wonder why I call you detective," Harrington scoffed. "Maybe you can investigate a social life. You're making me depressed."

"Look, this is all very interesting," Brindle said, standing and sliding his blazer over his shoulders. "But let's go grab some food. I need some fresh air. It's late, and I'm hungry."

Niko rubbed his eyes, realizing how exhausted he was. Perhaps Harrington's remark about obsessing wasn't entirely off-base.

"Yeah," Niko agreed. "I could use a break." He stood and swayed, catching himself on his desk. *And there's the hunger setting in.* Black dots swam before his eyes. Danielle called them "fishies." *Damnit,* he thought, as an ache crept into his heart.

"You okay?" Brindle moved over and held Niko up by the shoulder.

He caught his balance again and gave his head a shake. Recalibrating. "Yeah, I'm fine," he lied. "Just a little lightheaded. I guess I'm hungrier than I thought."

"Right," Brindle said, releasing his grip. "Let's go then."

Niko took a step, and his knees popped. Harrington and Brindle both shot him a bemused look.

Shit. Niko sighed.

"Whoa, Grandpa," Harrington joked. "You starting a fireworks stand? Holy hell. And I thought Brindle was old."

"Need some oil there, tin man?" Brindle clapped him on the back.

"Yeah, ha-ha," Niko said, snatching his blazer from his chair. "Let's go, smartass."

Brindle turned to Harrington. "Want anything?"

"Nah." Harrington waved him off, his focus never leaving his monitor.

Brindle nodded and made his way to the elevators with Niko. The walk to the lobby was quiet. Niko hated the quiet. His house had been like that since Danielle left. It was unsettling, so he absorbed himself in his work as a distraction.

Why the gap? The question irked him. *You should call her.* The ache returned, and he coughed to dispel the silence.

"How's your caseload looking?" he asked Brindle.

Brindle turned to Niko, raising his eyebrows in mock skepticism. He turned back and thumbed the elevator call button. "It's fine," he said, shoving his hands into his pockets, waiting for the doors to open.

Niko shot him a suspicious look. He seemed off. Distant and quieter than normal.

"And how is your caseload, Ortez?" Fleeger rounded the corner.

Niko's heart sank, and he groaned his disapproval. Mirroring Brindle, he shoved his hands into his pockets.

Fantastic, he thought. *Three more months. Just suck it up.*

"It's, um," Niko cleared his throat, casting a glance at Brindle who shook his head. "It's fine, sir. Just getting my notes organized. I should have this all settled next week."

"Settled?" Fleeger droned. "I'd double-check your work. You don't want to make a careless mistake. It would be a shame if your last assignment here were marred with mediocrity, agent." He snapped the "t" in agent and studied Niko.

Niko clenched his jaw. The elevator doors opened, and Fleeger stepped on. Brindle and Niko didn't follow.

"Are you getting on or not?" Fleeger held the door open, which surprised Niko.

"We'll take the next one," Brindle said.

Fleeger pursed his lips but let the elevator doors slide shut. Brindle waited a moment before hitting the button again. "Prick," he huffed.

Niko chuckled. "Yeah, you're not wrong. I didn't know he bothered you so much."

"Yeah, well, that's because I don't bitch about every little thing that irks me."

Niko recoiled but let the issue drop, which leant an uneasy silence to the elevator ride and the walk to the car. He *really* hated the quiet. But he had learned Brindle would broach the issue in his own time if he wanted. Niko received his reprieve as soon as they left the compound.

"You're a real piece of shit, you know that?"

"What?" Niko shot him a confused look.

"You." Brindle rested his head on his fist. "I shared personal details with you. I wanted to help you, and you spit in my face."

"What are you talking about?"

"I'm talking about how you constantly bitch and moan about Danielle," Brindle snapped, throwing his hands up in frustration. "Someone gives you advice, and what do you do? I opened up to you, trying to help you, and you…" Brindle shot a hard look at Niko and sighed. "You love this girl. I know you do."

"Yeah, I love her," Niko said.

"And yet, you let her leave."

"It's more complicated than that."

Brindle laughed callously. "You remind me of myself. Too much so. Every mistake I ever made, I see it in you, and I'm trying to save you the heartache that I went through. But you're just too goddamn stubborn."

"Where is this coming from?"

"I told you to let the little shit slide, or you'd regret it, and what happened? You let her walk away because her dad was a little abrasive with you."

"It's not some little thing, man," Niko said. "Her parents are a huge part of her life. Who am I to make her choose between her family and me?"

"That *is* the little shit," Brindle said. "Of course, her dad is going to hate you. That's his little girl. What, you think because you have a big-boy job he's just going to let her go? Your job is dangerous. You almost died once already, and she was a wreck over it, I remember. If I had a daughter, I'd be worried too."

"But you don't have a daughter, so why are you up my ass about this?"

"Because you're too blind to see what's happening." Brindle gripped the wheel with both hands. "She left because you put her second. Yeah, she's attached to her family because you're not giving her a foundation to hold on to. You're too focused on your career and following in your father's footsteps, and you're ignoring her. Does that sound familiar to you? Is that the life you want?"

Niko adjusted himself in his seat, fidgeting from nerves. The thought of biting back at the comment came and went. He knew Brindle had a point. But he didn't expect the shot at his father. Not from him. He tried to force the thought out of his head but failed, and the pain of Danielle leaving hit him. He became acutely aware of how alone he was. A hot rage heated his face.

"I'm not ignoring her—"

"Lie to me then, but you can't lie to yourself. And when she's gone, that's it. I told you not to make the same mistakes I did."

"This isn't your life, though," Niko said. "So, stop making the comparison."

Brindle shook his head. "You're so fucking thick."

"Yeah, and your life is so goddamn perfect, right?"

"At least I know what I want. You have no idea. You're a lost puppy."

"That's not true."

"Then what is?" Brindle snapped. "Huh? What is the truth?"

"I love her, all right?" Niko shouted. "I love her too goddamn much, and it hurts to know that I may never get the chance to spend my life with her, all because her dad has a chip on his shoulder about me. I fight every day for her, and I'm losing!" He sat in quiet reflection, breathing through his anger until it turned to sorrow. "I'm losing her…And what kind of fucking friend are you? This isn't your life. You had your chance."

"Yeah." Brindle clenched his jaw and twisted his hands on the steering wheel. "Yeah, I had my chance, and my wife was the best thing that ever happened to me." Brindle's voice shook. "Your dad was there for me at the worst point in my life, and it's because of him that I'm making sure you don't fuck yours up." Brindle composed himself with a heavy breath. "It's your relationship…I know that. But you can be so damn stupid."

He leaned back, rubbing a shaky hand along his forehead.

His face flushed as he battled his anger or whatever warred within him. Brindle inhaled deeply, exhaled, and broke into sobs. Niko studied him for a moment, trying to process the wave of emotions and grasp the situation. Then it came to him. Washing his anger away, the guilt hit him like a brick.

"Shit," Niko breathed. "It's today, isn't it?"

"It would have been thirty-four years," Brindle muttered.

Niko sank into his seat. He said nothing, giving Brindle space to grieve.

"You're right. It's not my place," Brindle said after taking a few breaths to compose himself. "I'm not your dad, but I see what you're doing. You're distracting yourself because it hurts to think about her. I've been there. I'm still there some days. But it's not the answer. So, do me a favor and call Danielle, or you'll hate yourself for the rest of your life because you didn't."

Niko stared into his lap, rolling the advice around in his head. He wanted to call Danielle, at least the logical side of him did, but some implacable voice resisted the thought. It was petty pride, he knew that, but he didn't want to break the silence first. He huffed and shifted his attention out the window. Thinking of his fractured relationship brought its share of pain. He didn't answer Brindle. Instead, he threw the notion aside. He would call her but not yet.

Why the gap?

11

REBEKAH

Rebekah woke to sunrise pooling through her bedroom window, casting an amber hue upon the room. Sheer curtains swayed to the rhythm of a breeze that whispered through the vent beneath. The aroma of cinnamon, maple, and butter wafted through the air, filling it with a comforting scent. Her lips curled into a smile. A perfect morning.

As she sat up, however, her head screamed in protest. Every sense intensified, amplifying her pain. The sunlight bore down upon her, exacerbating the throbbing headache. The once enticing smell of food now turned her stomach, evoking waves of nausea. Her throat and arm ached, and upon her forearm, a reddish mark adorned her skin, resembling an ominous handprint. The area beneath was taut and radiated heat.

It's just a burn, she tried to convince herself, but her memory refused to support the delusion.

The void of that phantom's face consumed her, its presence too vivid to dismiss as a mere nightmare. It was real. And the other presence she carried with her from that grim place, like an otherworldly interloper, served as a stark reminder.

Music eased her discomfort. "I Am Woman" by Betty Wright offered a bittersweet recollection of simpler times. Memories of her mother dancing in the kitchen to that song as she cooked—bubbly and smiling—rushed back. But that reality was a distant echo, a time before Nicole's death. Fighting the pain, Rebekah forced herself from the bed and down the stairs. An absence greeted her as no pictures bedecked the foyer.

Entering the kitchen, the music vanished, stealing the warmth it brought with it. The house stood empty. An implacable sense of dread surrounded her as the orange glow of sunrise dimmed to the dark of nightfall. The room around her crumbled into decay. Varnish peeled away from the cabinets and counters, exposing age-worn wood and rusted metal parts. A sinking realization took hold of her.

"This can't be real," she whispered, her voice filled with disbelief. "I'm still trapped in this nightmare."

"Rebekah?" A cautious voice crept through the darkness.

She turned, and her gaze fell upon Nicole. Her mind battled against logic, unable to fathom what stood before her, but it was her. Nicole looked wretched. Exhaustion darkened her eyes, which held no sign of sanity, and her tangled mess of curls framed her face in a ghastly exposé. Yet, she hadn't aged a day.

Rebekah's knees trembled, and she reached a hand out to steady herself against the decayed counter. Was she witnessing a ghost? The sight before her seemed too surreal to be true. Rebekah's hand covered her mouth, tears welling in her eyes. With a hesitant step forward, she spoke.

"Nicole." Her voice quivered.

Nicole approached with caution, her demeanor laced with uncertainty. "No," she gasped, her eyes widening in horror. "No, you're not her. You can't be her! She can't be here! Leave!" She retreated, faltering as she missed the step down from the kitchen, and collapsed. Pushing herself back into the living room, she clutched her face, convulsing in a fit of panic. Tears streamed down her cheeks as she repeated her denials, clawing at and marring her own flesh. Nicole's impetuosity compelled Rebekah to rush to her sister's side, grasping at her arms to stop the paroxysm. But Nicole screamed and pushed her away. "You're not her," she continued. "You're not her! You can't be her. Get out! Get out!"

Rebekah persisted, fighting her sister's protests. She grabbed

Nicole's shoulders, pulling her into her arms. Nicole struggled and screamed wildly, beating Rebekah's chest to extricate herself, but Rebekah clenched her eyes against the pain and hugged her sister tightly. "Nicole, stop!" she cried. "It's me. It's Rebekah. Please, stop!"

"No, you can't be her. Please," Nicole begged. "You're lying. Let me go!"

Rebekah shushed her sister, her voice filled with anguish. "Listen to me. It's me. This is real. I'm here. I *am* here." She attempted to steady her voice to offer solace to her sister, but her emotions overwhelmed her, and she burst into tears. Still, her sister thrashed feebly within her grasp, her screams fading into heavy sobs, her body growing limp.

"God, Nicole," Rebekah cried, hugging her sister. "I missed you so much. I am so lost without you."

The thrashing stopped, and Nicole shivered feebly in Rebekah's embrace.

"You shouldn't be here." Her voice was weak.

Rebekah loosened the hug and took in her sister, who looked frail and gaunt. "What do you mean?"

"This is a prison, Rebekah. This is *my* prison."

"Well, this is a breakout." Rebekah smiled down at her sister.

Nicole managed a weak laugh before resting her head against Rebekah's chest. Rebekah cradled her sister, running a hand along her back, feeling the bony ridges of her spine and shoulders. She bit her quivering lip, savoring the moment for what it was. She had her sister back. Whatever else held little significance.

They sat in contented silence, their embrace a sanctuary from the decay that surrounded them. Rebekah leaned down to plant a kiss on her sister's head but halted at the faint aroma of soot emanating from her hair. The scent shattered her complacency and jolted her back to the grim reality. Nicole was a prisoner, her soul trapped and tormented, and Rebekah couldn't help but feel responsible. Nicole looked up at her, and Rebekah saw a flicker of fear in her eyes.

"If he finds you here, it'll be your prison too," Nicole muttered. "It's you he wants."

"Who?"

"I don't know his name. He doesn't speak to me. But the things he does…" The life sank from Nicole's eyes, and her already pallid complexion lost what color remained. Rebekah squeezed her sister's shoulder, offering what comfort she could, but Nicole baulked in response, raising her arms as if instinctually defending herself. When her eyes returned to Rebekah's, they held a deep-rooted fear.

"I'm not leaving you," Rebekah vowed.

Nicole's eyes welled with tears. "You must. You have no idea what he's capable of."

"Not without you. There has to be a way to free you from this place."

Rebekah's eyes darted around the room, searching for an answer, but her efforts were in vain. She refused to accept defeat, determined to find a way to escape the nightmare, until a hand gently caressed her cheek, directing her attention back to Nicole. A weak smile formed on Nicole's face.

"You've grown so much," her sister said. "You're not the little girl I remember."

"No." A tinge of shame flushed Rebekah's face. "That little girl was relentless with hope. I've abandoned it entirely."

Nicole's expression shifted, displaying stern confidence. "No, you haven't. I feel it in you. It's what feeds what little strength I have left. This may sound strange, but when I'm at my lowest, I close my eyes, and it's like I can feel you with me. I can speak and sense your response."

"That doesn't sound strange." Rebekah smiled. "You visit me in my dreams. Everyone thinks I'm crazy to believe that, but I feel your presence."

"What a sad life they must lead not to believe in the idea that love transcends worlds." She returned Rebekah's smile, and it ignited a long-forgotten spark in Rebekah's heart.

Nicole's smile faded as a low hum filled the room. Abruptly, she pushed away from Rebekah and rose to her feet, her eyes fixed on the encroaching shadows at the room's far end. Rebekah followed her sister's gaze and witnessed the phantom peeling itself from the darkness. She rose to her feet and Nicole stepped in front of her, shielding her.

"Stay away from her!" Nicole cried. She charged at the creature, only to be ensnared by its grip around her throat, lifting her from the ground. Its gaze turned to Rebekah, who stepped forward, determined to free Nicole, but her body froze. Paralyzed, she fought against the invisible restraints, but her efforts were in vain. The sensation of a hand coiling around her head returned.

Stop, a voice said.

The room lengthened before her eyes, and the spectre looked around at the phenomenon before returning its focus to Rebekah. It snarled.

"Guardian!"

"Rebekah, run!" Nicole's voice strained beneath the creature's grasp.

There is a way to save her, but you must leave now, the voice of the stranger spoke urgently.

"Let me go!" Rebekah screamed.

If we stay, he will kill us both, and I don't have the strength to force you from this prison. Stop fighting me, and let me help you. It is the only way to save Nicole.

"Save Nicole" broke Rebekah's resistance, allowing her better judgement to rise into her conscious mind. "What would you have me do?" she asked.

A familiar warmth surged through her being, radiating from her core. A brilliant light flooded the room with Rebekah as its source.

"No!" The creature hissed, discarding Nicole, and hurtled toward Rebekah. The dust of the decaying room billowed in its wake.

A strange pulse emanated from her, an inexplicable surge of power. The distance between her and the phantom widened, impeding its advance.

Find where your sister died. The voice was strained under significant effort.

The light pouring from Rebekah intensified, transforming the warmth into searing pain. The phantom descended upon her, and the voice in her head screamed. Her body weakened as the pulse dissipated.

Rylos, she thought. *It's you, isn't it?*

Her body compressed and tightened as the blinding light enveloped the room. The towering figure recoiled, shielding its face. A deafening pop echoed through the air, and Rebekah was once again engulfed in the effervescent light.

12

REBEKAH

THE OVERHEAD FLUORESCENTS DRAINED of light as Rebekah woke, gasping and drawing life back into her body. Air entered her lungs with a sharp inhale, causing her to hack and cough. Waves of pain shot through her body. Had she died? Dizzying nausea settled in her stomach, and vomiting seemed likely. Anna sat near her bed, hugging her knees, a look of terrified surprise painted on her face.

"Rebekah…" Her voice trembled.

The world revolted, assaulting Rebekah's senses, and her vision swam. The lights pulsed in cadence with her throbbing headache. She gave Anna a dazed look.

Anna shot forward. "What the fuck!" Jumping to her feet, hands pressed to her head, she paced the small curtained-off room Rebekah recognized as the school clinic.

"What?" Rebekah asked.

Anna shot a grave look at her friend, still pacing, and hugged her arms against her chest. She then stopped. "I—I—I don't know where to start. After I heard you were in the clinic, I came to check on you, and you were tossing in your sleep, speaking to yourself. I thought you were having a fit, but you started speaking in a different voice. It was fucking scary, Becks. You screamed like you were in pain. I thought Nurse Peterson was gonna have a heart attack when she rushed out of the room.

We tried to wake you up, but you were thrashing and…and tensing like we were hurting you."

"Anna, I need to tell you some—"

"And then your eyes started glowing, and these damn lights, like, *exploded* and filled the whole room." She motioned up to the fluorescents. "Your body jolted and *lifted* from the bed like you were possessed. I mean…what the fuck!?"

"Anna!" Rebekah sat up in the bed. Tremors of pain shot down her spine, and her vision flashed for a moment. Fatigue made her unsteady. "I saw my sister."

Anna froze, hugging her arms against her chest once more. The look she gave Rebekah was riddled with an uneasy fear, implying her disbelief in what Rebekah had to say. Still processing what she saw, she made to speak, but Rebekah cut her off.

"I saw my sister, Anna," she repeated. "I know that sounds insane, but I *need* you to believe me. Her soul is trapped in this—this place. I don't know where or even what it is. But it's guarded by that ghost I keep seeing. I think I can save her, but I need to get out of here."

Anna's stare remained incredulous, eyebrows curled up dubiously, pensive and unyielding. Rebekah could imagine the conflict in her friend because even though everything was happening to her, she struggled to grasp it. But she hadn't stopped to question it. She was afraid of what rationalizations her mind would construct to convince her to dismiss it, but it was the closest thing to hope she'd had in a long time. So, she pulled at the thread given to her.

"Okay." Anna surrendered, though unconvincingly. "But the ambulance is on the way. They'll be here any minute. You hit your head pretty hard, so I don't think they're going to let you just walk out of here."

"Can you distract them?"

Anna hesitated, her eyes wrought with concern. She gnawed at her lip, considering the request and seemingly battling her better judgement.

"Anna, please. You have to believe me."

Anna spoke slowly and with apprehension. "Normally, I wouldn't. I mean, what you're saying sounds crazy, but after what I just saw..." Despite the worry in her eyes, she resigned. "Yeah. I'll distract Nurse Peterson. Just hurry."

Rebekah jumped from the bed and began collecting her things, battling through the woozy rush that attacked her mind.

Anna slid the curtain back and stopped at the door. "Rebekah, please be careful."

"Thanks, Anna."

Nurse Peterson's voice perked up beyond the doorway as Anna grabbed her attention. Rebekah focused on gathering a small list of supplies. Feeling the bandaging on her head, she grabbed extra gauze pads and wrap from the cabinets, stuffing them into her backpack along with crackers and bottles of water from the mini fridge. She threw her pack over her shoulder and fled the room, taking care not to pass in front of the office where Anna was talking to the nurse.

She worked her way through the empty halls as her heart raced from the growing fear of being caught. Rounding the corner toward the entrance, she froze as paramedics wheeled a gurney through the doors, escorted by the principal. Eyes glued to the EMTs, she raced to the other side of the hall where she ran into Devon. She clapped her hands over her mouth to cover a small shriek.

Devon grabbed her shoulders and steadied her. "Hey, easy. Please, don't fall over again," he said.

"Jesus," Rebekah hissed. "You have a knack for scaring the shit out of me."

Peeking around the corner, the paramedics made their way down the hall, oblivious to her presence.

"Are you okay?" he asked.

She glanced around nervously. "I need to leave."

"Are you sure that's a good idea? You hit the lockers hard when you fell. You probably have a concussion."

"I know, but I just *can't* go to the hospital. I need to get out of here."

"Bekah, I don't think—"

With an angry grunt, she pushed past Devon. He grabbed her arm and studied her for a moment. With a sigh, he said, "Let's go."

He ushered her down the hall, guiding her through the locker-lined corridors. As they rushed through the senior locker column, Rebekah noticed a substantial dent adorning the one below her own. Blood still spotted the floor. Turning, they entered the Academy hallway, somewhere Rebekah had never been, reserved for specialized learning. Devon opened a door at the back of the school that led around to the loading dock and dumpsters.

"You should be able to get to the senior parking lot from here. Your car is there, right?"

"Yeah." Rebekah squeezed past Devon as he held the door for her but hesitated as she passed him, her eyes locking with his.

A swell of emotions fluttered inside of her, and she kissed him, catching them both by surprise. Despite her reckless abandon, he didn't pull back. He pressed his lips tighter against hers, and a strange sensation prickled over her flesh, something new and unfamiliar. Easing back, she caught his eye once more.

"Thank you, Devon."

"Um," he stammered, "you're welcome."

Rebekah sprinted for the parking lot, retrieving her keys from the side pocket of her backpack. They danced at the end of the tattered GMU lanyard her sister had given her. George Mason University—the college she never got to attend.

Rebekah eased along the curvature of the school's exterior, peering around the brick-laden enclosure where the dumpsters sat. The flashing lights of the ambulance caught her eye. Two officers were posted at the front of the school, speaking with the school administrator, Ms. Greene. Her nerves assaulted her, turning her legs to jelly. Sweat beaded her forehead and slicked her palms. Glancing toward the parking lot, she found her car about forty yards away. Forty yards through the open basketball courts, two officers, and a nosy school official who Rebekah helped for extracurricular points at the start of the school year. Daunting was an understatement.

She leaned back against the wall and took slow and controlled breaths to ease her nerves. It helped. Sort of. Peering around the wall again, she could see the two officers. Their backs were turned, and Ms. Greene was flaunting her best "pick me" attitude, flipping her hair, popping her hips, and smiling stupidly. The display was pathetic. If there was a time, she supposed it was then.

Pushing off the wall, she sprinted for her car, the keys bouncing wildly at the end of their frayed tether. As she raced across the courts, making for the grass median that separated them from the parking lot, a snap sounded, and the weight in her hands lessened. The keys sprung loose, hitting the pavement with a dull metal slap. She paused. Her eyes were glued on the officers, who seemed to be unaffected by the commotion. So, she snatched her keys from the blacktop and continued to her car.

Rebekah approached her Honda hatchback with the lanyard in hand. She inserted the key into the lock and opened the door. She didn't have the lavish luxury of power locks like some of her classmates. Her backpack preceded her, flying over the center console to the passenger side before she dropped into the driver's seat. She jerked the belt over her shoulder, buckled herself in, and started the car.

"Hey!" Ms. Greene shouted. "That's her car! Rebekah!"

The heavier-set officer started toward her at a brisk walk. Rebekah threw the car into reverse and peeled from the parking spot, surprised she didn't hit either car beside her. She sped past the bulky officer, who hunched over in winded defeat, and made for the light at the entrance to the school. She saw Ms. Greene charging into the building in her rearview mirror. The light was red, so she made a sharp right turn to avoid the wait and the risk of being caught.

The roads were empty, and the new tar shone jet black under the midday sun. Not a cloud in sight. She exhaled a victorious breath followed by another that broke into contented laughter, the rush of adrenaline from her escape easing. Leaning back in her seat, she moved into the right turning lane toward the highway. Pinnacle Beach was on her mind—the beach that carried so many fond memories from her childhood, all of which were tainted by her most devastating recollection: her sister's death.

She traveled down Interstate 95, hand hanging out the window, gliding against the rush of wind. Her Jimmy Eat World CD blared throughout the car. It was during the change of songs she heard her cell phone ringing. Killing the music, she cranked her window up before fishing through her backpack to retrieve her phone. Glancing at the road to keep the car in her lane, she flipped it open.

Four missed calls from her mother.

Pausing a moment to allow her thumping heart to settle, she called her mom back. Pinning the phone between her ear and shoulder, she gripped the wheel with both hands as the phone droned its dreadful tone.

"Where are you?" Her mother didn't sound too pleased. "I left work because your school told me you were going to the hospital, and then I got a voicemail from them saying you *ran away*. Are you okay?"

"Yeah, Mom. Everything is fine."

"What has been going on with you lately?" Her mother's tone straddled gentle concern and distress. "You've been so distant and bitter."

"I know," Rebekah said, her emotions swarming inside of her. "It's been really difficult for me, and I've been struggling to get by, but I think I figured out what I need. It's hard to explain, but I want you to trust me on this, okay?"

"Fine," she huffed. "We'll talk at home."

"I'm not coming home," Rebekah said, wincing in anticipation of her mother's outrage.

Instead, she hesitated. "Where are you going?"

Rebekah pulled the phone away and choked back a sob. With a shaky breath, she returned the phone to her ear. "Pinnacle Beach."

The phone was silent for a long while, and she understood why. The mere thought of returning felt like lead in her chest, but if there was a chance to help her sister, to free her from that miserable prison, she had to try, right? Amid the considerable quiet, Rebekah checked to make sure the call hadn't dropped.

"Mom?" she asked.

"Yeah, baby, I'm here." She sounded devastated, on the verge of tears. "Why would you want to go back to that place?"

"It's a lot to explain, but this is something I need to do."

She thought of confessing to her mom but decided it would only make the situation worse.

"Okay," her mom said. "I'm in my car. I'll meet you there."

"No!" Rebekah barked. "No, this is something I need to do on my own."

"Rebekah Jean Daroh, you are out of your mind if you think I'm going to let my seventeen-year-old daughter go to the beach on her own. You're not even old enough to book yourself a room."

Shit. She hadn't thought of that. "I'll figure it out. Please, listen to me. I need to do this."

"I don't know what's going on in that head of yours, but I am coming. That's final."

"Mom!" Rebekah cried. "You're not hearing me."

"Excuse me, but I heard you just fine. If you're going, I'm going with you. It is too damn dangerous for a young girl to be at the beach alone."

"I won't be alone," she lied. "Anna and Josh are spending the weekend at the beach for their anniversary."

There was a pause. "So, you're going to be staying with them?"

"No," she faltered. "It's their anniversary, so I'm not sharing a room with them."

"Mm-hmm. Then where is a child with no reservation and no money going to stay?"

"I said I'll figure it out. Look, I appreciate the sudden concern, but I've handled myself just fine for almost a decade. I don't need you to step in and help now."

She shouldn't have said that. In fact, it tasted like regret the second the words left her lips. Why couldn't her mom just listen to her?

Tension hung in the air.

"I know things haven't been easy for you," her mother said. "And I know that I haven't been there for you. I can't get those years back, and I hate myself every day for that." Silence settled again, broken by small gasps as her mother cried on the other end of the line. Rebekah's heart climbed into her throat. "If this is something you need to do, then fine. I don't understand, and I'm *not* okay with it, but fine. I'll call ahead and book a room with Mr. Wymer, all right? Do you remember how to get there?"

"Yeah." Tears framed her face. "Thank you."

Her mother's voice shook. "Please, *please* be safe, baby. And call me as soon as you arrive."

"I will, Mom. I love you."

It was the first time she had said that since she was a child, but the words tasted sweeter than she remembered.

"I love you too."

Rebekah pulled the phone away from her ear and flipped it closed. Pressing the back of her shaking hand to her face, she coughed out heavy sobs, sending tremors through her body. The full effect of seeing her sister bore down on her, coupled with the swell of emotions from her mother's candor and vulnerability as well as her own cruel attack. The strength in her body shrank away. She wailed in her solitary capsule, pouring her pain into that empty metal shell.

The car vibrated, catching the rumble strips, and the realization she was veering off the road toward the drainage ditch sobered her enough to jerk the car back on course. She peered around, but there was no one else on the road, fortunately. She exhaled and shuffled in her seat, wiping the tears from her eyes.

Rebekah reached for the dash and eased the volume up on the radio. An empty sensation settled in her heart. Her family hadn't been to the Armitage since Nicole died, and she hadn't intended to go back. Why would her mom send her there?

It had been years. The boardwalk had grown, and nicer hotels had been popping up even when they still frequented the beach. The thought of seeing so many familiar faces connected to such a devastating memory frightened her, but she was left with little choice since she had no money. And her mother was right—she couldn't book her own room.

Her stomach gurgled, and she fished a pack of saltines out of her backpack along with a bottle of water, trying to ignore the ominous feeling that loomed over her.

Rylos, are you with me? she thought, but the question went unanswered.

13

NIKO

NIKO REGARDED THE AGE-WORN hotel with revulsion but grabbed his briefcase and proceeded toward the entrance all the same. Fleeger wasn't kidding about the meager per diem. He clenched his jaw at the thought of him laughing at his expense.

Silver lining—the owners have been here for decades, he thought as he crossed the cracked and weed-blistered asphalt of the parking lot. *That should help with the investigation, at least.*

He peered around at the monolithic hotels that surrounded the Armitage. Well-maintained and modern, they blocked out the sun, leaving his tattered, vintage hotel in the shade. One positive he found was the diner attached to the hotel. Maggie's Dive was overflowing with customers.

So, that's how they've kept this shithole afloat. Niko wrenched the door open. *No automatic doors? Christ.*

He made his way to the receptionist, noting the construction tarp sectioning off a portion of the hotel to his left. A young and bubbly blonde greeted him at the counter with an uncomfortably inviting smile and sultry affectation to her voice.

"Welcome to the Armitage," she said. "My name is Leslie. Are we booking a room today?"

She was cute.

"I have a reservation already, actually." Niko brushed his blazer back, reaching into his pocket to retrieve his wallet.

"Oh, are you a cop?" Her eyes shifted from a curious squint to bulging realization. "You must be that detective who's staying with us this weekend." A small blush flushed her cheeks.

Niko looked down at his exposed shoulder holster and quickly threw his blazer shut to conceal his weapon. "Yeah. Niko Ortez." He removed his ID and handed it to her.

She beamed at him. "Love the name."

"Thanks. Is Robert Wymer around by chance? I was hoping I could have a word with him."

"Um, yeah, he's in his office," she said, tapping at the keyboard. Niko was surprised they had a computer at all. "Let me go get him."

She spun on her heels and sauntered off, casting a smiling glance over her shoulder and catching Niko staring. *Shit.* He shook his head, returned his ID to his wallet, and tucked it back into his pocket, mindful of his blazer.

Beyond the reception desk and elevators stood the archway to the restaurant. Ridged and patterned metal decorated the entrance along with vivid pops of color, reminiscent of a fifties-style diner. Niko eased toward the eatery to get a better look. The noise coming from within was substantial.

As the restaurant came into view, the scene was staggering. Pictures, posters, and memorabilia decorated every inch of the wall, neon signs were scattered throughout, and a jukebox sat at the far side of the room, humming "Sympathy for the Devil," though it was lost beneath the chatter of the customers. Even the waitress, a fit-looking older woman—well, older than Niko's twenty-four—donned a salmon-colored uniform with white lapels, puffed shoulders, and a scalloped white apron tied at the waist.

"Detective Ortez." A gravelly voice pulled his attention away from the diner and toward a portly, older man who emerged from behind the reception desk. "Wonderful to meet you, young man. I'm Robert Wymer, the proprietor of this fine hotel."

Fine hotel? Niko thought. *Not a humble man, it seems.*

Robert held a shaky hand out to Niko, and he wondered if it was Parkinson's or arthritis. He gripped Robert's hand firmly and shook it. The man's knuckles were crooked and swollen, so he relaxed his grip a bit.

"Nice to meet you, sir."

"I have your room key here." Robert handed him a traditional silver key with a matching metal room tag hanging from it. Both were finely polished. "So, you're here on an investigation. Is there something I should be concerned about?"

"Not at all. I'm just following up on dated cases that are missing some information. Do you mind if we discuss this in your office?"

"Absolutely. Right this way." Robert extended an arm, inviting him behind the reception desk, and he obliged.

He opened the door to a hallway that held a small room, a storage closet, and a modest printer and fax bay. Niko stepped aside in the cramped corridor to allow Robert into his office. A bitter musk graced his nose as Robert squeezed by, and Niko crinkled his face in dissatisfaction.

A soft giggle caught his attention and he found Leslie watching him. She gave a flirtatious smile and brushed her hair behind her ear. Niko closed the door and joined Robert.

"Looks like you're doing some remodeling," Niko said.

"Ah, yes," Robert replied. "A necessary headache. I've been hounded the past year by these chain-hotel moguls trying to buy up my property. It's prime real estate—an ocean view on the boardwalk. I tell you, this hotel used to be *the* spot. It was one of the nicest on the strip and booked full every week."

Must have been before my time, Niko thought, casting a judging glance around the aged and cluttered office.

"My grandfather founded the Armitage, and my father took it over before handing it down to me when he died. Now, with these mammoth hotels all around us, I can't keep up, and they've gone and poached some of my best help. So, it's either modernize or die, and I'll be damned if I give up this hotel without a fight."

Robert slapped his hand on documents that littered his desk, sprawled over what looked like blueprints. "I've got some fine ideas in here to help bring the Armitage back to its former glory. A total face-lift. Hell, half of the building is out of commission, top to bottom. A new pool…new lounge…and upgrading the rooms to start."

"And get rid of these novelty keys." Niko laughed, holding up his room key.

Robert's face dropped, and his brows slanted in disapproval. "I like the keys. They're tangible. They make you feel like you own something."

"Well, it's no insult to you," Niko said tucking his key in his pocket. "Today's generation doesn't have the same appreciation for ownership that yours does."

Robert waved a dismissive hand. "Kids today are too damned spoiled. No offense."

"Well, there wasn't any until you said that." Niko chuckled.

"I've been rambling," he said. "Tell me how I can help you, detective."

"As I stated, I'm following up on some cases. Some of them date back decades, and many are sensitive in nature. I would like your help filling in the gaps for the older cases or pointing me in the right direction."

"I'm not sure how much help I'll be." Robert barked out a wheezy laugh. "I'll certainly do my best, but I tend to stay out of the drama and gossip. You're welcome to talk to Maggie, though. Her diner has seen its share of folks, locals and tourists alike. I imagine she's heard her share of things and could be useful to you."

"I'll look into it." Niko fished a folded slip of paper from his blazer pocket and slid it over the desk to the man. "That's a list of people who may have been patrons of your hotel. I need confirmation of the dates they stayed and any other information you might have."

Robert plucked the paper slip from the desk and snatched a pair of reading glasses from his shirt pocket. Unfolding the list, he said, "It'll take me some digging to find the information on these people, if I even have it. Anything older than five years I've boxed and stored, and I'll be honest, I wouldn't call it organized."

"So, it may be a shot in the dark." Niko folded his hands in front of him and watched the man eye over the list, noting the slight twitch at the corner of his mouth. "Still, any help you can offer is better than the nothing I currently have. Since I'll be staying in your hotel, I'd also like your permission to conduct my investigation from here, which may include interviewing patrons who were around for some of these cases. I see at least two families who are local to the area. I don't intend to disrupt your business, but I need to know if you'll allow me to conduct mine on your property."

"Well, I wanted to talk to you about that," Robert responded. "See, when I heard you were coming, I reached out to some friends on the local force. They have the idea that you're *not* a special agent for the FBI but a file clerk. Strikes me as a bit odd that a file clerk would be out here investigating old, unsolved cases."

"And you would have every right to feel that way. However, by title, I am still a special agent. I'm filling a file clerk role while a previous case is under review."

Robert eyed him suspiciously before a wicked grin etched across his face. "You're on probation," he said in a haughty tone. "Those details are not—"

"Even if you are still a special agent, isn't it common practice to present a badge? And further, you're investigating *local* missing persons. Why would the FBI have any interest in such matters?"

He's guarded, Niko thought. *Off to a rough start.*

"Well, as I implied earlier, several of the cases concern vacationers. People from out of town. And most of the cases, local and non-local, are over a decade old. It would stand to reason that they may have crossed state lines, which brings them into federal territory."

Robert weighed Niko, the expression on his face ponderous. After a moment, he nodded. "That's a fair point." He leaned forward in his chair, placing his hands on the table. His voice shifted from congenial to firm. "I don't see a problem allowing you to conduct your investigation, but I'm reserving my right to revoke that permission should it prove to be disruptive."

"Understandable." Niko leaned back. "I'll be a ghost. Except for the moments where I need your help, you won't know I'm here, and after a few days' investigation, I'll be out of your hair."

There was a knock at the door, and Leslie poked her head in. "Mr. Wymer, there's someone here to see you."

Robert grumbled and grunted as he climbed out of his seat, chuckling when he stood. "Age is a cruel bitch. Excuse me, detect—sorry. I mean, Niko. It appears it's a busy day."

Robert limped from the room, and Niko leaned down to collect his briefcase.

"My goodness. Rebekah Daroh!" Robert's voice boomed from the lobby. "It's been years! God, you're all grown up."

Niko hesitated. *Daroh. Where have I heard that name before?*

He racked his brain, but the answer eluded him. It had been a long day. He grabbed his briefcase and fled the office. As he appeared from the back, his eyes landed on the young woman talking to Robert.

She even looks familiar.

Making his way from behind the counter, he approached the two as they conversed. The young girl caught him from the corner of her eye and broke from the conversation. Niko noted a crescent-shaped discoloration on her left eye, thinking he would have remembered a detail like that.

"Apologies for interrupting," he said, holding out his hand to Robert. "I appreciate your time. I'm going to grab my things and head up to my room. I'll leave you to catch up with…"

His eyes hovered over her again. He couldn't escape the sense of déjà vu.

"Rebekah," she said.

"Niko Ortez." He shook her hand. "Nice to meet you."

"Rebekah's father and I go way back. He's one of the best lawyers in Northern Virginia." Robert smiled down at her.

"Are you a cop?" Rebekah's eyes drifted to the holster beneath his blazer.

"Special agent, technically." Niko pulled his suit jacket closed again. He couldn't wait to take the damn thing off.

"I have your key ready, ma'am," Leslie called from the counter.

"Let me escort you up," Robert said. "It's been a long time, and I'd like to catch up a bit if that's all right with you. I can help you with your bags."

"Sure," Rebekah responded. "But it's just my backpack." She tucked her thumbs under the straps slung over her shoulders, removing them when Robert handed her the key. Niko noted the number, 213, hanging from the polished metal placard.

"You didn't bring any bags?" Robert gave her a concerned look, like a father might give a child.

She shrugged and gave him a tired smile. "The trip was kind of spontaneous."

"Well, it was nice meeting you, Rebekah," Niko cut in with a slight bow and a final handshake. "Robert, I'll catch up with you later."

Robert gave a tight-lipped nod and chaperoned Rebekah to the elevators.

She looks miserable, Niko thought as he eyed the teenager. Her wild mass of curly hair, sunken eyes, and bowed posture screamed fatigue. Niko noted a dried clump in the back of her hair that resembled blood.

Leslie smiled at him from behind the counter. "Do you need help getting your bags up to your room?"

"No, thank you." He kept his attention trained on Rebekah until she disappeared into the elevator with Robert. "I can manage."

He returned to his car for his duffle, throwing the strap over his shoulder. The sun concealed itself beneath an overcast sky, and the temperature had dropped a few degrees. A faint roar of thunder sounded in the distance.

Looks like rain. Great.

He closed the trunk and made his way back to the hotel. A group of drunk college kids burst through the door as he approached, knocking into him. He had to grab the handle to steady himself.

"Ah, sorry about that, man," one of the boys slurred, stumbling over his feet, the whole group cackling like asses.

Niko held the door for the others to exit. "Not a problem."

A heavy gust of wind threw his blazer open, exposing his holster again, and he quickly worked his way inside, heaving the door shut behind him as he struggled against the wind. Pulling his blazer closed, he fastened the button. Something he should have done earlier.

Retrieving the room key from his pocket, he examined the number on his placard. Room 417. He tossed the key up in the air, catching it as it came back down, and made for the elevator. Hesitating, he returned to the counter.

"Do you have a gym here?"

"Mm-hmm," Leslie responded. "Past the elevators and to the left. Just beyond the pool and before the construction area."

"Thanks." He gave her a smile and headed back to the elevator, glancing at his watch as he walked.

4:42 p.m. He had time to work out and shower before dinner. Thunder growled—louder than before—and lightning lashed at the sky, the power in the hotel flickering. Niko glanced at the lights.

Go figure, shitty wiring.

He looked out the window to see heavy winds tormenting beach goers and tearing umbrellas from the sand as people gathered their things and charged for their respective hotels. Thick droplets of rain started pelting the windows as another strike of lightning cracked in the sky. The snarl of thunder that followed shook the entire floor. Not many people ran back to the Armitage, though. Even the diner emptied substantially.

That makes sense, he thought as he turned back to the elevator and punched the call button, but a detail gnawed at him. Robert's aggression—his discomfort with the investigation—roused Niko's interest.

14
REBEKAH

Rebekah collapsed on the bed the moment she entered her room as the strain of the day caught up with her; she was more exhausted than she realized. Before comfort could set in, she groaned and rolled off the bed. There was something she had to do. Fishing her phone from her backpack, she flipped it open to call her mom—no signal. *Strange*. Tossing her cellphone aside, she reached for the landline and dialed nine—no tone.

Perfect. A shrill ring echoed in response to her slamming the phone down. *Good start to mending the relationship*.

A violent clap of thunder sent tremors through the room, and the lights flickered. She rushed to the window and ripped the curtains open. Dark gray clouds hung over the ocean, hurling droplets of rain at her window. The black sea below resembled an abyssal maw devouring the world. A spear of lightning struck a lamppost at the end of the pier, sending sparks into the night, carried off by the torrential winds. Rebekah stepped away from the window and a knock sounded at her door.

"Rebekah, it's Mr. Wymer. Are you there?"

Making her way to the entrance, she unlatched the chain lock and opened the door. Mr. Wymer stood with a maintenance man at his side. A tool belt hung from the man's waist, and he held three heavy metal flashlights.

"Ah, there we are." Mr. Wymer smiled. "Sorry for the disturbance. I know I just got you to your room, but it seems we're on the cusp of a harsh storm. Weathermen didn't catch it, at least as far as I saw before the cable went out. We don't have the best cable line feeding this old hotel, something I'm having upgraded along with the modernization." He chuckled, which turned into a cough. "Anyways, I thought I'd bring you a flashlight should the power go out, which it's looking like it might."

The maintenance man, whose nametag read "Jorge," handed Robert a flashlight. He passed it off to Rebekah, after testing it a few times.

"There. That should do."

"Thank you," Rebekah said.

"We have emergency lights on a generator, but to be honest, we haven't tested it in ages. Jorge and I are going to take a peek, but hopefully we won't need the backups. In any case, you have the flashlight if you need it."

Rebekah pursed her lips and held the flashlight up in confirmation. "Yep. Thanks again."

"All right, I'll let you go back to settling in. Looks like you could use the rest. If you need me, though, I'll be in my office, or Leslie can hail me over the radio. Come on, Jorge." And with that, the two men were off.

Rebekah closed and locked the door, placing the flashlight, glass down, on the dresser. She plopped onto the end of the bed and slumped over. Not only was she exhausted but sore. Her body ached fiercely, and her head most of all.

Rylos?

The thought echoed through her mind, met only with silence. She'd never met him but found herself worried about him as she would worry about a friend. He risked his life to save her. Or was it self-preservation? Though freeing her from that place had exhausted him, she could feel his strength leaving as if it were her own. That could explain her fatigue. Just like the power that had pulsed through her. Was that source within her? Or had it come from him?

She needed a shower. And with the threat of a power outage looming, she decided to do it sooner rather than later. She made for the bathroom and got the water running. Her mother had scarred her and her sister for life with an old wives' tale that one should never bathe during a thunderstorm. As a little girl, she was terrified by the thought of being struck by lightning while showering. It was an irrational fear, much like her fear of spontaneously catching fire after learning about stop-drop-and-roll.

The water heated quickly, and soon a dense fog filled the room, clouding the mirror and adding a thickness to the air. Rebekah undressed as the thought struck her she had no change of clothes. In her impetuousness, she forgot the barest necessities, save for a small ration of water and saltine crackers.

Lovely.

She took a moment to laugh at the absurdity of it all before putting her hair up, not wanting to deal with wet curls, and climbing into the shower. The warm water was refreshing and amidst the imitation rainfall, she mulled over her situation. She traveled on impulse to carry out some delusional mission to rescue her sister from a spiritual prison at the suggestion of a voice in her head. Still grappling with the reality of the situation, a strong case could be made for insanity. But the shower helped. Somewhat.

Grabbing the metal handle for the shower tap, Rebekah eased it closed, water still cascading down her body. She climbed out of the shower, grabbed a towel from the rack, and wrapped herself. She then slipped on the wet tile, nearly crashing to the ground. Her hand on the grab bar, she caught something scrawled on the mirror:

find me.

-N.

What the hell?

She stared at the note, deciphering its meaning, which only took her a moment.

"Find me. –N."

It was a note from Nicole. She was sure of it. When they were younger, they used to leave messages for each other on the bathroom mirrors. Invisible at first, the steam from the shower, sink, or their breath would expose them. But how the hell was she supposed to find her?

Rylos, where are you?

She hated the dependency, but she was so far out of her depth and needed guidance. What was her next move? Impatience gnawed at her, but with the weather, she wasn't going anywhere. With no real options, she put on her old clothes, lending a grimy texture to her freshly cleaned self. A slight pain drummed in her head. She clenched her jaw against the pain, grabbed her key, and left the room. She was hungry, and Maggie's had the best chicken tenders. Just the thought of them inspired hungry groans from her stomach. Maybe a shot of nostalgia would do her good.

She turned left when she exited the room, used to taking the stairs with her family, and noticed the construction tarp sectioning off part of the floor, so she turned back toward the elevators and got on the first one that arrived. When it opened to the elevator bay, she found her exit blocked by five, clearly drunk, soaked-with-rain, boys.

The group of kids, who appeared to be college-aged, were laughing. One was wringing out his shirt on the tiled floor. When they caught sight of Rebekah, silence entered the space, and their eyes roved over her greedily. Her expression transitioned from surprise to discontent, but a flicker of fear settled beneath her stern resolve.

"What do we have here?" asked the shirtless one. "A little mocha princess? Where you goin', gorgeous?"

Just what I need. The scent of alcohol poured into the elevator.

"Oh, Joey, good find," the shortest of them said. "You know I love dark meat."

"You can't be serious." Rebekah scoffed as she pushed her way through the drunken cluster.

Joey, the shirtless one, grabbed her arm as two others blocked her exit. "Whoa, what's the hurry, beautiful? We were getting to know each other." He grabbed her ass hard, causing her to shriek in pain, and whispered in her ear, "Look at that potential. You really shouldn't waste it."

She cocked her shoulder up as the heat of his breath slithered around her neck, sending shivers through her body. Seeking an escape, she glanced toward the empty lobby, finding the reception desk blocked from view. Joey's hands crawled around her waist as he pulled her to him, thrusting his hips forward. His dick pressed against her, and a sick sensation plummeted in her stomach, driving away all thoughts of food. Heat flushed throughout her body, and she threw an elbow back, shoving the boy off her.

"She's a fucking wiry bitch," another slurred.

Rebekah turned and threw a punch, aiming at Joey, but she didn't care who she hit. She was hot with rage. Unfortunately, she missed, and the boys erupted with laughter. One of them grabbed her when the momentum, coupled with the slick tiled floor, threw her off balance. The boy clasped her arms behind her back and clapped a hand over her mouth. An angry buzz sounded from the elevator as the cluster of young men barred the doors from closing.

"Hoh, she's a fighter!" one of the boys exclaimed. She didn't see whom.

Joey stepped in front of her and ran his hands under her shirt. "Whatchu hidin' under these baggy clothes, huh?"

His clammy hands slid up her stomach. She tensed and struggled, but two other boys held her legs in place with their own, keeping them spread. His hands climbed under her bra, and his tentacular fingers fondled her nipples. She twisted, tears wetting her cheeks, grunting for him to stop beneath the firm grip of the boy's hand. But Joey's eyes were alive with malicious intention. He licked his lips as a wicked grin formed, his hand sliding back down, teasing the waist of her pants. Buried in the huddle of drunken deviants, concealed from view, a new fear took root in her mind.

"What the hell is going on here?" Mr. Wymer's voice boomed

through the lobby, and the young men stepped back immediately, stumbling about stupidly.

Rebekah shook off the one still holding her and moved away quickly. Mr. Wymer took her into his arms.

"I suggest you boys walk away before I call the cops. I don't tolerate that shit in my hotel."

The boys laughed and stepped onto the elevator. Joey gave Rebekah the finger and puckered his lips. Mr. Wymer rubbed her arms as she trembled.

"My God, are you okay? Did they hurt you?" he asked.

"N-No, I'm…f-fine," she lied, sick with shock as tears soaked her cheeks.

"The hell you are. Come with me." He ushered her off to the diner, where "Hotel California" serenaded the nearly vacant room. A handful of people were scattered about the place, which was somewhat of a relief. The receptionist, Leslie, darted around taking orders. "Sit here." He guided her to a booth by the window. Heavy rains slicked the pavement, and the trees and brush thrashed in the wind. "Maggie, if you could."

Maggie arrived at the table, older now but still as heavily tanned, if not more so. Skin like rough leather freckled with liver spots and the pepperminty smell of her gum gave Rebekah a dose of nostalgia.

"Well, I'll be goddamned," Maggie said, her chewing gum slapping between her teeth. "It's like I'm seeing a ghost. Rebekah?"

"Hi, Ms. Berman," she muttered.

"You are the spitting image of your sister, God rest her soul. But what's wrong? You're shaking like a dog."

"Some drunken assholes just tried to have their way with her out in my lobby. Damn fools." Mr. Wymer huffed a wheezy breath. "Could you bring something to warm her up and maybe something sweet to calm her nerves? It's on me."

"Absolutely," Maggie replied. "I'll be right back, dear."

"Mr. Wymer, I'm heading back," Leslie called as she exited the diner.

Robert waved a hand in acknowledgement before turning

back to Rebekah. "Look, I need to go take care of some things. This storm is a nightmare for this old hotel. I feel terrible leaving you like this, but I'll be sure Maggie keeps an eye on you. Is that all right?"

Rebekah nodded, and Robert gave her a sympathetic frown.

"Oh, and about those boys. I'll be writing a report and filing it with the proper authorities. They'll face their justice, don't you worry." He patted her on the shoulder, lingering a moment before making his way from the diner, leaving Rebekah to stew over her recent encounter.

A lump rose in her throat as she battled back an onslaught of tears, forcing her to take fast and labored breaths. The gravity of the situation settled on her like a dark cloud. She could have been raped. She almost was! What would have happened if Mr. Wymer hadn't been there? A sudden longing for her parents swept what little breath she had away, and she wished she hadn't told her mom not to come. Even her father would do. She needed comfort to dispel her loneliness.

"Here we go, dear." Maggie returned with a steaming mug of hot cocoa and a plate of her renowned gelatin parfait, which she'd named "Maggie's American Dream." It was a blue gelatin base, nestled under a cream cheese icing and loaded with pretzel crumbles and a cranberry purée gelatin topper. Once Rebekah's go-to dessert, it sat warming under the diner lights as she sulked in the booth. Steam from the mug teased her, so she attempted a sip. It warmed her stomach, but the taste soured in her mouth, stealing away what little appetite she had.

Setting the cup aside, she stood from the booth and wandered to the brick wall beside the bar. Various photos hung beneath an etched wood sign that read "We Remember..."

It didn't take long to find Nicole's picture among the various others. The beach and vast ocean made up the backdrop, depicting her on a clear, sunny day, wearing those gaudy pink sunglasses Rebekah had given her. Nicole had enough compassion toward her sister to delight in every gift and wore it no matter how horrible it looked. They looked atrocious, but Nicole's confidence brought a unique elegance to the glasses.

Rebekah slid a gentle finger along the framed photo, smiling at the years of memories as they returned to her. Her eyes found the necklace Nicole wore, another gift from Rebekah—a series of interconnected crescent moons, varying in size, crafted from obsidian. She had almost forgotten about that.

Your sister's necklace…

A smile lifted her cheeks, touching her eyes and sending tears tumbling down the curves of her face. An emptiness had opened up within her at Rylos's absence, filling again with his return, and she realized his presence was one she'd known all her life—something she'd equated to home.

Welcome back, she thought in reply.

How did she come by it? Rylos's voice, as weak as it were, was a relief, and his re-appearance emitted brought with it a new warmth.

The necklace? I gave it to her.

How did you come by it, then?

I woke up one day wearing it when I was younger. I thought it was a gift from my parents, but they had never seen it before. I gave it to Nicole when she was in the hospital with pneumonia. I told her that it was magic and would cure her. Rebekah lowered her hand from the frame, sinking into her own thoughts. "I suppose it did," she said aloud.

Iunctura mentem, he spoke with a distant, musing tone. *Material objects passed through coalescence…*

What?

There was no response, and the silence that settled had a heaviness to it. She could sense his mind turning with questions as if they were her own, though the knowledge behind the questions lay far beyond her understanding.

That amulet is ancient, Rylos said, an artifact of great power. Strange that it merged into your world.

How do you know that?

Because it belonged to me. Somehow, when my consciousness fused with your own, I passed it to you.

Rebekah's mouth bobbed, wanting to speak, but she couldn't articulate her thoughts, let alone find the right questions to ask. What he said made sense, but she couldn't explain how. It was just a feeling of knowing. There was a power within the necklace—she remembered—but over time, she equated it to her childish imagination, which was what led her to give it to her sister. She had told her it would give her strength, but she hadn't realized how right she was.

Where is it now?

"It was lost when she went missing," Rebekah replied.

And this is that place?

"Yes." Sorrow touched her heart as she spoke that truth. It was merely hours ago she had spoken to Nicole, which challenged Rebekah's grasp on reality. Nicole was dead, Rebekah had come to accept that. But…was she? Death held permanence. If she could still communicate with Nicole, it became less enduring. There was a comfort in knowing there was a connection to her.

I feel its presence, Rylos said. *It is near. Stranger still…*

"Excuse me." A voice came from behind Rebekah, startling her out of her head. She turned to find the detective she had met earlier. Niko, wasn't it?

15

THE MAN

The acrid smell of hydrochloric acid filled the room. Despite the mask, the pungent chemical assaulted his senses, bypassing the rubber seal. Using the last of his stores, the washtub contained just enough of the putrid acid to soak the sections of skin taken from Edward Smith. Boiling was his preferred method to extract the collagen, but the encroaching storm had him wary the power wouldn't hold, and boiling took time. Had he replenished his citric acid stores, he could have been spared the rancid odor, but it would suffice.

He had removed the heavy rubber gloves and hazmat suit he donned but kept the mask on—the ventilation in the space wasn't optimal. Rolling his chair over to his workbench, he slipped on a pair of nitrile gloves and began removing the marrow from the last of Eddie's bones. Halving the husks lengthwise to ease the process, the loose marrow collected in a waiting bowl as he opened the skeletal chutes, a grim harvest.

he mused, his thoughts mingling with the rhythmic, Darth Vaderesque breathing of the mask.

An unsettling stillness hung in the air, an absence he hadn't experienced since his sinister companion first invaded his mind years ago. The quiet seemed foreign and suffocating, enclosing him in an unnerving cocoon. Setting the bowl of marrow aside, arranged with the assorted ligaments and tendons, he took the bones to the sink, meticulously cleansing every fragment of remaining tissue.

Returning to the workbench, he gripped a cleaver, hacking the bones into smaller fragments before transferring them into a grinder. After a single pass, the grated pieces were poured into a food processor and ground down to a fine powder. The resulting bonemeal joined the contents of a fifty-five-gallon plastic drum, ominously labeled "Fertilizer," half-filled with osteal matter.

Finally, he made his way back to the freezer, retrieving several slabs of ground meat and a tub brimming with separated fat.

Eddie à la carte. He chuckled.

Pressure gripped his head, and he nearly collapsed, salvaging his haul by tossing it on the workbench, freeing his hands to catch himself as a familiar presence returned to him.

The voice of his companion.

You must prepare for another, it said.

So soon?

The man regained his balance but sat as the headache traversed his skull. There was an anxious energy to his counterpart.

This will be the last.

After all these years, you've found him? the man asked.

Yes.

Finally. He breathed sweet relief. *I can be rid of you, and this curse you've burdened me with.*

His companion loosed a shrill cackle. *You were burdened with demons long before I entered your mind. I simply gave them purpose.*

"No, I had given up those demons," he said aloud. "You invited them back in. But it's almost over. Soon, I will have peace."

When this is over, you shall have your peace. But it will not taste as sweet as you imagine.

"I don't need your cynicism," the man spat. "Let's just be done with it."

I have done my part. The girl is here, the voice said. *The rest is on you.*

"I will do what needs to be done as I have many times before." The man retrieved sheets of plastic packaging and a vacuum sealer, but he hesitated, glancing toward the burled-wood box. "And the blade?"

What of it?

The man eyed it greedily, attempting to conceal his thoughts from the intruder. "Why must we use it? I have plenty that I am more comfortable with."

It is the only way to sever the bond they share, the voice stated. *It was crafted in the Heart of the World by the Mystics as a deterrent for the Guardians. They feared their own creation.*

"Will it remain here when you're finished?" He hoped his subtleties would mask the avarice in his voice.

His associate cackled again. *Ensnared you, has it?*

It had. The dagger carried a voice of its own, and the man heard its song each time he wielded it. A softer contrast to that of his companion, it was a tonic to the bludgeon the trespasser used.

The blade remains because I allow it to. Phantom crystal cannot maintain corporeal form in this realm without an Ethereal to wield it. When I leave, it goes as well.

Tearing his gaze from the box, the man began separating the ground meat into portions dedicated to various sizes of bags, considering what to do with the new stock. What remained of Eddie would last three months, he calculated. A fresh inventory may sour before he could get to it. He could dispose of it, but there were inherent risks to that. Perhaps he could thin out his stock. The storm would obscure the exhaust, alleviating suspicions. It was safe.

Bring her in as usual. I will confront him on the other side. The girl's spirit will linger in that place—a waste, but there's nothing for it. My purpose will be fulfilled.

A strange sadness sank into the man as the realization of losing a piece of himself, as he'd come to think of the voice, dawned on him, but he held his tongue and continued his work. He both loved and hated his companion. And feared him. But more than all else he had grown complacent with his company.

Still, he sought escape, and a plan, years in the making, took root.

In another steel washtub, he poured sulfuric acid and turned to ignite the furnace.

"If this is to be done, then let it be done carefully," he said. "I will be the one to suffer the consequences when you're gone. My body will linger here, and I would like to have something left to live of my life."

I don't care how it's done so long as you deliver him to me.

Tossing the excess vacuum-sealed packaging into the tub as the acid hissed and sputtered, devouring the contents, the last remains of Edward Smith dissolved. Heat quickly filled the room as the furnace rose to temperature, and an open vent dispelled the smoke. Fishing the skin from the hydrochloric acid, he cast it into the fire, slammed the door closed, and triggered the vent fan, which whirred to life with a breathy wail.

"This girl." The man began dumping the bowls of marrow, ligaments, and tendons into the acid but left the bowl of excess fat untouched to replenish their supply of soap. "Who is she?"

Her name is Rebekah.

16
NIKO

NIKO SPREAD THE CASE files across the dresser chest, the overflow nearly swallowing the round table in the corner. Beads of sweat trickled down his forehead as he unpacked his spare suit, the energetic beat from his Discman filling the room. After carefully hanging his spare suit in the armoire, he arranged the rest of his casuals in a single dresser drawer.

On the bed, his discarded shoulder holster concealed his federally issued Glock 23. Niko unclipped the gun from the holster and proceeded to perform the ritual he knew too well—removing the magazine and clearing the chamber.

Not the smartest move to leave a loaded gun lying around, he chided himself, securing the gun in the nightstand. Unsurprisingly, the hotel room didn't contain a safe.

Next to the Glock sat his father's old snub-nosed Ruger, the one he had learned to shoot with. He picked up the gun, slid it from its holster, and turned it over in his hands, feeling the weight of the memories it held. *Miss you, Dad.* A satisfying swish sounded from the suede interior as he returned the gun to its sheath and tucked it back in the drawer.

With the busy work completed, he shed his sweaty gym clothes, laying out fresh ones on the spare bed. Coiling the headphone cable around the Discman, he set it down beside his casuals. A sudden clap of thunder rattled the room. Niko fished his phone from the pocket of his slacks, hesitating for a moment. Considering Brindle's advice, he decided to call Danielle.

"Hello?" she answered.

"Hey, uh." He realized he hadn't planned out what he wanted to say. "I just got down to the beach, and I thought I would give you a call and see how you're doing."

"I'm fine," she said, the sound of silverware clinking. Crowded conversations clouded the space between her words. "I'm out at dinner right now."

"Ah, sorry to bother you," Niko said. "Look, I wanted to apologize. I said some things that... Well, in hindsight, I acted like an asshole. I'm sorry."

"Yeah," she said, the background noise diminishing as she escaped to a quieter room. "We both kind of said things we shouldn't have."

"This isn't on you," he said. "I've been selfish. I didn't consider your feelings in my pursuit to restore my status, and after talking with your dad, I realized I never thanked you for everything you did for me while I was recovering. I didn't... I guess I never considered what I put you through."

"I appreciate that." Her voice was marred with static. "Listen, I want you to be happy, and I know that your career means a lot to you. I'm not trying to change that, but—"

"I know you're not." Niko ran his hand along the back of his neck. "But I want to be honest with you. Being an agent *is* important to me, and it's not something I want to give up on, not yet at least. I want to be with you, though, and I hope you can accept that."

More static hissed over the line, wavering back and forth in strength.

"—you want to do, then—"

The reception quality degraded. Niko held out his phone, examining the signal strength. One bar. He maneuvered around the room, searching for the best spot.

"—I was hoping to—" Danielle kept talking in broken sentences. "—talk more when I get—"

"Call ended" flashed on the screen, and Niko cursed. He slammed the phone shut and flung it onto the bed, clenching his fists tightly. Running his hand through his sweaty hair, he sighed. At least the conversation went better than expected. What more could he ask for?

Deciding to shake off the tension, Niko prepared for a shower, draping a towel over the back of the toilet and laying another on the floor. Grabbing a travel-sized bottle of shampoo from the sink, he noticed the intriguing packaging on a bar of soap labeled "Armitage" in decorative green letters instead of the usual branding.

Interesting.

Curiosity piqued, he turned the shower handle, waiting for the water to heat up. When it finally did, the scalding stream hit him unexpectedly, forcing him to lower the temperature. As he washed his hair, the name returned to his mind.

Daroh, he thought.

A sense of familiarity tormented him. He hurried through the remainder of his shower, abruptly stopping when the realization struck him. Turning the handle off, he jumped out of the tub, wrapped a towel around his waist, and made for the scattered files. He fumbled over a few before finding the one he wanted.

With one slick hand, the other holding his towel in place, he flipped the folder open to see the picture of a young girl he knew as Nicole Daroh.

"Daroh!" he exclaimed. "Nicole Fucking Daroh!"

Snatching the picture from the file, he rushed to the bed and threw his clothes on over his water-streaked body, leaving dark splotches to dapple his shirt. Grabbing the room key from his discarded slacks, he hung a "do not disturb" sign on the door and hurried through the hall, slicking his wet hair back and out of his face. The elevator tested his patience, but it finally spit him out in the lobby. Leslie perked up behind the counter as he approached.

"I met a girl here in the lobby a couple of hours ago," he said.

"She was talking with Robert, and he escorted her to her room. Rebekah Daroh?"

Leslie's smile wavered. "Yes, what about her?"

"I need her room number."

"I can't, uh…" Leslie cleared her throat and bit her lip, glancing around nervously. She dropped her voice to a whisper. "I don't think I'm allowed to give that information out, even to an FBI agent."

Niko groaned and stepped back from the desk. But a fleeting memory held him in his tracks—the number he'd glimpsed when Robert handed her the key. Room 213. He rushed back to the elevator, but after a brief wait, he opted for the stairs. His legs, stiff from his workout, propelled him up the single flight and through the corridor to her room. He knocked, catching his breath. After a moment, he knocked again and a third time when there was still no response.

Double-checking the room number, uncertainty gnawed at him. *Did I get it wrong?*

Despite his doubts, he knocked a final time. No answer.

Great.

Hunched over, defeat settling in, he took a deep breath. Reluctantly, he worked his way back to the elevator.

A growl of protest snarled from his stomach. Punching the call button, he decided to take Robert's advice and seek out Maggie. Rebekah wasn't going anywhere, not with the storm raging outside. When he landed back in the lobby, he turned left, not noticing if Leslie was looking or even there, and made his way into the diner to the tune of "Hotel California."

Good song.

Entering the nearly deserted room, he spotted Maggie, the fit, older waitress, attending to a tipsy customer at the bar. After Niko caught her attention, she gestured to the available seats, and he nodded gratefully. A few steps into the diner, he spotted Rebekah standing in front of a brick-laden wall adorned with photos. There were so many it looked like a memorial.

He did a double-take and approached cautiously. It was

harder to be sure from behind, but the clothes and the dried clump in her curls confirmed his suspicions. It was her.

Is she talking to herself?

"Excuse me," he said, startling her.

The faint light of a thought retreated in her eyes as she turned, like the light of a candle flickering out. Her cheeks were wet with tears, and looking beyond her, he understood why. A picture of Nicole sat at eye level with her, and it was uncanny how alike they looked.

"Rebekah, right?" Niko asked.

"Yes," she replied, brushing the tears from her cheeks.

"We met previously. I'm Niko."

"I remember."

"Well, I'm following up on some cold cases, and I discovered one of them is your sister's." He fished the picture out of his pocket and held it out for her to see.

Rebekah's eyes widened at the photo then snapped back to his, remnants of tears still clumping her eyelashes together. She cleared her throat. "What do you need from me?" She avoided eye contact.

Niko slid the photo back into his pocket. "I was hoping you might be able to shed some light on gaps in the case. There were a string of testimonies and interviews but nothing from you."

"I was only ten."

"I understand. Do you have time to sit and discuss it now?"

"I'd rather not." Rebekah glanced toward the ground and picked at her fingers.

"How about some dinner then? It's on me."

"I actually already have some food." She nodded her head at a booth behind Niko with a plate of untouched dessert and a mug of what looked like hot cocoa.

"Okay, well, I'm starving. So, how about I order myself something, and you can tell me about your sister? Not as an investigator, just an ear to vent to. Sometimes, that's all people need."

Her brows furrowed as she assessed him, still fidgeting nervously and gnawing at her lip.

"Okay," she agreed, though her breath carried reluctance.

Maggie approached. "Everything all right, Rebekah?"

"Yeah, Ms. Berman, everything is fine." She avoided eye contact with her as well.

"Special Agent Niko Ortez." He held out an introductory hand.

"Maggie Berman," the woman replied with a suspicious stare, but she shook his hand.

"Rebekah, do you mind if I have a quick word with Maggie?"

Rebekah nodded and escaped to the booth. Niko waited for her to wander out of earshot before turning back to Maggie.

"I don't know what you want with that girl," Maggie started in on him, "but she's already had a hell of a day on top of everything else. I told Robert I'd keep an eye on her, and I intend to do just that, agent or not."

Ignoring the threat, Niko asked, "Is she okay? She seems tense, and she's dodging eye contact. Both are signs of someone in danger."

Maggie shifted, hesitating briefly before stumbling through her response. "She was assaulted just a few moments ago by some drunken misfits in the elevator lobby. I thought my dessert might help. It used to be her favorite, but she hasn't touched it."

"Drunken misfits? Were they a group of college kids?" Niko asked.

"I'm not sure. Robert wasn't particularly detailed. All I know is they were drunk and being inappropriate, and Robert intervened. She's been quiet and shifty ever since."

"Did anyone call her parents?" Niko asked.

"Wouldn't do much good," Maggie replied. "Storm took out the phones, and I haven't been able to get a signal."

"Hmm, okay." Niko stared back at Rebekah. "Give us about five minutes and bring out some coffee. Some dinner for both of us about thirty minutes after that. Give her whatever she likes, and just bring me a cheeseburger. Can you do that for me?"

Maggie weighed him carefully before nodding her head, loudly chomping her gum as she turned back to the bar.

Niko approached the booth. “Do you mind if I sit?” Motioning toward the bench opposite Rebekah, he waited for her shy, approving nod.

17

REBEKAH

"My sister was the only person I had in my life, except for my parents. I loved my parents, and they were around a lot before Nicole died, but my sister was the one I went to when I was scared or angry. We were seven years apart, so she pretty much had a handle on her independence when I was born. My parents made sure of that. Even with me, they were heavy advocates of me learning to do things on my own."

"So, there was discord even before Nicole died," Niko said.

"No," Rebekah replied. "My relationship with my parents began like most children, I suppose, but as I grew, I related more to my sister. I still loved my parents, but Nicole was my confidant, the one who kept my secrets, and the one who knew me at the deepest level. I wanted to be just like her and still do.

"Nicole was brilliant and so compassionate. She spoke with a soft tone and always wore a smile. I never saw her lose her temper. If she ever did, she did a good job concealing it from me. But what mattered the most was her ability to put my needs above her own, no matter what pressures she had. It sounds selfish to me now, but when I was a kid, it meant everything. She welcomed me with genuine happiness, as if I eased her stress."

"She sounds like a great person," Niko said before lifting his mug for another sip of coffee.

"She was," Rebekah replied, prodding the lukewarm gelatin dessert with her fork and watching it jiggle.

Niko smiled, returning his mug to the table. "I mean, the way you describe her makes her sound like a parent."

Rebekah chuckled softly. "Yeah, she kind of was."

Zoning into the steam dancing from the mug of coffee Maggie had brought, Rebekah reminisced.

"Would you say your sister had the greatest influence on your life?" Niko asked.

"Yeah, she practically raised me," she responded.

"Interesting."

"What do you mean?"

"Well, I've never met a seventeen-year-old who talks quite like you." He chuckled. "Not that I've met the best and brightest, being a cop. But you seem more mature for your age. I think your sister would be proud."

Rebekah's face flushed. She smiled and peered down at her drink. "Thank you."

"So, how is it that everyone around here is so familiar with you?" Niko asked.

"We came here every summer, two or three times a year for as long as I can remember. It was like a second home for us. My dad helped Mr. Wymer out with some court thing. He's a lawyer. So, Mr. Wymer let us stay here for cheap."

Rebekah set her fork aside and sipped from the steaming cup, not so much for the taste but for the warmth it brought her. A flush swept over her skin, and a weightlessness hung from her chest. Glancing out the window, she noticed the storm outside had intensified. The gray clouds sank to a darker shade, and harsh waves clawed at the shore.

"But you stopped coming when your sister went missing?" he asked.

"Yeah." Rebekah looked down, cupping the warm mug in her hands and rolling it beneath her fingers. A dull pain throbbed in her head again from her earlier injury at school.

"What do you remember about the last time you were here?"

"It was a challenging time for us. We stayed for two months, working with the police to try and find her. There was this detective—uh, Rossi, I think—who led the case. My dad didn't like him."

"Why not?" Niko casually sipped from his cup, maintaining eye contact.

Rebekah glanced up, meeting Niko's eyes. He was good-looking. She wasn't particularly loquacious even at the best of times, but something about him allowed her guard to drop somewhat.

"He was a lazy prick," she said. An amused grin split Niko's lips, which he quickly covered with another sip of coffee. "He spent most of his time hanging around the bar, and he treated my family like shit, shrugging off our concerns and giving us as little attention as possible."

Nodding, Niko asked, "Did he run his operation from this hotel?"

"I don't know." Rebekah snatched up the fork and stabbed at her dessert; feeling the fork plunge through the soft layers pacified her anger slightly. "There were cops all over the place and volunteers for the search party, so maybe. They met at the diner every morning before they conducted their search, but I never saw them at night."

Rebekah dropped her fork again in frustration as the nerves rattled inside of her. Feverish tremors crept through her flesh, accompanied by a flush of anger. She breathed deeply, attempting to slake the anxiety.

"Maggie and her brother Stuart made these big breakfast platters most days. One day, they even closed the diner to join the search."

"So, did he hang around the bar during the day?"

"Detective Rossi? Not at first," Rebekah said. "After a couple weeks."

"Interesting." Niko's brows drew together as he set his cup down. "Do you remember anything about the search?"

"Yeah, they had us canvassing a few miles from here and working our way back toward the hotel each day. It didn't make any sense. We walked so much my feet started to hurt, and my dad had to carry me on his back some days. I stopped going because of that, so I'd stay at the diner, and Detective Rossi was always there.

"Eventually, he stopped going out, leaving only my parents and a few officers still searching. The volunteers were less each day until no one showed up at all. Detective Rossi pulled the officers after a while and relied on missing posters and their own resources. My dad was pretty furious."

"I can imagine," Niko said.

Maggie arrived at the table with their food, chicken tenders and fries for Rebekah and a large burger for Niko.

He threw a napkin over his lap and reached for his meal. "Do you mind if I—"

"Go ahead," Rebekah responded, plucking a single fry from her own basket to nibble on. She sat in introspection as she grazed. It was relieving to talk about Nicole, and despite the morbid context, it brought her close to her sister again. But that didn't ease the frustration in revisiting the memory. After she finished a solitary fry, she attempted the chicken, but her stomach rolled in protest.

"You seem a little furious as well," Niko said, setting his burger aside.

"Obviously!" She shoved her food away and brought her knees to her chest, pinning them between herself and the ribbed metal band that wrapped the tabletop. "Why wouldn't I be? He gave up on us. He left my sister to die!"

Tears threatened to cascade down her cheeks, and she inhaled deeply. Shaking her head and fighting the anger swelling inside of her, she worked hard to hold them back. Drew's words swam through her head. *Just another dead Black kid. Who would care? I mean, who cared when your sister died?* Apparently, the answer was no one, and that realization infuriated her. She looked at Niko, who studied her with an empathetic stare.

"Were people receptive when you went door to door?" he asked.

"We only went to the various businesses and shared her photo around. It was mostly hotels along the boardwalk, but some of the owners led us through the hotel, room by room, and even through the maintenance locations to search for her. We spent one day scouring the beach and around the pier. I was terrified that we would find her body washed ashore."

"But you never found her?" he asked.

"No." Rebekah gave him a curious look. "But you already know that."

"Well, I have an open case, which would imply that she was never found. But everyone I've spoken to refers to her as dead. It's strange."

A crash startled them both as a beach chair collided with the window, sending a cracked web sprawling throughout the glass. A fierce howl whistled outside, and a thunderous boom growled through the dark sky. Lounge chairs were thrown violently along the boardwalk, and another flash of lightning showed the chaos further out on the beach. The trees bowed low against the heavy wind, giving obeisance to the ferocious storm.

"Jesus," Niko said. "This storm is getting worse. Let's move away from the windows."

Captivated by the weather, Rebekah nodded, picked up her food, and followed Niko to a table closer to the center of the room. Her heart raced but not from the storm. She'd held onto the hope Nicole wasn't dead until she found her in that horrible place, but she hadn't realized she projected that outwardly. Could she tell the agent the truth? No, that wouldn't bode well. The padded penitentiary would find a new occupant. Best to keep the less rational thoughts internalized. Her silence earned pressure from Niko's insistence.

"As I was saying, the situation is odd, wouldn't you agree?"

Rebekah fumbled with her food. "I think it's been years, and people tend to assume that after so long, it's likely that she's dead. You start to lose hope."

"You don't strike me as that type," Niko said. "When you were standing by her photo over there, I heard you talking to yourself. You said, 'it was lost when she went missing.' That's a curious statement, don't you think?"

Rebekah's eyes met his, and he weighed her with steady

resolve. A chill crawled over her flesh, like someone who was caught where they shouldn't be.

"Are you accusing me of something?" She steadied herself and pooled her confidence, but a defensive anger surged within her.

"Not at all." Niko leaned back in his seat. "Again, you don't strike me as the type. But when left to your own thoughts, you refer to her as missing. With me, you acknowledge her death."

Rebekah scoffed. "I don't find that strange." Even she wasn't convinced by the lie, though, so she attempted to redirect. "What type of person do I strike you as?"

A smirk worked its way onto Niko's face as she avoided the topic, and she got the feeling he knew what she was doing. "I think you're exceptionally intelligent and clever. Not as much as you might think, though. You're incredibly devoted, especially to your sister, but I don't get the feeling that you have many other people in your life, certainly not your parents. Not anymore."

"That's a brash assumption."

Niko smiled at her. "Maybe. But a seventeen-year-old girl, even as impressive as you, travelling to a place of trauma is curious. You've been wrought with grief and depression, judging by that scar on your wrist. I don't see a well-adjusted and loving family letting you travel here alone. But I'm not judging you, and I'm not judging your parents. I understand.

"I lost my mother when I was younger to a drunk driver, and my dad poured himself into tracking the bastard down and putting him behind bars. He succeeded, but his pursuit left me to bear her loss on my own. It was challenging and I lashed out. It wasn't until I met Danielle, my girlfriend, who grounded me and comforted me, that I was able to return to something close to normal. She helped me through it. She helped me through a lot."

He paused and took a deep breath. Rebekah could see the emotional toll of his confession wash over his face. Another headache thrummed in her head and she closed her eyes to battle through it.

"Anyway, my dad eventually came around and tried to make amends. We were on a good path. But cancer got him shortly after, and I never got the opportunity to let him know that I forgave him. I didn't get to tell him how much I loved him before he died."

Niko finished his story with a mournful sigh, and whatever defensive anger Rebekah had used as a shield dissipated when she caught a familiar sorrow in his distant eyes. His pain mirrored her own, and the thought of how selfishly hateful she had been toward her parents pushed itself to the front of her mind.

"My mom booked me the room," Rebekah said. "I told her not to come. I wish I hadn't done that."

"I imagine she listened because she wants to mend the relationship."

Rebekah nodded and reached for her coffee.

"My dad was the same way," Niko said. "I can't imagine it sitting well with your mom, especially with this storm. She's probably sick with worry. Have you had the chance to talk to her yet?"

"No." Guilt hit her again. "I couldn't get a signal, and the landline in my room is down."

"I may be able to help." Niko leaned forward and snatched up a fry. "When I was in Robert's office, I noticed he had an old analog phone. They don't require the extra phantom power that the digital ones in the rooms do. You should see if he'll let you call your mom. I don't see him having a problem with it."

A smile lifted Rebekah's cheeks. "Thank you. I'll ask him about that when he's done running around."

There was a pause as they both returned to their meals, a little colder now, but Rebekah's appetite returned, so she reached for the chicken again. Another beach chair collided with the diner window, expanding the web of cracks. Rebekah watched as Maggie rushed behind the counter and disappeared into the kitchen. The old man at the bar dropped some money in front of him and stumbled from the stool, throwing his hat over his head. Before long, Rebekah realized she had downed half of her meal and caught Niko staring at her with a slacked jaw.

"What?" she asked.

He laughed. "I was just getting concerned since you hadn't come up for air. Thought I might have to do CPR."

Rebekah covered her mouth and blushed. "Sorry. I didn't realize how hungry I was."

"No need to apologize. It sounded like you had an eventful day."

Rebekah swallowed back her food and wiped her hands on her napkin as a sudden nervousness crept over her. She hoped he wouldn't bring up the lobby incident. "Yeah," she said.

"I don't mean to pry, but when I met you earlier, when Robert escorted you to your room, I noticed some dried blood clumped in your hair."

Her eyes widened and she threw her hand back, feeling through her curls, and sure enough, there was a dried clump knotted in her hair. "Oh shit," she said. "That's embarrassing."

Niko laughed. "Not really." He shuffled his food around on its tray as a solemn expression washed over him. "It's none of my business, but if you got cut, or if you banged your head hard enough to draw that much blood, it must have hurt. Do you want to talk about it?"

Rebekah shook her head.

Okay," Niko replied. "Fair enough. But I do want to talk to you about those boys in the lobby."

Before Rebekah could respond, a loud crash sounded, drawing their attention to the windows of the diner, where a beach umbrella had just speared through the glass. The torrential winds outside whistled through the newly formed hole, and rain misted the air like steam through a vent. Maggie emerged from the kitchen, dragging a piece of plywood, with Stuart trailing behind, adorned in his grease-soaked apron. They threw the wooden sheet over the window, dampening the sounds of the storm, and Stuart began driving screws into the frame to secure the board in place.

Wild screaming brought their attention deeper into the

restaurant. Rebekah gasped and clapped her hands to her mouth, and Niko sprung from his seat.

"Maggie, I need water and towels. Now!" Niko screamed as he hurtled a table.

The drunken gentleman from the bar was sprawled on the ground, the elbow of his left arm missing. A trail of blood soaked the floor, leading to where the beach umbrella sat beneath a pile of toppled chairs. Howls of pain erupted from the man as he flailed his arm, spewing curtains of blood from the wound. His forearm, now a limp marionette tethered by a thick web of skin, bounced around uselessly from the end.

18

NIKO

NIKO SLID ACROSS THE tiled floor and pinned the guy down, stopping him from throwing his arm around. The other diners, a young couple and an elderly man, watched in shock as Niko dropped a knee on the man's bicep and pressed his hands onto his shoulders to both limit the blood flow and his movements.

"Steady, steady." He worked to calm the man while reaching for a belt that wasn't there. "Shit. Maggie, I need a belt or—or twine. Something to make a tourniquet. It's all right, buddy. I got you. I got you."

The man's skin looked pallid and waxy, and his screams and movements weakened. Niko shifted his knee and pressed down harder, but blood continued to pool from the arm. Maggie rushed from the kitchen with butcher twine and an armful of clean towels.

"Oh my God!" she screamed as she caught a closer look at the man. "Oh no, Henry! Hang in there. It'll be all right."

Maggie handed Niko the twine, and he bound the man's arm with three tight wraps, tying it off at the end. The crimson flow slowed, but by then, Henry was unconscious. Niko checked his neck for a pulse, then sighed in relief. He reached for the towels and laid a few over the red puddle, mopping up the mess. Once the floor was relatively clear, Niko used a stack of clean towels to elevate Henry's arm. He then turned to the older bystander.

"Sir, what's your name?"

"It's Jim," the man replied.

"Jim. I need you to find Robert Wymer, the hotel owner, and see if he has any medications, preferably some antibiotics and painkillers. Have him call an ambulance too."

Jim nodded and fled for the elevator lobby just past the diner entrance.

"Okay...okay." Niko thought for a moment, assessing the situation and muttering to himself. "Ideal scenario, ambulance comes through in maybe eight minutes." He glanced back toward the windows. "Maybe thirteen in this storm. Worst case? No ambulance. What would I need? Shit. Think."

He stood, attempting to avoid the mess on the floor, holding his hands awkwardly at his sides to avoid bloodying up his clothes any further.

"Hmm," he pondered, gesturing through the scenario with his hands. "Clean and cover. Uh, it would need to be bandaged. I would need to...amputate the forearm to separate the pieces so I can dress the wound." Niko's hands shook as the adrenaline fed his nerves.

"You'd need salt," said a voice from behind him. He turned to find Stuart.

"What?"

"Salt to clot the wound. Then cauterize it."

Niko nodded, considering the advice, then he turned to Maggie. "I need a browning torch, uh, packing salt, and something sharp to cut the excess. Bring some alcohol too."

Stuart dropped to the floor and began examining the damage closely, making mild adjustments to Niko's tourniquet and nodding in approval. Maggie rushed off to the kitchen. He placed a hand on Henry's chest, feeling the shallow breaths rise and fall, then pressed two fingers against his neck and checked his watch. After a moment, Stuart stood and took a step back.

"Do you have any medical training?" Niko asked him.

"No."

"So, how did you know to use salt to clot the wound?"

"We cure our meat with salt because it draws out moisture.

Drawing moisture from blood compresses the cells, causing them to clot."

With that, Stuart fled, disappearing into the kitchen. Robert rushed into the room with Jim nipping at his heels. Leslie brought up the rear and shrieked at the grisly scene.

"What in the hell happened?" Robert cried as his eyes darted around the diner.

Niko blurted out, "Robert, did you call for an ambulance?"

"I did," Robert said with an unsatisfied tone. "They can't send anyone out right now. Storm's too bad."

"Fuck. This man needs medical attention immediately." Niko's eyes darted around. He knew what would need to be done but didn't know if he had the prowess to do it.

Fuck. Why me?

"Here we are." Maggie returned, maneuvering around the tables with a two-tier cart loaded with supplies. "Here's everything you need, and I brought more water and towels. I threw in some gloves as well."

"Thanks," Niko replied.

Looking over the cart, he hesitated, planning his approach, but he also hoped someone with more experience would step up to save him from the task. He grabbed the liquor bottle and poured some over his shaking hands to sterilize them. Maggie handed him a pair of nitrile gloves, which he slipped on before pouring another swig of alcohol over those. A meat cleaver sat on the cart. He collected it and examined his pale, uncertain face in the reflection. Sinking to his knees next to Henry, he took a final shaky breath. Sparing a sympathetic glance toward the unconscious man, he apologized and took a heavy swing of the meat cleaver, severing the skin and the brittle fragment of bone that was still attached.

That wasn't so bad, Niko thought, sliding the severed forearm away from Henry.

"Hand that here," Maggie said.

Confused, Niko snatched the arm from the floor, still warm and dribbling blood, and turned back to Maggie, who presented a cooler filled with ice. Niko carefully placed the arm in the cooler, and Maggie snapped the lid shut and latched it closed.

"That should hold it over for a while," she said.

"Smart thinking," Robert noted.

Niko grabbed the bottle of alcohol and retrieved a handful of packing salt from a bowl on the cart. He poured a dash of alcohol over the wound. The crimson pool became a slurry mixture with tendrils of clear liquid weaving throughout. Henry woke in a screaming fit, thrashing around violently as Niko cupped his hand around the man's stubbed arm. Niko slid his knee onto Henry's chest and used his free hand to pin the wound down. The man's good arm clawed at Niko's shirt and hair, attempting to throw him off. He was stronger than he looked.

"Help!" Niko growled as he struggled to restrain him.

The young woman from the couple slid in and pinned Henry's free arm down, but the man's feet still kicked about wildly, toppling over the supplies on Maggie's cart.

"Towel!" Niko called.

Maggie unfolded a small hand towel from the cart and thrust it at him. He pressed the towel against the wound, securing the salt, and tied another wrap of twine around the top of the cloth to hold it in place. The man's fit grew weaker until he lost consciousness again. Niko grabbed a few more towels and created a pile. He rested Henry's arm on it to keep it elevated. He then rocked back on his knees and wiped the sweat from his head with his forearm.

"We won't be able to cauterize his arm if we can't sedate him or strap him down. Then again, we may not need to if the tourniquet holds." Niko stood and removed the gloves, discarding them on the cart.

Robert stepped forward. "Anyone care to tell me what the hell happened?"

"Beach umbrella," Niko said. "The wind threw it through the window. Best guess is it hit the floor here." Niko pointed at a spot of broken tile. "Likely ricocheted and hit Henry. Damn near took his arm off, as you saw. It stopped over there."

Robert stepped carefully around Henry and followed the splattered trail to the toppled chairs. He lifted a few to reveal the ravaged umbrella, the canopy of which was torn and shredded, still attached to a bent pole that had been severed. It exposed a jagged edge that was coated in blood, a mass of carnage lodged in it. Robert inspected the umbrella closer and turned away in nauseous revulsion, heaving dryly.

"Ah, that would be Henry's elbow," Niko said with a grim affectation.

Scouring the cart of supplies, he found a kabob skewer. Presenting it to Maggie with a concerned look on his face, he shrugged and shook his head. With the skewer in hand, he dislodged the bone fragment and added it to the ice box with Henry's arm. He wasn't sure if it would be of any use, but he didn't want to take the chance.

"This has been one hell of a day," Robert managed after composing himself.

"Yeah," Niko replied, wiping his hands on a fresh towel. "Not over yet. Were you able to find any medicine?"

"Well, I found some antibiotics, but they're expired. No painkillers, unfortunately."

"Okay." Niko sighed. "That's better than nothing to help fight the infection, and we can give him some alcohol to numb the pain. It doesn't look good, though."

"Well, from the looks of him, you've done the best you can do for now."

Niko glanced back toward the kitchen, remembering Stuart's advice. He considered the options for a moment before speaking again.

"We need to place another call to emergency. Even if they can't get out here, they can walk us through steps to keep him stable until they can. For now, we'll make him comfortable, administer the medication, and monitor him. We'll need a thermometer of some kind to check for a fever. If an infection sets in or the bleeding doesn't stop, we'll probably have to cauterize the wound."

Niko squatted over the man, feeling for a pulse and timing

the beats with his watch. "Looks like…sixty beats per minute, give or take. Let's start a log for vitals. We'll document everything we know, everything we did, and everything we do going forward."

"Sounds like a plan. Let's get him up to his room, then." Robert started for the man, gesturing for Jim to help.

"We need to keep him on this floor. We don't want to make time a bigger challenge than it already is. Do you have any available rooms close to an exit?"

"Leslie!" Robert glanced around until he found the young receptionist. "Check the vacancies, would you?"

"Sure." She fled on shaky legs, looking queasy over the grim display.

"Let's clear the cart," Niko said. "We can use it to roll him to the room."

The three men worked to move the supplies from the cart to the various tables around them. Once it was empty, Niko unfolded a larger towel and draped it over the top, which earned a skeptical look from Robert.

"Easier to move him to the bed," Niko said.

Robert nodded in agreement, and the three men heaved Henry from the ground. The cart started rolling as they maneuvered him, and Niko placed a foot behind the wheel to stop it. The awkward angle added immense pressure to his knees, and he grunted in pain as they set the man down, his limbs dangling over the edges. They folded Henry's arms up, crossing them over his chest. The damaged arm lay propped atop the healthy one.

Winded, the three men worked the cart toward the lobby. Jim pushed while the other two helped steer. Niko limped in matching style to Robert, his knee a tight knot on the verge of popping.

As they emerged in the reception area, Leslie called from behind the computer, "Room 127 is vacant!"

"Thanks," Robert responded as he hustled off to meet her at the reception area.

Niko and Jim waited while Robert had a brief conversation

with Leslie, who nodded and disappeared into the back office. Robert returned with the key and pointed down a hallway just beyond the elevators. They made their way through the empty corridor, past the gym and the indoor pool. The lights flickered again, accompanied by a roar of thunder.

"Goddamn electricity," Robert said.

"Any chance we'll lose power, Bob?" Jim asked.

"Good chance. But we have the backup generator gassed up enough to get us through thirty-six hours. Two days if we're conservative."

Robert held his hand up as they approached the room, which sat just beside an exit door. He unlocked it and entered first to turn the lights on.

"Hang tight, gents," he said. "Leslie is bringing a few things to prep the room."

Right on cue, Leslie came jogging down the hall carrying extra towels, bedsheets, and pillows as well as a plastic tarp. Niko shot Robert a look.

"I don't need to soak a mattress in blood and take a whole room out of commission. These renovations are throttling my bank account as it is," he replied.

Niko chuckled and followed him into the room, helping Jim lift the cart over the threshold. Henry stirred and groaned at the jostling movement. As Leslie and Robert wrapped the mattress in the plastic protector, Niko approached the window and threw back the curtains. The tides had climbed the beach and were now threatening the boardwalk. A thick puddle of water collected on the patio outside the room, so Niko knelt and prodded around the bottom of the sliding door, checking for signs of moisture. He found nothing to suggest the seal wouldn't hold.

After Leslie finished refitting the sheets, the three men grabbed the towel and hoisted Henry onto the bed while Leslie held the cart steady. They propped a few pillows behind his head and a few more under his arm to keep it elevated. Leslie started jotting notes into a notebook.

"What's that?" Niko asked her.

"Mr. Wymer said you wanted me to document everything we are doing for him. You said sixty beats per minute, right?"

"Right," Niko replied.

She finished writing and set the notebook and pen on the bedside table. Niko leaned over to review the notes. She had the gist of it.

"No need to keep this room locked up," he said. "Let's prop the door open and leave the key hanging outside."

"Good idea," Robert said.

"We'll work a rotation and have someone check on him every hour or so," Niko offered. "Jim, you take first shift, then Leslie, Robert, and me. Mark his vitals down, and put your initials by the record along with the time you came in. Let's be as detailed as possible."

"You're the boss," Jim said.

Robert placed a hand on Henry's shoulder. "Hang in there, Henry. We'll get you help as soon as we can."

Leslie set the bottle of antibiotics and a glass of water near the notebook. She then placed a fifth of whiskey on the bedside table before the party evacuated the room, leaving the lights on behind them. The trek through the hallway was silent, save for the rolling thunder snarling outside. Niko returned to the diner to check on Rebekah—the whole event had pushed her from his mind—but only Maggie remained, mopping up the carnage on the floor while wearing an old-style personal gas mask. A pungent scent struck Niko, and he moved closer.

"Is that…ammonia?" he asked.

"Bleach and ammonia," Maggie replied. "Need to do it now, or the floor'll stain."

Niko wafted the scent away and fled the diner, hacking up harsh breaths as he left. Inhaling the clean air of the lobby, the thought struck him to check Rebekah's room to see if she was okay. But he was exhausted, so instead, he decided to return to his room. There were notes he needed to document while the conversation with Rebekah was still fresh in his mind. A lot had happened, and he didn't want to risk forgetting the important details he had mentally logged.

19

REBEKAH

REBEKAH COVERED HER MOUTH, unnerved by the grotesque scene. There was so much blood. Nausea worked its way through her stomach, so she flew from the diner and made for the elevator. Swallowing back the bile rising in her throat, leaving a bitter taste, she slapped the button for the second floor. When the elevator opened, she charged through the hall, fished the key from her pocket, and burst into her room. Vomit erupted from her mouth just as she flipped the toilet lid open. Harsh, burning liquid rushed through her throat, splattering the porcelain bowl as it evacuated. A weakness settled into her body, crippling her legs.

She took heavy, gasping breaths between episodes, fighting back the swell of puke amassing in her throat and choking her. The image kept replaying in her head of that man's flailing arm, and sheets of blood whipping through the air. It fueled her nausea, and she vomited until nothing remained but acid. Her legs curled under her, prickly and numb, and her arms dropped weakly to her sides as the onslaught diminished. She reached for a towel to wipe the debris from her face and flushed the toilet to relieve herself of the smell.

She was languid—famished—but her appetite was absent. *So much for the chicken. Maybe some crackers would be a safe bet.*

Hoisting herself up, she closed the lid of the toilet and gripped the sink to steady herself. The walk to the bed was arduous, but she made it. Digging through her backpack, she retrieved a sleeve of crackers and another bottle of water. She gulped down several swallows of the drink to remove the vile taste in her mouth before unwrapping the crackers and nibbling on one cautiously. The salty flavor was welcomed, but the dry crumble soaking up the moisture in her mouth was dissatisfying. Still, she stomached it enough to eat through half of the sleeve, restoring some semblance of strength.

The clock on the bedside table showed it was nearly 9:00 p.m. She groaned and collapsed back on the bed. "Why can't this day be over?"

Exhaustion consumed her as she laid back. It was as if the very sheets of the bed swallowed her. Dizziness sent the room into a spinning frenzy. The injury on her head pulsed, shooting waves of pain through her skull. Closing her eyes, she palmed her head with a shaky hand, but the motion continued, unsettling her stomach once more.

A chilled wind crept through the room, and goosepimples crawled over her flesh. Her body shivered wildly as the frozen air gripped her. Her eyes opened to complete darkness, challenging her knowledge of whether she'd even opened them at all. Save for a column of breath exiting her mouth, lit by an unseen source of light, the space was stark.

"Hello?" she called, chased by an echo through the cavernous void.

Glancing around, and as far as she could sense, she was alone but certainly no longer in the hotel. At least, her consciousness was no longer there.

"Rylos?"

The fading echo of her voice met only silence. So, she walked. To what end, she had no idea, but the movement helped warm her. For what seemed like hours, she walked with no company but the reverberating clap of her footsteps. The cold bore deep into her flesh, and she hugged her arms over her chest. The chill was sharp and penetrating.

The strident sound of scraping metal coupled with distant

screams echoed through the space, sending a chill through her, more biting than the icy air. Rebekah stopped. Peering into the dark around her, she looked for signs of movement but to no avail. A loud thud sounded from behind her, and she whipped around. Light splintered the darkness, throwing a luminous cone across the floor as a door opened.

"Is someone there?"

The silhouette of a man stepped into the opening, dragging a weighted bag behind him, obscuring the light.

"Who are you?" Rebekah called.

The silhouette halted. "You," the voice said. "But how?"

The man turned and fled. Rebekah gave chase, but a pillar of smoke erupted in the open doorway and shaped itself into the spectre. Several small, dark figures rose from the light-splashed floor as the phantom raised its arm, summoning them. The non-human creatures dashed toward her, disappearing as they abandoned the light for the shadows. In a panic, she stumbled backwards and crashed to the ground. The fiendish gnashing sounds of the creatures' greedy teeth ornamented the atmosphere as the clicking of sharp claws against the hard floor drew closer.

"Nox!" a voice boomed through the stark space.

All movement ceased beneath the commanding tone, and Rebekah turned to find a rugged older man, wearing an aged and tattered lace-top tunic, silver streaking through his black, tied-back hair. A gray-flecked beard covered his face, and a translucent glow framed his image.

Rylos? she thought.

"Guardian," the phantom snarled.

With a wave of his hand, Rylos dispelled the creatures into wisps of smoke. He stepped forward, stopping beside Rebekah, and with a fierce gaze, he held the phantom.

"End this, Nox," he said.

So, it has a name.

"You have no power here, Guardian."

Dark tendrils erupted from Nox like twisted vines and lashed at Rylos. A pulse of light exploded from the Guardian's outstretched arm, forming its own spires that severed the tentacles of shadow. The figure of Nox sank into the ground, and the door slammed closed, blanketing the space in darkness once again.

An eerie stillness gripped the room, save for Rebekah's panicked breaths. A soft glow emanated from Rylos, which lent some measure of light to the void.

Nox emerged behind Rylos, who turned as the phantom latched a gnarled hand to his throat, hoisting him up. Rebekah shrieked and scrambled to her feet. Rylos struggled, gasping for air, clutching at the creature's arm. The light emitting from Rylos brightened, nearly blinding Rebekah, and ignited the room with white color. Nox recoiled and dropped him. From his knees, Rylos pushed with both arms, emitting a force that drove Nox back and sent him sprawling to the ground.

Rylos reached down and placed a hand to Rebekah's chest, filling her with that familiar warmth, and transported them away from danger.

The rolling tide and misty spray of water brought her back to the black-sand beach. Though disjointed from the jolted teleportation, as she had been each time before, she opened her eyes to a speckled sky with damp sand shifting beneath her fingers. She grew familiar with the pulse of magic within her and the feeling of its use, though she lacked the focus to attune her attention to its source.

"What you did," Rylos said, "was incredibly foolish."

Rebekah sat up and saw him sitting beside her, gazing up at the sky with his arms resting on his knees. A patterned brand the color of ash adorned his right forearm. Light faded from the design, which she imagined to be the power within him retreating. His eyes met hers—luminous gray eyes, resembling the moon, not dissimilar to the crescent shape of her own iris. They studied her.

"What?" she asked.

"You invaded the consciousness of another. Worse, a mind inhabited by Nox."

"I—I don't know what happened," Rebekah said. "I was feeling sick, and I laid down to rest. I don't know how I did that."

Rylos stood and peered down at her, his brows furrowed in curiosity. Gazing back, she hoped he had an answer to slake her confusion, but instead he sighed and held out an arm to help her stand.

"Don't worry yourself," he said. "You will learn in time."

Learn in time?

The permanence of the situation never occurred to her. Would that be her life? She assumed once Nicole was free, she would be as well, and the random sequence of events could be played off as a series of bad dreams. Rebekah brushed the sand from her clothes and peered around at the landscape. The moon reflected off the gentle cresting waves, the mountain ranges in the distance, and the dense forest butting against the shore. It all seemed so peaceful. Save for the memory she had of Nox, peeling himself from the darkness of the forest. Her breath caught in her throat as the thought arose it could happen again. She turned her sight back to the water, a more serene view.

"I've been here before," she said. "What is this place?"

"This is Idromir," he said, gesturing his arms wide. "It is the nexus for all life across the realms. Once held by the Guardians, those your kind knew as gods, now lost to the Shadow… It was my home."

His eyes poured over the land, decorated with a regretful longing. The emotions churned within her chest the same as they stirred within him. The place held a great deal of significance to Rylos. He motioned toward the stars, where another red comet plummeted from the sky.

"Each star you see is a soul or rather the materialized consciousness of one. Every speck of light gracing this sky is a life filled with happiness or sorrow, challenges and mystery, a universe unto itself."

"And the falling stars?" The answer came to her before he gave it.

"They are those who have been abandoned and left to die."

The red star flickered and blinked out. Rylos stood in quiet reflection, grief darkening his face.

"What do you mean abandoned?" she asked.

"There were once Reapers who judged the souls and ferried them to their next life."

"Where are they now?"

"Centuries ago, the Reapers rebelled and waged war against the Guardians. The battle spanned decades, ravaging these sacred lands, claiming the lives of many Guardians and Reapers alike, until only Nox and I remained—the last of our kin. He has left this land in ruins, allowing the shadow to conquer, and without intervention, it will pour into the realms and spread its plague. No life will remain."

Rylos dipped his head, and a solitary glowing tear fell, shattering like glass against the dark beach, leaving luminous specks of light dotting the black sand. "I am sorry that you were dragged into this conflict," he said. "The burden of your sister's death and of your suffering weighs on me. But I must act to stop Nox before the realms tip out of balance."

"What about my sister? You said you could free her."

"And I still intend to. Though, we must take care in how we act. Nox built the prison that holds her, and he will not hesitate to threaten you with her life."

"Then we kill him," Rebekah stated.

"I'm not sure I could defeat him, not in my weakened state. And even if I could, I wouldn't. Nox is the last Reaper just as I am the last Guardian. If either of us should perish, Idromir could fall, and life would cease. No new souls would be born, and all life would eventually flicker and die, with nothing to take its place."

He gestured to the stars as three more blazed a bright red and fell.

A voice came from behind them. "And we must not let that happen."

Rylos turned and smiled. "Numenos."

"It is good to see you again, friend," Numenos said.

A creature resembling a faun approached, one that looked born of the forest, unlike his brother who looked more akin to a sea creature. Bark adorned his legs and arms, moss clung to his chest, his hair and beard resembled willow branch, and his horns were twisted trunks of aged tree, protruding from his temples. His back was hunched, and he walked like age had ravaged his joints. A flowered cloak dragged behind him, and he carried a green-flamed lantern attached to a staff. He approached Rylos, and the two embraced.

"What happened?" Numenos asked.

"It is a long story, friend, but we have more pressing concerns. Walk with me, both of you."

He gestured for Rebekah to follow him, and the three paced the beach as he explained the amulet and its disappearance. Numenos walked in ponderous silence, considering the situation. Rylos's arms were tucked behind his back, gripping the leather bracer on his left wrist. To her right, a creature emerged from the sea. Another faun-like being, though younger in appearance. As it approached, Rebekah realized she had seen it before.

"Aegeus," Rylos said.

"Ah, the Guardian himself," Aegeus replied. "How I have missed you."

The two men embraced, leaving the front of Rylos's tunic soaked. Aegeus caught sight of Rebekah over Rylos's shoulder, pushed off the man, and bowed curtly.

"If I may, a proper introduction." He bowed lower and held his hand out. Rebekah took it. "I am Aegeus—"

"Brother," Numenos cut in. "There is a problem. The Heart of Idromir is lost."

"You lost it?" Aegeus shot a vexed glare at Rylos.

"I need to visit Reyja," Rylos said.

"The witch?" Aegeus laughed sardonically, gesturing toward Rebekah. "With her? Are you mad?"

"I don't like it, but what choice do I have?"

“There are other ways. Safer ways,” Numenos said.

“I know what you would say, but I won’t,” Rylos replied. “And it’s hardly safer.”

“But the things Nox has done—”

“Yes, he has done monstrous things in his anger, but to destroy the last Reaper would resign every soul to extinction.”

“That is not known,” Numenos said. “As long as a Guardian remains, the shadow can be held at bay.”

“And if you’re wrong? What purpose would that leave for us? I will not sacrifice all for one.”

“You are holding out hope that some piece of your friend still lingers,” Numenos said. “That is dangerous, Rylos. Look at the havoc that has been wrought while you’ve suffered your internal conflict.”

“Kalen is gone,” Aegeus stated. “And like any soul that has partnered with the shadow, whatever remains of him is a twisted and tortured spirit.”

“That’s not true,” Rylos said. “There is humanity left in him. I’ve felt it, but it is spoiled with anger and vengeance.”

“More than anger and vengeance,” Numenos said. “Being a Reaper bears a heavy toll that ravages the soul of the cloaked. Characteristics the shadow craves, it is what drew them together. He has turned, Rylos.”

“Damaged he may be but not lost. I will not kill him.”

“Then what will you do?”

“Find the amulet,” Rylos said.

“And while you search, more souls perish,” Aegeus replied.

“My sister had the amulet when she died,” Rebekah stated. Aegeus groaned, and Numenos quieted him. “If I could see her again, she may remember something that could help us find it. Rylos felt its presence. It is close.”

“She speaks the truth,” Rylos said matter-of-factly. “But we cannot go back to that place.”

“What? Why not?” Rebekah protested.

“That prison was built by Nox. I fear we won’t be as likely to escape again.”

"My sister sent me a message. I think she's in trouble. I need to go back."

"That was likely a ruse to draw you in. Nox would use your sister to bait you. Don't be foolish."

"And if it's not?" she challenged.

"Then you would simply put her *and* us in danger. Understand, he has no further need for your sister except as leverage to manipulate you. It's best not to draw his focus to her. Doing so would certainly endanger her."

Rebekah held Rylos with a fiery gaze, and an uneasy silence settled on the beach, lending room for the tides to whisper their song. Frustration rattled around Rebekah's mind as the prospect of seeing Nicole once more was taken from her. But she bit her tongue as rationality entered her mind. As much as the truth angered her, Rylos was right. Nibbling at her lip, she gave a rueful nod.

"So, you seek the witch," Numenos said.

"So, I seek the witch," Rylos replied.

"Fine," Numenos agreed, much to Aegeus's chagrin.

"You would act without the council?" Aegeus protested.

"It is as you said, brother," Numenos replied. "Consulting with the council will take time and more souls will perish."

"But—"

"It is done," Numenos interjected. "Go with light, Guardian."

Rylos nodded and gripped Rebekah's shoulder. The familiar warmth flooded through her, and a bright light shone from beneath his hand. Rebekah's body tightened and compressed as the jolt of movement carried them to their destination.

20

NIKO

THE WIND WHISTLED OUTSIDE the window as Niko hunched over the table, jotting notes in his leatherback book. The solitary cone of soft light from the desk lamp eased his aching eyes. He had been writing for hours, piecing together the bits of information he had received and comparing them with the details contained in the case files. Detective David Rossi had signed off on several forms absent of any reasonable information.

Lazy prick is an apt description, he thought.

He compiled a registry of each case Rossi was involved in, which was quite a few, and each one contained a scarce amount of usable information. The writing had been incredibly verbose, but the important details were vague or missing. He hadn't noticed it before because he was so consumed with the timeline of events he never bothered with the more granular details. Something didn't sit right, and he made a note to dig into the detective.

The power flickered again, pulling him from his thoughts, and another roar of thunder sounded. The ice in his drink rattled against the glass. Niko stood and threw back the curtains to a black sky. The streetlights were on, igniting the heavy downpour, and the tides continued to spill over the boardwalk.

A flash of lightning gave him a brief view of the pier, where the sea was near level with the wooden walkway.

This is more like a hurricane, he thought.

Another spear of lightning struck at the base of the Armitage, sending sparks streaming into the dark, swept away by the wind. The power in his room blinked out, and the boom of thunder that followed shook the floor.

"Christ!" he muttered.

He stumbled backwards and stupidly felt his way through the dark to his duffle. Sifting through the bag and throwing loose clothes out of the way, he found the cool metal shaft of his flashlight. The room erupted with light when he clicked it on, throwing shadows from the dresser, bed, and his luggage across the room, swaying with the movement of his hand. A moment later, a dim light flicked on.

Emergency lights. Good.

He clicked the flashlight off and pocketed it before making his way to the drawer to retrieve his Glock. Holstering his sidearm and clipping it to his waistband, he wandered back to the desk, closed his files and notes, snatched up the room key, and fled into the hall. The dim lights in the corridor blinked weakly as another rumble shook the building, and he pulled his flashlight from his pocket again. Just in case. He opened the door to the stairwell, but it was pitch dark.

"No lights for the stairs?" Niko muttered.

Powering on the flashlight again, he worked his way down the steps. An irrational fear from watching too many monster movies struck him as he approached the darkened corner of the landing. The old-style hotel had fully walled-in stairs as opposed to the railed-off ones in more modern buildings.

A creaking sound echoed from above him, followed by quick footsteps clapping against the hard floor. He knew it was someone from a higher level making their way down the stairwell, but in the absolute dark, terror set in. He moved a little quicker until he reached the door to the lobby. The unseen person stopped at a higher floor, signaled by another door slamming closed.

The entrance was better lit than the rest of the hotel. The overhead fluorescent lights had backups running parallel in the mount. Upon examination, he found the lights were recently upgraded, likely part of the renovation. He approached the reception desk, but no one was there. Not unexpected since it had to be nearly midnight, if not later, but a crack of light spilled from the back-office door and hushed tones snarled from within. Niko crept forward and overheard Maggie chastising Robert.

"What do you expect me to do?" Robert asked with a harsh whisper.

"That's not my problem, but if you don't do something, then my entire inventory is ruined. How do you think that would go over?"

"I told you we should have bought a separate generator years ago."

"Don't flip this on me, Robert. My restaurant is the only thing keeping this wad of shit afloat."

Robert derided her. "I'd like to see you try to take your business somewhere else."

Niko eased the door open a little more to better hear the conversation. A slight whine squealed from the hinges, and he winced.

There was a lull in the conversation, and Niko worried they had heard him. A creak sounded, and he quickly retreated to the lobby. He stopped by the elevators just in time to see Maggie storm out of the office. She jumped in shock when she saw him.

"My God! You scared me half to death." She held her throat and released a heavy breath.

"Everything all right?" Niko inquired. "You seem flustered."

Maggie threw a thumb over her shoulder toward the office. "Not at all. I was just, uh, having a word with Robert about this power outage. My freezer went out, and I have thousands of dollars of meat and produce in there and—" She threw a hand on her hip. "It's no matter to bother you with. What are you doing down here?"

"Well, the power's out." Niko said.

"Yes. And?"

"And I wanted to check in with Robert. I'm happy to lend a hand. Also, it's my shift to check on the injured gentleman, Henry." He praised himself for the quick cover. "By the way, I'd like to get a minute of your time. Robert told me you'd have the greatest breadth of knowledge to help me fill in the gaps for these cold cases."

Maggie waved him off and started toward the diner. "Not right now. I wanted to sleep, but it appears I have work to do and a mess of inventory to sort through."

"It's best to keep the freezer door closed," Niko said.

She stopped and turned to him. "What?"

"The seal on the freezer door keeps the cold in. Leaving it closed will keep the temperature stable for longer. It should buy you some time and delay the thawing process."

"Thanks," she said, giving an impatient nod.

That should be common knowledge for a seasoned restaurant owner, he thought.

Maggie waved a hand and rounded the corner to the diner. Niko turned and found Robert emerging from behind the reception desk, hobbling on a cane.

"Ah, Mr. Ortez," he said. "I know you're likely here to see me, but there are things I need to tend to. So, please excuse me."

"I understand." Niko motioned to the cane. "Are you okay?"

"Fine," Robert replied as he hobbled past. "Age hasn't been kind, and I've not had a moment to sit because of this damned storm. My joints aren't as limber as they used to be. I really must be going, though."

"I'd like to catch up when you have time," Niko said. "There are some things I want to discuss."

"Later," Robert stated, grabbing the radio from his hip. "Jorge, meet me in the mechanical room please." He disappeared around the corner beyond the elevators, heading toward the construction zone.

Niko waited a moment in the quiet lobby and then worked his way back toward the office. Something seemed off. He wasn't sure what, but he intended to find out. The door was locked, however.

Of course, he thought.

He peered around and fished his wallet from his pocket, pulling out his Blockbuster membership card. The good thing about the old hotel was the security was also outdated. Niko pressed his shoulder against the door and worked the laminated card around the bend, shimmying it to catch the latch. With a quick slide forward, it popped, and the door swung open. He had to grip the handle to keep from toppling over.

The room was pitch black, save for the spill of illumination pouring through the opening. It took a moment for Niko to locate the light switch, which he flicked on without giving it further thought. It was only when room ignited, the realization hit him. He glanced up to find the same parallel light set up as in the lobby.

Tied a few key areas into the backup generator, he thought.

Closing the door behind him, and leaving the lock engaged, he entered Robert's office. He glanced around the cluttered room, giving his eyes a moment to adjust to the mess.

Fumbling through the various filing cabinets and cardboard boxes overflowing with paperwork, nothing stood out. Mostly, he encountered guest complaints, receipts, reservation details, logistical documents, and purchase orders. Commonplace documents one could expect in a hotel manager's office. Skimming over a few of them, some details popped out that piqued his curiosity, but there was nothing condemning, and he was under a time constraint.

Blueprints sat on the side desk. He recalled them from his initial visit and eyed them inquisitively. There were several documents stacked on top of each other, various floors, rooms, and structural diagrams bundled into a packet. He noticed they all carried a version number printed in the bottom right corner, opposite the name Halder Construction, LLC. A few versions, however, didn't match up. Iteration nine seemed to be the most current, but even that was over a decade old. Flipping through the pile, he found an age-worn copy stamped with version three.

The first thing that caught Niko's eye was an entire section of the hotel that didn't appear in any of the newer drawings. Typically, he wouldn't have thought twice about it. It could have been an addition that was later removed, except the section of the hotel in question was underground. He studied the page for a while. Blueprints weren't a familiar format to him, so it took him a moment to orient himself, but it looked like the structure sat beneath the right wing.

Muffled voices filtered through the office door. Throwing the blueprints aside, he reached for the analog phone hanging on the wall. Keys rattled as the hall door unlocked, and Robert and Jorge made their way into the office, stopping when they caught Niko.

"Can I help you?" Robert's voice was an amalgamation of confusion and outrage.

Niko held up a finger and spoke to the dial tone humming in his ear. "Yeah, look, the owner just walked in so let me let you go. Bye." Niko hung up the phone and turned to Robert. "Sorry, what was that?"

"I said can I help you?" Robert took a few steps into his office, considering Niko skeptically.

"Oh, no. Sorry. I was thinking about Henry while I was out in the lobby, and since there's no chance of an ambulance coming tonight, I decided to bug a buddy of mine who's a medic in the military, hoping for some advice. I remembered seeing this old analog phone when I was here earlier. I hope you don't mind. All the other phones are down."

Robert looked perplexed. "After midnight? I locked my office. How did you get in?"

Niko shrugged. "It opened for me. And you know us younger guys tend to chase the midnight sun." Niko laughed to cover the tension in his voice, hoping his bluff would satisfy.

"Uh-huh," Robert said, taking a few more steps into the room and glancing over the contents of his desk.

Niko worked to maintain his composure as Robert's eyes fell

on the disheveled stack of blueprints Niko had been examining. His skin flushed slightly.

"Well, in any case," Robert continued, leaning over his cane with both hands, "I went to check on Henry. Hadn't had the chance to so far. He's awake and asked to see you."

His tone was flat and chilled. Niko interpreted it as suspicion but didn't want to elevate it if it was, so he remained as impassive as he could. "Glad to hear it," he replied, releasing a genuine breath of relief. "I'll go pay him a visit, if you don't mind."

"Wasn't there something you needed to discuss with me?"

"Part of it was about Henry," Niko said. "The rest we can catch up on later. You said you had your hands full, right?"

"If it's important, I can spare a few minutes."

"It's not. Taking care of the hotel takes precedence. As I said, I don't want my work to interfere with yours."

"Fair enough," Robert replied.

Niko nodded and exited the office, mentally reprimanding himself for his misstep. It was an opportune moment with Robert having his hands full. He didn't think the lie would have gone over as well if the day had been calmer. Though, he also would have been more discreet had he not been so exhausted. He needed to act with more tact moving forward.

Niko wandered the corridor to Room 127, considering the recent puzzle piece. He wasn't sure how it fit in with his theory, if it even did, but it was an odd circumstance he kept a mental note of.

The room at the end of the hall had its door propped open, the key still sitting atop the fire alarm in the hall, though it was difficult to spot beneath the dim emergency lights. A soft glow flashed from within. He knocked as a courtesy and waited for the man to acknowledge him and invite him inside.

"How are you doing, Henry?" Niko asked.

"You the man who cut off my arm?" Henry responded, his voice weak and raspy.

Niko sat on a chair that was propped near the bed. A small gas lantern sat on the dresser, filling the room with something akin to the blaze of a warm campfire. Hazy shadows danced throughout, and there was a plate of mostly untouched food on the end table.

Niko sighed. "Yeah. Sorry about that."

"Don't apologize," Henry said in a sorrowful tone. "I hear you saved my life, doin' what you did."

"How does it feel?"

The man examined the stump of his arm. "Like shit. But it's better than dyin', I guess. So, thank you." Henry held out his good hand in introduction. "Harold Rossi, but everyone calls me Henry."

Are you fucking kidding me? Niko thought.

He shook his hand. "Niko Ortez. You wouldn't happen to be related to David Rossi, would you? The detective?"

"Yeah, he's my brother." Henry then launched into a coughing fit.

What an unfortunate accident. Watching him writhe in pain while coughing up a lung, one foot in the grave, compelled a measure of pity. Henry groaned as the fit ended, and he could get comfortable again.

"He was stationed at Chesapeake, right?" Niko asked.

"Yeah."

"I just got there a few months ago and never met the man. He retired?"

"About four years now, but it's not a surprise that you never met him."

"Because he retired before I got there?" Niko asked with a chuckle of sarcasm.

"No. Because he's dead. Do you mind?" Henry gestured toward the liquor bottle.

"Oh, sure." Niko rose, headed to the end table, and poured the man a glass, grappling with the information Henry had just dropped on him. Taking his time with the drink, he worked to remain unrevealing.

"Dead? I'm sorry to hear that," Niko said.

"Don't be," Henry responded. "My brother was a jackass. It was no great loss."

With a confused look, Niko handed him the glass, and Henry took a healthy swig, reveling in the flavor, or maybe the warmth it provided. The contents had lowered quite a bit from when Niko last saw the bottle. Henry was clearly more than a few drinks in, on top of what he'd already had at the bar. His slurred words were evidence of that.

"But he was your brother. You're not upset about it?"

"Not really."

"Can I ask how he died?" Niko returned to his seat.

"Suicide," Henry replied.

"When did that happen?"

"Shortly after retirement. Didn't even make it a year."

Niko ran his hands through his hair. *Dead end.* He let loose a heavy sigh and sank back into his chair. It didn't make sense. Had his hunch been so far off?

"You don't find that strange?" Niko asked. "Did he seem suicidal to you?"

Henry laughed. "I wouldn't know. I hadn't seen him for years. But isn't suicide common among retired detectives?"

"Unfortunately," Niko admitted. "Why'd you keep your distance from your brother? Rift in the family?"

"You could say that. Then again, David and I were never close. He was a temperamental prick, and I got the brunt of his bad moods when I was younger. Didn't really seal the bond. But it wasn't me. He's the one who kept his distance. He protected me through high school, but after that, he didn't much speak to me."

Niko started to sink into a comfortable rhythm with the conversation, his questions coming more naturally. Henry being drunk helped. "Were you local boys?"

Henry nodded. "Small town outside Norfolk called Schib Creek."

Niko cringed. "Ah, 'Shiv' Creek. Rough area."

Henry chuckled. "Yeah, you ain't kiddin'. I don't know, I tried my hand and traveled around for a few years, but nothin' fit right. So, I made my way back here. This place ain't much, but it's home to me."

"Were you military brats?"

"Fuck no. Virginia boys through and through. Though, with the base and port nearby, there were lots of comings and goings. Plenty of military folk, but our local group stuck together, kept to ourselves. Still do. I mean, I graduated with Stuart and my brother with Maggie." Henry's face crinkled in pain, and he rolled the shoulder of his left arm.

"Keep it elevated," Niko said, shuffling a few pillows under him.

"Thanks," Henry said after polishing off his drink. "Still not used to it being gone. What do they call that? Phantom limb?"

"Something like that." Niko laughed and poured another glass, handing it to him. "So, you guys kept in touch?"

"Yep. Wasn't many people in our class, and we were thicker'n thieves. Kinda friendship that keeps."

Henry fell into another coughing fit. He was looking pale and weak; he needed to rest. His slur started to thicken, and Niko figured it wouldn't be long before he passed out, so he stood.

"Get some rest, Henry."

"Yeah, all right," Henry said, shooting back his drink and setting the empty glass aside. "Well, thanks again, Nick-o. For e'rything."

Niko shook the man's hand one final time. "Don't mention it."

He left the room, pondering the conversation he had just had with Henry. It was too much to unravel with the weight of exhaustion, but he needed to make more notes. So, he didn't dawdle and made his way to his room, igniting the stairwell and braving the stairs with heavy legs. Hoping he could keep his eyes open long enough to document his thoughts before passing out, he pulled out his key as he exited the stairs and trudged down the corridor back to his room.

21

REBEKAH

THE TERRAIN WAS HARSH, with jagged spires of luminous obsidian jutting from the hillside. Several times, Rebekah lost her footing and nearly went careening down the rocky slope to the valley below, where the sharp formations were most dense. Geysers sprayed hot misty water speckled with bioluminescent flecks, and the larger droplets scalded her flesh when they landed. Aside from the unforgiving and dangerous obstacles, the view was picturesque. Everything was alive with color, illuminating the landscape, and her vantage point provided a broad sweeping view.

Rylos trekked the hill with ease, clearly familiar with the dynamic terrain that Idromir had to offer. Rebekah imagined the alp would be easier to scale in daylight, then caught herself wondering if daylight ever graced the realm.

"No," Rylos answered.

She had forgotten his consciousness was tethered to her own, so her thoughts were hardly private.

"The sky is always dark. The world is lit only by the Eye of Idromir." He gestured to what Rebekah had thought was the moon.

"The Eye of Idromir, the Heart of Idromir," Rebekah recited breathlessly. "Couldn't you have thought of more creative names?"

"Idromir is the name of the Celestial we inhabit." With no further explanation, he continued his climb toward the peak.

Rebekah fumbled to grasp what she'd heard. "A Celestial? Like an astral being? We're *inside* a Celestial?"

She glanced around with a new perspective, struggling to comprehend the *how* of it all but appreciating the wonder. She wasn't as affected by the newfound knowledge as she expected, and that bothered her. Had she become so complacent with the surreal changes that they no longer phased her?

"Yes. A dead one," Rylos said. "The mystics built this world and brought the realms together. Harvesting the body of the Celestial Titan, they served to augment their sortilege and craft tools and pathways to traverse the various worlds."

"Mystics?" Rebekah grappled with the overflow of information.

"You've met Numenos and Aegeus. Reyja is kin to them. She was among the first, and she crafted the amulet from the Heart of Idromir." Rylos stopped and turned to Rebekah. "Reyja deserted her kin, forsaking her vow of servitude, and pledged fealty to no one. Her turn from the light has corrupted her, making her volatile and dangerous if crossed, so take care what you say. She is clairvoyant and will use your emotions against you."

His eyes carried stern sincerity, flashing a warning Rebekah couldn't ignore, and she swallowed those words with the solemnity with which they were delivered. She nodded her acquiescence, and Rylos turned back toward the rocky slope, resuming his climb.

"Can I ask you something?" Rebekah inquired.

"I imagine you can."

"Is it possible for a soul in this realm to appear to someone in another realm, like a ghost?"

"Surely by now you've seen it is possible."

"Right, but I'm not talking about a Reaper or a Guardian or whatever," Rebekah said.

"We are called ethereals."

"Okay. Ethereals. Is it possible for a non-ethereal?"

"You sound as though you have something on your mind. No need to skirt the issue. Tell me."

"Before all of this, I had felt like my sister was visiting me in my dreams, or like she was watching over me at times. Something that was amplified when it rained."

Rylos stopped and glanced over his shoulder, regarding Rebekah with a look of curiosity.

"There are ways that non-ethereals can appear in your realm, typically when a soul is trapped in the fabric between them. You call them ghosts. But your sister is not trapped in that sense. Water is a spiritual conduit, and a strong enough emotional connection could cause that anomaly. But your dreams are something else entirely. I don't believe it was your sister visiting you but a manifestation of your mind. A way of coping with her absence."

Rylos lingered on the slope, his eyes fixed on Rebekah's. He must have either seen the change in her expression or sensed her disappointment because he gave her a sympathetic look and apologized before turning away, continuing forward. Rebekah lingered for a moment, processing the wave of emotions.

So, Mrs. Harrity was right, she thought with bitter reluctance. A tear slid down her cheek as she contended with her anger and grief.

"Come, Rebekah," Rylos called after her. "We are nearly there."

Rebekah rushed up the slope to catch up with Rylos, struggling to navigate the terrain at times. Near the peak of the climb, they came upon the mouth of a cave that had been outfitted with a makeshift home front. A round wooden door set in fabricated walls sealed the tunnel. Iron-caged lanterns containing purple flames framed the opening, and red glowing runes were etched around the curve of the door. It reminded Rebekah of a hobbit hole, though a more sinister version.

Rylos looked upon the door for a while, and Rebekah could feel the conflict whirring inside of him. There was a form of fear mixed with an emotion she couldn't read that lent to the hesitancy, rooting his feet. Rebekah moved to the door and knocked, sending deep hollow thuds echoing through the interior. The sound jarred Rylos from his stupor.

A low, guttural hum resonated from within, and the door flew open with a gust of breathy wind, which carried a foul stench. Rebekah covered her nose to stifle a gag as tears filled her eyes. "Ugh! What is that smell?"

"You are entering the den of a witch," Rylos said. "Nothing here will be pleasant." He placed a hand on Rebekah's shoulder. "Remember, steel yourself. Do not let her control you."

Rylos entered the exposed, dark tunnel. Rebekah imagined him entering the throat of a dormant beast, and a sense of unease washed over her as what courage she thought she had retreated. She walked into the passageway after Rylos, and the door creaked closed behind her, removing all light from the space. Rylos's translucent glow lit the cramped cavern, where a hot moisture imparted a restricting quality to the air. It may have been a hallucination, but the tunnel appeared to be shrinking as they proceeded.

"How deep is this tunnel?" Rebekah asked.

"As deep as Reyja needs to deceive us," Rylos replied.

"What? Is that some kind of riddle?"

"No. Our eyes are being cheated. Use your other senses. We are in a trap. Reyja was aware of our presence the moment we arrived on the mountain."

"You knew?"

Rylos nodded.

"And you led us here anyway?"

"Our intention was to come here. I was not naïve to think that she would be blind to our approach. This was a journey we needed to take."

"You could have warned me," Rebekah said.

"Would you have come if I had?"

Rebekah considered his words and acknowledged the truth. Not knowing saved her the anxiety of the decision and allowed her instincts to kick in, guiding her response. Her fear may have stopped her when the climb became difficult or kept her from approaching the door as it had done to Rylos.

"How do you know it's a trap?" she asked.

"You cannot trust your sight as it is betrayed by her illusion, so you must rely on your other senses. Focus."

Rebekah concentrated. She could feel the uneven floor beneath her footsteps, but her muscles were not weakening nor was her breathing labored from exertion. The pain that had settled in her shins on her climb was easing, giving no indication she was moving. The humid air had a subtle scent to it, but not the rotten scent of sulfur she expected a volcanic tunnel to carry. It was sweet and inviting. Her head responded to the aroma, and her legs became heavy and unstable. She fumbled to her knees, looking up at Rylos, who was unaffected.

"Why are you…Why is…" Rebekah's eyes were heavy, and talking was suddenly exhausting.

"I am a projection from your mind. I am not physically here."

Rylos's voice sounded distant, and she could no longer see him. Rebekah fell prone, paralyzed and straddling her consciousness. "What?" Her voice was a hoarse whisper.

The question lingered in the air with no answer, and Rebekah found herself alone. Both in the dark space and within her mind. She struggled, but her body wouldn't respond. Her heart rapped at her ribs as fear consumed her.

"Rylos?" she called, answered only by the echo of her own voice.

Mentally battling the enchantment, she brought her arm up and tried to rise from the ground. The resistance of weight was immense, and her arm shook fiercely before she collapsed again.

"Rylos!" she cried.

The resolve inside of her resisted the toxic fumes, fighting with every ounce of will she could muster, but her consciousness shrank into the distance, leaving her in a shadowy dream. Wisps of smoke wriggled in the dark and constricted her.

22

NIKO

FRENZIED KNOCKING DRAGGED NIKO from his dreamless slumber, still drunk from lethargy. At first, he believed it to be a dream, but as his delirium faded and consciousness returned, alarm took over, and he sprung out from beneath the covers.

"Niko!" Robert's voice called from beyond the door. "Wake up!"

Without dressing, wearing nothing but his underwear, he unlatched the chain lock, turned the deadbolt, and threw the door open. Even in the dim emergency lights, he could see the sweat decorating Robert's face. The man was winded.

"What's wrong?" Niko asked.

"It's Rebekah," Robert replied between frantic breaths. "I went to check on her. She wouldn't answer. I opened the door, and she's not responsive."

"What?"

"She was writhing around, and I thought she was having a seizure, so I tried to help. But now she's stiff as a board, and I can't wake her." Robert offered one of the mugs he held. "I brought you a coffee, so get your ass in gear."

"Shit. Okay," Niko said charging from the room, but he paused and looked down. "Let me grab some clothes first."

Niko closed the door, rushed to the dresser, and pulled an outfit out, quickly throwing his things on. He reached into the nightstand drawer and clipped his holster containing the Glock to his waistband—force of habit. He then exited into the hallway and followed Robert's hurried limp to Rebekah's room. Taking the mug, he threw back a large sip. The warmth was a welcome relief, but the coffee tasted awful.

The stairwell was still dark. Fortunately, Robert had brought a flashlight. Leading the way, he huffed and wheezed as he descended the steps. Niko stumbled, missing one, and spilled a splash of coffee on Robert's shoulder.

"Ah, Christ!" Robert howled in pain, shifting his coffee to the hand holding his cane, and swatting at the spot.

"Sorry about that," Niko said.

Robert turned and flashed what Niko assumed was an angry look, but his face was blanketed in shadow as the light pointed ahead of him. Robert grumbled and proceeded down the steps at a relatively limber pace. They exited the stairs and hurried to Room 213, where Robert used a master key to gain entry. He stepped aside to let Niko ahead of him.

Robert propped the door open, and Niko rushed to the bedside where Rebekah lay, setting his coffee mug down on the end table. Unable to see much until Robert pointed the light at her, he climbed onto the bed to get a better angle. She was sprawled across the mattress diagonally. Her skin was clammy and tepid. Droplets of sweat dotted her forehead. Niko tried moving her, but her body was rigid and unyielding. A feverish shiver shook her.

The light bobbed up and down from Robert's arthritic hand, making it difficult to examine Rebekah in detail.

"Robert, I need a constant light source. Do you have another gas lantern?"

"Yes, I do. I'll be right back," Robert responded before taking his leave, and the light, with him.

The clack of Robert's cane disappeared into the hall, and Niko drooped his head with a reprehensive sigh. *I should've thought that one through. But I suppose he needs it more than I do.*

Unable to do anything more to help the girl until Robert returned with some light, Niko stumbled to the chair in the corner of the room. An eerie silence settled, textured with Rebekah's shallow breathing. The realization dawned on him it was the first moment of peace he'd had since he arrived, and his mind began to wander.

The quiet dark became a space of meditation, with Rebekah's consistent breaths fading into white noise. Rain pelted the window, and a low howl of wind reminded him of the storm still raging outside. His mind churned and stumbled its way over topics he had been avoiding: the deaths of the officers he blamed himself for, his neglect of Danielle, and his selfish obsession with self-gratifying ends.

Rosenberg's voice climbed into focus in his mind, reminding him of his breathing techniques and methods of transference, but he pushed it aside and allowed his pain to surface. Exhaustion brought a sense of masochism, and his desire to feel pain overflowed. Wet tears slid down his cheeks.

"It's strange," he said aloud. "I've been fighting so hard for what I thought I wanted, but I haven't been happy for months. I'm not even sure if I was happy before the incident. I wanted this career because my dad loved it, and it brought me closer to him. But am I chasing this for him or for me?"

Niko wiped his eyes and stewed in the dark, mulling over the question.

"I know you can't hear me," he said to Rebekah. "But I need to get this off my chest. And well, you won't judge me, will you?" He chuckled. "I know that the last twenty-four hours don't represent a normal day—far from it—but I'm exhausted. Maybe the past few months have changed me more than I realized, or maybe my fuckup is what did it. Is my pursuit to reclaim my status pride more than desire? I don't know. But I'm starting to understand. It's been festering for a while, but I refused to face it. Danielle was right, I think. Her father was right."

It pained him to admit it, but there was a truth to the words. An orange glow lit up the door as the clack of a cane sounded through the hall. Robert turned into the room with a gas lantern, huffing heavy breaths. Setting it on the dresser, and turning the valve to increase the light, Robert glanced at Niko.

His face scrunched with curiosity. "Were you crying?" he asked.

"No." Niko rubbed his eyes and yawned. "Just tired."

He rose from the chair and returned to Rebekah, who shifted into sharp, rapid breathing. Her body convulsed, and Niko immediately hoisted her onto her side. Rebekah grunted with the strain, and Niko turned to Robert.

"We need to call her parents," he said. "I know they won't be able to get out here with the storm, but they need to know that their daughter isn't well. Can you handle that?"

"I think I should stay here," Robert said. "I want to be sure she's okay."

"Neither of us have authority over this child," Niko said. "Her parents need to be notified, and we need their permission to treat her in any way. Unless you want to administer care while I go call her parents. But if anything happens, blame goes to whoever's care she's under. It makes more sense for that to be a federal agent than a hotel owner, but you decide."

Robert gave a wary scowl but spun and left the room again. "I'll be back shortly."

Niko turned to Rebekah. Her spasms had begun to lessen. Loosening his grip, he allowed her body to move, applying only enough pressure to keep her propped on her side. Letting her body ease back naturally as the fit came to an end, he removed his hand, and she gently rolled onto her back again. He wasn't a doctor, but he was intimately familiar with seizures from junkies and those his mother had in the hospital after the car crash. Rebekah was not having a seizure, so that added a level of comfort to ease his worry.

"It's all right," he said. "You're gonna be all right."

Sweat glistened on her forehead, and strands of curly hair clung to her skin. He gently plucked them away and brushed them to the side before easing off the bed and heading to the bathroom. After wetting a cloth with cool water and ringing out the excess, he returned and placed the compress on her head. Her breath eased back to a steady tempo.

"I wish I could do more to help you," he said. "But I'm the best you've got right now thanks to this storm."

He glanced at the drawn curtains. Hearing the rain and wind persisting beyond the window, he didn't need to throw them back to know things hadn't changed much. Moving to the end of the bed, he sighed and rested his elbow on his knees, burying his face in his hands. He was fucking tired, and he wondered if his thoughts were genuine or mixed with the delirium of sleep deprivation.

He sighed again. "I need to figure this out."

23

REBEKAH

BRIMSTONE MINGLED WITH THE scent of death as, once again, consciousness returned to Rebekah. The soft orange glow of a fire filled her sight as her eyes fluttered open. Pain reverberated through her head, causing her to wince in discomfort. From her seat at a rough-edged stone table, she took in the environment.

To her left, a stacked-stone hearth cradled a blazing fire beneath a black iron cauldron, its contents simmering. To her right, shelves overflowed with books and tomes and miscellaneous trinkets, none of which she recognized.

At the other end of the hovel, beyond a gauntlet of bone chimes hanging from twisted and burled wooden rafters, sat a workbench, adorned with various glass containers. Runes, glowing a fiery red, were etched throughout the space, most prominently along the wooden beams and posts.

A pale creature with a long mane of thinning black hair toiled at the table. Deep jagged scars ran down the length of its back. Folds of leathery skin hung from its bones in weathered drapes, swinging from its arms as it retrieved a fine gray powder from one of the jars. Inky black fingers tipped each boney hand like long, spidery claws capped with sharp nails.

Rebekah could hear the raspy gargle of the creature's breath as it worked. It retrieved a pestle from the table, and Rebekah heard the grinding of coarse stone materials. Under the cloak of noise, Rebekah tried to move.

A tremor of pain shot through her spine that was unimaginable. She screamed in agony. Her body's natural reaction was to tense up, which only furthered her torment. Gritting her teeth, she relaxed her muscles. The silence following her outburst was unsettling. Yet, the witch in front of her, who she assumed to be Reyja as clarity cut through the fog in her mind, didn't so much as flinch.

Reyja turned from the bench, carrying an oblong stone bowl toward the cauldron. She walked on white-haired legs resembling a goat's legs, much like her kin. She dumped the contents into the simmering liquid. Dense fog poured over the edges of the iron cask and slithered to the floor, beginning as a white miasma and shifting through shades of purple until it sank to a pitch black. The fog thickened to a viscous tar and pooled on the ground, reflecting the dancing flames like a black mirror. Rebekah recoiled from consternation, only to find the witch inches from her face.

Another violent tremor rattled her spine as she jerked away in shock. Sunken eyes examined her, purple flames burning within their lifeless sockets.

"You sought me out," Reyja said, her voice a grating croak. "Are you satisfied with what you've found?"

Sharp spears of teeth rested in her mouth, and her breath carried a rotten stench that caused Rebekah to scrunch her face up again.

Rylos, Rebekah thought, seeking comfort in the moment.

Reyja loosed a shrill cackle, her boney black fingers reaching for the rafters and pointing out the runes. "The Guardian is not welcome here. You'll find you are more alone than you know."

Reyja slid her face next to Rebekah's and inhaled a rattled breath. The witch's cold and clammy flesh grazed Rebekah's ear, sending a chill through her. When Reyja pulled back, a curious expression obscured her features. There was a chink in the witch's armor hidden in that expression.

"Who are you?" she asked with sharp impatience.

"Rebekah Daroh, and I sought you out to find the Heart of Idromir."

Reyja laughed. "And why should I help with such a quest?" She moved away and returned to her workbench, retrieving the mortar and pestle and collecting more ingredients. Rebekah thought for a moment to justify her demand but found her own reasoning lacked foundation. Her actions were solely motivated by her sister, and she held no hope her answer would persuade the witch.

"Nicole," the witch said, glancing back over her shoulder. "You place your life in danger for your sister. Why?"

"Because I love her."

"Don't lie to me!" Reyja whipped around in a fury. "You serve a more selfish purpose. You love her, yes, but you have deeper motivations."

Rebekah's confidence wavered. "I am here because I owe her that much. I love her and would see her freed from that prison."

Reyja appeared before Rebekah faster than she could see the movement, a sharp finger pressed against the bottom of her chin. The tilting of her head caused pain to shoot throughout Rebekah's body, but she gritted her teeth, choking back her reaction to starve Reyja of the satisfaction.

"And what does that freedom mean to you, child? You think it will bring her back? You think it will undo the years of abandonment? Or change your spirit into what you imagine it should be?"

Rebekah regarded her with ire. The witch knew her too deeply for her to be illusive, meeting her artifice with sharp words. Reyja laughed at the pain settling in her soul.

"I will free her," Rebekah said on the verge of tears.

"As you tried to free yourself?" Reyja gripped Rebekah's wrist and thumbed over the scar.

"That was not made by my hand."

"You may not have swept the blade, but your mind was not strong enough to stop it. You were a prisoner of your suffering and sought escape. But it would not have brought you the peace you seek."

"You speak of what you do not know."

"The string was there for Nox to pull. He cannot create. He can only manipulate."

Reyja's eyes flashed purple and pierced Rebekah's soul. She could feel the creature rifling through her mind, turning stones and unlocking doors as the memory of that night brought tears to her eyes. She knew she could have resisted, even then, but she didn't. Why? It happened because she allowed it to, and that realization shook her to her core. Mustering as much grit as she could, she forced her mental will to drive the witch out, but it was swatted away.

"You cannot keep secrets from me, child. I have lived for eons. There is no stone in this world that I have not unturned. There are no happenings in this place that escape my sight."

"Then your inaction is benign neglect," Rebekah said as a loathsome heat rose within her. "And for that, all things that transpire under your *omnipresent* gaze are your responsibility."

"You pull on strings that have long been severed," Reyja replied. "You'll find no sympathy from me."

"You detach yourself not out of strength but fear," Rebekah said, unsure where the knowledge came from. "You're alone. You feel it in your very core."

A dark rictus twisted Reyja's lips. "You speak obdurately for a pawn placed by the hand of happenchance. You think yourself special, but you are an ordinary being. You will be discarded once your use is spent."

"Happenchance?"

"Yes." Reyja's presence slithered through Rebekah's mind, leaving a naked feeling in its wake. "It is a sorely accepted rationalization: coincidence. But you were an anomaly. Unforeseen. Your purpose is not divine. You were not chosen. You are a cog upon which Kismet thrusts its will. Many have come before you, and many will come after. None have had the power to change their direction."

Agonizing spears of pain snaked their way through Rebekah's skull as the witch's grimy fingers delved into the depths of her psyche, unearthing vulnerabilities she had long buried. Each memory she touched projected itself in her mind like a still-frame embossment, ravaging her emotions. A dormant energy, hidden deep within her, cracked and surged forth like an unleashed tempest, coursing through her entire being.

In a deafening scream, Rebekah unleashed that newfound power, a primal force that reverberated through the room with an unbridled fury. The bone chimes hanging from the rafters swung in a wild frenzy, clattering and chiming in chaotic discord. Reyja was hurled backward, tumbling over the stone table. Books toppled from their precarious perches on the overstuffed shelves, and glass jars shattered upon impact with the workbench.

As Reyja staggered to her feet, Rebekah sensed a flicker of fear. Puzzlement, without doubt, but fear as well.

"Who *are* you?" Reyja asked, the question delivered with more importance than before.

Rebekah's headache returned, bringing with it immense pain. The threat of death became real. Her body pulled in two directions, tearing her mind along with it. She could visualize two places overlapping one another—her hotel room, where that detective sat talking to himself, and the hovel, where the witch examined her with interest. When the pain subsided, Rebekah felt weak and depleted.

Reyja approached her cautiously, gliding a hand along the textured stone of the table.

"I couldn't see it," Reyja muttered. "The pieces are scattered, unaware of each other. A riddle in the dark seeking purpose." Her voice was low as she whispered to herself, and Rebekah strained to hear. The after-echoes of pain still shot through her skull, diluting her concentration.

"What is happening to me?" Rebekah asked through gasping breaths.

"You are broken, child. Broken by those who have claimed to love you and those who sought to help you. Perhaps you *were* chosen but for what purpose?"

"What? What are you talking about?"

"Your mind is at war with itself," Reyja said. "There are many elements at play, but the Guardian's presence within you is at conflict with your own spirit. They broke the seal. That was the catalyst. If not for my enchantments, you would have thrown your consciousness to distant worlds."

"But why?" Rebekah asked. "Why is this happening? I have no control of my body."

"The injury to your head plays a part, but the Guardian trapped in your mind is the poison. Never have two ethereals inhabited a single body, and with the seal broken, no barrier exists to contain the Guardian's energy. The convergence will rip you apart."

"Two ethereals?"

Reyja's eyes locked with hers. "There is more to you than you know, child. But it is hidden deep within."

Rebekah studied the witch, rolling the information around in her head. One piece flashed into focus. "Wait. I'm dying?"

"Yes. As the Guardian gains strength, you will weaken. It is the ebb and flow of dominance—his presence seeks to overtake your own. It is not within his power to control it. You, however, can stop it. There is a power in you. But I suppose the Guardian did not tell you." Reyja laughed. "And yet you view *me* as the enemy. I wonder why."

Rebekah spoke softly, doubting herself. "I don't believe you. They told me of your corruption. How you abandoned your kin for your own selfish desires."

"Smoke and mirrors, child. It is easy to deceive the ignorant, and make no mistake, you *are* ignorant. The shadow dances with my kin. Through their greed, they have sealed their fate. That is why I abandoned them, and they marked my body for it."

Reyja lurched toward Rebekah, pressing both thumbs into the center of her forehead as gnarled fingers slid beneath the skin of her face. A cold sensation sank into her body, chilling her to the bone. Reyja muttered incantations as a shadow spread through her eyes, darkening the iris and spanning over the sclera.

"What are you doing?" Rebekah shrieked, panicked. "What is this?"

"An answer to my curiosity," Reyja said.

Immeasurable pain gripped her, throttling her spine, and she writhed in agony. The chair twisted beneath her, rattling against the dirt floor to the groaning chorus of splintering wood. Her sight blurred, and her fingers dug into the arms of the seat. She could feel herself screaming, the harsh air grating against her throat, but no sound came. Her body went numb and rigid. Ringing entered her ears as time stopped, trapping her in that agonized pose, in a state of perpetual torture.

In an instant, it all ceased, and Reyja stood before her winded, steadying herself against the stone table. Her eyes rose to meet Rebekah's with a shine of reverence.

"You," she breathed, raising a sharp finger. "You are a descendant of the Liverium." Reyja's voice dropped to a pensive whisper as she muttered to herself. "The essence of the Arcanum lives."

She darted to the shelves and began searching among the trinkets. Rebekah wanted to probe further, needing answers to the questions racking her brain, but her mind was riddled with exhaustion and struggled to maintain consciousness. Her head sank, and realizing she was no longer held in Reyja's trap, she toppled out of the chair.

Fighting to maintain some semblance of awareness, she watched her breath push away clouds of dirt. The fire danced before her, still reflecting off the black mass on the ground which was drying to a waxy sheen. Thudding hoofbeats approached her, and Reyja peeled her from the ground. Placing her back on the chair, she squeezed Rebekah's cheeks and forced a cool liquid down her throat. The taste was sickening, and Rebekah hacked and wheezed through the thick elixir coating her esophagus.

Reyja placed a stopper over a glass vial containing a velvety purple liquid and set it aside on the table. The pressure in Rebekah's head eased, and clarity took its place. Energy swam through her, replenishing her.

Rebekah coughed. "What did you do to me?"

"Spared your life or prolonged your suffering. Time will tell." Reyja regarded her with fierce purpose. "The elixir will subdue the headaches, but they will return. Here." She pushed an object into Rebekah's hand. "This will guide you to what you seek."

Reyja maneuvered back to her workbench and sifted through the chaos. Rebekah turned the stone over in her hand. A smooth, glossy black oval with a violet light pulsing within.

"You're helping me?" Rebekah asked.

"More than you know," Reyja said amidst the clattering of broken jars. "The storm provides, child."

"The storm?" Rebekah's brow creased in thought. "That was you?"

Reyja returned to Rebekah with a broken jar filled with a golden powder. Snatching a handful from inside, she spared Rebekah a final sympathetic glance.

"You are not safe, and your journey is far from over. I pity you for what's to come."

Before Rebekah could respond, Reyja opened her hand and blew on the fine powder. Particles of golden dust flew toward her, light growing within each grain until the cloud blotted her sight, blinding her with an all-too-familiar light.

24

NIKO

SEATED AT THE EDGE of the bed, bathed in the soft orange glow of the lantern, Niko buried his face in his hands, fighting off his fatigue. The coffee was spent, and Robert was still off making the call to Rebekah's parents when the bed shook from movement. He turned back as Rebekah hurriedly sat up. Gagging signaled vomit.

Niko rushed to grab the closest trash can and set it on the floor just as Rebekah leaned over the edge of the bed, bile spewing from her mouth. It was then Niko realized the waste bin was mesh metal. The vomit sprayed through the side holes, painting the carpet in a dotted pattern.

Well, fuck, he thought, his shoulders sinking in defeat.

Sitting beside Rebekah, he pulled her hair back from her face as she took miserable, heaving breaths.

"It's all right," Niko said. "You'll be all right. Just get it out."

The sickness was brief, but Rebekah appeared weak when it ended. She rolled back onto her pillow. He could relate. Niko noticed a half-empty bottle of water on the bed and spun the cap off, handing it to the girl.

"Here. Small sips," he said.

After a few mouthfuls, Rebekah pushed the bottle away. "What are you doing here?"

"Well, Robert came to check on you for…something. I don't

know. But he thought you were having a seizure, so he came and grabbed me for help. He's calling your parents right now."

Rebekah jolted up. "What? Why?"

"You need medical attention, Rebekah," he said. "That's not something I can provide without their permission since you're a minor. Emergencies, sure, but you'll need a hospital as soon as we can safely get you to one. That's something they'd want to know."

Rebekah scoffed and laid back, resting the back of her hand on her forehead. "I wouldn't be so sure."

"Be realistic. Whatever problems you guys may have, I promise you they care. More than you know."

Triggering an epiphany, he was drawn back to his conversation with Charles, and his perspective shifted. Was it possible Charles wasn't as much of a prick as he thought? Perhaps he was just a concerned father whose daughter was involved with someone in a dangerous career. He understood that danger and considered its effect on his life. Again, he questioned if his introspection was a symptom of his fatigue or if he truly held the desire to leave his job.

Rebekah rose, seemingly considering his sentiment as she propped herself up against the headboard.

"So, then what happens now?" Rebekah asked.

"Nothing much we can do except monitor you until the storm passes," Niko replied. "Rest and take it easy. Once it's safe we'll get an ambulance out here and I'll be heading back to Chesapeake."

"I thought you had an investigation to do."

"My per diem only carries me through the weekend. I think I have enough information, though. It'll need to be reviewed, and then a decision will be made if further action can be taken."

"Action?" Rebekah gave Niko a pensive stare.

"It's nothing you need to worry about. I want you to rest. Robert will be back soon, and then I have some things to take care of."

"I heard you talking earlier. You said Danielle was right. About what?"

Niko chuckled, thinking how he had felt safe confiding to the unconscious girl. *All things come back around, I suppose.* "It's a long story," he said.

"According to you, there's nothing else to do."

"It's also personal."

"Okay," Rebekah replied. "I guess we can sit here and listen to the rain drum against the windows."

Niko shot her a sideways glance, which she mocked right back at him, crossing her arms over her chest.

"Come on," she groaned. "The campfire glow of the room, the rain outside…Tell me a story."

Niko sighed and stood, pacing the room. "Okay. Long story short, I was on probation, and my status as a special agent was under review. I'd petitioned to be reinstated, and shortly before taking this trip, it was approved—with some conditions. Danielle isn't happy about it. The job is dangerous, and a prior incident made her understand—made me understand as well—how real that danger can be. But my obsession with being reinstated has brought its share of problems, and it's forcing me to reexamine my priorities."

"So, you chose your job over her?"

"Not exactly."

Rebekah laughed. "What would you call it? She doesn't want you in a dangerous job, but you go for it anyway. Of course, she's pissed at you. I would be too."

"All right, well, that's my story," Niko said plopping down on the chair.

"I'm sorry," Rebekah said, crossing her legs and picking at her fingers in her lap. "She helped you through a lot, right? I think maybe you feel guilty for what you did…for chasing your career. I'm guessing you two have been together a while, and I can tell that you care about her, just in the way you talked about her. Maybe it's not my place, but I think you're doing the right thing, reexamining your priorities."

Niko regarded her with curious interest, nodding his head in consideration. It wasn't lost on him how incredibly observant she was or how she was more intelligent than he initially thought. She'd make a good agent.

"Thank you," he said. "Sometimes, it's difficult to know if the decisions you're making are the right ones."

Rebekah gave a gentle smile and glanced back toward her active hands, reminiscing. "I know the feeling," she said.

Niko leaned forward in his seat, his mind wandering over the numerous tasks he needed to address.

"My sister and I used to do this," she said. "Have late-night, exhaustion-fueled conversations."

"Danielle and I used to do the same." Niko smiled in his musing. "I used to sneak over to her house late at night and lay on the hood of my car, parked beneath her window. She'd lean out, and we'd talk until sunrise. She always worried that I'd get caught by her dad one morning. I think that's what helped me overcome my anger and short temper. I used to close myself off and try not to feel anything. I don't know. There's something about the high you get from sleep deprivation that allowed me to drop my guard around her. It's where we really found each other."

"You're not giving up on this case, are you?" The orange glow flickered in Rebekah's glossy eyes. "My sister…This case deserves to be solved. Don't abandon it."

"I agree," Niko said, leaning forward in his chair. "And I plan to solve it."

The clack of a cane sounded again from the hall as Robert returned, speaking from the hallway before entering the room. Niko realized he had left the door propped open.

"I've got some upsetting news, Niko." Robert halted when he caught sight of Rebekah propped up in bed, his chest heaving winded breaths. "Oh, thank goodness you're all right. You gave me a hell of a shock, but I'm glad you're up because this concerns you as well."

Robert maneuvered into the room, sitting on the empty bed closest to the door. Setting his cane aside, he struggled to catch his breath. Niko and Rebekah glanced at each other as Robert wheezed several times.

"I called Rebekah's home, the only number I have, but no one answered. I called a few times. Then, I got an unpleasant feeling and decided to call some of the nearby hospitals."

"Why would you bother calling local hospitals?" Niko asked.

Robert gave a cautious look to Rebekah. "Don't be mad at me. I was doing as your mother asked. You see, when she called to procure your room, she booked one for herself as well. She was very clear that her room needed to be apart from yours, and she was adamant that I not mention it to you.

"It's not my business to ask questions, so I did as she said and didn't think much more of it, though I had my suspicions. I half expected you to mention something to me as we're a cash-only establishment. I don't know how you thought your mother was paying for your room. Anyways, that's why I called the nearby hospitals, and sure enough, my third call was to Leigh Memorial, where your mother is currently at. Your father's there too."

Niko glanced at Rebekah. He didn't need to imagine how she felt. Her expression made it clear. Tears streamed down her cheeks as her hands covered her mouth. There was a silence while she collected herself enough to speak, and even then, her voice was choked.

"What happened? Is she okay? Is everything all right?"

"She's fine, according to your father. She's banged up pretty bad, but the doctors seem optimistic about her recovery. As for what happened, I don't have the details, but it sounded like your mother's car ran off the road, and she's been unconscious since the accident. They called your father, and he rushed down immediately. In my opinion, he was lucky to make it through the storm."

"So, you spoke to her father," Niko cut in. "Did you talk to him about Rebekah?"

"I'm getting there," Robert replied. "I did talk to him about Rebekah, and he…" Robert glanced at her again. "Well, first you should know that he is extremely worried about you. He had nothing but questions about what happened and what we've done for you. We got his blessing to take care of you and to have you brought to Leigh Hospital as soon as this storm allows. He wants you there so he can be sure that you're safe."

Niko glanced Rebekah's way again. "Are you doing all right?"

"Yeah," she replied with a distance in her eyes. "It's just a lot to take in."

"Everything will be fine," he said. "The storm should pass soon enough, and you'll be with your family."

Rebekah nodded, but Niko could see the gears turning in her mind. Curiosity entered his own, but he pushed it away and decided to leave it alone. She was going through enough, and he had his own concerns to address.

"I need to step out for a moment." Niko stood, sparing a final glance at the young girl. "You sure you'll be all right?"

"Yeah," she said.

"I won't be long," he said to Robert, who nodded.

As he left the room, Robert began his mental check on Rebekah, asking the same superfluous questions and getting the same vague replies.

Moving quickly, Niko wanted to get his notes from his room and head to Robert's office to call Brindle. He needed a second opinion to see if his theory held any water. He didn't trust his mind under the veil of exhaustion.

It wasn't until he reached the stairwell he realized he never had a light with him. Two floors he needed to climb, and he wasn't excited to do so in the pitch black. The door slammed shut behind him, and he gripped the rails tightly. Uneasily, he felt for each step, though after rounding the first landing, he started to get more comfortable. It was a challenge to suppress the irrational fears pressing on his mind of monsters springing at him from the dark, but eventually he opened the door to the hallway on the fourth floor.

A sigh of relief accompanied his exit from the abyssal stairwell, and he shook off the nerves as he trudged down the corridor toward his room. Approaching his door, he reached for his key, only to find an empty pocket. Stopping in the hall, he haphazardly patted his other pockets and even his chest, for some reason. Nothing.

"Fuck!" he screamed into the empty space.

Throwing his hands up and gripping his hair, he proceeded toward the door with the unlikely hope it would be open. The door was closed. As he approached, however, he found splintered wood framing the lock. Someone had kicked in the door. He rushed inside, searching the dresser for his flashlight. The moment his hand grasped the metal shaft, he clicked the button, and a beam of light ignited the chaotic scene. His case files had been thrown to the floor and his duffle emptied over the bed. Hectically searching the mess, he discovered his leatherback book was missing.

Instinctually, he lurched for the nightstand, fearing the worst, but sighed in relief when he found his father's gun still sitting in the drawer. He loaded six rounds into the revolver, stuffed it into its holster, and clipped it to his belt at the base of his spine. He then adjusted his shirt to conceal it.

Giving the room a final scan in case he overlooked his notebook, he left dissatisfied. Tucking his gun carefully into his waistband, he raised his flashlight and made his way into the hall, running into unexpected guests. The drunken group of college kids. One of them had stumbled into Niko and shoved him against the wall.

"Watch where you're fuckin' goin', man," the kid slurred, planting his hands on Niko's chest and pushing him once more.

"You ran into—" Niko caught himself and thought better of it. "Look, you're right. I apologize. You guys have a good night."

"Yo," the kid said, grabbing Niko's shoulder. "You run into me, and now you're just gonna walk away?" The kid stumbled around as he talked, struggling to find stable footing. Niko kept the flashlight trained on the group, pointing it at their eyes, using it to skew their vision as a defensive tactic.

"You tell him, Joey!" one of the others yelled.

"Fuck him up," a second said.

"Look, guys." Niko held up his free palm in a gesture of peace. "You're all clearly drunk, and it was just a mistake. Let's brush it off and go our separate ways."

"Oh, brush it off, he says." Joey turned to his cackling group of morons. "Who the fuck are you to talk to me like that?"

"Special Agent Niko Ortez of the FBI. I'm here on a case. So, let's just call it a night, all right?"

"Whoa, special agent," Joey mocked. "Get the fuck outta here, man. You look like you're our age. What are you, twenty-one? Twenty-two?"

"Twenty-four." Niko chided himself mentally for the knee-jerk response.

Joey and his group broke out in a chorus of laughter. "Yeah, special agent my ass."

"All right," Niko said, slowly backing away. "Again, I'm sorry for bumping into you. Have a good night." He turned, his flashlight held down by his side, putting the boys behind him in the dark.

"Don't you walk away from me," Joey said.

As Niko turned, Joey's fist collided with his jaw, sending him stumbling aside. The kid and his friends laughed.

"Yeah, what now, bitch!?" he yelled.

Niko stood, and Joey took another swing, which Niko parried. He followed with a right hook to Joey's stomach and a left to his jaw, and Joey went down. Before any of the kids could move, Niko drew his Glock and leveled it at the group, taking a few steps back to create distance from Joey.

"Back up!" Niko shouted. "Everybody back up!"

"Whoa, shit," one of the kids said. "Take it easy."

Niko tongued the inside of his cheek, tasting blood, and spit on the ground. It had been a long day, and he was toeing the edge of his patience. Taking a deep breath, he relaxed to control the situation.

"Your friend is drunk," Niko said. "I suggest you pick him up and walk the other way."

"Yeah, all right," the same kid said as two boys ran to grab their friend.

Joey laughed as his buddies dragged him away.

"I'm gonna fuck you up, Niko," he said. "You better watch your fucking back!"

"Joey, chill," one of the boys hissed.

"Watch your back, Niko," Joey continued. "Power outage, bitch. No rules. I'll find you."

That was the last Niko heard as the group rounded the far corner. When they were out of sight, he lowered his guard and rubbed a hand against his cheek. The taste of blood coated his mouth. He chuckled at the sheer stupidity of the entire encounter and turned, resuming his trek back to Rebekah's room. His original intention was to be tactful, but his room being broken into changed the situation, adding more weight to his hunch.

I'm getting close, and someone knows it.

He paused outside of Rebekah's room and tucked his gun into his waist, covering it with his shirt. There didn't need to be a scene. After everything Rebekah had been through, he didn't need to add further stress.

"Robert," he said as he entered the room, startling both Robert and Rebekah. "I need to make a call. Do you mind letting me into your office?"

"Uh, sure," Robert said, studying him before turning back to Rebekah. "Give me a moment. I'll be right back."

Rebekah simply nodded before the two men exited the room. Robert's slow limp tested Niko's patience as they worked their way through the hall, down the stairs, and finally to the bright lights of the lobby. After unlocking the office, Robert didn't linger.

"I'll be with Rebekah when you're finished," he said before shuffling from the room.

Niko took a moment to compose himself and collect his thoughts. It also ensured Robert was out of earshot. Snatching the headset from the base, he dialed Brindle's home number. He couldn't be sure of the time, but it had to be close to four, which would be around the time Brindle would be getting up to start his day. The phone rang several times, and Niko began to think he wouldn't answer, until the dial tone cut short and shuffling noises blurted through the speaker.

"Kevin Brindle." His voice was groggy, so it must not have been quite four yet.

"Hey, Kev," Niko said.

"Ortez? Jesus, this is early for you."

"Yeah, tell me about it. Look, I don't have a lot of time, but I need you to do some digging for me when you get into the office. You got something to write with?"

Brindle groaned. "Give me a minute."

There was more shuffling and scratching through the headset as Brindle scrambled for a pen. A drawer slammed shut, and the microphone muffled in and out before he spoke again.

"Okay, go ahead."

"I need some background on some people. Robert Wymer, Maggie Berman, Stuart Berman, and a retired detective named David Rossi."

"Rossi?" Brindle asked. "Isn't he dead?"

"Yeah," Niko said. "Wait. Did you know him?"

"I wouldn't say I knew him. I saw him around the office from time to time. He was a grumpy bastard who always looked like he was having a bad day. Came as no surprise when he offed himself after he retired. Plenty of people saw it coming and offered all kinds of support to try and prevent it."

"Well, he was the lead on most of these cold cases, and I can't say that they were thorough. I ran into his brother Harold. He, uh, had a bad run-in with a beach umbrella, and he's not looking so good. Actually, do you mind adding him to the list as well?"

"Sure thing. Harold Rossi," Brindle said. "Anything else? Want an order of fries?"

Niko chuckled. "Smart-ass." It hadn't been that long, but he missed the banter. "Look, someone broke into my room and took my notes. I have a good feeling that my hunch was on the fucking nose."

"What? That the cases are connected, and there's some kind of serial killer on the loose?"

"Exactly. It's a reasonable assumption because I'm pissing someone off."

"Well, if that's true, that means you're in the den with a psycho who's likely working with someone else. And you're trapped in that building with them."

"That crossed my mind too. But they fucked up breaking into my room. They gave me a hammer."

"Probable cause," Brindle agreed. "I could get a warrant issued on that."

"First, get some background on those names. We'll need it. Then, see if you can get some people out here. Storm or not, we can't risk them making a run for it when the weather breaks."

"I'll see what I can do. Start poking around. You'll need some physical evidence if you want anything to stick. But be smart. If you have suspicions, keep them close to your chest, otherwise you're looking at a hotel of potential hostages or the risk of this psycho slipping through your fingers."

"I know," Niko said. "I'll play nice for now, but I could really use some backup."

"Hard for a file clerk to round up a TAC team, but I'll make a call. You just be careful."

"I will," Niko said. "My cell reception is shit because of the storm, so you won't be able to reach me, but I'll try and call you back in a few hours."

Niko returned the handset to the base and lingered for a moment, considering everything that had happened. He yawned and rubbed his eyes; he needed more coffee or a good night's rest, though he didn't imagine either happening. Emerging from the office into the lobby, he dragged his feet. Robert came limping around the corner past the elevators.

"Niko," he said, struggling for breath. "Rebekah's gone."

"What?" His overtiredness fled as his focus returned.

"I went back to her room, and she wasn't there. The door was still propped open, but the room was empty."

"Damnit." Niko palmed his face. "Well, she's gotta be somewhere in the hotel, right? So, let's split up and search for her."

"Okay. Let me get you a radio."

Robert limped off toward his office and returned a moment later, dialing in the proper channel on a bulky radio that looked like some Circuit City dinosaur.

"You take the upper floors. My legs can't handle the stairs anymore. We'll meet back at Rebekah's room."

"Fine," Niko said, noting the radio dialed to channel five. They made their way toward the stairwell.

25

REBEKAH

THE SILENCE THAT REMAINED in the wake of Robert and Niko leaving gave Rebekah time to reflect on everything that had happened with the witch. Retrieving the stone she had concealed beneath her pillow after waking, she rolled it over in her hand. Orange firelight flickered from the lantern and danced along the glossy black surface. There was a certain gravity to the conflict within her.

The witch gave you a praesagium stone? Rylos's voice returned to her head, its presence less welcome than before.

"You knew you would be forced from that place," Rebekah said. "You knew her enchantments would bar your entry."

A long silence followed her accusation, bridging the gap before he spoke next.

Yes, he finally said.

"So, you led me there and put my life in danger to serve your own end."

We would not have succeeded otherwise.

Rebekah stood from the bed and paced the room, still examining the glossy cover of the stone. Pushing aside her anger at Rylos's deceit, she shifted her focus to her sister. That was all that mattered.

"What does this stone do?"

It gives you visions for what you seek, he said. *You need but grip the stone in your hand and ask, but your mind must be clear and unburdened.*

Rebekah paused, turning the rock over again. The violet light pulsed within, but it was faint and nearly indistinguishable, even in the dark of the room. The rain pelting the window sounded weaker, but the roar of thunder was still close and powerful. Her fingers curled around the stone.

"Reyja told me that I was a descendant of the Liverium," Rebekah said. "Did you know? Did you know your presence within me will kill me?"

The Liverium? The children of the Arcanum? No, that's not possible. The Arcanum was lost—

"Did you know?" Her voice was imperious.

No, he said.

Her jaw clenched in frustration. "What am I to you then?"

I have told you, Rylos said. *You are a victim of circumstance. Nothing more. But for that, I am sorry. Like a coward, I fled from Nox and concealed myself among the conscious stars. I did not intend to fuse with your spirit, nor did I intend to trap myself. But if you are a descendant of the Liverium…*

Understand, we are all beings of energy—ethereal, mortal, it makes no difference—and as such, we are governed by our restrictions. There must always be a balance. Guardians and Reapers controlled that balance because if left to the will of kismet, the correction would be catastrophic. If you are Liverium, then when I concealed myself within your consciousness, it must have created an imbalance. That must be how I… It was not something I foresaw.

"So, I'm just a pawn to you," Rebekah said. "I'm collateral."

No. Our relationship may be fortuitous, but it is not without purpose. If we find the amulet, I can sever the tie that binds us, freeing us both as well as your sister.

Rebekah considered the alternative. If they remained tethered, she would die. The witch said as much. No matter how much she fought it, that was unavoidable, and her sister would be left to bear an unimaginable fate. So, she was left with little choice to bicker over.

"Fine," she resigned. "Then let's find the amulet."

Unfurling her fist, she gave the stone a final cursory glance. After a few meditative breaths, calming the turmoil in her mind, she curled her fingers back over it and focused her thoughts. A slight heat permeated her palm, and an energy shot through her arm, something she likened to being shocked. Much like being electrocuted, her body went rigid and locked as a series of visions flooded her mind. She recognized much of the hotel—the dark corridors, the brightly lit lobby, the diner. But a location flashed by she wasn't familiar with. A dimly lit area, but in place of walls, there was a skeletal framework of metal studs, unburdened by drywall, with veins of electrical wiring and copper piping running throughout.

Within that room was a complex furnace, the fire within lending light to the space. Images flashed of a large area with a steel table at its center. Storage shelves framed the room, adorned with an array of chemicals, and scattered workbenches broke the monotony of tiered shelving, each seemingly serving a specific purpose. Above one sat a pegboard where a solitary cone of light lit the display, spotlighting what appeared to be a shrine of trophies. Marking the centerpiece of an assortment of other jewelry, the amulet sat, swinging softly, casting a dance of colors from the white of the overhead light to the orange of the furnace.

Trying to absorb and memorize as much detail as possible, Rebekah's focus slipped, and a new series of images shot through her mind, carrying physical feelings with them. One disturbing vision that stuck with her was a dark room, where ominous silhouettes surrounded her, laughing and mocking her. Pain stung her face, and an unfamiliar sensation plunged into the lowest pit of her stomach. Though unfamiliar, she could guess what was happening—rape.

In her shock, she dropped the stone, ceasing the assault of images, carrying the pain away with them and making them seem like a distant memory. But that didn't remove the terror the vision brought. Rebekah collapsed to the floor and clapped her hands over her face.

What is it? Rylos asked. *What did you see?*

Rebekah remained silent, shaking with fear, unable to string together coherent words to speak. Calming herself, she rationalized it as an obscure event. Not a possibility.

"Does the stone predict the future?" she asked.

No. It provides visions to guide you to what you seek. Did it show you where the amulet is?

"Yes, but..." Rebekah considered confessing to Rylos, but if what she had seen was not in her future, then she figured it best to leave the vision alone rather than give it power.

But?

"N—Nothing," Rebekah said, shaking off the anxiety. "Let's go."

Grabbing the stone from the floor and pocketing it, she fled the room. In her vision, her thoughts had drifted from the amulet, and in the chaos that followed, she couldn't recall where her thoughts had fallen. Fear fluttered in her stomach, and the urge to decipher what she had seen nagged at her, but she shrugged it away. Finding the amulet was her focus, and the vision related to that seemed a facile task.

What is our destination?

"Somewhere on the first floor," she said. "Across from the diner is a construction area. I think what we seek is somewhere within that space."

You are sure of this?

"Not really," she admitted. "But it's a start."

In the darkened corridor, she made her way to the elevator, trapped in her own thoughts. She slapped the down button and waited for a moment, pressing it again before the realization struck her the power was out. Her exhaustion from the long day and the chaos of all that had transpired had blinded her to the situation around her. Suddenly, the lantern in her room and the darkness of the hallway connected in her mind. She shook her head in embarrassment for not realizing sooner.

Turning back, she hesitated, remembering the stairwell closest to her room was buried behind the plastic curtain walling off the construction zone. Instead, she made for the other stairwell just beyond the elevators. Entering the hallway, she encountered the group of college kids once more, and fear rooted her to the spot. Pausing and drinking in the situation, a smile cut across Joey's face.

"Well, well," he said.

Rebekah turned and rushed past the elevators, charging down the corridor, her thoughts solely on safety. She shot past her room and threw aside the opaque plastic tarp, disappearing into the darkness of the construction zone. The emergency lights were scattered. Some hung from the wires powering them, obscuring their light against the freshly laid drywall. Dust and debris decorated exposed flooring. Rebekah's foot slipped on a rogue screw, throwing her against a wall, where her shoulder punched a dent into the drywall. Near the end of the hall, the metal framing beneath the wall sat exposed. Strands of cabling dangled from the ceiling and between the joists.

Ducking a section of scaffolding and slipping between two joists, she felt a hand clasp the cloth of her shirt. Her momentum was enough to break free, though it threw her to the ground. Rebekah found herself in the cramped framework of a bedroom, the boys bearing down on her. She maneuvered around and worked her way behind the group of enraged deviants, who struggled to squeeze through the scaffolding.

"I'll get you, bitch!" Joey screamed.

Rebekah spared a glance back as he slipped through the exposed joists and back into the hall.

Stairs. I need to get to the stairs, Rebekah thought.

Racing through the corridor, her foot caught a coiled extension cord, and she crashed to the ground, bringing a collapsed A-frame ladder down with her and nearly hitting Joey. Untangling her foot from the cord, she clambered to her feet, slipping on the dust-slicked floor. Throwing the construction tarp open again, the cleanliness of the air hit her, making her aware of the musty woodchip smell that clouded the construction area.

Thudding feet bore down on her, and despite the burning in her muscles and lungs, she pushed harder, turning once again at the elevators. Hands gripped her shoulders and dragged her down to the ground, her face sliding against the rough carpet. Joey pinned her down, trapping her arms beneath his knees. Heat licked at her cheek where the rug had dug in.

"You're fucking ballsy. I'll give you that," he breathed heavily into her ear. "But you're mine now."

As the rest of his group caught up, they jerked her from the ground, restraining her arms and legs and dragging her into the next hall. She kicked and screamed, trying to bite at the boys' hands, grazing the knuckles of one with her teeth. A fist connected with her face—first the cheek, then the temple—sending her vision into a blurred and spinning frenzy.

"Let's get her to the room," Joey said. "Grab the door, Zack. Quick!"

Despite her dizziness, she struggled feebly, refusing to submit. She swung her knees back and forth and attempted to throw her arms over her chest to break the hold, but the boys' grip tightened and overpowered her. Rattling keys scraped the wooden door, searching for the lock. The arms of one of the boys slackened as they waited for Zack to open it.

"Are you fucking kidding me?" one of the boys said. "Hurry up!"

"I'm trying!" Zack complained. "It's too dark. I can't see."

Zack hissed a "yes" as the key slid into the lock, and he turned the deadbolt back. As Rebekah was crammed through the doorway, she threw her head back, connecting with one of the boys, and contorted her limbs in a desperate attempt to break free from their grasp. She slipped their grip and crashed violently against the cold, tiled entryway, a jolt of pain reverberating through her skull. Determined, she crawled deeper into the room, clawing for space to pull herself up from the ground. Her respite was short-lived, however, as three of the boys pounced on her, lifted her, and forcefully slammed her against the wall. Two pairs of hands gripped her arms tightly, rendering her defenseless. Joey, his lips wet with anticipation, approached, his brow sporting a visible cut from her headbutt, even in the dimly lit room.

"No one coming to save you now," he sneered, throwing another punch that landed sharply on her ear.

Sounds became muffled, replaced by an intrusive ringing. Joey uttered words she couldn't decipher, but his fist found its mark once again, connecting with her jaw.

"Take it easy, Joe," the boy restraining her right arm cautioned. "I like her face. Don't bruise it."

"It's pitch black in here, Zack," Joey retorted. "Can't even see her face."

His next punch found her abdomen, sending tremors coursing through her legs and weakening her knees. Seizing her shirt by the collar, he yanked downward with a fierce tug. The seams strained, threatening to tear around her neck and shoulders, but the shirt clung defiantly, refusing to surrender to his brutal desires. Joey gave another forceful jerk, wrenching the shirt loose and exposing her skin to the chilling air that washed over her body. It caused goosebumps to rise and a wave of nausea to surge within. In a flash of lightning, the room ignited, granting Rebekah a horrifying glimpse of her assailants, their eyes filled with a predatory hunger as they leered at her vulnerable, exposed form.

"I'm gonna enjoy this," Joey said.

Sliding the bra strap down her shoulder, revealing her exposed breast, he licked at her nipple. A guttural scream erupted from her, and she lunged toward him, her claws poised to rip at his flesh. But the boys holding her only laughed as they forcefully thrust her back against the wall. A merciless fist struck her face again, dislodging her lower jaw and leaving a searing ache in its wake.

"Maybe we should move her into the room," Zack suggested.

"Yeah," Joey said. "Get her over to the bed. Face down."

In a desperate act of defiance, Rebekah spat at Joey, drawing twisted amusement from the others. With a cruel laugh, Joey's open palm struck her across the face, leaving behind a tingling ache that danced along the surface of her rug-burned skin, mingling with the pain of her throbbing jaw. Zack and another boy seized her, wrenched her away from the wall, and flung her mercilessly across the room, her body crashing onto the bed. The resounding thud of the door closing sealed her grim fate.

A fleeting moment of freedom granted Rebekah a surge of hope. She writhed and struggled in a futile attempt to assume a defensive position. But her defiance was swiftly quashed as two boys seized her arms, restraining them with their knees, pressing them into the soft mattress, while another forcibly spread her trembling legs apart. The metallic sound of a belt being undone pierced the air, heralding the impending horror that loomed between her vulnerable thighs. Fear clawed at her chest as images from her vision flashed before her, reminding her of what she had seen—and what was about to unfold.

"Strip her pants," Joey commanded, his voice dripping with sadistic pleasure.

"No!" Rebekah's anguished scream filled the air. "Please, no. Stop! Don't do this."

"Shut up, bitch," one of the boys hissed, forcibly silencing her with a cloth gag.

Hands clawed at the waistband of her pants, tugging and tearing, threatening to pull her underwear with them. The fabric split at the hem of her left leg, the button giving way. It allowed her pants to slither down her trembling legs. Summoning every ounce of strength she could muster, she twisted her body, rolling onto her back just enough to launch a desperate kick at Joey's chest.

A twisted satisfaction flooded Rebekah as her foot made contact, eliciting a high-pitched squeal from Joey. He crashed against the dresser, coughing and gasping for air, momentarily incapacitated by the unexpected assault.

"You…fucking cunt!" he screamed, punctuated by ragged breaths.

Her momentary triumph was brief as the other boys swiftly rolled her back onto her stomach. Joey, fueled by unbridled vengeance, delivered a punishing kick right between her legs, unleashing a wave of excruciating pain that radiated through her hips and spine. The intensity of the assault left her certain her pelvis had been shattered. Grunting through the dull, throbbing agony, Rebekah fought with every ounce of her being to free her legs once more, but her efforts were in vain. Joey's hand callously pushed her underwear aside, laying bare her most intimate vulnerability.

Her heart pounded in her chest, a desperate rhythm of survival, as her mind waged a battle against the harrowing reality. She desperately clung to the hope it was a nightmare or some horrible hallucination. Seeking refuge from the impending trauma, her mind recoiled, distancing itself from the horrific event and invoking a disassociation. It was a fragile defense against the impending echoes of trauma.

A flicker of light caught the corner of her eye, emanating from within her very being. Power surged through her, bringing with it an intoxicating warmth and, more importantly, strength. It was a sensation she knew well, having experienced Rylos's magic before, with her as the conduit.

"What the fuck!" Zack's terrified cry pierced the air as he released his grip and stumbled back in disbelief.

Rebekah's vision was flooded with a blinding light, her mind retreating to a place of dreamlike serenity. Only the strained cry of Rylos echoed, imploring her to halt. But control was lost, consumed by raw, untamed power, leaving her with no recollection to anchor herself to. Her vision dissolved into an inky abyss, liberating her from the weight of anxiety. It was replaced with a sense of safety and satisfaction, an enigmatic solace that settled deep within her soul.

When consciousness returned to her, she found herself surrounded by a grotesque scene. Disoriented and confused, she grappled with the reality of it. The room was a canvas of horror, a chilling sight that sent shivers down her spine. The five boys lay scattered, their bodies sprawled in twisted poses. Swaths of blood decorated the walls and furniture, accented with thick droplets and misty sprays. Lightning briefly illuminated the gruesome carnage in vivid detail—the severed limbs, the disemboweled remains, and the sight of Joey's decapitated head resting on the dresser, painted with a look of horror.

Clapping a hand to her face, she recoiled at the sticky wetness that clung to her skin. In the dim light, she saw her forearms were coated in a thick layer of blood, dribbling from her trembling fingers. Nausea stabbed at her stomach as she stumbled through the slaughter, losing her footing as she slipped over a dismembered arm. The tiled entryway proved treacherous, slick with liquid and offering little stability. Reaching out a hand to steady herself, she left a smeared crimson imprint along the wall.

Rebekah sought refuge in the darkened bathroom. She fumbled for the sink handles, the threat of vomit scraping at the back of her throat. Clutching the knobs, she turned on the water, unbothered by the scalding heat. Furiously, she scrubbed her hands, desperate to rid herself of the repulsive residue and shift her thoughts to anything but blood to satiate her sickness.

In the mirror's faint reflection, she glimpsed her silhouette, astonished to find a soft white glow emanating from the crescent-shaped mark of her eye. Tentatively, she placed a hand over the spot, watching as the glow disappeared only to reappear once her hand was removed.

Rylos? she asked. *What is happening to me?*

There was no answer, and a profound emptiness settled within her, reminiscent of the emptiness she had felt when Nicole disappeared—a void that her parents' neglect had fostered. Yet she longed for their presence and comfort. The reminder of her mother's accident brought her to the floor, and she wept, her tears coalescing with the bloodstains.

"Rylos!" she called once more, finding only silence.

Was this how it would end? Was her connection to the Guardian severed? And what of her mother? Hope for her mother's recovery intermingled with self-reproach. She had been foolish to believe she could brave the endeavor alone, and she was reaping the consequences of her ignorance.

A sudden realization dawned on her, causing her heart to plummet into the pit of her stomach. The boys in the other room—she had killed them. Even if she could argue self-defense, which she decided wouldn't absolve her, there was no justification for the grotesque disfigurement of their bodies.

The evidence soaked her clothes and stained the floor. Her footprints traced a trail of horror across the entryway, and her handprint marked the wall. Should she confess? Morally, it was right to seek out the detective and admit her guilt, hoping for mercy. It was a terrible plan, but it was the right thing to do, come what may.

She staggered to her feet, her weary legs threatening to buckle beneath her. With each step, her body swayed in a dance of exhaustion and disorientation. Stumbling from the room, the draft that swept through the hall reminded her of her nakedness. She was dressed only in her underwear. Steeling herself, she ventured back to the beds, where the feeble emergency light cast a pallid glow on the pools of crimson.

With cautious determination, she waded through the blood-soaked carpet to retrieve her crumpled jeans from the floor, their fabric saturated with the sickening evidence of the horrors she had endured. The torn leg seemed like a minor inconvenience compared to the vulnerability of being exposed, so she squeezed into the cold, damp pants and fled the room.

Tears streamed down her face, mingling with the remnants of blood and anguish. The tumultuous storm of emotions threatened to consume her, a tempest of relief mingled with a profound terror. She had narrowly evaded the unspeakable, but the cost of her survival weighed heavy on her conscience.

Navigating the corridor, she felt utterly lost, her sense of direction elusive. She passed the stairwell and the elevators, walking aimlessly in the opposite direction of her room, lost in her own turbulent thoughts. Beyond the prospect of confession, her mind fixated on nagging questions. What had happened? Had Rylos saved her?

No. His resistance, his pain, was evidence he hadn't intervened. It had been her.

Denial, of course, crept into her thoughts. She couldn't—*wouldn't*—believe she was capable of such horrors. Yet, the absence of recollection only deepened her uncertainty. What was that blinding light? It was the last fragment of memory before her consciousness had abandoned her. Then she remembered Rylos and his arm on that darkened beach. The light had been present then too. But to lose conscious control to the extent of mercilessly killing five boys much larger and stronger…

Anxiety tightened its grip around her chest. Unanswered questions weighed heavily upon her. She came to a halt, feeling like a stranger in her own body, reminiscent of that night three years ago when she teetered on the precipice of death. Falling to her knees, she wept, her cries echoing through the empty hallway.

Suddenly, the sound of footsteps rushed from behind her. Before she could turn to see who approached, a brutal blow struck the back of her head, casting her into the realm of unconsciousness.

26

NIKO

AMID THE THOUSANDS OF other things on his mind, searching for Rebekah was shy from the top, and that brought Niko a measure of guilt. Nevertheless, he explored the fifth floor to no avail. He had run into the younger couple from the diner, slowing his search as he answered a few questions about how Henry was recovering and if he knew anything about the power outage.

Making his way through the fourth floor, he chewed on the questions compounding in his head. His hunch about Detective Rossi led him nowhere, and though he had his suspicions about a few characters, there was a wrench in the gears. Still fixated on the anomaly that broke every theory, he pondered the question further still. *Why the gap?*

Metal clanging drew his light to the dust-spattered tarp at the end of the hall, obscuring his view to the area beyond. He removed his firearm and maneuvered his flashlight hand beneath the magazine of his gun, crossing his wrists. It was a common stance known as the Harries Technique, which he preferred to the FBI technique; it allowed him to move tactically. Brushing the tarp aside, he strode into the dimly lit area.

His training would've had him announce his presence as an agent, but he decided against it, knowing the legality of any following events would not be in his favor. He glided through the hallway, maintaining the debris clustering the floor in his peripheral to avoid any missteps. Plastic sheets scaled the walls, covering the skeletal metal beams. It looked as though the drywall for the ceiling had recently been done, and the guts of the lighting dangled awaiting final fitment.

Hushed voices sounded from ahead, causing him to thumb off the light and slow his steps. Keeping his gun ahead of him, the few emergency lights and the uncovered windows of the rooms gave him vague silhouettes to work with to establish his surroundings. Passing by one room, he caught two shadows in the faint light of a window.

Flashing the light on, he pushed past the tarp and shouted, "FBI! Freeze!" He immediately lowered his gun when he entered the room.

Leslie, the receptionist, was bent over a rolling tool cart, covering her bare breasts in surprise as the young man behind her stumbled backward, erection flopping around uselessly. The boy was someone Niko didn't recognize, but it seemed Leslie knew him well enough.

"Holy shit, man!" the guy cried. "You almost gave me a fucking heart attack."

"Detective," Leslie said, scrambling to gather her clothes. "What are you—"

"Why the hell are you in the construction area?" Niko chided, averting his gaze and lowering his light to give the couple some privacy. "Can't you get a room?"

"Well, Jason was waiting for my shift to end to drive me home, but the storm hit, and we got stuck here. Please don't tell Mr. Wymer about this!"

"I'm not going to say anything," Niko said, tucking his weapon back into his waistband. "But I don't think he'd care much if you and your boyfriend were—"

"He's not my boyfriend," Leslie cut in, clasping her bra and covering her breasts.

"Whatever," Niko replied. "I don't think he'd care. But next time, get a room. This is just…dirty."

"Yeah, we've done that before, and he almost fired me when he found out."

"But there are plenty of unoccupied rooms here. Why would he care?"

"Trust me, he's a hard ass," Leslie said. "He cares."

"Fine. I won't mention this to him, but since we're here, I have a few questions for you."

"Um, okay," Leslie said, sliding her pants up. "Do you think now is the appropriate time?"

"If you want me to keep this quiet." Blackmail wasn't the best approach, but desperate times…

"Fine," Leslie huffed.

Jason edged toward the door. "Is it cool if I—"

"No, it's not," Niko interrupted. "Finish getting dressed, and go relax by the window. I don't need you wandering off."

Jason rolled his eyes and finished buttoning his shorts. Snagging his shirt from the floor, he scuttled off to the window where rain clouded the glass, but the storm beyond seemed to be easing.

Niko turned back to Leslie, who was buttoning her blouse. "How long have you worked here?"

"Almost a year, I think," she said.

"Had you worked in hotels before?"

"Well, no, but I worked in customer service, and I was a waitress before I came here. I think that's why Mr. Wymer hired me."

"How do you mean?"

"Well, part of my job is waiting tables at the diner during the busy hours. Two of the cleaners help out too."

"You work reception *and* waitress at the diner?" Niko clarified. "Who works the front while you're working the diner?"

"Mr. Wymer does," Leslie said. "Not like it matters much. We don't see many customers."

"Yeah, I believe that." Niko glanced around at the construction. "So, how is he paying for all this?"

"How would I know?" She scoffed. "I don't handle any of the finances."

"You seem like a smart girl, though," Niko said, earning a blushed smile from Leslie and a scoff from Jason, who lit a cigarette.

"Well, the diner is where most of the money comes from. That and Stuarts's business. So, I'd assume that's how they're paying for the renovation."

"Isn't the diner Stuart's business?"

"No." Leslie sneered, jumping up and sitting on the tool cart. "He cooks there, and that keeps him pretty busy, but he's a butcher and some kind of craftsman. I don't know, but he ships stuff out constantly. Mostly meat from butchering whatever the local hunters and fishermen bring in, but he also makes his own soaps, lotions, candles, and fertilizer."

Thinking about the handmade soap he found in the bathroom upstairs, Niko said, "I imagine he supplies the hotel with its share of soap too."

"Yeah, he does. Robert has some partnerships with a few of the bigger names that he bulk orders from occasionally, but Stuart donates a couple boxes to Robert each year. A few hundred bars of soap at least."

"This hotel houses what…two hundred and fifty people?"

"Two-twenty," Leslie said.

"It's almost spring break, and you guys have maybe ten percent occupancy. Is that normal?"

"Yeah, we don't get a whole lot of people throughout the year. That's why the diner is the major source of income. It's a hot spot, being right on the boardwalk. I help them out more than I run the hotel desk."

"So, that soap likely lasts most of the year," Niko muttered to himself.

He mused about the situation. Strange, but it made a measure of sense. He had to give Robert credit for the crafty business approach and delegation of labor. Still, there was something deeper he was failing to see. There was no doubt the Armitage was the nexus point of his suspicions, and how fortunate it was he had ended up there. He paced the room before finding an unlabeled toolbox he used as a seat.

"Can you tell me about schedules?" Niko asked. "Let's start with you."

"I work a twelve-hour shift at the hotel. Eight to eight. Then two ten-hour shifts at the diner on weekends."

"So, you technically work two jobs."

"I'm trying to pay off my student loans and some other debts. But it's not really a big deal. I do the same thing at both jobs and make the same. I'm just in the books under two different positions."

"Yeah, and it allows Robert and Maggie to exploit you without breaching any labor restrictions. They also dodge paying you overtime."

"What?" Leslie asked.

"Look, it's none of my business, but you're being fucked over."

"Not really," Leslie said. "The pay is considerable, and I even get to keep my tips from waitressing, which is all cash. Thanks for the concern, though."

Niko noted the ire accompanying her tone and dialed back the personal probing, something he should have kept out of in the first place. It was good to keep in mind Robert and Maggie had bought and paid for her loyalty, which called into question the bias surrounding her testimony. However, her insecurities over losing her position were volatile, which he could use.

"I apologize," Niko said. "Okay. What about Robert then?"

"Oh, he lives here," Leslie said. "Literally. He stays in a room on the first floor, so he's always around doing something."

"And Maggie?"

"A little looser with the schedule. She comes in around the same time I do since the diner doesn't open until ten. But she's here pretty late since they're open until two in the morning. I've stayed back a few times to grab a bite with friends, and she was still waiting and bussing tables on her own. She's a workhorse for sure but a really nice woman and a great boss. Robert too."

"Hmm. And Stuart?"

"Um..." Leslie considered for a moment. "To be honest, I'm not sure. I don't think I've ever seen him leave, and he's always here when I get here. I think he might live at the hotel as well. I don't really interact with him too much."

"Why is that?"

"There's no need to," she replied. "In my first month working here, I ran back to the kitchen to grab some extra things for a table, and he was stepping out of the freezer. He went off on me about how I wasn't allowed back there and was just really aggressive. Maggie grabbed me and calmed him down, but ever since then, I've stayed in front of house."

"What did Maggie say to you about that?"

"She just told me that Stuart is very particular and enjoys things a certain way. Said it would be best to keep to the tables and bar area. So, that's what I did."

"And how does Henry fit into all of this?"

"Oh, God. Henry." Leslie's face went pale, and she scooted to the edge of her seat. "Shit! I was supposed to check on him."

Niko held his palms out, reassuring and calming her. "It's okay," he said. "Robert went and checked on him. He's fine. I saw him a couple hours ago, and he was doing much better. Just relax."

Leslie eased back on the tool cart, taking a breath. A heavy sigh came from the window followed by the waft of tobacco. Jason had lit another cigarette and was lolling his head back against the wall. Niko returned to the conversation.

"Tell me about Henry."

Leslie let out a sigh before speaking. "I don't know much about Henry. He's just always kind of…around."

"Hanging at the bar?"

"Yeah, usually. He's a regular. We have a few of them. Jim, the guy who helped you get Henry to his room, is another. I don't really pay them any attention. Maggie usually serves and handles them."

Garbled noises chirped over the radio, followed by a mild hiss of static before silence. A moment later, Robert's voice came through. "Niko, you there?"

Unclipping the radio from his belt, he fingered the talk button. "Yeah, I'm here."

"I'm heading up to the second floor now. Have you found her yet?"

"Not yet. I'm on the fourth floor, still looking."

"Okay. I'll let you take the third floor, and I'll just wait outside Rebekah's room when I finish my check."

"Roger that," Niko said, setting the radio aside.

"What's going on?" Leslie asked.

"Rebekah, that girl that Robert knows, is missing," Niko said. "That's what I was doing here in the first place. Look, before I go, I have one more question, but it's a long shot."

"Okay?" Leslie donned a quizzical look.

"Does this place have a basement?"

Leslie's brows furrowed in thought. "Uh, actually, I think there is. I've never seen it, but I've heard Stuart mention a basement to Maggie."

"No shit," Niko said, his mind flying into overdrive. "Okay. That's all I have. I'll let you guys get back to…whatever. But seriously, you guys are young. Use a rubber. Don't fuck your lives up."

Leslie blushed, turning to Jason, who sat uninterested in his window perch. Niko grabbed the radio from the floor and clipped it to his belt. Throwing the tarp aside, he made his way from the construction area back to the stairwell. Doing his due diligence, he searched the third floor but held no expectations of finding Rebekah. Something seemed off.

27

THE MAN

THE GIRL WAS HEAVIER than she looked, making it difficult to handle her with any sort of grace. But the man maneuvered his way through the hallway with Rebekah hanging over his shoulder. After all, he had handled far bigger victims than her. But he was weak, more so than what age alone had done to him. Despite it all, he powered through, focused solely on reaching his destination as quickly and discreetly as possible. He supposed the power outage worked in his favor. As much as it was an obstacle, it acted as a blessing as well. And the pitch-black stairwell certainly proved to be an impediment—he nearly lost his footing several times.

The stark contrast of the brightly lit lobby as he exited the darkened stairwell took a moment to adjust to. Muffled voices exited the office behind the reception desk, causing him to power across the entrance and into the darkened diner. Robert spoke to someone, likely the cop, about finding the girl. Without hesitation, he rushed through the diner to avoid being seen. Everything hinged on discretion. With the detective lurking around, the stakes were especially high. Freedom from the burden of his otherworldly passenger, the voice in his head and the hand that corrupted his mind, was coming to fruition. Though that presence had been more frequent as of late. He envied his partner for that reward of peace.

Through the rain-stippled windows of the diner, the first glimpse of sunrise colored the horizon. The clouds had cleared, and the rain was mild; the storm was coming to an end. Pushing though the saloon-style doors of the kitchen, he navigated the darkness as one familiar with the landscape. Vague silhouettes of appliances and tables haunted the space, but he made his way to the light switch with deft movements. He requested that the kitchen lights be tied into the backup generator but was unaware if that task had been completed. With bated breath, he flipped the switch and was greeted by the satisfying buzz of the fluorescents and a brightly lit room. The man smiled.

Dire pain erupted in his skull as the hand coiled around his head. Rage poured from the presence like magma, dripping from it and cooling on the surface beneath.

You have the girl? Nox asked.

Yes, yes, I have her, the man replied.

Strange…I do not feel the Guardian's presence around her as I had before.

Setting the girl down on the age-worn tiled floor, hesitating to be sure she was still unconscious, he unlocked and unlatched the freezer door, fumbling with the key and lock in his hand. Rolling the storage carts aside to access the floor panel, he raised the hatch, exposing access steps with a grooved slide notched into the sides.

Should we not proceed? Is she not the one?

Prepare the girl, and call the other, the voice commanded.

Why do we need him?

Because I feel how weak this body is. You do not have the strength to wield the blade.

Then, why not summon him yourself? A pang of spite decorated the man's voice, something he regretted the moment the words escaped his mouth.

Your friend is refusing me, Nox said as anger pulsed through him, causing heat to scour the man's skull.

He snarled in pain, clenching his jaw to suppress a scream. *How? How is that possible?*

Nox fumed. *He has found a way. But if you wish to keep your mind intact, you will summon him and finish this task.*

With another hesitant glance toward Rebekah, he disappeared into the basement and retrieved a type of gurney he mounted to the grooves—an invention of his own.

There is much to be done, the man said. *The girl has murdered several others. If we do not—*

Yes, the Guardian acts through her, Nox said. *Much like how I act through you. That was not a strength born from the girl. You need not worry.*

But if the Guardian—

He cannot harm you whilst I protect you.

But about the girl, the man persisted. *The mess she's left behind. We need to dispose of—*

Pain brought him to his knees as Nox tightened his grip. *I care not for what petty troubles you bear! Prepare the room, and summon your friend.*

Lifting the girl back onto his shoulder, an uncomfortable tightness gripped his lower back as he stood. Shifting the weight to his legs and moving the strain to his upper thighs, he hoisted her up and carried her to the gurney. His legs were weak under the tense muscles, and he dropped the girl, hard, onto the gurney and paused. He worried his misstep would rouse her. Strapping her in, he made his way down the steps first, then gently eased the gurney down behind him. Unstrapping her, he carried her to the next room, where a table rested in the center, close to the drainage trough. The warmth from the lit furnace was stifling after his exertion, but his work was not over yet.

Glancing around the room, a sense of languor came over him as he remembered it needed to be prepped. It wasn't his usual task. Shaking off the sensation, he bound Rebekah's ankles together with duct tape. He did the same just above her knees. Finally, he retrieved a pair of cloth-lined manacles, aged but sturdy, and bound her wrists. Using the chain, he raised her onto a meat hook until her feet barely toed the ground.

"You've left quite a mess behind," he mused while he labored.

"Unfortunate. It's more work for us with that detective stalking the halls. Best to kill him and be done with it, but that's not my decision to make. Still, I don't envy your fate."

Gathering supplies, he brought them to the workbench near Rebekah. Thinking and counting the rolls of plastic sheeting, he shrugged and continued. *Less than I need, but I can make do.*

"If it were up to me, I'd cut your throat right now. Spill all that pretty blood over the floor and deal with the mess later. Or not. We could leave the mess, including the one you made, and just run off. We've labored at this task far too long, and I want the life I had back. This one has far too many rules."

The man pressed his face between her breasts and inhaled, glancing up to the girl's unconscious eyes. Thoughts ran through his mind of what he would do to her and what he wanted to do to her sister. However, the torture he'd endured for questioning the rules soured his thoughts, and his face twisted into a scowl.

"Not long now," he said. "Not long."

He slid his hand along her flesh, goosebumps crawling across his own, and stepped away. The desire was strong, but the fear of retaliation from the others—from Nox in particular—deflated his lust. He had much to attend to still.

The room contained two doorways branching off to other rooms. The fluorescents there hadn't been added to the grid since they had to keep the area removed from the blueprints. They had only the original emergency lights to rely on—those and the fire from the furnace as well as a solitary light exposing the trophies along the pegboard. It was enough to work by. Retreating to the stairs, he closed the access panel, concealing the workshop, before moving through the space to the storage room to gather more supplies. Returning to the workbench, he retrieved a radio from its charging dock and dialed channel three.

"Who's on?" he asked. Static garbled when he released the talk button.

"What do you need?" a male voice responded.

"Deep clean. Room 232. Three men, carpet removal, sanitize.

We have a detective scouring the building, so be quick and be discrete."

After a moment, the radio hissed again. "On it."

28

NIKO

EVERY STEP OF THE investigation created a litany of questions rather than answers. Niko's theory evolved, transformed, and eventually branched into layered thoughts. But one thing he was certain of was the Armitage was the axis around which all evidence revolved. The *who* began to take many shapes, and the names he provided Brindle started to seem less like a suspect list and more like a list of accomplices. Still, a wrench remained in the gears, begging the question, the only thing that broke all other theories apart, why the gap? For that, he was absent even speculation. But suspicions nagged at him, somewhere out of reach and hidden in the dark.

Lost in his thoughts, he wandered the third floor, lacking any situational awareness. It wasn't until the plastic tarp sectioning off the construction area brushed against his face, jolting him from his musing, he returned to reality. His flashlight ignited the opaque sheet, casting a brilliant but hazy glow that nearly blinded him, so he clicked it off.

Rubbing his eyes, heat flushed his face from embarrassment, and tiny black spots—*fishies*—darted behind his lids. His sight cleared, and a faint light shone beyond the tarp, illuminating a silhouette. Massaging his eyes once more, certain enervation was the culprit for his hallucination, he looked again.

There was, without a doubt, the vague shape of a person in the shadows.

"Niko," a voice whispered.

Ripping the Glock from its holster, he gently pushed his way through the tarp. He clicked his light, but nothing happened. Giving his hand a rough shake, the battery within clanking against the metal casing, he tried again but still nothing.

"Who's there?" he called to the dark silhouette, easing his gun up and employing the Harries Technique again, despite the light being out.

Succumbing to his irrational fear that the silhouette was more phantom than person, he stopped. Two beads of light resembling eyes shone in the darkness.

You're losing it, he thought to himself. *Get your shit together.*

"Who are you?" he asked again.

The figure didn't move, even as he cautiously approached. Gently sliding his feet along the floor, he brushed aside debris and construction hardware. The cadence of the *swish-thump* of his steps unnerved him in the still space.

The whisper came again. "She needs your help."

"Who needs my help?" he asked, his police training kicking in. More to calm himself than anything. "Just tell me where they are, and we can go help them."

The statuesque shadow couldn't have been more than ten feet from him, resembling a child in a hoodie. Still, the figure was shrouded in darkness, and he couldn't discern any features.

Just a kid lost in the hotel, he rationalized.

"They have her…" the voice whispered.

The unyielding calmness panicked him, sending goosebumps across his flesh. Swallowing hard, his steps slowed as if the figure warded him off, and an uneasy feeling crept up his back.

Suddenly, his light shot on, and he nearly jerked the trigger in shock. Easing his grip on the pistol, he exhaled sharply, releasing his tension with the breath. A vacuum cleaner with a hoodie hanging from it sat in the hall. His light danced off the chrome shaft of the machine, and he couldn't help but laugh.

Lowering his weapon, he ripped the sweatshirt down and tossed it aside. Sticking the gun back in its holster, he shook his head incredulously. Relief flooded his mind, but a flush of humiliation accompanied it. Fatigue had impaired his judgement, despite his battle against it. That was how he justified it, anyway.

A metal clang drew his attention back to the construction tarp, which wavered slightly, and the sound of footsteps disappeared into the distance. Without thought, he took off, and though he was sure it was exhaustion drumming up yet another hallucination, he chased the echoing footfalls.

"Stop!" he shouted.

The muted pattering of footsteps tramping the carpet sounded around the corner before the tinny whine of door hinges wailed through the corridor. Cutting the corner past the elevators, his light swung before him, bringing the hall into view just in time to see the stairwell door clicking closed. Ripping it open and throwing the flashlight beam into the dark space, Niko's heart stopped. There was a foot rounding the corner of the steps, pale and dirt-speckled. The pungent odor of sulfur contaminated the air, something rotten—like death.

He rushed down the stairs, chasing the sound of the door from the floor below as it slammed closed. A maniacal cackle echoed in the hall beyond. Niko slowed as he approached the door and retrieved his Glock once again. Slowly easing out of the confined stairwell, he shone his light through the crack in the door before exiting completely. There was no sign or sound of life. He turned to the left, knowing the elevator lobby was in that direction, but a whisper in his head told him it was the wrong way.

Swinging in the other direction, he found a large commercial trash bin heavily lined with plastic set beside a rolling tool cart, much like the one he had seen on the fourth floor. As he approached the supplies, a solitary thought ran through his mind.

Why is this here?

Using the light, he surveyed the hall in both directions, but he was alone. Desperate for a bearing, he examined the ceiling and floor for any sign of construction work. As an act of providence, his light glinted off dark, wet footprints staining the carpet. Reaching down, he pressed on one of the marks. Blood seeped onto his fingers. Maneuvering his flashlight, he followed the path of prints toward the elevator but stopped. Instead, he traced them back, finding them disappearing beyond the door to Room 232, where the trash bin and cart sat. Examining the supplies on the tool cart, he found nothing bizarre, but a familiar smell hit him.

Hovering the light over the trash bin, he found thick, black plastic bags inside. Lifting one, the weight was surprising. He untied the knot that sealed the bag, and the odor that poured out made him cough and gag. Moving his light back to the trash, his jaw dropped. The interior plastic was splattered with blood, and within, sitting atop various other carnage, was a severed arm.

Niko covered his nose, using the wrist of his flashlight hand, and glanced up and down the hallway again. Had he stumbled across the killer in the act? If so, they couldn't be far. Niko shone the beam back on Room 232. His thoughts returned to the person he was chasing, considering they may have been a victim. When the door swung open, shock riddled the face of Robert Wymer as the light swam over him. Blood ornamented the rubber smock he wore.

The air was still, like the calm before a storm. Commotion sounded from within the room. At least one other person was with Robert, unaware of the gravity of the collision of fate that had befallen them.

"Robert, close the door," a voice said, and it was one Niko recognized. *Jim.*

"Niko!" Robert gasped.

He leveled his gun at the hotel owner, and Robert threw his hands up, dropping a black trash bag Niko could only assume carried another body part. Just over Robert's shoulder, a bloody handprint decorated the wall.

"Back," Niko said, filling his voice with as much severity as he could muster.

Robert immediately moved back. As the light poured into the room, the grisly scene came into view, and two men froze in fear. Jason, the guy who had been having sex with Leslie, had been removing the bedsheets, while Jim and Robert disposed of the bodies. Bloodied footprints decorated the tiled entryway, a small puddle of blood eked from the carpet over the tiles, and remnants of various other bodies littered the room. The kills were fresh.

"What the fuck?" Niko asked, eyeing the room in horror. "What the fuck did you do?"

To his left, Jason jolted, making a move at Niko, but he swung the gun in his direction and fired a solitary round above the man's head, stopping him where he stood. Jason's face wasn't filled with surprise or fear but anger. Niko motioned with the gun for him to move toward the balcony, where the other two men had congregated. As the light maneuvered over, Niko got a good look at the three of them.

"You guys are in a world of shit," he said.

"This isn't what it looks like," Robert replied.

"Looks like three men in wading suits, disposing of four... maybe five...brutalized bodies, and judging by the footprints, I'd say one of your potential victims got away."

"Victim?" Jason scoffed. "She's the—"

"Shut it, boy," Jim snapped.

"I had my suspicions about you, Robert," Niko said. "Nearly thirty years of unsolved missing persons cases, and I had a feeling they were connected. You've been murdering innocent people for thirty years."

"That's a damn lie!" Robert snapped, dropping his arms and coiling his fists.

"You're standing in a pool of blood with your partners in tow. Good luck convincing a jury you're innocent, Robert. And Jim, you look a little pale."

"I've never killed anyone," Jim said. "My boy and I just work construction."

"Boy?" Niko's eyes flicked toward Jason. "Ah, father and son business. I suppose you'll tell me this is his first time as well. You just happened to have rubber wading suits on hand in case there was a last-minute construction emergency."

"You don't know what you're—"

"I said shut it, boy," Jim snarled again.

Niko surveyed the room, and a thought occurred to him. No sooner did it hit him than Robert spoke.

"What's your move now?" Robert asked. "You got no handcuffs, no backup. You can't shoot us."

"Make another move, and I'll have no choice," Niko said.

But Robert was right. Three killers stood before him, accomplices at the very least, and he had no way of detaining or holding them. He racked his brain, but he wasn't familiar with the hotel, and he couldn't trust moving them through the dark. There was no radio to call for backup, his cellphone was in his room (which wouldn't matter because the reception would still be shit), and the landlines in the rooms were dead. He couldn't let any of the men go, nor could he show them he had few options. He had to get them talking.

"Where is she?" Niko shifted his light over to Robert.

He scrunched his face stupidly. "Who?"

"The girl!" Niko screamed. "Don't act fucking stupid. Rebekah. Where is she?"

"The hell if I know," Robert barked. "I'd love to find out since she's the one who did all this."

An amused chortle escaped before Niko could stop it. "That's why you're here cleaning up, is it? Because a teenage girl, who couldn't be more than a hundred pounds, gruesomely murdered five much larger boys?"

"This wasn't us," Robert said, a stern look adorning his face.

"But Nicole...That was you."

Robert sighed. Beads of sweat caught the light as they glided down his forehead.

"Thirty years, Robert," Niko noted. "And I know it's not just you. Maggie and Stuart will share the punishment. I imagine the only reason you lasted so long was because of local police support. Someone like Rossi. Like a merry village of fucking psychopaths."

At that point, he was speculating, using the various pieces of data he had collected and hoping to rouse them into confessing or revealing more.

"David's reports were ignorantly devoid of information, too much so to be benign neglect. I figured he had to be hiding something or covering for someone—his childhood friends maybe. I imagine his suicide was out of guilt or fear of being discovered when the cold cases were revisited.

"Now, with Jim and his boy Jason. Halder is it? As in Halder Construction? Robert didn't trust anyone else to work on this hotel, and after seeing the basement you redlined from the drawings, likely when the county started requiring inspections and permits for renovations, I can imagine why. You're not fooling anyone anymore, so I'll ask again. Where is Rebekah?"

Jim bobbed his mouth, but his eyes fixed on Niko, but Robert cut in. "He can't do anything to us. He's just trying to fish for information. His word. That's all he has."

The room was silent as the three men stared at Niko with a mixture of unease and anger. Every moment of silence was another moment wasted. Niko had to guess Rebekah was with Maggie or Stuart, and the section of hotel he had seen on the blueprints was likely where they were holding her, assuming she was still alive. Room 232 was an anomaly, and he was inclined to believe Robert wasn't responsible. It made sense they had to clean the mess to avoid the search that would inevitably follow, which would uncover all their dirty secrets. But he also didn't believe Rebekah could be responsible for, or even capable of, the gruesome scene before him.

It was clear none of the men would provide an answer. But a crazed, exhaustion-fueled plan formed in his head. It was unstable and likely wouldn't work, but time was slipping away, and he needed to act.

"Give me your master key, Robert," Niko demanded.

"What?" Robert's voice wavered.

"The master key. Set it on the edge of the dresser here."

Robert fished the key ring from his pocket with a shaky hand and limped toward Niko. He tossed the keys onto the wooden top, and they nearly slid off the edge. They stopped when they hit Robert's cane leaning against the piece of furniture. Niko motioned for Robert to move away before collecting the keys.

He worked his way back to the door, keeping his gun poised at the three men. Propping it open, he moved to the tool cart and seized a hammer. Returning to the room, he used the hammer to break the interior handle off the door. It was more difficult than he imagined, trying to monitor the three men in case they attacked. When the metal handle clanked onto the tile floor, Jason laughed.

"This is stupid," the kid said. "The balcony is right there. We're on the second floor. We can just jump down."

"Goddamnit, shut up," Jim said, shooting a crazed look at his son.

"Maybe you can, Jason," Niko said. "But Robert has arthritis and a bum leg, and your dad looks like he's pushing seventy. I doubt they'd make the jump. Even if they did, none of you would make it very far. The entire bureau will be looking for you. Speaking of which…"

Niko snatched Robert's cane. Closing the door, he grabbed a power drill from the tool cart and drove four screws through the frame from floor to ceiling. He could only hope it would contain them, but he was pessimistic. As an added measure of security, he rolled the cart to the door, which was just tall enough to pin under the lever handle. He figured it would prevent them from being able to turn it.

He dabbed at the sweat forming along his brow, examined his handy work for a moment, and then made for the stairs. Reaching the bright lights of the lobby, he hesitated. It was quiet, quieter than he remembered, and he could see the orange sunrise peeking through the windows. The storm was over. Good. He turned toward the reception desk and made for the back office to make a call.

29

REBEKAH

CONSCIOUSNESS DANCED ON THE fringes of Rebekah's mind, wavering in and out. Muffled voices, sharp and argumentative, clawed their way into focus, but the words were indecipherable, distorted by the murky haze. The darkness receded, giving way to flickering glimpses of light, casting eerie shadows that lent form to the figures engaged in their heated debate. A groan escaped Rebekah's lips, a feeble protest against the raging torment in her brain.

Her hands were bound above her head, and the cold iron shackles bit into her flesh. Dangling above the floor, a foot barely scraping the hard surface, her wrists were tender, near breaking from her binds. The fabric that separated her skin from the cold metal offered little solace, and her shoulders ached from the weight of her unconscious body. The relentless throbbing in her head shattered any coherent thought, leaving only excruciating agony in its wake.

"Where am I?" she croaked, her voice a mere whisper in the oppressive silence. She didn't know who remained to hear since the silhouettes had vanished. "What happened?"

The room remained still, punctuated only by the faint clinking of chains and the low, guttural hum of the furnace. Rebekah's eyes scanned the space, drawn to a single light illuminating a workbench. Above it, a pegboard displayed an array of trinkets, a chilling tableau of souvenirs and an echo from her vision. The centerpiece, the amulet, was absent. On the bench top, the praesagium stone glistened, its reflection playing with the flickering flames of the furnace. They had stolen it from her pocket—her own contribution to the mosaic of mementos.

Rylos, she spoke in her mind. *The amulet is gone. It's not here.*

She squirmed, desperate to free herself from the unforgiving grip of the binds. The rough, splintered metal tore into her flesh, releasing rivulets of warm blood that trailed down her arms. With each twist and turn, she gritted her teeth, biting back the searing pain.

Rylos, she called once more.

She probed deeper but found nothing. No comforting presence, no guiding voice. She was utterly alone. The absence of Rylos brought a chilling sense of isolation, a haunting reminder of the depths of her solitude. Fear clawed at her, intertwining with the memories of his anguished screams. Had she drained him of his energy? Had she killed him?

A pang of sadness welled up within her, constricting her throat. But amidst the sorrow, a resolute determination ignited. She wouldn't surrender to despair. With a burst of strength, she twisted her wrists once more, ignoring the spurs of the shackles sinking deeper into her palms as her wrists inched closer to freedom. The pain was sharp and focused, and she clenched her jaw against the frightened, negative voice in her head. Her right arm slipped free and fell limply to her side, allowing her to plant a foot firmly on the ground. Droplets of blood splattered the plastic sheeting beneath her, a testament to her tenacity and the price she paid for her freedom.

Examining her hand, she found deep gouges running over the pads of her palm. She traced them along the outside edge to the knuckle of her pinky. The back of her hand bore smaller cuts, but she disregarded the pain, clenching her fist and testing its mobility. Satisfied, she steeled her nerves, preparing to free her other hand. Persistent determination surged within her like an unyielding flame, urging her forward.

The screech of hinges jolted her senses, and a beam of light sliced through the darkness, illuminating the floor just beyond the doorway. A shadow materialized, accompanied by the clap of footsteps on metal. Rebekah's heart raced as she raised her right arm, gripping the chain of the shackle, hoping her progress would go unnoticed.

As the figure rounded the corner, a sinking feeling washed over her. It was Stuart, his head bowed, softly humming a mournful tune. He carried a small bag, his movements deliberate. Oblivious to Rebekah's presence, he approached the workbench and unzipped the bag, revealing an assortment of tools. His humming abruptly ceased when he met Rebekah's gaze and her open, watchful eyes.

"No," he said. "No, it's too soon."

He whipped back around and unsheathed a needle and small vial. Extracting the clear liquid with deft precision, he discarded the empty container and flicked the needle.

"Stuart?" Rebekah asked once the fog of shock dissipated. "It…it was you? You're the one…My sister…"

"It is too soon," Stuart repeated.

Brandishing the needle, he inched toward her. A sudden pressure gripped Rebekah's mind, an oppressive hand stealing control. Her arm shot down and gripped Stuart's throat, lifting him from the ground.

"Butcher" a gravelly voice snarled from Rebekah's mouth.

Stuart's eyes shot open. Fear expanded his pupils as he garbled out an incoherent rattle. Rebekah pulled him closer to her face, but every fiber of muscle lay beyond her control. His feet kicked in a feeble attempt to find the ground. The man struggled beneath the grip of her fingers, the echoes traveling up the branch of her arm, but she had no control of her body. The presence was similar to Rylos's, only hot with rage and teeming with power. There was something deeply corrupt pulsing within his presence.

"I'm sorry," Stuart managed through choking breaths. "I…I… tried. I can't…"

Rebekah's eyes flicked down at a glint on Stuart's chest. The presence inside of her, no doubt Nox, swelled with rage as her fingers eased their grip on the man only to tighten again around the leather strap of the necklace. Stuart fell, and the leather strap broke. Hanging before Rebekah was the amulet, the Heart of Idromir.

Get out of my head. Rebekah rallied to no avail.

The Reaper examined the necklace through her eyes. His demeanor momentarily softened before a surge of rage engulfed him once again. Rebekah found the presence in her mind, something tangible, and pushed back, attempting to dispel it. Instead, she touched Nox's consciousness. In an instant, a vision consumed her akin to the power of the praesagium stone, and she was transported.

Through Stuart's eyes, she observed her sister being stalked and studied. A young Rebekah was also there. Nox's voice echoed through the man's head, poisoning his mind and commanding him to seize Nicole.

She's the one I need, he had said. *I sense the presence of the Guardian. She possesses the amulet. It is her.*

Darkness enveloped the scene as nightfall approached. They dragged Nicole into the room, tearing her clothes from her. She fought back, but another man whose face was obscured by the shadows struck her over and over again until she stopped fighting. Whimpering pleas and desperate cries for mercy filled the air as he placed her on the table. Stuart remained idle, a passive observer, as the man continued his macabre work.

"You could help," the man said, his voice heaving.

"Retrieving the target is your responsibility. It always has been," Stuart replied.

"Things change."

"After you abandoned us, didn't you have to hunt your prey, Hank? Or is it Roger? Or any of the other aliases you frequent."

"You know what? Fuck you!" the man retorted, his face concealed by the room's shadows. "It's because of you that I'm caught up in this mess again. Everything was perfect until you sent your…" He tapped his temple with a finger. "Friend."

"He's our friend now," Stuart calmly maintained. "And you're not the only one trapped in this. I was happy to leave this life behind. Now, let us finish this."

Stuart fetched a bucket of soapy water, and both men proceeded to sponge Nicole's body. Stuart hesitated when he reached the leather strap of the amulet.

"Why are we doing this again?" the man inquired. "Killing them would be so much easier. What's the point of cleaning her off?"

"There is safety in taking precautions," Stuart replied as he carefully retrieved the amulet from beneath Nicole's shoulder.

The man scoffed and resumed scrubbing, focusing the brunt of his efforts on Nicole's breasts and between her legs.

Slipping the necklace over her head, Stuart briefly admired it, relishing the glimmering lights dancing off its glossy surface.

"No," Nicole weakly whispered.

"Silence," Stuart commanded.

Placing the amulet aside, he retrieved a burled-wood box and extracted a blade resembling white opal, set in a handle carved from a fragment of bone.

"What's that?" the man inquired.

"This is the blade we must use—the one Nox provided."

They secured Nicole to the table, inverting it so her head hung over a drainage trough. Without hesitation, Stuart swiped the blade through Nicole's neck.

He watched, and Rebekah watched through his eyes, as the color drained from Nicole's skin. Bulging eyes stared back at him. With a final surge of energy fueled by adrenaline, she fought against the restraints that tightly bound her naked body. Panic filled Nicole's eyes. Rebekah watched, her sister gazing back at her, as the life force within her faded. And then, the vision receded into the distance, returning Rebekah to her own body.

Fury consumed her, and she unleashed her pent-up rage. She fought with all her strength, battling against the creature's iron grip, but it held her tighter than Rylos ever had. In that moment, she began to grasp what Rylos meant by his own weakness. His power, impressive as it was, paled in comparison to this...

From the floor, Stuart struggled to his feet, clutching his throat, desperately trying to catch his breath. With a dismissive gesture, Nox cast the amulet aside, and it careened onto the cluttered workbench, bouncing off the bag of tools and landing on a folded cloth.

As Stuart rose, a wicked smile creased his face. In a blink, he jabbed the needle into Rebekah's neck, and the frigid liquid surged through her veins. But instead of despair, Nox etched a sly grin onto Rebekah's face. Suddenly, the pressure that had weighed on her mind slithered away. The oppressive presence vanished, and with it, her smile. Stuart's eyes widened, and darkness consumed all color within his irises. Moments later, he crumpled to the floor, shrieking and writhing in agony.

Freed from Nox's insidious influence, Rebekah summoned her last reserves of strength and pulled once more, wrenching her remaining wrist free. Excruciating pain shot through her arm, and warm blood trickled from her fresh wounds, but at last, her arm slipped free, and she crashed to the ground, gasping for air as the impact stole her breath away. Clutching her throbbing hand to her chest, she coughed, fighting to fill her lungs with air.

Struggling to her knees, she attempted to rise, but her legs betrayed her. She grasped onto the edge of the table, her feet sliding over the blood-splattered sheeting, her own crimson handiwork. She fought for balance. Once she gained stable footing, she made her way to the workbench and retrieved the amulet and the stone, ensuring she kept a safe distance from Stuart's writhing form.

Turning her gaze to the column of light beckoning from the adjacent room, she stumbled forward on unsteady legs, navigating the treacherous path of slick plastic. Falling onto the doorframe, clutching it for support, she surveyed the room ahead. Stuart's tortured screams echoed behind her, his desperate apologies ringing hollow. No doubt Nox was exacting vengeance for his betrayal. Her knees quivered as whatever drug Stuart injected her with coursed through her veins, draining of her strength.

Moving into the room, her breath began to return, easing the pressure on her chest, but the drug robbed her legs of their vitality. Leaning against an open plastic drum that emitted a putrid stench, she recoiled. The word "Fertilizer" was scrawled across its surface, though all she could see inside was a gritty white powder. Shaking off the unsettling thought, she reminded herself to stay focused as she maneuvered toward the beckoning light—a radiant beacon from above the steep metallic staircase. Clinging to the rail for support, she ascended the steps as quickly as her waning strength allowed.

Emerging from the cramped darkness, she found herself standing behind the door of a meat freezer. The coldness enveloped her, though not as chilling as she would have thought. Tugging at the latch and slamming her shoulder against the door, it wouldn't budge. Again, she tried, and again, her frustration mounted. She pounded her fist against the unyielding barricade and cried for help. Through the tiny window of frosted glass, she caught a glimpse of the barren kitchen of the diner—a place she remembered from her childhood. Maggie used to let her sit there, watching her as she diced vegetables while her parents and the police searched for Nicole.

Her emotions caught in her throat at the memory, realizing who was truly responsible for her sister's death. She hammered on the door once more, though impaired by the insidious effects of the drug. Leaning against the unforgiving metal, its icy touch seeping into her flesh, she cried. Reyja's words circled her head: *You are broken, child. Broken by those who have claimed to love you and those who sought to help you.*

Suddenly, the door swung open, and Maggie stood over her. Her expression, first an amalgamation of confusion and annoyance, shifted to something resembling concern.

"Oh my God," she said, helping Rebekah up from the ground. "What are you doing here?"

Anger surged within Rebekah, shattering the fragile façade of politeness she had once worn. "You," she hissed, locking eyes with Maggie. "You killed her."

Maggie's friendly, empathetic face transformed into one

of darkness and malice. Without uttering a single word, she gripped the freezer frame, planting her foot against Rebekah's chest, propelling her backward down the stairs. Rebekah's hands desperately clung to the shelves, causing them to topple over, sending plastic containers and metal tins crashing to the floor. Her arm collided with the unforgiving freezer floor as she tumbled into the access opening, and a searing pain shot through her. The ridged metal steps struck her shoulder, spinning her head over heels until she crashed to the floor below, plunging her into unconsciousness as her head collided with the hard surface.

30

NIKO

NIKO CONSULTED THE BLUEPRINTS in Robert's office, attempting to determine where the entrance to the basement area was. The plans were weathered and faded. Time in storage, coupled with the aged printing, gave the finer details a hazy, blurred appearance. Between exhaustion and the close face examination under a bright flashlight, Niko's eyes became dry and sore, causing his vision to wane in and out.

That's just great, he thought, rubbing his eyes in frustration.

Locating a symbol he assumed indicated an elevation transition, the entrance rested somewhere in the kitchen of the diner. Not unexpected, but he couldn't discern an exact location. He flipped through more recent drawings, comparing them with the old to try and place the marker. The kitchen had seen a wide array of improvements in the last few decades, making it hard to line up where the entrance could be.

Pressed for time, he pushed off the desk, hoping that seeing the layout in person would give him a better idea. A creeping fear sank into his heart he would be too late, turning his thoughts to the officers he had failed. Shunning away visions of Rebekah's mutilated body, much like what he'd found in Room 232, he exited the office and bumped into Leslie at the reception desk. She sported a black eye and busted lip, which she quickly tried to hide by turning her face away.

"What happened to you?" Niko asked.

Tears wet her eyes before she started speaking. "Jason."

"What did he do?" Niko guided her to a chair.

"He wasn't happy that I talked to you...so he hit me." She shifted her eyes away from Niko's. "I don't know what I did wrong. He just started beating me, telling me I shouldn't have done that."

She broke down crying, covering her face with her hands. Niko studied her a moment before his more vulnerable compassions broke down, and he brought her into his arms. He rubbed her back as she sobbed into his shoulder. However, the weight of time slipping away blanketed over him, forcing a focus shift. Grabbing Leslie by the shoulders, he held her at arm's length, staring into her wide, fearful eyes.

"Leslie, there's something I need to do. Can you stay here?"

"What?" she said, wiping the tears away.

"I have to go."

"But..." she protested, her eyes glancing around fretfully.

"Jason isn't going to bother you," Niko replied.

Leslie nodded apprehensively and eased back into the chair, clasping her hands in her lap. Niko spared a final glance, and a pang of guilt touched him for her suffering. Catching the swollen cheek beneath her darkened eye and the split skin on her lip he was ultimately responsible for reminded him of the negatives of a heavy-handed approach. His carelessness had avoided him, to some degree, but it had been redirected to others. He shuffled away from the reception desk and beyond the elevators.

In the diner, the rising sun cast oblong shadows off the tables and chairs, obscuring the shape of the room. In the light of sunrise, save for the boarded-up window, there was no evidence of the chaotic scene that had transpired only hours ago, leaving Henry gravely injured. No glass shards or umbrella. The chairs and tables had been reorganized. And there was no trace of residue from the carnage Henry had left behind.

The fleeting memory of the event graced Niko's mind, and he realized his actions then were not marred with his anxiety.

A situation arose, and he responded. Despite not having the knowledge, he had worked to save a man's life, and that filled him with a measure of pride and bolstered his confidence.

A loud crash drew his attention to the kitchen, where beyond the closed and locked takeout window gate, the lights were on. Glancing around the diner at the dead overheads, the thought occurred to him the kitchen power might have been tied into the backup generator.

I'm getting close, he thought. *But why would the kitchen lights be tied in and not the freezer?*

He eased his gun from its holster and dropped his flashlight in his pocket. As he pushed open the saloon doors to the kitchen, he heard another heavy door slam shut, causing him to duck and halt, listening for movement.

Satisfied with the silence that followed, he stood and glided through the kitchen quietly, checking the corners and ensuring he kept his back to a wall. The space had been thoroughly cleaned, save for the slick, tiled floors, which held a persistent oily layer—a culmination of grease that had compounded over the years.

He approached the freezer door and peered through the window. Toppled shelves mounted over a mass of spilled food and overturned containers sat inside. But beyond the mess, he found an open access panel in the floor, exposing the basement. Jerking the lever handle, the freezer door opened with a wispy breath of air, warmer than he would have expected. A stale aroma, bordering the scent of rotten food, invaded his nostrils. The room had been used often.

It took a good deal of effort to navigate the slick puddles of food and scattered containers while stepping over and between the heavy metal shelving. He nearly lost his footing when he reached the access panel, catching himself on the wall while staring down the steep steps to the dark basement. He held his position for a moment as he worried that the metal clank of the gun against the wall may have alerted whoever was down there.

But as silence settled, he heard muffled voices from below that seemed undisturbed by his embarrassing lack of dexterity. He could blame it on his sleep deprivation, and it may have played a part, but sadly, the gaucherie wasn't out of pocket. Composing himself, and maneuvering back into a stable position, he cautiously descended the stairs. At the base sat a packaging room. Only faintly lit from the kitchen above and a few emergency lights, it was hard to make out much. A doorway sat to the right, covered by a sheet of hazy plastic, behind which the voices argued.

"This is unnecessary," the woman hissed. "Just get it over with. Slit her throat and be done with it."

"No," the man argued. "I have a process, and it has kept us out of the spotlight so far. There is no reason to get careless now."

"Careless?" the woman barked back. "She nearly escaped. If not for me, she would have. Then what?"

"I had given her a half dose of ketamine already. She wasn't going anywhere."

Niko crept as silently as he could, closer to the plastic sheeting where three silhouettes could be seen, lit by a large fire deeper in the room. An industrial furnace, he guessed.

They're cremating the bodies.

"There's a damn detective snooping around, so we don't have time for your obsession over details. Just fucking do it already."

"Stop," Niko said as he pushed through the tarp, gun drawn.

31

REBEKAH

REBEKAH'S MIND FOUGHT AGAINST the sedative's grasp, clawing its way back to consciousness. Harsh, hissing whispers dragged her from the void. Struggling to focus, she saw Maggie and Stuart locked in a tense exchange, but the words remained distant, shrouded in a fog of confusion.

From the shadows, Niko emerged, his grip firm on his gun. His presence embodied that of a sentinel. He barked the order to stop, and Maggie jumped while Stuart concealed himself behind Rebekah, pressing a knife to her throat. The blade bit into her flesh, and the threat became all too real. Once again bound at the wrist and suspended on the meat hook, she dangled helplessly. Her body was limp from whatever concoction they had pumped into her veins, leaving her like a puppet on a string.

"Put the gun down!" Maggie seized her own knife from Stuart's assortment.

Niko, his voice level and unwavering, tried to reason with Maggie, but she was a tempest, a force of malevolence with nothing left to lose. Depravity shone in the depths of her eyes, reinforcing her will. The walls of the room seemed to close in, suffocating everyone as the tension tightened like a noose around their throats.

"This doesn't need to get out of hand," Niko said, unyielding behind his gun.

"I'm not going to jail." Maggie's voice was as steadfast as the detective's.

Niko's measured steps brought him closer, his voice steady and resolute. But Maggie's unwavering resolve sliced through the room like an icy blade.

"Think, Maggie," Niko implored. "This doesn't have to end in bloodshed. Let her go."

"We're beyond that, detective," Maggie said, brandishing the blade at Rebekah, its sharp tip threatening to puncture her flesh. "Someone here will die. Will it be you? Or her?"

Her voice cut through the silence, a venomous vow that sent chills down Rebekah's spine. Niko's calm demeanor belied the urgency of the situation, but Rebekah knew he was strategizing, searching for any opening to resolve the nightmare.

Stuart's trembling hand illustrated the dichotomy, betraying his façade of cold-blooded composure. He had heartlessly taken Rebekah's sister's life, but he quivered when faced with his own mortality. Rebekah knew the darkness within him was far worse than any fear she might feel.

Relentless, Niko inched ever forward, maneuvering around the table, drawing closer to get a bead on Stuart, who cowered behind Rebekah.

"Calm down," Niko said, his tone flat. "Don't do anything rash—"

"If you want her dead, then by all means take another step," Maggie interrupted. "I'll cut her fucking throat myself."

In that moment, Rebekah saw the raw truth of the situation. It wasn't about reasoning. It was about survival. There was no room for negotiation when lives hung in the balance. Niko's gun remained steady, his eyes steadfast, but Rebekah's heart pounded with uncertainty, never more aware of her vulnerability. In their perilous dance, one wrong move could lead to irreversible consequences.

"What's it gonna be, Niko?" Maggie pressed the blade tighter against Rebekah's throat, drawing a thin line of blood.

Niko stopped. The room held its breath, teetering on the edge of catastrophe. The taste of danger hung thick in the air. Rebekah's life in the balance, the battle for her survival raged on, fueled by the raw and primal instincts of those entangled in its deadly game.

"You're not thinking it through," Niko said.

"I've seen enough bloodshed to be numb to it," Maggie sneered, her voice venomous. "I'll cut her throat and watch her die, and it won't cripple my conscience. But what about you, detective? Can you live with her blood on your hands?"

"And what about your brother? You'd risk his life?"

Stuart's fingers adjusted their grip on Rebekah's shoulder.

"Test me, and we'll find out." Maggie's voice taunted Niko, almost desperate for him to accept her challenge.

Niko didn't answer, keeping the gun firmly directed at Maggie. Rebekah's heart pounded as she witnessed the morbid exchange, her life being weighed as currency. Fear clenched her stomach like a vice, and she prayed for a miracle, a savior in the depths of her own psyche.

Rylos, she thought. *Please. Are you there?*

But there was no answer within the caverns of her mind. With a jolt of tension, Stuart writhed, his blade bit deeper into her throat, and an agonized scream escaped her lips.

Amidst grunts of pain, Stuart's fingers clamped down harder. His weight dropped, clutching at her shoulder and digging the bindings deeper into her wrists. The blade slid down her neck, scraping against her flesh. The pain was searing. Fighting against the haze of the sedative, her instincts roared to life as her mind cleared.

"He's here!" Stuart screamed, unable to restrain himself. "Please. The amulet."

"Time's up, detective," Maggie said. "Drop the fucking gun or she dies!"

Niko hesitated, trapped in a vise of moral dilemma. Rebekah could see the gravity of the situation bearing down on him. Finally, palm raised, he lowered the gun.

"Okay," he said. "Okay, I'm putting the gun down."

Yet, the nightmare only deepened as Stuart's grip on the blade tightened, and he pressed the sharp edge harder against her neck. The pain ignited her senses, and she cried out for salvation.

"Kick it over." Maggie's impatient command sliced through the tension like a razor, and Niko complied.

Maggie's blade was withdrawn from Rebekah's neck as she claimed the weapon and trained it on Niko. With the gun surrendered, she turned her attention to the workbench where the amulet lay. Passing it to Stuart, she kept the gun poised on the detective. Stuart surrendered his grip on Rebekah, freeing the blade from her neck, and lunged for the necklace greedily. A moment of relief washed over Rebekah as the threats to her life retreated. As the trinket settled around Stuart's neck, a calm enveloped him, seemingly soothing his inner demons.

The unexpected sound of a gunshot shattered the room's fragile equilibrium. Niko crumpled to the floor, blood misting the plastic sheeting, and Rebekah's scream tore through the air. Squirming, the rough edges of the manacles gouged her wrists. The bindings refused to surrender their grip, but still she struggled, hurling obscenities at Maggie like venom. Watching the people responsible for her sister's death get away with murder gnawed at her sanity.

Rushing to Stuart's side, Maggie gripped his arm and pulled. "We need to leave!" she barked, her voice a chilling blend of urgency and cruelty.

"I need to catch my breath," he replied weakly, leveraging the workbench to hold his weight.

"We don't have time for that!"

"Give me a minute," Stuart said. "I just need—"

Another gunshot echoed through the small, plastic-lined room.

The pegboard of trinkets and jewelry became an easel, capturing the spray of blood. Stuart fell, lifeless, to the ground, his eye a chasm of carnage. Rebekah's struggle ceased as she fixated on the gruesome sight before her. Maggie's horrified scream brought a cold satisfaction to her.

She turned to find Niko propped up on the ground, holding a revolver. The sound of a final gunshot pierced the air, and Maggie's screams ended abruptly.

With the bodies of her tormentors sprawled before her, Rebekah released a shaky, gratified breath. Niko gripped his shoulder, blood seeping through his fingers, a testament to the price he had paid for her life.

"Fuck. This hurts," he said. "Did I ever tell you I was shot in this shoulder before?"

A smile creased Rebekah's face, bringing warmth to the cold, dark space, the place where her sister had been murdered. It was an image that plagued her mind even then. From the floor, Niko nursed his wound beneath meditative breaths.

Her respite was short-lived. Seething pain stung Rebekah as something sharp plunged into her left shoulder. A hand gripped the curls of her hair, jerking her head backward. She yelped as a haunting voice whispered in her ear, chilling her to the core.

"You're mine, Guardian."

A man screamed in protest, lost beneath the haze of panic gripping her mind. Another gunshot echoed in the dark room, and the fingers gripping her hair loosened. Her eyes darted around wildly, desperate for an explanation. Stuart and Maggie remained lifeless on the floor. So, who?

Her life drained as if it were being siphoned from her body. Shadows swam into her vision as torrents of blood cascaded down her chest. The room reeked of blood and death, but in the midst of the macabre, Niko rushed to her side.

With trembling hands, he lifted her from the meat hook. The relief of pressure on her shoulders was lost amid searing pain. Every movement was torture. Agony ignited within her, but Niko's voice cut through the chaos, a lifeline, urging her to stay alive.

"Hang on," he said. His voice, trembling, echoed somewhere in the fading light. "Help is on the way. Please, stay with me!"

It was the last thing she heard before the world went black.

32

NIKO

THE WEIGHTED BLANKET OFFERED its share of comfort as did the desperately needed coffee. Still, a sense of gloom settled over Niko. Once again, he wasn't quick enough. He wasn't smart enough either. Sitting in the back of an ambulance, sipping on his lukewarm coffee, he watched the scene unfold around him. Cops were everywhere, and curious citizens gathered beyond the yellow tape line. News vans were unloading equipment, and Robert Wymer was being escorted from the building followed by Jim and Jason Halder. It should have been a proud moment, but Niko struggled to find the joy in it. His passion for the job had vanished.

Brindle leaned against the ambulance, slipping a cigarette from the pack, and lighting it. After a hearty drag and an impressive cloud of smoke, he said, "You must be the only guy I know who could find a reason to mope around after uncovering a decades-long killing spree. Digging it up through a shit heap of cold cases no less."

"It doesn't bring peace to the families, though," Niko droned, watching Robert, Jason, and Jim being loaded into individual cars.

He thought less about peace for the families and more about his own peace, but he didn't need to share that. Brindle was a great friend and mentor, but Niko wasn't in the mood for counsel. He wasn't in the mood for much at that moment, especially as the painkillers amplified his already palpable exhaustion.

"Yeah," Brindle said, taking another drag from his cigarette. "Peace is something they find on their own. It's not something that can be given. You'll find yours too." He gripped and patted Niko's shoulder, causing him to wince in pain.

"Ah, shit." Brindle jerked his hand back. "Sorry about that."

As the gurneys rolled out, topped with zipped-up black bags, that sense of gloom returned. Peace seemed unattainable. So, he simply nodded and took another sip of the shitty coffee. He tugged the blanket tighter around himself, bumping the sling and wincing again at the ache in his left shoulder. They had bandaged him up nicely, better work than last time, but then again, this one hadn't been as bad.

"Here. Officers pulled this off that Jason kid. I'd recognize your chicken scratch anywhere." Brindle handed him the leatherback notebook.

Niko took it and flipped through the pages. His notes appeared to be intact, meriting a sigh of relief. So, Jason had been the prick who broke into his room. Well, at least he had a face to stitch to the event. He'd put the investigation notes to good use.

"Thanks," Niko replied.

"Anytime," Brindle said. "Now, perk up and get your shit together. Rogers just got here and is making his rounds. He's gonna want your briefing. Oh, and here's the background you asked me for."

Brindle handed Niko a brown folder and cast his cigarette aside, snuffing it out against the wet pavement with the ball of his shoe. He began to walk away.

Niko called to him as he left. "Hey, Brindle! Thanks. For everything."

He gave a nod and shuffled off into the cluster of officers discussing the details of the scene.

Niko sighed. He was sore and buried beneath a leaden sense of melancholy. There was a glimmer of hope, though, and he decided to focus on that as he gazed up at the cloudless blue sky. His mind weighed over the thoughts he'd had in the hotel. About his job. About Danielle. He wanted to call her, but it wasn't the right time.

Niko opened the folder and reviewed the contents within. His eyes widened as the last piece of the puzzle came into focus. The question that had been nagging at him from the start. The answer to the gap in the kidnappings.

Rogers approached with Rodriguez in tow. "Niko," he said.

"Sir," Niko replied.

"How's the shoulder?"

Niko glanced down and rolled it slightly. "Tender, but I'll be all right."

"Glad to hear it," Rogers said, taking a heavy breath to segue back to business. "Listen, we have five men in custody and seven bodies. News crews are lining up, and I'll be expected to issue a statement. So, tell me. What happened?"

Rogers had been a no-nonsense, straight-to-business guy for as long as Niko had known him, but occasionally he loosened the tie and let his humanity show. On that day, however, he kept the business tight. Niko sighed and gave a nod.

"The short version is that Maggie and Stuart Berman have been behind every cold case I'm assigned to. They kidnapped and murdered several dozen people over the span of thirty years, give or take. Robert Wymer has been the owner of the Armitage the entire time and has known about their affairs and even helped cover them up since the diner brought in the business that kept his hotel afloat. Though, I think there's more to it than that. He's not the only one. There was a local detective, David Rossi, who also protected them by manipulating data in his reports to draw off suspicions."

Rogers signaled silence with a raised hand. "David Rossi was covering for them? Why?"

Niko pushed the blanket off his shoulders and stood, stretching his back. Undoing the Velcro strap of the sling, he eased his arm down, scrunching his face at the stiffness and discomfort. He retrieved a fresh shirt Brindle had brought him from his luggage and tossed it over his head, struggling to raise his arm through the sleeve.

"There were a couple oddities that kept pulling me away from the answer, Rossi being one. He grew up in this area, and, as I learned, graduated in the same class as Maggie. There was also a sizeable gap in the killings. Eight years where there were no reported disappearances. It took me a minute to piece that together, but I found the answer. Henry Rossi."

"David's brother?" Rodriguez asked.

"Yeah," Niko replied. "He and Stuart were working together. At first, I thought David was covering for Maggie and Stuart because of their history together, but then I realized that he had been covering for his brother. I spoke with Henry—hell I even saved his life before I knew—but when we were talking, he mentioned he had left the area for a while."

Niko held up the brown folder for display, a smile creasing his face and excitement pumping through him. "Henry Rossi travelled for eight years before coming back. Eight years. And during that time, not a single missing person's case went unsolved. We discovered at least one alias to account for some of that time, but I believe there are more that will corroborate my claim."

"Before you go any further, we need hard evidence. I'm assuming you have some."

"Well, I stumbled across Robert, Jason, and Jim in the act of disposing of the bodies in Room 232. Five college kids. Beyond that, I have some suspicions that a few of the officers are investigating, and labs should be able to support my theory."

"Which is?"

"Armitage-brand soap," Niko said. "Every room in the hotel has unbranded soap, packaged in custom Armitage labeling. Questioning the receptionist, Leslie, I found out that Stuart runs his own business making soaps and lotions as well as a few other things the officers are investigating. I think that he was rendering the soap and lotions from the skin and fat of the bodies—as a means of disposing of them. He also has a commercial-grade furnace, which I believe he used to cremate whatever remains he couldn't process. Oh! And not to mention, Henry stabbed that girl, Rebekah Daroh. I shot him. He's in our custody, and I'm sure we can get him to talk."

"Well, if your investigation yields anything, we have Maggie and Stuart, but they're dead. We have a strong case against Robert and the others for the murder of those kids and potentially aiding and abetting."

"I think if we pushed them hard enough, they would buckle on Henry. He's the last major player in these murders."

"That's a gamble," Rogers said. "And we'd have to give leeway somewhere. Maybe offer amnesty."

Two officers jogged up to Niko and Rogers, interrupting them. Wide, unbelieving eyes adorned their faces, Frye and Jones on their nametags.

"Sir," Officer Frye announced. "You're gonna want to see this."

Sharing a questioning glance, Niko and Rogers, with Rodriguez in tow, followed the two officers. Keeping silent until they entered the hotel, where the young couple was being checked out and dismissed by Leslie at the front desk, Officer Jones started.

"We did as you asked, Agent Ortez, and dug into the basement area of the kitchen. We found a pallet worth of soap and several loose bottles of lotions. We've sent a few off for lab work, but we also found a tub of bonemeal labeled as fertilizer. We sent those off for analysis as well, but I think your theory holds water."

The tables and chairs in the diner had all been pushed aside, the saloon doors were propped open, and the kitchen was crawling with analysts, Harrington among them, assisting with taking photos of the scene. He gave Niko a cursory nod.

Power had been restored to the hotel not long ago, but work lights were still positioned in the basement, feeding off the outlets in the kitchen. The toppled shelves in the freezer had been removed, and numbered placards marking spots of blood decorated the floor. As Niko descended the steps to the basement again, the memory of Rebekah bleeding out in his arms flashed into his head. Shaking it off, he shuffled aside, following Officer Frye into the room at the base of the steps with Rogers tucking in behind him.

Officer Jones grabbed a loose piece of plastic containing a red liquid substance and handed it to Niko. "It's labeled 'Edward Smith' and dated early February," he said. "We have another that went in for processing, but the analysts believe that's myoglobin, and it ain't from an animal."

"What are you saying?" Rogers asked.

"They were…feeding them to—" Niko stifled a gag.

"Yeah," Officer Jones said. "We've found traces of the same residue in the kitchen. Some of it appears to be animal. We found packaging labeled pork, beef, and chicken in the freezer, too, but there were various unlabeled ground meat mixtures where we believe human meat was ground together with animal meat. We're having samples tested to confirm."

Niko held his hand over his mouth. His stomach lurched, and vomit rose in his throat. Frye handed him an empty trash can. All he could think of was the burger Maggie had handed him. He couldn't shift his mind to anything else, and he began throwing up.

"You okay, Niko?" Rogers asked, planting a comforting hand on his back.

"I ate…" he tried to explain, but another wave of sickness cut him off. "I ate a burger from here," he said through gasping breaths.

A groan of sympathetic "oh" resonated from the officers and Rogers, but they allowed him a moment to collect himself. Once the onslaught of nausea passed, Niko set the can aside and wiped his mouth.

"Sick fucks," Niko said, spitting into the trash.

"Well, hang tight," Officer Frye said. "According to the purchase orders we found, they have been shipping product, including the meat, all over the country. We found orders dating back to the late eighties."

"Okay," Rogers said, muttering "fuck" under his breath. "I'd say we have everything we need, but keep this shit out of the media. We need to gather all the information we can before we break the news to the public. Otherwise…" Rogers shook his head while the others, Niko included, nodded in acquiescence.

It wasn't a story Niko wanted to break to anyone. Not only wasn't he sure if his stomach could handle thinking about it again, but he also didn't want to be the cause of that misery for anyone else.

"Get someone to track down every purchase order," Rogers said. "We need to know where they went. Hopefully, these people didn't know what they were buying. Prioritize the recent shipments first so we can try to stop any more of this shit from being consumed. Niko, walk with me."

Niko followed Rogers up the steps as Officers Frye and Jones barked a "yes, sir" behind them. As they charged through the kitchen, Niko could hear Rogers muttering to himself. In the diner, he turned around.

"You did good work, Niko. Great work, actually. I'll be happy to have you back once your psych eval is completed."

"About that, sir," Niko started. "I was giving it some thought, and I don't know if I want to continue my career as a special agent."

"What?" Rogers's brow creased in confusion. "I thought that's what you wanted."

"It was, but after this weekend…Look, I was chasing this career because it was what my father did, and it helped me feel closer to him. But it's not something I want anymore. I want to start a family, and Danielle doesn't like the risk this job brings with it. Truth be told, I'm kind of over it myself. I don't want to leave the bureau, so I'd be happy if you just stuck me in an analyst position."

Rogers threw back his blazer and placed his hands on his hips. His eyes scanned the room in thought.

"I'm sorry to hear that," he said. "But I want to offer you a compromise. I don't want to lose someone with your mind and attention to detail. Plus, I feel some obligation to your father. It's because of him that I'm where I'm at today, and I believe you're every bit the man he was."

Rogers turned back to Niko and squared up, crossing his

arms over his barrel chest. His lips curled, and his eyes studied his colleague. "Agent Stewart requested a transfer to another station. I've been sitting on it for a few weeks because I was waiting you out. I was hoping to offer the position to you once you completed your psych evaluation."

"You want to bump me up to ASAC?"

"If you're willing," Rogers said. "It's not entirely risk-free, but it keeps you out of the field more often."

Niko hesitated, his thoughts drifting to Danielle. "Can I think about it?"

"Of course." Rogers patted a hand on Niko's right shoulder. "I've got the press to handle, but take the week and get back to me. Good work on this. Your father would be proud."

Rogers stepped away, and a smile crawled onto Niko's face. Suddenly, his thoughts shifted, and he called after Rogers. "Oh, sir!"

Rogers turned.

"Where'd they take Rebekah?" Niko asked.

"She's at Leigh Hospital with her family."

"Can I—"

"Yeah, you're done here." Rogers smiled before turning back to exit the hotel.

Niko returned to his room to gather his things. Unloading his guns, he picked up his father's revolver. "Thanks for saving my ass, Dad."

Just then, a knock came at the door. Niko loaded rounds back into the revolver and slipped it into its holster at the base of his spine. The hotel was swarming with police, but anything could happen. Another knock came just as he approached the old-school, outdated door that didn't even have a peephole. Taking a breath, he turned the handle and swung the door open. There stood Danielle, accompanied by Brindle.

She smiled at him. "Hi."

"I gave her a call before you left for your trip," Brindle said. "I figured you were too proud to do it, so I did it for you."

Niko laughed.

"I thought about telling you on the phone, but we got disconnected," Danielle said. "After Kevin called, I took the next flight home. I was planning to surprise you when you got back."

"So, you're not still mad?" he asked.

Danielle laughed. "I was never mad at you. I was scared. I was…I don't know…conflicted, I guess. I needed some time to think."

Brindle cleared his throat. "I'll, uh, leave you two lovebirds alone."

With that, Brindle left hastily. The two shared a look and chuckled. Danielle leaned in to give Niko a hug. He sucked in a breath as she bumped against his shoulder.

"Oh, I'm sorry," she said, glancing down at the sling. Her face twisted in concern. "Were you shot *again*?"

"Well…" Niko hesitated. "Yeah."

She gave a sly giggle, and he pulled her in for a kiss, half expecting her to pull away. But she didn't. It was nice. He had missed her and was glad to have her back. He wanted to share the news of Rogers's offer with her right then, but there were still things to take care of.

"Hey, I need to take a little trip," he said. "Care to join me?"

33

REBEKAH

DARKNESS SWALLOWED REBEKAH, DRAGGING her down into a foreign place, deep into a distant void. Wispy black smoke surrounded her, entangled her. The shadow invited her in, welcomed her, and filled her with wanting. All pain subsided. Her worries and fears were absolved. She simply sank into the deep black nothingness. What she did feel was empty. The presence she had grown acclimated to—that had become a part of her—was gone.

Hands cradled her shoulders and gently pulled her from the darkness, bringing her into a familiar embrace. The warmth and comfort were a welcome reprieve, and Rebekah rested her head against the figure, listening to the heart beating beneath the surface. It could have been her own, but it didn't matter. It didn't matter who it was or what was going on around her. Lethargy was all she knew, and she let that be who she was. Weak and tired, she wanted to sleep until the stars faded from the sky.

"It's not time for that yet," a familiar voice spoke to her.

Rebekah raised her head and gazed into the eyes of her sister. Brilliant radiance. Like a beacon in the dark, Nicole carried the same effervescent glow Rylos had held, and Rebekah couldn't help but smile. It was a weak and fragile smile, but it was there.

She had so many questions, but even their presence in her mind consumed too much energy. She had to rest.

Once again, her head fell onto Nicole's chest, and she listened to her heart's beautiful song. It spoke of life and love, and Rebekah couldn't have asked for more.

"How?" Rebekah whispered. That was the most strength she could muster.

"Rylos," Nicole said, and that was answer enough. "Rest, sister. Close your weary eyes and sleep."

So, she did.

Steady pulsing beeps drummed in her head as light and consciousness returned. Blurry shapes danced in front of her as she opened her eyes. But clarity brought with it reality. She was in a hospital room, wires snaking from her body and an oxygen tube respiring into her nostrils, but she was numb. She went to move her arm and couldn't. Instead, her fingers twitched in response. In her mind, she envisioned climbing from the grave, drawing as much life and strength as she could, but the siphon was feeble. Still, little by little, she returned to herself.

Pillars of light streaked the room from the half-cracked blinds. Misty particles of dust drifted between the columns, and "Georgia on My Mind" hummed softly over the radio, drawing her attention to where her father sat beneath the window. Hunched over a mess of files, glasses perched on the tip of his nose, he gently hummed along, something she hadn't heard since she was a child. The sound relaxed her and transported her to a better time. She closed her eyes and smiled. Unaware of what would come next, she sat in the ambiance and simply collected the memory.

"Rebekah?" her father said, and she turned to him. "Rebekah!"

He shot from the seat, bumping the table as he rose, sending files cascading to the ground. His fervor startled her, and she recoiled, but he didn't falter. Bringing her into his arms, his body shook from his sobs. He ran a hand along the back of her head where the sore spot was still tender, but she didn't stop him. His other hand clutched at the clothes covering her back, quivering. As she adjusted to the moment, her eyes slicked with tears as well. She had never seen him so vulnerable, and to be so for her sake was as jarring as it was touching. Buried in his chest, she wanted to reciprocate the hug, but her arms wouldn't move. That stung her heart.

"Thank God," he said, his voice quaking. "My baby, thank God." Easing her back so he could examine her, he asked, "How are you feeling? All right?"

His glossy eyes danced around wildly, examining every detail of her face, while one hand still cradled the back of her neck.

"Yeah," she said. She wanted to say more, but her voice was hoarse and grating. Even the energy needed to muster such little speech weighed on her, and she realized how truly spent she was. It didn't seem right. "What happened?" she croaked.

Her father wiped tears from his eyes before explaining, "You were stabbed, baby. You lost a lot of blood. We were so worried you wouldn't..." His lips pursed, and his face contorted.

She could see the struggle in his eyes and how difficult it was for him to relive the emotions. The sudden weight of time washed over her, begging the question. "How long was I—"

"Three days," her father said before she could finish, and her heart sank.

Three days?

It didn't seem possible. Revisiting the dream...Only it wasn't a dream, she realized. Nicole had pulled her from the darkness. That was real. Had she died? Had Nicole brought her back?

On the bedside table were vases of flowers and various cards. While still vibrant and beautiful, the flowers were showing early signs of decay, and a few stray petals decorated the tabletop. On her other side, a blood bag was suspended, feeding a catheter in her forearm. So, it was true. Despite that revelation, her mind drifted to the one thing that concerned her.

"And Mom?" she asked.

"She's doing better." He smiled. "She stepped out to get breakfast, but she should be back any minute."

Rebekah sighed gratefully, but impatience raged within her.

She had so much to say, so many questions she needed answers to, but her body lacked the strength to carry out her wishes.

"It's okay," her father said, brushing her curls from her face. "Everything will come in time. I'm just happy you came back to us. You lay back and rest. I'll go get the doctor."

With a hesitant but smiling glance, her father left. The commotion of thoughts in her head was overwhelming, tempting her patience to break, but she stifled the impulse to throw herself from the bed, force her body into motion, and rip the wires off. Instead, she let her thoughts drift to Nicole, deciphering what she knew from that brief interaction. Nicole was free of her prison thanks to Rylos, which she also assumed meant their tether had been broken. She was free.

She was *free.*

But what did that mean?

In some ways, she wished she could take it back. Despite everything, her worst fear rose to the surface. Even though she had liberated Nicole, she had severed their connection as well. Of that, she hoped she was wrong, but the sinking feeling in her stomach suggested she wasn't.

The sound of a cane tapping the floor came into focus, and Rebekah turned to the doorway. Her mother walked in, and her face turned to shock. She dropped the tray of food she was carrying and rushed to Rebekah's bed, tears already wetting her cheeks.

"Oh, my God!" she cried. "My baby, thank God!"

Collapsing on the bed, her mother planted a tear-soaked kiss on her forehead and gave her a hug. Still, Rebekah couldn't lift her arm to embrace her. She ignored that and appreciated what she did have. She leaned her head against her mother's and hugged her against her shoulder until the pain erupted in her body, rallying against her movement. Her mother recoiled.

"Oh, no," she said. "I'm so sorry." She caressed Rebekah's face, her eyes curled into their own smiles. "But look at you. My baby is so beautiful."

Rebekah returned the smile, too weak to summon words, and it soon quivered into a frown. "You came for me..."

"Of course, I did, baby," she said. "I know I've made my share of mistakes as a mother, but when you told me you were going back to that damned place…I was terrified. After everything we had suffered there, all the horrible memories, I was terrified."

Rebekah gasped a harsh breath, fighting back tears and choking back her regret. "I'm sorry, Mom." Her voice wavered.

"No, no," her mother said. "No, I'm the one who should be sorry. I shouldn't have…" She fought back the riot of emotions. "I should never have agreed to letting you go on your own. I had a feeling in the pit of my stomach, but I ignored it. I wanted to try and win you back, I guess, so I let you go. But I decided to follow you anyway to keep an eye on you."

"Win me back?" Rebekah rasped, her brows creasing in dire confusion. Dots speckled her vision, and the world sank away. Her mother cried in the distance, calling for help as darkness swallowed her once more.

When Rebekah woke again, hours had passed, and the orange light of dusk colored the room. A whole day had gone by, but some of her strength had returned. At the sound of her parents' hushed conversation, she remained still and feigned sleep.

"The doctor says her vitals have stabilized," her mother said. "The CT scan showed no signs of damage, but I may request an MRI just to be safe. I want to schedule with a neurologist as well for a second opinion."

"Is this something we need to worry about?" her father asked.

"I don't think so. I mean, it's not uncommon for seizures to happen in cases of traumatic brain injury. She was dead for thirteen minutes. The lack of oxygen in the brain for that amount of time can have side effects."

"So, this may happen again," her father said.

"It's possible," her mother replied. Rebekah heard the familiar doctoral tone in her delivery. "I'll ask the doctor for a prescription of midazolam to take home. Just in case. But…" she paused, exhaling. "Until she gets her strength back, we'll need to keep a close eye on her."

"She's not the only one."

"Don't start, Victor. I'm fine."

"You should be resting," her father said. "Your leg is still in bad shape, and the bruises on your ribs look horrible."

"I look worse than I feel. I'm fine. I'm just worried about our daughter. I'm scared."

"I know, I know," he said. "I'm scared too. But the worst is behind us now, right?"

"I think so," she replied. "The doctors all seem optimistic, and her charts look good to me, so…I think so."

The room was silent for a while, and Rebekah considered opening her eyes. She was horribly uncomfortable and wanted to reposition herself but didn't want to risk disturbing the peace. There was some semblance of the family she used to know in that room, and she wanted to hold onto it for as long as she could. The whine of the leather couch broke the silence, followed by the soft clap of footsteps.

"We could use some food," her father said. "I'm going to get us some dinner. After we eat, we'll talk about what needs to be done. For now, rest."

"You know I won't rest." Her mother chuckled, following up with a more earnest tone. "But I'll try to relax."

Rebekah peeked through her lids to see her father offer his hand to her mother. She stood, and the two embraced and gently swayed as her father hummed the melody of a song Rebekah didn't know.

"Mmm, I've missed this," her mother said. "We've been so focused on everything else that we forgot about each other."

"Well," her father responded, "my thoughts have never been far from you."

With a soft laugh, her mother said, "After all this time, you still know how to make me blush."

They held each other for a while, her mother's head resting on her father's shoulder, and a broad smile decorating her face. It was peaceful, and Rebekah had to fight back her own grin to maintain the illusion she was sleeping.

"Okay," her father finally said, and Rebekah snapped her eyes shut. "I'll be back in a bit. I love you."

"Love you too, hun," her mother replied.

Rebekah waited, listening as her father's footsteps left the room, and her mother situated herself on the noisy leather couch. Giving time for silence to settle back into the room, Rebekah broke it moments later.

"That was adorable," she said.

Unsure how her jest would be received, the brief quiet that followed seemed tangible. But her mother returned the volley. "Excuse me, young lady. You were supposed to be asleep."

"Who could sleep with all that…whatever that was. Was that flirting? Is that what was happening?"

"Okay. Your mama still has moves." She paraded a sassy finger. "Back in the day, your father couldn't keep his hands off me."

"Oh God, Mom!" Rebekah laughed. "Can you just…That plug right there. Just pull it. Please? End my misery."

Her mother joined in her laughter. She wasn't sure where the sudden comfort came from, but she welcomed it. Part of her stoked those old emotions, encouraging her to shut down and guard herself, but she doused the flames and let the moment live. She was happy, and her mother and father were happy. It was the life they had before, reinvigorated. Like welcoming home an old friend. It didn't matter how it came; it was what she had been longing for.

"Oh, you've had a visitor," her mother said. "He's been by every day to check on you. Wonderful young man."

"Mama," Rebekah said. "Behind Dad's back?"

"Oh, hush." She laughed. "No, it's the FBI agent who saved your life. And speak of the devil."

Rebekah turned to see Niko stepping into the doorway of her room, a mug of coffee in his free hand while the other arm was done up in a sling. A backpack hung from his good shoulder. The evening glow of sunset creeping through the blinds cast him in an almost angelic light, and for a moment, Rebekah saw Nicole occupying that glow in place of Niko.

"Hey kid," Niko said, a soft smile lifting his cheeks.

34

REBEKAH

NIKO CROSSED THE ROOM with a certain familiarity and gave Rebekah's mom a hug. Rebekah wasn't quite sure what to make of that. In an instant, two worlds collided. The part of her life she had known with Niko had been marred with pain and trauma, none of which was his doing. In fact, he was the light amidst it all. But seeing him there, talking with her mother, made everything real. A fleeting moment of anxiety pressed on her chest as the memories of what she had suffered flashed through her mind.

"Niko," her mother said, "would you mind keeping an eye on her? I've been trapped in this place for days. Victor won't let me leave. If I don't get some fresh air, I think I might lose my mind, and I'd take Victor with me."

Niko chuckled. "I understand. Yeah, go ahead. I'll watch her."

"Thank you," she replied.

She seized her cane and sped from the room, the clicking sound chasing her down the hall. Niko stood for a moment, watching the door with an amused look on his face. Then, he turned to Rebekah.

"Glad to see you're awake," he said as he took a seat next to the bed, setting his bag beside him on the floor. "I was starting to think you didn't want to come back. How are you feeling?"

Rebekah glanced around the hospital room. "I've had better

days. But all things considered, I'm doing okay. Thank you for that."

"You don't need to thank me." Niko took a long breath. "I feel like I'm partly to blame for things." He gestured at the whole of Rebekah. "I let my guard down. I wasn't paying attention when Henry stabbed you. I could have stopped him."

"Henry?" Rebekah asked. "The old guy from the diner who lost his arm?"

"Yeah, caught me by surprise too," Niko replied.

"But how?"

"There was a backroom where they kept supplies. I guess he heard me come in and laid low. I'm not sure why he came after you, though. He's in custody now, and we've been interrogating him. I have a follow up with him tomorrow. From what we uncovered, he and Stuart had been working together for a while. He's going to plead insanity, of course. It's bullshit. He's playing the cliché about a voice in his head making him do it. Claims Stuart heard the voice as well."

Rebekah shrank into her own head, Niko's voice trailing into the distance. She recalled the vision she had when she invaded Nox's mind. She saw them capture, torture, and kill her sister.

The cadence of the beeps pumping through the monitor increased, mirroring the drumming in her chest. She knew. She had felt it through Nox. He controlled them both, used them both—hunter and butcher—to enact his torment on innocent people for his vendetta. His war.

"Hey." Niko's voice dragged her from her stupor. "Are you all right?"

"Yeah." Rebekah shook her head to flush the thought. "Just zoned out. So, you don't believe it?"

"Fuck no," Niko said. "Even if it were true, the asshole deserves to rot in jail."

Rebekah couldn't argue with that. "But you don't believe people hear voices in their head, I mean."

"Well, my father's family is Puerto Rican, so we believe a lot. But this guy? Not a chance."

Niko took a sip of coffee and appeared to zone into the bed. His brow creased in thought.

"Something on your mind?" she asked.

"No," he said. "It's just..." He sat in reflective silence for a moment, opening his mouth to speak then reconsidering. Finally, he said, "You know, it's crazy, but I heard a voice at the hotel as well."

"What did it say?"

"It told me that you were in trouble."

"Sounds like intuition."

"No," Niko said. "No, it was different than that. I even chased someone that I thought was you. It led me to the first domino, the chain of events that brought me to you in that meat freezer."

Rebekah studied Niko's face as he puzzled his way through the situation. It wasn't impossible for Rebekah to believe. Not with all she had been through. But she wondered what he made of it all. Instead, she offered him an out.

"It was a strange weekend," she said. "None of us got much sleep. Maybe it was just exhaustion playing with our minds."

"Maybe," he replied, his expression showing he wasn't entirely convinced. "Anyways, I'm sorry for what happened to you."

"No," Rebekah responded, "you saved my life. Without you, I..." She shook her head, sliding a free hand up to the bandaging on her shoulder. "I'll take this instead." Reaching her hand out, she slid back the collar of Niko's shirt, exposing the bandaging on his shoulder. "Looks like we have matching tattoos."

He chuckled, glancing down at his own wound. "Yeah, I suppose we do."

He looked back at her, and she could see the gears turning beneath his sympathetic eyes. Instead of speaking, though, he sighed and lowered his gaze to his lap.

She studied the detective for a moment, her own thoughts dwelling on the quiet that filled the hospital room. She churned through ways to break it, fearful of the emptiness it carried, but the only vision surfacing in her mind was that of her standing in a pool of blood with the dismembered bodies of the boys around her. She wondered if they had been discovered and imagined not. Otherwise, the conversation would be far less friendly.

Rebekah turned her head to a folded piece of cloth on the bedside table. "What's that?" she asked, snapping him from his stupor.

"What? Oh," he said, following her gaze. He reached for it and handed it to her. "I brought this for you. I noticed it after the ambulance took you and grabbed it before forensics arrived."

Rebekah unfolded the cloth, revealing the amulet, her sister's necklace. The orange glow of sunset danced along the glossy black curves, carrying with it every memory she had of Nicole but also the warmth she had known with Rylos. She closed her eyes and held it to her chest. A smile found its way onto her face.

It seemed such a small thing. Everything she suffered in pursuit of it, and it was simply handed to her. All her happy thoughts became tainted by the harsh reality. The presence of the amulet made everything real. All her struggles and strife could no longer be shouldered as a bad dream.

Holding it out to examine it again, she was reminded her connection to Rylos—and worse, her sister—had been broken. Laying it in her lap, she turned to Niko. "Thank you," she said in a near whisper.

"I hope it helps you find peace through all of this," he replied.

"And you?" Rebekah's face shaped into concern. "What about your peace?"

Niko gave a half-hearted, throaty laugh. "I'm sure I'll think of something." He reached into his bag and retrieved a small, felt-covered box, turning it over in his hands.

"Is that…"

He held it out more plainly. "Do you think she'd say yes?"

Rebekah weighed him carefully, searching for a spark of life behind his eyes. There was a flutter of excitement in her own chest. She barely knew the man, but there was a certain comfort with him, something familiar, and she was happy for him. Recalling their conversation in the hotel room, she knew there was an obstacle. She knew nothing else about the girl than what he had told her, but she had a feeling.

"What about your job?"

"I plan to break the news tonight over dinner," Niko said, bringing the box back into his lap. "I accepted a position as assistant special agent in charge—or ASAC as we say—under my old boss, someone my father mentored. It keeps me out of the field, managing a few teams. Less dangerous."

"And you're happy with that?"

Niko nodded slowly, as if considering it. "I am. I was ready to leave so I could be with her. Rogers, my boss, gave me this alternative. Of course, I have three months left of a psych evaluation before I can move into the position, so I was thinking that would be a good time to propose."

"I think she'll say yes." Rebekah smiled. "But maybe lead with you being ready to leave for her."

Another smile cut across Niko's face. "Noted."

"So…can I see it?"

Niko's smile widened as he extended his arm and peeled open the small box. Inside rested a beautiful diamond ring, catching the evening sun, throwing prismatic colors around the room. A simple round-cut diamond nestled in a thin white-gold band.

"It's beautiful," she said.

"It was my mom's," he replied.

"I think she'll love it."

35

REBEKAH

Four months later…

EVENING SUNLIGHT FILTERED THROUGH the window as Rebekah lay on her bed reading. She had cracked the spine of her latest book, *The Lovely Bones*. Music danced through her room. Not her music, though. Her mother's. "A Sunday Kind of Love" by Etta James played somewhere on the floor below. The smell of bread baking chased the song and filled the room with warmth, adding a cinnamon flavor to the air.

Rebekah draped the book over her chest, tears slicking her cheeks as she finished the first chapter. She wondered if Nicole was looking down as Susie Salmon had done in the novel and reached for the necklace that had fallen behind her shoulder. She clenched it in her fist, and an almost imperceptible warmth radiated in her palm. Taking a deep breath, she inhaled the sweet smell and smiled. It was as perfect an evening as she could have asked for.

A typical Thursday night would have her bracing her nerves for another indecorous duologue in therapy. Ignored, undermined, and manipulated. That was her. But she'd been surprised when her father gave her the option to continue after the Armitage. She never cared much for Mrs. Harrity, so she declined. Comparatively, catching up on reading was far more therapeutic.

Placing a bookmark before chapter two, she set the story

aside and crossed the hardwood floor with bare feet. In the bathroom, she drew open the tap and plugged the drain to collect warm water in the sink, prepping for a face scrub. Not something she did often, but the mood struck. A good thing, too, since her mascara had smudged to form large black circles under her eyes.

Focusing her attention beyond her face, she caught the scar on her shoulder, poking out from beneath the strap of her top. Like a memory embossed on her skin, it was a reminder of everything that she had lost. Or everything she'd gained. Running a finger along its shape, like the blind deciphering braille, she recounted the events of that weekend. Though she lost her connection with Rylos and Nicole, she had filled that void with a renewed relationship with her parents. It was something to adjust to. There was a lot of that going around.

Steam clouded the mirror while she scavenged her thoughts, hiding her reflection behind a hazy filter. She lifted her hand to swipe away the condensation but hesitated. Instead, she took a finger and drew in letters, just as she and her sister had done when they were younger.

Are you with me?

The fog licked at the trenches carved through the moisture, and before long, the words were hardly visible. She held her breath, unsure what to expect, though she had an idea. Hope rallied regardless. But when the words faded from the mirror completely, she released a long sigh and closed the tap. A brief sting of loneliness visited her before she washed it away with the warm water from the basin.

Tramping down the stairs, the smell of lasagna and banana bread drew her in. She stopped, as usual, at the family photos in the foyer. Many of them had changed from four months ago, and more had been added. New faces—smiling faces—adorned the table. A picture of her trip with her parents to the

Florida Keys. Another from their trip to Vegas to celebrate the victory of her mother's lawsuit. She had been thrilled to retain her medical license, and Rebekah was happy for her as well.

It had been a busy summer but in the best of ways. It was as if her parents tried to scrub away the trauma with positive experiences, something Rebekah could appreciate. It was working too. There were more photos of her with her parents littered around the mosaic of Nicole photos than ever. It had become cluttered. But Rebekah protested when they considered taking a few of Nicole's down.

"Smells good, Mama," Rebekah said, entering the kitchen.

"Mm-hmm," her mother replied. "I'm trying something new with the lasagna. I added mushrooms and peppers. And I baked a chocolate chip banana bread for dessert."

Rebekah hovered over the casserole dish and took a deep breath, complimenting her mother with a "mmm" and a smile. "Need any help?" she asked.

"Yes, please," her mother said. "Your father should be home soon, and I'd like to surprise him."

"Special occasion?"

"Hopefully. He met with a new client today. He's been nervous about this meeting all week. It would be a huge win for his firm. So, I wanted to have a celebration ready."

"What if he didn't win the client?"

"Then we have something to lift his spirits. Could you set the salad out?"

Her mother pointed to a large bubbled-glass bowl, and Rebekah seized it from the counter. The tongs were already dipped in the salad. She carried it to the table, where candles were lit, and a flowery display decorated the center. The memory struck her of how dinners used to be—the arguments and insults, the tension and distance—and she smiled at what her family had become. Setting the bowl aside, she made minor adjustments to the bouquet to clean up the appearance.

Rebekah checked the placemats. Her mother had even used the good china. As she was making haphazard adjustments, she noticed extra seats prepared.

"Mama, why are there five plates set?"

"Oh, Niko and Danielle are coming tonight," she said. "Since he helped your father set up the meeting, it's the least I could do. And I thought this could be a small celebration for their engagement."

Rebekah whipped around, a broad smile on her face. "She said yes?"

Her mother smiled back as she made her way to the table with the casserole dish, a slight limp still burdening her steps. The doctor told her to rest, but her mother, being as stubborn as she was, used that time instead to treat the family to their various vacations.

"Well worth the sacrifice," her mother had said.

Rebekah agreed until she saw the reversion in her mother's health. She supposed she hadn't understood what was being sacrificed, or she had been blinded by the joy of the family reunion. Whatever the reason, Rebekah teamed up with her father in concern for her mother's health. She took the dish from her and finished the trek to the table.

"Thank you, baby," her mother said. "And yes, she did. There's a lot to celebrate. I have no doubt your father's pitch to the client was successful. He has a way with people."

The phone in the kitchen went off, followed by the echoing chimes from the handsets littered throughout the house. It took two rings before her mother could snatch the receiver and answer the call.

"Hello?" her mother said.

Rebekah finished bringing things to the table, motioning for her mother to take a seat as she did. Not everything was ready. A mix of vegetables still simmered in a pan, but she did what she could. Deciding to give her mother some privacy, Rebekah wandered from the kitchen and back to the photos.

Over the past four months, the entryway table felt less like a shrine and more like a symbol of rebirth. A catalogue of her own family's second chance. Scanning over the pictures hanging from the wall, she found the ripped photo of her and her sister, which had been repaired to some degree, framed, and placed off to the right of Nicole's senior photo. The jagged white strip still etched down the center where it had torn. It always brought a smile to her face, her favorite photo of the two of them. They were young, joyous, and unburdened by the pressures of growing up.

Beneath Nicole's, Rebekah's senior photo hung, encircled by various moments from her childhood. Examining her sister's picture, she saw the necklace—the one Rebekah had reclaimed after her death—ornamenting her neck. The worn leather strap looked out of place between the manicured hair and velvet black dress, but it wholly personified Nicole's character. It was a gift from her younger sister, something to be cherished, no matter how it clashed.

Rebekah caressed the amulet hanging from her neck. When Niko had returned it to her, she vowed to never take it off. It had become an emblematic memory of her sister, and wearing it was the best way to honor her. She smiled and reached out her hand, touching the necklace in Nicole's photo.

"I miss you," she said.

A knock came to the door, startling Rebekah from her reverie. Opening it, she found Niko dressed in a fine suit, carrying flowers and a bottle of wine. Clutched to his arm was Danielle, the tall blonde—taller than Niko even without the heels. Rebekah smiled and gave an excited greeting before inviting them in.

No sooner than she'd closed the door she said, "So, I hear congratulations are in order."

The words couldn't be restrained. Despite her attempt to bite them back, they broke free of her control.

"Shared the news already, did she?" Niko replied.

"My mom can't keep secrets," Rebekah said. "You'll learn. Let me see it!"

Danielle flashed her hand, decorated with the ring Rebekah had seen mere months earlier. It had been cleaned and polished since then. The diamond attracted every light in the house and threw it into a beautiful prism of colors.

Smart man.

Rebekah took Danielle's hand with genuine awe, complimenting and congratulating them both. When she returned to the kitchen, her mother was off the phone and back to scurrying around, cleaning the mess left from dinner prep.

"Evening, Mrs. Daroh," Niko said.

"Ah, right on time." Rebekah's mom turned. "Come in, and make yourselves comfortable."

Niko presented the flowers and wine, Danielle hugged Rebekah's mom, and they exchanged the usual pleasantries. Rebekah watched from just beyond the kitchen. It was a strange thing how it had all fallen together so naturally. It had never occurred to her until just then, but in its own chaotic way, it made sense. Niko carried a certain comfort within him Rebekah had felt early on. Her parents must have felt it too since they had welcomed him and Danielle into the family. Though it could have been the sacrifice he made to save Rebekah's life that left her parents feeling indebted to him. It didn't matter.

"Victor should be home any minute," her mother said, grabbing a vase from the cabinet to put the flowers in.

"Have you heard how his meeting went?" Niko asked as he uncorked the wine, transferring the contents to a decanter.

"Nothing yet. Knowing Victor, he'll let me marinate in suspense. He believes important news should be delivered in person. Old-fashioned."

"Ah, mum's the word then," Niko said.

Rebekah's mom gave him a curious glance. "Do you know something I don't?"

"Not a clue." Niko slipped two cigars from his blazer's inner pocket and rested one beside his plate.

He shot a sly grin at Rebekah and set the other one next to her father's plate. Rebekah couldn't help but smile. Her mother had turned back to preparing the flowers and missed the subtle exchange. It was then her father entered through the garage door, his blazer folded over one arm. He set his briefcase aside and greeted the family, giving his wife a kiss on the cheek and hugging Rebekah. A firm handshake was offered to Niko, with a "thanks again" muttered between them. And there it was.

The life Rebekah had longed for unfolded before her. She was glad to be alive to see it. Not long after her father returned home, dinner was set, and everyone took their seats at the table. Niko shared first, recounting his story of the proposal, Danielle's eyes glued to him, biting her lip. A look dripping with enamor. Rebekah's father was next, sharing the good news about his meeting, which won him an excited "congratulations" from her mother, followed by a loving embrace. Then, the conversation turned to Rebekah.

"So, I heard," Niko said. "Scholarship to Georgetown University. That's impressive. Congratulations."

"Thank you," Rebekah said.

"Have you broken the news to Anna?" her mother asked.

"Yeah," Rebekah replied. "She's happy for me. I offered to turn it down so I could go to Roanoke with her, but she said I'd be stupid to turn down Georgetown."

Her father chuckled. "I know that's right."

"What's your major going to be?" Niko asked.

"I'm doing a double major. Criminal law and psychology."

Niko gave an impressed nod. "Following in your father's footsteps?"

"Actually, I was thinking of entering the FBI." Rebekah glanced around the table nervously, weighing the looks from her parents.

"What made you choose that?" her father asked.

"Well, after everything with Nicole—and with Detective Rossi—I wouldn't have even considered it. But after meeting Niko and everything that happened at the Armitage, I realized there are good people who want to do the right thing. I want to be one of them."

Her father smiled and gave an approving nod. "I think that's an excellent idea."

"Really?" Rebekah asked.

"Yes," he replied. "All I ever wanted was for you to find something that would give you purpose. Something respectable. The dangers of the job, though..."

"I'll keep an eye on her," Niko said.

"I'd appreciate that," her father replied.

"Speaking of which," her mother chimed in. "Whatever happened with those boys from the hotel? Did Robert really kill them?"

"It appears that way," Niko said. "He denies it tooth and nail. He's still insisting it was Rebekah who did it, but her testimony checks out. In some sick way, she was fortunate Henry grabbed her, otherwise that room could have been her coffin as well."

"It sends shivers up my skin just thinking how close Rebekah came to…" Her father gulped. "I thought I knew Robert. Hell, I defended him in a zoning case years ago when I still practiced real estate law."

"Some people are very talented at hiding who they truly are," Niko said. "In my profession, you see it every day. But as for those boys, as bad as it may seem, they deserved it. Especially with what they did to Rebekah."

Rebekah shot a cautionary look at Niko, which earned a curious glance from him.

"What did they do to Rebekah?" her mother asked, snapping her focus to her daughter.

Niko's eyes darted between them before he resigned from his commitment to break the news.

"Rebekah, what happened?" her father inquired.

She gave a sigh and set her fork down. "It was a long time ago. I don't want to get into it."

"It was only a few months ago," her mother said.

"I just want to forget about it," she said.

"Did they hurt you?" her father asked.

Rebekah glanced at Niko, who gave her an apologetic look. "No," she lied. "They tried. C—Can we just get back to dinner? I don't want to talk about this stuff."

Her mother sighed. Concern decorating her face, she said, "Okay, but I still want to hear what happened when you're ready."

"Okay, Mom," Rebekah replied.

It didn't take long for the conversation to swing back to a happier subject. Before long, dinner had passed, and everyone was finishing their dessert. Rebekah's dad and Niko resigned to the back porch with their cigars, discussing details of the meeting, among an array of other things.

Rebekah fled the kitchen, leaving Danielle and her mother to indulge in their gossip. She headed to the shower. Her mind had snapped back to that weekend, something she fought to avoid the entire summer. She knew she needed to face her trauma. Mrs. Harrity had harped on it in numerous sessions when Rebekah was still attending therapy. As painful as it was to admit, she had been right, and in due time, she would, though with a more competent therapist. Finding Nicole in that prison, however. She would keep that to herself.

Rebekah primed the water, waiting for it to heat, and wrapped her hair back into a bun. Catching herself in the mirror, she gave another look at the scar on her shoulder. It was something she hadn't grown used to, but she would. She had grown used to the scar on her wrist, after all.

The shower was the tonic she needed to draw the events of the Armitage from her mind. Before long, amidst the dancing steam, she was singing melodies from her favorite songs, putting on her own personal concert for the toiletries, even borrowing a shampoo bottle for a makeshift microphone.

She turned the shower handle off, retrieved her towel from its wall-mounted rack and wrapped herself. Freeing her hair from its bun, she flicked her fingers through the curls to return its shape. As she made for the door, she stopped. The steam on the mirror held a message in response to the question she had asked earlier. Tears stung her eyes accompanied by a smile. She exited the room, leaving the bleeding condensation to melt away the lingering letters.

The story continues in *Heritage*,
book 2 in the Children of Arcanum

Keep reading for an excerpt from *Heritage*...

Acknowledgements

First, to the reader. If you're here, you've made it to the end, and by that feat alone, I am ineffably grateful. Whether you loved the story or hated it, it doesn't matter. You read it. You took a chance on an independent author, and that is all I could've hoped for. So, from the bottom of my heart, thank you!

Piecing this work together has been no small feat. A culmination of several years of planning and structuring that could not have been accomplished without the help of some extraordinary people, most of all from my family and friends. There were several iterations of this work before it evolved into what it is today, and each iteration passed through friends and alpha readers, who offered incredible advice to help push me to transform this story into something far greater than what it began as.

The original blueprint for this novel was a simple Crime/Mystery, surrounding only Rebekah. Paranormal elements were added in the form of Nicole reaching out to Rebekah to help her solve the mystery of her death, and there was even a child who went missing that fueled Rebekah's search, uncovering clues along the way. It wasn't long before I decided to add in a detective, thus Niko took shape. He began as a simple side character and grew solely because I loved his potential and the background he portrayed.

And then, finally, leaning full tilt into the paranormal element, I merged this story into another that was also years in the making. Rylos was the first character I ever created (which was sophomore year in high school). Idromir was his world, and he had a story all his own that was intended to be my magnum opus. Instead, this all converged, thanks in large part to inspiration derived from Stephen King's *The Dark Tower* series and his skill at weaving his worlds together. And thus, the evolution of *Armitage*. Though, Rylos's story may still come about. The ideas are there, and I was careful in my web spinning to work his story into the lore of this novel series, should it ever come.

For this final iteration, I must thank my wife, Melissa, whose patience with my incessant rambling and prattling of ideas and concepts, which had no end (still to this day doesn't), was invaluable; a highly important friend, Steven, who was thrust revision after revision and chapter after chapter throughout the book's evolution; my beta readers, who I will list below; and lastly, the wonderful Elizabeth Merck, my editor, who polished this piece of work from something degenerate, into something to be admired.

I truly hope you have enjoyed reading this story and if you did, *please* be kind enough to leave me a review, whether it be on Amazon, Goodreads, Barnes & Noble, etc. Reviews are so incredibly helpful to indie authors like myself (any author in general, really), and beyond that, I love to see the feedback, good or bad, and love interacting with people who enjoy reading, movies, music, games…whatever! You can also reach out to me via my website (which I have included at the opening of this novel and will include on the next page) or through any of my social media accounts.

Until next time, my friendly reader!

BETA READERS:

J.C. Ceron, author of *Death of the Ice Angel.*
Andie Matei, author of *Fear of Flying.*
Claire Paton, author of *The Future is Set.*
Amber (amberlilyreadin on Fiverr).
Danielle (localwriting on Fiverr).
Jasmin (jwolffrath on Fiverr).

Visit my website:
www.atlascreedauthor.com

Please, be kind enough to leave a review!
Amazon, Barnes & Noble, Goodreads, etc.

Thank you for reading my novel, your support goes beyond words!

Here is a QR Code to my author website, where you can find links to purchase my books, my social media accounts, and other things to explore.

GLOSSARY

Aegeus (age–ee–us) – A mystic on the council of elders, devoted to the rivers and seas on Idromir. Shares kinship with his brother Numenos.

Armitage (arm–ih–tidge) – Once a grand and thriving hotel in its prime nestled along the boardwalk of Pinnacle Beach, has been reduced to a dilapidated relic, struggling to hold on.

Arcanum (ar–cane–um) – The source of energy in Idromir, the heart of the light that created all light.

Berman, Maggie – Owner of Maggie's Dive, the Armitage's renowned diner. Sister to Stuart.

Berman, Stuart – Head Chef of Maggie's Dive, with a myriad of side businesses including soaps, lotions, and meat processing. Brother to Maggie.

Brindle, Kevin – File clerk with the FBI who worked alongside Niko's father and stepped in as a father figure and mentor after Niko's father passed.

Corbin, Mike – Notorious school bully known for his disruptive antics with his friend Drew.

Daroh, Evelyn (dare-oh) – Talented neurosurgeon currently under attack by an association of doctors for false allegations of medical malpractice. Mother to Rebekah and Nicole; wife to Victor.

Daroh, Nicole – An intelligent and compassion sister and daughter with near limitless potential who was tragically taken too soon, leaving her family distraught and struggling to carry on.

Daroh, Rebekah – A strong-willed, intelligent young girl who experienced heavy trauma from the loss of her sister and the fracturing of her family, desperate for the family she once knew.

Daroh, Victor – A prestigious lawyer who has worked numerous legal issues, currently helping his wife with her malpractice suit.

Ethereals – Beings blessed by Idromir's light and imbued with the power to control and manipulate the energy around them.

Fleeger, Richard – Mid-level supervisor with the FBI with a chip on his shoulder and a reputation for being an asshole.

Greene, Rachel Ms. – Administrative assistant at Rebekah's high school with a bubbly personality and advocate for her students.

Guardian – A being imbued with the power of light and placed in charge of caretaking the souls of mortals.

Halder, James 'Jim' – Owner and operator of Halder Construction with a long working relationship with the Armitage hotel, being its primary contractor.

Halder, Jason – Son of James Halder and employee with Halder Construction.

Harrington, Michael – Data analyst with the FBI, regularly seen with Kevin Brindle and Niko Ortez; ambitious career aspirations.

Harrity, Jenorah Dr. – A tenured, over-the-hedge therapist with unorthodox practices, but a long and successful career.

Heart of the World – Mysterious location where several powerful artifacts have been crafted.

Idromir (id–droe–meer) – Celestial Titan planet and protector of light whose corpse has become a nexus for life, light, and souls.

iunctura mentem (ee–unk–tour–rah, men–tem) – Phenomenon occurring when objects are forced through the ethereal plane to the corporeal world when an ethereal converges with a mortal's consciousness.

Joey – A vagrant and disturber of the peace at the Armitage hotel.

Kismet (kiz-met) – The ever-present energy that guides the course of time, fate, and corrects imbalances when necessary.

Liverium (lie–veer–ee–um) – Known as the "Children of Idromir," a prophesized group said to protect the light since Idromir passed.

mystics – Servants of Idromir, born from his light and tasked with preserving his legacy until the liverium return.

Nox 'Kalen' – A rogue Reaper who abused his power and started a rebellion against the mystics and Guardians destabilizing the ecosystem of Idromir.
Numenos (new–men–os) – A mystic on the council of elders devoted to the lands of Idromir. Shares a kinship with his brother Aegeus.
Ortez, Niko – Budding FBI special agent on probation from an on-the-job incident that led to the death of three officers. Eager to prove himself and follow in his father's footsteps. Dating Danielle.
Peterson, Stephanie Nurse – School nurse at Rebekah's high school.
phantom crystal – Mysterious artifact given to Stuart by Nox to help fulfill his purpose.
praesagium stone (pray–sage–ee–um) – Powerful stone with many abilities including the ability to guide one to what they seek.
Reaper – A being adorned with a cloak imbued with the power of shadow responsible for caretaking mortal souls that have passed.
Reibach, Charles – Renowned and prestigious doctor currently overseeing a council heading a malpractice lawsuit. Danielle's father; suing Evelyn Daroh.
Reibach, Danielle – Paralegal and loving and devoted daughter; girlfriend to Niko Ortez.
Reibach, Lisa – Clinical psychologist. Wife to Charles and mother to Danielle.
Rodriguez, Burton – ASAC to Brent Rogers and helping oversee Niko's probation case.
Rogers, Brent – SAC for the FBI D.C. office and Niko's previous supervisor before his probation.
Rosenberg, Shelly – Supervisory Special Agent for the Behavioral Analysis Unit (BAU) assigned to evaluate Niko following an incident on the job.
Rossi, David (ross-ee) – Ex-FBI special agent stationed in Charlottesville who oversaw several missing persons cases along Pinnacle Beach. Suspected of covering for his brother Henry.
Rossi, Harold 'Henry' (ross–ee) – Virginia local and discovered serial killer who operated under multiple aliases. Lost his arm to an over-zealous beach umbrella.
Reyja (ray–zsa) – Fromer mystic on the council of elders, cast out by her kin. Serving the will of Kismet.

Rylos (rye–los) – Last of the Guardians who failed to stop the fall of Idromir during the Reaper/Guardian war. Powerful energy manipulator who holds the power to correct Idromir's course.
Shadow, The – Mysterious scourge of darkness determined to reclaim its domain by eradicating the light.
Smith, Devon – Amid Rebekah's friend group; attracted to Rebekah, but lacks confidence.
Smith, Edward – Unfortunate soul caught in Nox's path on his search for the Guardian.
Sorbach, Drew – Notorious school bully known for his disruptive antics with his friend Mike.
Stewart, Jennifer – ASAC to Brent Rogers and helping oversee Niko's probation case.
Turner, Leslie – Receptionist and waitress at the Armitage hotel.
Warner, Josh – Amid Rebekah's friend group; dating Anna.
Weaver, Anna – Rebekah's best friend since childhood, the bubbly and optimistic counterbalance to Rebekah's pessimism. Dating Josh.
Wymer, Robert – Owner of the Armitage hotel seeking to restore his hotel's position and reputation even through unconventional means.
Zack – One of Joey's goons causing disruptions at the Armitage hotel.

ABOUT THE AUTHOR

With the release of his debut novel "Armitage," Book One in the Children of Arcanum series, Atlas Creed subverted genre norms and cemented his creative, character-driven approach to storytelling. Winning an IPPY (2025) for Mystery/Thriller audiobook, as well as two BookFest Book Awards (1st place in Supernatural Thriller and 3rd place in Urban Fantasy) for his book Armitage, Atlas Creed cemented his position as an ambitious up and coming novelist. As a writer, Atlas seeks to create new worlds for readers to explore, with stories being developed in several genres. He focuses primarily on characters, ensuring that their development resonates with readers. "We are not perfect, and those imperfections, as we embrace them, shape who we are."

ABOUT THE AUTHOR

With the release of his debut novel "Armitage," Book One in the Children of Anathem series, Atlas Creed defied genre norms and cemented his creative, character-driven approach to storytelling. Winning an IPPY (2023) for Mystery/Thriller audiobook, as well as two BookFest Book Awards (1st place in Supernatural Thriller and 3rd place in Urban Fantasy) for his book Armitage, Atlas Creed cemented his position as an ambitious up and coming novelist. As a writer, Atlas seeks to create new worlds for readers to explore, with stories being developed in several genres. He focuses primarily on characters, ensuring that their development resonates with readers. "We are not perfect, and those imperfections, as we embrace them, shape who we are."

HERITAGE

The following chapter is from book 2 in the Children of Arcanum series, titled *Heritage*...

Heritage takes place a year and a half after the events of *Armitage*.

REBEKAH

THREE WEEKS...

Three weeks without respite from the nightmare. Never wavering, like some inescapable horror that transformed Rebekah's bed into a prison she loathed to return to. The thought of sleep brought with it an inescapable anxiety. Three weeks of fighting—and losing—against her wits amplified the terror of the nightmare, devastating her health in the process. Battle fatigue reared its head.

Therapy had its benefits, and under the support of Dr. Bower, the campus counselor, Rebekah was recovering from her ordeal at the Armitage. But, some memories, like scars, linger even after healing. And from those unremitting memories, the dream poured forth.

It's just a dream.

It's just *a dream.* She repeated, yet the words offered no comfort.

The haunting echoes of Joey's fingers skated up her thighs and touched the spot between her legs. A chill flitted across her flesh, and her shoulders shivered in revolt. Nausea threatened her stomach. She tugged at the hem of her shirt and swatted at hands that weren't there. It didn't matter. Nothing changed. The sensation remained, leaving behind an unclean feeling.

Despite the events of the Armitage being more than a year ago, she couldn't shake the tainted memory of the event.

The need to scrub away the impurities drew her to the shared dormitory bathroom, nestled between her room and her neighbor's. Locking both doors, she primed the shower and shed her clothes. As the water heated, she hugged herself and collapsed to the floor.

There, she cried.

She wanted to scream—to thrash about wildly and fling whatever dark cloud followed her away. To free herself from the shackles of her past. But instead, she breathed, and once more, slowly. She climbed from the floor, finding confidence in her footing. It was, after all, only a dream, and she had conquered those before.

Steam from the shower climbed the mirror, where Rebekah locked eyes with her reflection. A slight flicker drew her gaze to the amulet, swaying at the base of her neck. A comforting memory of her sister planted itself in her mind along with a small, but fleeting smile on her lips.

There were two things she knew. First, Joey was dead. The memory of his decapitated head was as fresh and as satisfying as the day it happened. Yet, his ghost lingered in the form of phantom signals of his violation of her. As if his fingerprints bore themselves into her flesh, grafting him to her.

Second, she was alone. And that loneliness tasted like abandonment. It had been more than a year since the last message with her sister. And now that she entered her sophomore year in college, that sense of aloneness was prodigious.

I NEED YOU

Her shaky finger carved through the condensation on the mirror. Erratic eyes scanned the message over once more before she jumped into the shower. There would be no answer. That was a reality she had come to expect.

The warmth of the cascading water was serene, dispelling such lugubrious thoughts and terrors from her mind. Soaping herself down changed the aroma to that of passion fruit with calming undertones of lavender. Within that aromatic sauna her stresses were minimized, reduced to trivial notions.

Beneath the gentle waterfall, she reminisced on the memories and visions of her sister, as brought to her by waters in her past. Rylos had said water is a conduit for souls. But, if that were true, then why could she feel nothing?

Had Nox's blade poisoned me and stripped me of that power? she mused. *Did it sever my connection with Idromir and my sister?*

It was a comforting thought, even if it tasted like a lie. The alternative was Rylos—and worse, her sister—abandoning her.

With reluctance, she shut off the water and stepped from the warm embrace of the shower to the chilling grip of the tile. Reprieve came when she wrapped herself with a towel, tucking the corner of the covering tightly at the center of her chest. The writing on the mirror was a ghost of its former self. Blots of water occupied the once defined lines and as expected, no response. She exhaled heavily to accompany the leaden weight settling in her stomach.

A thought occurred to her. She retrieved her discarded jeans from the floor and fished her phone from the pockets. With a flip, she opened it and thumbed through the contacts, stopping on Anna's. She pressed call.

The phone rang.

Again.

And again.

"Hey, this is Anna, leave your message after the beep. Thank—"

Rebekah flipped the phone closed and sighed. She ruffled her damp curls—she had tried to keep them dry—as her mind raced about. Anna didn't know about the dreams; Rebekah hadn't told her. But if anyone could help, it was her. Anna was the only other person who knew the full extent of her trauma, the only one aware of the other world Rebekah had visited. But if not Anna, there was another person close by. Not aware of the situation, but enough to lend a comforting shoulder.

She flipped her phone open once more and searched for

Devon's contact, opting to text him rather than call—they weren't quite there yet.

'r u free?' she sent.

Before she could set the phone down it buzzed in her hand, *'ya. wanna meet?'*

'coffee?'

'k. 20 mins. shoot me the address.'

Standing in the tepid, sticky bathroom collecting condensation, she considered the impulse. She needed an ear to vent to, but should she give Devon background to understand? Perhaps, it was best for him to be a distraction from the chaos. It would do.

Collecting her discarded clothes, she unlocked both doors and escaped back to her dorm. After dumping the soiled laundry into a hamper, she chose a new outfit. Not normally one to stress over clothes, she found herself being more selective than usual. After a moment of running her hand over the various fabrics in empty abstraction, she settled on an outfit she deemed more mature: a white cotton summer dress that once belonged to Nicole, and black vans—no need to abandon her style entirely. She even went as far as consulting her meager collection of makeup, only to settle on some lip gloss.

Devon hadn't come home the previous summer, so this was their first get together since high school. She was nervous. She wasn't sure why, but the fluttering in her stomach and thinness of breath spoke volumes.

Stepping outside, the beautiful autumn weather greeted her with a soft breeze and the gentle kiss of sunlight. She made her way down Library Walk. The first signs of fall showed in the faint yellowing of leaves, even if the weather didn't feel like it. The occasional breeze complimented the dry eighty-degree heat.

Café Republic had opened earlier that year on the corner of 35th and O street. Being a seven-minute walk away meant Rebekah was familiar. It was a good place to find peace and enjoy her pastime of people watching. Georgetown was in no short supply of subjects to observe. It was Friday, which meant America-man would be up to his usual antics, covered head to toe in star-spangled glory, carrying an oversized American flag and marching backward down the sidewalk. She wondered if Devon had ever seen America-man.

George Washington University, where Devon attended, was less than two miles away, after all. Rebekah had been excited to have a familiar face nearby, but that excitement died when the demand of their course schedules left them little time to socialize. Before she knew it, she was a sophomore. It was a surprising yet welcome miracle that her whim of a suggestion for last minute coffee panned out.

Emerging from behind Healy Hall, she turned and passed before the grand building—one of her favorites on campus. She paused at the cannons flanking the clock tower entrance to admire the architecture. At orientation they described it as an amalgamation of styles representing both Romanesque and Gothic Revival intended to exude academic grandeur. Though, her own interest was in the feeling elicited by the monument. With its intricate stonework and various soaring spires, it symbolized the change she recognized within herself. The drab monolith, given life by the stained-glass—a riot of color amidst the gloom—epitomized her own dreary past, mottled with life-giving color in the shape of her friends and the trials she'd endured.

Passing the statue of John Carroll, she proceeded toward O street. Her shoes beat against the red brick walkway, perpetually edged with parked cars. A few leaves decorated the copper-colored walk, where trace weeds patterned a maze through the seams in the pavers. A peaceful splash of nature against a backdrop of industry.

Two blocks down, she turned into Café Republic. The immediate and powerful scent of coffee and buttered confectioneries greeted her entry. It was a mild morning, with only a few scattered customers. Devon not among them. "I'd Do Anything" sounded over the radio, giving Rebekah pause. Thoughts flitted in and out of her mind, painful reminders of what she had, and had so shortly after lost. She took a breath and shook off the melancholy.

She approached the counter with a familiar greeting to Jerald, the owner. Her typical autumn order would be the café au lait with whipped cream and a cinnamon dusting, but the warmer weather left her craving a cooler alternative. So, she opted for the iced vanilla latte—keeping the whip and cinnamon, of course, but adding a caramel drizzle.

Her eyes wandered over the pastries warming in their display on the counter, and she considered a buttered croissant. But the mention of the name Harold Rossi on the news drew her attention to the ceiling mounted TV.

"The trial of Harold Clint Rossi, also known as Henry, concluded today, finding the defendant guilty of first-degree murder of fifty-two individuals," the news anchor, Brent Moore, stated. "However, through the trial, it was discovered that for eight years, from 1984 to 1992, Harold traveled the country under three different aliases and is believed to be responsible for the murder of at least six others. Pending investigation, a separate trial will be held for those charges at an undisclosed date. Details on sentencing to come."

"Fuck that guy," a voice sounded behind Rebekah, startling her.

She turned to find Devon, and a smile planted itself on her face. The two hugged, and she caught the sweet scent of sage as her face brushed past his neck. It paired nicely with the warmth of Devon's embrace. His hands stacked one over the other comfortably at the middle of her back. She was only a few inches shorter than him, but she leaned into the hug, giving way to a floating sensation.

"How've you been, Becks?" he asked.

"Good," she lied. "I've been good."

"You okay with…all that?" He gestured toward the television.

Rebekah contemplated briefly, her thoughts whirring about, flicking through memories of the Armitage. Strangely, Henry was the least of it. Joey held the most stubborn residence in her head. "Yeah," she replied.

"Here's your coffee, Rebekah," Jerald said. "Can I get your friend something?"

"Uhm, sure." Devon pulled out his wallet and stepped toward the counter. "Hot cocoa, please. I got hers as well."

"You don't have to do that," Rebekah said.

"I know. But I want to."

Once Devon paid, they took an open table by the large bay window at the front. Café Republic's logo was printed over the glass, and a neon "open" sign gently hummed off to one side.

"You look good," she said.

"Me?" He gave her a polite, approving lookover. "Look at you."

Heat flushed her cheeks. She smiled and brushed a lock of hair behind her ear.

"But can we move past the small talk?" he said.

"What do you mean?" Her smile disappeared.

"I mean, it's great to see you, but I don't think you hit me up out of the blue to catch up. I can tell something's bothering you."

Rebekah's brows lifted. She didn't know this Devon—no longer the standoffish boy from high school. He was older now, more direct. A certain confidence had surfaced, and it intrigued her.

"You don't have to talk about it," he said. "I just wanted to let you know that I'm here if you need me."

"Thank you." Her smile returned, though decorated with a tinge of melancholy. "Why didn't you come home over the summer?"

"I moved in with my dad in Brookland to save on dorm costs. That's home now."

"Really? Wow. You're a local now."

He chuckled. "Yeah, I guess so. Plus, mom moved to Georgia with her new boyfriend, so."

"Sorry to hear that."

He shrugged. "She's happy. Dad's happy. That's all that matters."

But Devon didn't look happy. His eyes shifted around the café and Rebekah sensed the same reservations she had within him; a secret sadness lingering just beneath the surface.

"You still could've come up to visit."

"I wanted to, but I didn't have a car. I spent the summer working at my dad's shop to save up for one."

Jerald brought out Devon's drink and a small plate of assorted pastries. "On the house."

They both thanked him before he ambled back behind the counter. The bell above the door rang as one of the few patrons left. Rebekah glanced back at the TV, but the news had shifted to the weather. A pang of sorrow stabbed at her heart as the mere allusion to the Armitage—and thus her sister—was enough to remind her of the abandonment. Following her sadness, anxiety crept in as the reminder of Joey's atrocity once again pushed to the forefront of her thoughts.

She inhaled sharply and fidgeted in her seat, willing her thoughts to change, as if to outrun the memory attempting to seize control of her mind. As her gaze fell back over Devon, she found him eyeing her under sympathetic brows.

"Talk to me," he said. "Please. What's going on?"

She looked down at her drink and took a sip.

He sighed. "Okay…"

The shrill rattle of a whistle drew her gaze towards the bay window. Coming into view, America-man tramped down the sidewalk backwards. As expected, he wore his American flag styled three-piece suit, marching with militaristic cadence, and wielding a single large American flag, supported by an honor guard leather sling. Only today he sported a black hat embroidered with the POW-MIA emblem in white stitching.

"What is that?" Devon stared, bemused.

"You don't know America-man?" Rebekah asked, failing to restrain a smile. "He does this every week."

"Why?"

She chuckled and shrugged. "I don't know. But he's become this odd routine in my little world."

Her smile faded as thoughts of that night relentlessly climbed their way into focus.

Closing her eyes, she breathed, and a tear slid down her cheek. Her attention shifted back to Devon who still watched America-man traipsing away down 35th street. "I was nearly raped," she said, her voice a near whisper.

Devon's eyes whipped back to her. "What?"

She looked down. "I've been having nightmares about it, and it's been causing a lot of anxiety."

"When?"

"At the Armitage."

There was a silent pause preceding his next words. "Becks, I'm so sorry, I—I didn't—"

"I know, it's fine," she said with a shake of her head and an attempt at a smile. "But that's what's been on my mind."

"Does Anna know?"

"No. Well, she knows about what happened, but not that it's been causing nightmares."

"And the guy who did it?"

"Guys," she corrected. "Dead."

Another pause, this time Rebekah looked up and Devon looked away. He pondered some distant thought, his focus trailing beyond the bay window.

"Good," he said. "They got what they deserved then."

She tilted her head and gave a slight shake. "But you don't know how—"

"It doesn't matter." His eyes met hers, a fury burning within. "To do something like that…" He glanced down and rolled his cup between his hands, breathed, then took a sip. "They got what they deserved."

Stillness settled over the table. Devon shrank into his thoughts, while Rebekah examined him curiously. This was not the Devon she knew. Yet, she found comfort in that. There was an instinct to him—something protective—but kindness as well.

While Devon appeared to labor over the frustration inside of him, Rebekah simply watched. She knew what it was like to wrestle with voices, with out-of-control emotions. Though, since the Armitage, with the exception of the nightmares, her mind had been still. A feeling so unfamiliar to her that it set her on edge for months. Relief gave way to unease, then to worry, and finally loneliness.

"Are *you* okay?" he asked, pulling her from her introspection. He shook his head before she could answer, muttering derisively to himself. "No, of course not. I—I'm sorry. Stupid question."

"It's all right," she said. "I'm..." She restrained from the knee-jerk guard of "fine," and cycled through words, but none seemed right. "I'm managing."

He considered her and nodded his head, sympathy creasing his brow. She held his hazel gaze, and in that moment, she felt like breaking—like confessing everything, but couldn't. She wasn't ready. Not for Devon to know. She had no reason not to be—she trusted him, and he had always been there for her. But still. She wasn't ready.

"I'm seeing a therapist on campus," she continued. "It's helping, but it's not something that I think I'll ever get over. So, she's helping me manage...the chaos...of it all."

The look of sympathy deepened on his face and shame flushed her own. Why? She knew that none of what happened was her fault. But shame settled all the same.

Her gaze dropped to the glaciers of ice bobbing in the froth of her coffee, caramel rivers capping some, while dots of cinnamon speckled the foamy surface. Devon's look wounded her. It wasn't even his fault. It was the first glimpse of the old Devon that she saw. He felt what she was feeling. Her pain became his own, and she hated that.

A warm hand enclosed around her own, drawing her attention up. Devon eased her hand closer, and she met his eyes once more.

"I'm right here," he said.

That was it. What little noise permeating the café, with its employees working behind the counters and empty dining tables, faded. That gesture was enough.

Another tear slid down her cheek. She closed her eyes and cried. He moved to the seat beside her, wrapping her in his arms. She pressed herself against his chest and he simply held her. They sat for a time, unmoving. The world shrank away from them, and Rebekah allowed her pain to surge.

The shrill ring of her phone shattered the peace and brought her crashing back to the present. It began so abruptly that they both jolted in response. She fished through her handbag. The name 'Niko' appeared on the screen, and she flipped the phone open. The voice on the other end, however, carried a grim affectation.

...stay tuned for more in book 2...

www.ingramcontent.com/pod-product-compliance
Lightning Source LLC
Chambersburg PA
CBHW010541020826
49168CB00029B/389

* 9 7 9 8 9 8 7 7 4 5 3 2 8 *